Emma Neale was born in Dunedin and raised in Christchurch, San Diego CA and Wellington. She has a PhD from University College, London. Her novels, *Night Swimming* (1998) and *Little Moon* (2001), and her collections of poetry, *Sleeve-notes* (1999) and *How to Make a Million* (2002) are also published by Random House.

She lives in Dunedin with her partner and their young son.

Double Take
Emma Neale

V
VINTAGE

The author gratefully acknowledges the Todd Foundation and Creative New Zealand for the Todd Bursary, which assisted in the completion of this novel. Thanks to Chris and Barbara Else of TFS.

for Dorothy Pearson

National Library of New Zealand Cataloguing-in-Publication Data
Neale, Emma.
Double take / Emma Neale.
ISBN 1-86941-560-4
I. Title.
NZ823.2—dc 21

A VINTAGE BOOK
published by
Random House New Zealand
18 Poland Road, Glenfield, Auckland, New Zealand
www.randomhouse.co.nz

First published 2003
© 2003 Emma Neale
The moral rights of the author have been asserted
ISBN 1 86941 560 4

Text design: Elin Termannsen
Cover photograph: GETTY IMAGES
Cover design: Matthew Trbuhovic, The Bureau
Printed in Australia by Griffin Press

PEAS IN A pod. Cherries on a stem. Jeffrey and Candy. A pair, a set, a perfect match, people seemed to so quickly think, looking from sister to brother and recalling stories from the *Woman's Weekly* or *Time* about twins who communicate in private code: cryptophasia, idioglossia, or ESP. They saw Candy and Jeff and thought of siblings studied by linguists, psychologists, even anthropologists; as if twins were a tribe of two with a secret understanding, existing in a self-contained, mysterious world. 'Yep, my two pearls,' their dad would say to those who asked. Years later Candy would sometimes feel she was still up against the ogling curiosity: a scientist on the Net saying she envied the parents of twins, 'who have instant access to this living laboratory!' or the front page story in a regional newspaper that announced: 'Flaw in Gene Responsible: Twins a Biological "Mistake"'; or magazine headlines: 'Nepalese Baby Girl Twins Separated by Surgeons', 'Film Star's Miracle Twins'. If twins were in it, it was twice the news, apparently.

'Aren't they sweet!' creaked elderly couples in the mall, making Candy feel they wanted to fondle and pick her and Jeff up like novelty salt and pepper shakers displayed in a sale. But how different are salt and pepper if you touch them to your tongue, she thought, looking at Jeffrey's green eyes that reflected her own, the small mole on his left cheek exactly where hers was on the right, the tiny flattening of the bone at the top of the bridge of the nose, as if someone had pressed gently with a thumb into the soft clay of them both before they had fully grown. Identikit, photofit, their mother's womb a copier, trying to perform a duplicate — and coming up with boy and girl. Even *better* than identical twins, relatives said: the perfect family all in one go! A pair, a set, a match. Was it only Candy who came to imagine red flint to strike alight? Or a contest, a series of games, the prize going to the opponent who won the greater number?

'Oh, they're so obviously twins!' murmured the kindergarten supervisor, the primary school principal, the swimming instructor, the clothes store assistant. '*Fraternal* twins,' their mother corrected. 'They're really no more alike than ordinary siblings.' Only nobody listened. The family resemblance was so close — so many of their mirror traits like those of identicals (Candy right handed, Jeff left; a whorl in Jeff's hair that grew in one direction, Candy's in the other) — that even their GP became excited about the Third-Type-of-Twins hypothesis, waving his hands as he described a theory that the egg can split before conception. Candy saw how Rose's mouth twitched. 'A theory is just that,' she said. 'A theory.'

Yet the resemblance persisted, well after puberty. Even Candy was startled by what happened at a bus stop once, near a downtown construction site, where she and Jeff waited to be collected by Rose. Aged sixteen Jeffrey was still boyishly slim, Candy still girlishly flat-chested. The dark curls on both their heads reached mid-neck, Jeffrey's tucked behind his ears to show his new silver studs. Candy wore a silver chain with a small guitar pendant. Both twins wore denim jackets and black trousers — Candy's jacket blue, Jeffrey's black. A builder whose yellow hard hat tilted back to show his broad forehead leaned out through some iron girders. 'Gidday, girls,' he grinned. 'Sweet *as*.'

Jeffrey answered back, voice consciously lowered. 'Gidday, mate.'

The builder jerked, his chin tucked in as he stared at them. 'Gender benders. Fucken — *poofters!*'

Expressionless, Jeffrey gave a quick hula with his hips, but, simmering with embarrassment and fury, Candy folded her arms and turned away.

'*Leave* it, would you, Jeff? I don't want to be gang-banged by the whole site crew.'

'Think a good deal of yourself, don't you?'

Candy closed her eyes and breathed in slowly, fighting down the quick, spiteful fish of habit that wanted to snatch at his bait and fight.

Push-me-pull-you. Janus, with two reflected faces, seeing opposing ways.

'Oh, look, kids, *twinnies!*' cried parents downtown.

'I was born six minutes earlier,' Jeffrey gave back automatically, when he was as young as four, and when he and Candy were in fact 'thick as thieves', as their father said. Jeffrey's admonitory tone disoriented people. They seemed to need to stare again, as if they might have been mistaken. Twins were about togetherness, and sharing, weren't they? But Jeff's voice was so grey and serious. Candy kept quiet and watched him also. The one first seen and held. Six minutes of separateness. Six minutes of air in lungs and against skin. Six minutes of being ahead, of being the only one.

But after they were born it was Jeffrey who had been behind. He had taken time to learn how to suckle, was fretful, sleepless, and the nurses swore he was thinning before their very eyes; it was such a terrible, unnatural thing to see a baby thin . . .

Candy, however, knew how to feed almost straight away, took her fill and then slept while their mother, Rose, fought her own fatigue to try to coax Jeffrey to latch on to her breast properly, sitting it inside his open, crying mouth, herself crying when Robinson, their father, tried to make light of it and said, 'He's a right little performer. A wailer, not a crooner, eh?' But Rose told them later that with all the attention (*Yeah, with all the attention*, Candy thought) soon it was Jeffrey who fed regularly, little loaf boy rising, and Candy who seemed to forget, to lose interest, once Jeffrey had the knack. And when she did feed, she clamped down in a way that hurt, as if she hit upon some tender duct or nerve that Jeffrey knew to avoid. Candy stayed small, a worry to her mother, worrying at her mother's raw nipples the way some people gnaw their nails, or pens, the chewing a thinking, something eating away at them.

'Right from the start they've been different,' Rose insisted when asked wasn't it difficult raising twins. Twice the work, surely, and wasn't it hard not to see them as a unit? Especially when, if they both wore trousers, and with that curly hair, those South Island river-stone green eyes, the similarity was *uncanny*. ('Is it a boy or a girl?' asked one four-year-old at kindergarten, looking from Jeffrey to Candy and back again.)

Rose certainly brought some of it on herself. She *would* insist on dressing them in the same colours. 'Boys' clothes are more practical,' she said, let alone that so often two for the price of one was hard to resist. And it did make the laundry loads so much easier if the children wore the same colours — not a factor to be scoffed at in a southern winter in the seventies, when the washing machine was so slow, and had no spin, so that you had to feed the clothes through a wringer, piece by piece, your hands turning red with the cold.

Those first months had been hard. The twins weren't ever supposed to know: that was something Robinson and Rose had agreed upon once Rose pulled through. But Candy found out. And although she could tell you exactly what things she had heard, and when, it was still as if she had always known somehow. As if there were an empty space deep down, waiting for a missing part, and yet when the part came it didn't fill the emptiness: it sealed it in place.

Candy and Jeffrey had often heard about Rose's problems with teaching the babies to feed properly: first one giving trouble, then the other. Their parents had both thought the other difficulties were all to do with that, initially. They thought it was just that Rose was worn out. She moved slowly around the house in her pink towelling bathrobe, taking hours to complete a single chore. Candy was never sure how she knew this story, but she knew that Robinson found Rose once, standing stock still in the laundry with her hands suspended over the disinfecting bucket. She had gone out there half an hour earlier to rinse out the nappies that had been soaking in bleach. They still sat in the bucket, and Rose didn't move when he spoke, nor when he touched her cheek, which was icy. He had to virtually carry her back to the house, arms around her bowed shoulders, as if he were leading her away from the scene of an accident. Apparently it was after this that the tears started. Doing the dishes, the ironing, watching TV, cooking, Rose's face streamed. She talked right through it often enough, behaving as if it were merely the symptom of something like a cold or an allergy. Feeding and changing the children, she wet their fontanelles with big heavy drips. Years on, she couldn't help wondering if that was why they both refused to put their heads under water when learning to swim. She said this to Robinson one afternoon in the car on the way home after their lessons, when she thought the radio distracted the children from adult talk. Robinson had laughed, even taken a hand off the steering wheel to lay it on Rose's thigh. But it was one of the things Candy heard. The things she stored away, a reluctant collector, as if concealing them, shoving them, crumpled, to the back of a cupboard. Yet she knew they were there. Like the regular discussion about household accounts, and the annual donations to Barnados, which Rose never once allowed the family budget to omit.

And then, of course, there was the clinching event — the fact that Robinson's mother came to visit from England only once. She had told Candy a story. Days afterwards, an uncharacteristically furious Rose shouted at Robinson as she stood in the centre of the living room, arms angled on her hips. 'I will *not* have her in this house again.' Rose seemed to rise up on her heels, a large pale bird preparing to become skyborne. 'She is a greatly dangerous woman.'

Which was a little bit like what Gram had said to Candy. 'Your mother is a woman who could have done great damage.' That was when she also said Rose wouldn't let Robinson go and live in

England again — although he didn't appear to want to. Candy had only ever heard her father say how long ago his time in England seemed to him now: 'like someone else's olden days'.

'Your father wrote to me about it all at the time,' Gram explained to Candy, as they sat in her room, folding all the clothes Gram had emptied out of Candy's bureau because she didn't think Rose knew how to use storage space efficiently. Candy hadn't minded Gram's intervention at first — before Robinson had said no, he definitely wasn't ever planning to shift the family back to England, Gram had been fun. She'd brought them all butterscotch and fudge, and little mechanised tin toys — even to Rose and Robinson, who had seemed to like being included in the separate Christmas of her arrival: the one that came nearly two months after the real Christmas, which she'd also sent presents for. And Gram had lots of astonishing stories about Robinson as a boy: stories that, initially anyway, made everybody laugh, and made Candy and Jeffrey look at their father as if he were a wonderful trickster. All the marvels and mishaps of boyhood so well concealed, but together he and Gram could draw them out, colourful, glinting, absurd: a juggling act of stolen suspenders, escaped white mice, trying to catch a bird by putting out cut limes on the lawn. Gram had told *the* story to Candy, with the same persuasiveness about when the twins were babies: as if she had witnessed it all. It was so detailed in fact that Candy had felt an upwards zigzagging fizz of confusion in her thoughts. She wanted to ask, why didn't you say something to her in the shop, why didn't you walk after her and turn her around? She couldn't shake the sense that her grandmother had *known*. When Candy was older she remembered Gram's look of satisfaction. Quietly savouring the scandal, her mouth as it was in photos: the corners slightly upturned in the permanent smile of a cat whose eyes don't share the muzzle's expression.

The story was about Rose taking the twins out in their double stroller, both of them bundled up in hand-knitted woollens and tucked in under sheepskin and crocheted quilts. Candy had thought about it so often — adding particulars of her own — that although the colours were faded, like an old *Look and Learn* magazine bought at a second-hand book stall, it was as if it were all happening again, right then, in another part of the city. The events would never go away, never stop, be undone:

Rose's raincoat whips between her legs as she walks, pushing the twins. The cold finds its way through her leather gloves as easily as it would through evening cocktail silk. She catches the bus to the centre of town and finds a Barnados shop. She manoeuvres the stroller in through the door and parks it under the wall-mounted gas heater, which later Candy knew — from those in old school halls — would have had dangling metal chains like the mechanism on a grandfather clock. Roaming through the clothes racks, fingering the stationery sets, Rose finds her pulse actually steadies when the bell on the shop door tinkles once, twice, three times, as lunch-break shoppers duck in, the confined space filling up. The bell gives a fourth ring: two women this time, about to enter. Rose holds the door for them before she passes through, smiling kindly in their general direction, although not meeting their eyes. The brown toes of her flat-heeled boots flash in front of her vision; it's as if some kind of visor has come down, and the glistening, wet patch of footpath where her shoes move — <u>one</u> and <u>one</u> and <u>one</u> and <u>one</u> — is all she can see.

Rose is reported, nearly two hours afterwards, by several motorists, seen along the city's exit motorway still walking — limping, in fact — and not on the roadside but in the middle of the busy, racing lanes. She is wet to the skin, frozen, and when her boots are taken off later the stockings have worn away. (The burst blisters and grated skin, which looks as if it has been chewed, leave dark stains on the white insides of her shoes.) Eventually a patrol car slows down beside her and stops to find out what is going on. The officer quickly decides it would be best to take her in to the nearest station, as the only thing he can get out of her is 'Please help my babies'.

When Robinson arrives with Jeffrey and Candy, Rose says, as soon as he steps through the door, 'I filled the bath with only hot. It will be cold by now.' Robinson crouches down, one hand still on the stroller, one in his lap with the car keys. (When Gram told the story she said, 'Miraculously, you twins had slept peacefully for hours.' But there was a strange prickling sensation on the outside of Candy's throat, which then fanned along her shoulderblades. She could *see* her mother in an orange plastic bucket chair, her wet raincoat drying in patches so it almost looked marked like leopardskin. She could *see* her father's profile as he squatted beside the stroller's metal frame. Candy felt the shudder of having to lean over into a dark, cold tarn and slowly immerse her arm up to the pit to retrieve something from amidst the lake weed, silt and rock. She wanted to shake the pictures off, but Gram had continued with Rose's words: 'I had to get the babies away from the house. Before I put them in the water.') In the place where this is all happening Robinson nods, trying to see into her downcast eyes. 'That's good, Rose,' he says. 'You did the right thing. You didn't hurt them. You didn't hurt them.'

'Your father withstood so much,' Gram had said to Candy when she finished the story. Then she frowned, gazing up at the art deco plaster moulding of the ceiling, which to Candy looked like thick pitchfork tines. 'Actually, *was* it both of the twins she left behind, or only one? It must have been both. But now, why would I even *think* it was only one?' Gram looked annoyed, her memory a hem caught in a door that had pulled her up short when she wanted to hurry on. 'Oh, never mind.' Then she had patted Candy's knee with a sorrowful look. Candy had to fight the urge to put her palm up to Gram's face and push it away.

At dinner a couple of nights later — after two days of brooding on it all — Candy had watched where her mother's eyes and smiles went. She listened hard to how people responded to Jeffrey when he said anything. Often he said what Candy had wanted to say. Instead of playing the game where she finished his sentences with him, which they'd always then round off with a series of hand claps — his palm to hers, straight on, then one palm up, one down — she gradually felt a slow, sad tiredness. Gram told new stories about their father when he was a boy, but tonight they clearly embarrassed him: two bulges came up on either side of his jaw, giving away that he was gritting his teeth. Gram just carried on. Something in her tone meant that during a break in an anecdote about a rabbit Robinson had left out too long in its cage in the sun without water, Candy eyed her and asked, 'So did *you* ever want to leave your children, while you walked away?'

That emphasis on *you*: the word acted like a pressed switch — the air and light in the whole room shifted. The faces around Candy were shocked, as if an explosion had been heard in the street, vibrated the windows of the house. Except, that is, for Jeffrey: he merely watched Candy, curiously, waiting for the explanation nobody else needed.

'No, I never did,' answered Gram. A layer of politeness cooled and stiffened over her. 'I always wanted both of my children.'

Later that night Rose came into Candy's room when it was time for sleep. She sat on her bed after she had been tucked in. It was still light outside, the last of the long summer evenings now that school had begun. Candy liked the curtains to be left open so she could watch clouds elongate, fold over, disperse. The sound of the TV and occasionally Gram's laughter came from the living room: slipping out through the keyhole, Candy imagined, a cartoon version of the smell of hot fruit pie, wafting through the air in a sugary white ribbon. That was Gram's laugh, anyway: too much sweetness forced into it.

Rose ran her hand up and down Candy's arm. 'I want to talk to you about what happened at dinner. What did Gram tell you exactly?'

Candy fingered the pages of the book she had been absorbed in when her mother tapped at the door. She kept her head down, talked stiffly, as if the answer were typed there in unfamiliar lettering she'd been asked to read out loud. 'That you left us, or maybe one of us, in a shop, and walked away along the motorway.' Candy waited for her mother to say which one of them it had been. She thought of Jeffrey, sitting up in his bed just the other side of the wall, dark hair still wet from his bath, pyjamas buttoned up to his collarbone, one of their father's magazines about mechanics on his knees. Jeffrey was like Robinson. Candy wasn't. Sometimes she wasn't like anyone much.

Rose frowned. 'What Gram doesn't seem to have explained is . . . that I wasn't very well.'

Candy focused hard on the chapter heading she had reached in her book. 'The Hut in the Old Man's Beard', it said. She tried to concentrate on rearranging the letters at the top of the page into new words, but couldn't help listening.

'Sometimes the mother is just so tired after giving birth, and it's such a big change from what she's used to, that she can't do anything, and it makes her sad. That's all. She gets over being tired eventually.'

Candy looked up. Rose's eyes reflected the window's silver squares of late evening light, which gave her a removed expression, like someone staring out across a flat sea to the thickened line between sky and water. But it seemed she was seeing elsewhere.

'That house we lived in then,' she said. 'Something about it. And that suburb. Its climate seemed different from the rest of the city. Hemmed you in like hills, like there were great slopes of cold shouldering in on you all the time, pressing against the walls, against your mind. A coldness that said there was really nothing else out there anywhere, either: everything was just temporarily built over it, to ward it off. But the cold and the damp and the dark always seeped through. I used to think, in that first house, that I'd brought the past with me, that I would never entirely leave it behind.'

Candy glanced out quickly to look at the blue sky, feeling a turn of anxiety in her stomach, a turn the size of the small wax-paper twist of salt that went into their school lunches sometimes, to accompany boiled eggs, the smell and taste of which made her queasy. The cold and damp must have followed Rose here, too, because there had been the bad times, when Candy and Jeffrey had thought their mother would never smile again, when her face was grey and heavy, sad and leonine.

Rose sighed. 'I wonder if it was the place, sometimes, as much as anything else.' She blinked. 'I'm thinking out loud. Sorry, love. Promise me you won't worry about what Gram said? It was a long time ago, and it doesn't mean anything now. I was sick then, I've been sick sometimes since, but I'm not now, and that's all there is to it. It was wrong of Gram to tell you about something that doesn't matter any more. Your dad and I have forgotten all about that time, okay? We've forgotten.'

Now reflected in her mother's eyes, looking from one to the other, Candy saw two of herself. And thought of the double stroller, in the rain, then pushed up under the heater. And her mother, striding, hurrying: still walking even when her feet blistered. Walking away.

'RIGHT FROM THE start they've been different.' Rose used to get so tired of the questions when the children were little that sometimes she'd have liked to move from their birth town altogether once they were ready for school. She'd even have been prepared to go to the trouble of finding a suburb big enough that she could send Jeffrey and Candy to separate schools: only the thing was, the twins had wanted to stay together. Dressing them the same, but insisting on their separation. Divided about them, you could say. In two minds.

At Rose's wish to send them to different schools Robinson had showed the curious dimples that appeared above, not beside, the corners of his mouth whenever he was trying to restrain a smile.

'I don't want them seen as odd,' Rose insisted, exasperated by Robinson's amusement, the way he had of laughing lightly at her most serious suggestions as if they were twenty-one again, back in her grandfather's shed, where she was trying on old fishing hats, pulling the floppy khaki brims down low over her eyebrows, fingering the rainbow-dyed feathers safety-pinned to the crown. Robinson would get a look in his eyes as if he'd soon be closing the shed door, drawing shut the fly-specked curtains and sliding a hand along her back, feeling for the tiny white-painted metal hooks on her bra. (The way Candy, by accident, had seen him do once or twice. It had both surprised and reassured her: and had made her feel infinitely wiser.)

'I mean it, Robinson,' Rose said, trying to erase his dimples with her stare. And he had to hear the barb of fear her voice had often put out after the birth of the twins: a thorn that snagged at him unexpectedly every time, so that he had to slow down and consider, work out how to unpick what he had unintentionally done. He was so proud of his 'little dittos', his 'two chips off the old block', his 'look-at-them-they're-spitting-images!' (coined when the kids were blowing milk bubbles side by side in their high chairs: he'd thought he was hilarious, but Rose just handed him a pair of fresh bibs). He was intrigued by the similarities of their small quirks and larger commonalities. There was the way both kids twisted their hair into knots — witch's stirrups, Gram had called them — on one side of their head when reading. The way both — despite Rose trying to teach them otherwise — put their T-shirts on neck first instead of sleeves first, and took them off by dragging at the back of the collars, which eventually pulled little holes in the top seams. The way they always started out kneeling, instead of sitting, on sofas and chairs, as if each of them forgot, every time, how uncomfortable they'd be in a few minutes. The way they never used the handles on mugs but held them from the opposite side, so when they moved on to hot chocolates, coffees, teas, they always had to wait for their drinks to cool. Funny little tykes. The way each one often took the lead when interacting separately with their peers, although when they were together it seemed Jeffrey was the slightly more assertive.

For Robinson, their twinship was a delight, and he'd have made more of it, somehow, if he could. But Rose didn't want the twins to stand out, he could see that. Stand out: outstanding. Rose's outstanding family, and how exposed they had made her feel as she had grown up. Grandfather in parliament, father a fine arts professor and respected painter, mother a history lecturer in the days when it was still fairly unusual for women even to finish secondary school, older brother now a choreographer living overseas, and not much in contact with people back home. Rose had grown up with another endlessly repeated question: 'Rose Greger? You're not related to Harry Greger, Phil Greger, Helen Greger, Bill Greger are you?' Expectations pressed in on her like the warm air in a stuffy room, sapping her energy instead of stimulating it, dulling her interest in most things academic, and even in dance, because it was so readily assumed that she should try them and Would Do Well.

When Robinson met Rose he had never heard of the Gregers. He had come to New Zealand from England for a working holiday at the end of his studies. The children grew to know the story off by heart, and could correct Robinson and Rose when they left out incidents. He knew Rose as the girl behind the counter at the vet's where he'd had to make several mail deliveries in his work as a postie. It had been an oppressively still summer, extraordinary for so far south, everything parched and desiccating, lawns blond like straw, surface of the asphalt rising and popping: black soup in a saucepan. It felt to Robinson as if even the population had been evaporated by the heat: the streets were void, ghostly after London. His colleagues at the post office kept reassuring him that it would change once term started again and the university students returned, but he doubted it. The information he had picked up about Dunedin said that it was one of New Zealand's coldest cities, but already his nose was through its fifth sunburn peeling. He didn't think he had been conned: just that he was learning that definitions of basic concepts were different down here. Cold was hot. So busy would still mean empty, even if the town did pick up a little at the start of term.

Rose was a comfort to Robinson in his feverish solitude even before they spoke. There at the reception desk, dressed in simple primary-coloured cottons — blue and white sailor's maillot, white button-fly-front trousers (zips for women were considered *fast*), her brown hair swept up in a ponytail, a silver snakelike bracelet clasped on her upper arm — Rose had seemed so — fresh. Drinkable. He had wanted her to notice him. Really notice. Not just say, 'Oh, great. The mail. Great. Thanks.' Robinson became uncomfortably conscious of how he sweated as he strode up and down hills, bag jouncing on his hip, letters and parcels slippery in his hot hands; he knew he must smell doggy, tried not to raise his arms too high as he handed her the post so the sweat marks wouldn't moon obscenely at her. He felt overpoweringly grimy whenever he came near her. Yet the self-consciousness had a thrilling jab to it also: he pushed himself through the vet's door every day like someone walking up to the edge of a magnificent, vertiginous precipice. When he looked back it seemed he had never felt so alive as when he was in this inarticulate suspense.

On a scorching New Year's Eve the vet's was his final delivery. Rose was closing the office early for a half day. 'Sorry to hold you up,' he said. Then, heart pounding so hard he was sure she would see the surface of his regulation shirt vibrate like the wing of a nervous insect perched on his chest, he said, 'Can I offer you a lift anywhere, in recompense?' His car was at least a twenty-minute walk away. He honestly didn't know if he wanted her to say yes or no. He just wanted to offer her something. She seemed to angle her gaze at his breast pocket, which made his heart kick harder, wanting to leap out of his ribs: stupid, tongue-lolling cuckoo from a clock.

She waited only a moment before she said no, but he could walk her to the corner.

As for Rose: it was the nearest thing to excitement she'd had all summer. She had thought she would get to help more in the surgery but she was stuck out there on reception, answering phones, filing, typing. And in an accent that showed he wasn't from around here, he had said a word like *recompense*. She hated herself for noticing, but the thing was, it was the kind of word which — had she used it — her last boyfriend would have labelled snobby. Why couldn't she speak like normal people? Rose couldn't quite work out where she fitted. The people who wouldn't mind 'recompense' would know about her family. They wouldn't let her just be Rose. But the one boyfriend who had not cared about the Gregers or their world wouldn't let her be Rose either. He had felt mocked by the words she used: 'Not all of us have had your chances; not all of us come from up your scale,' and she had floundered, stuck with the sentences that she swore just came to her like oxygen. She had realised during that boyfriend's glowering sulks how much a part of her family she was, speaking its tongue, despite all her resistance to being known as one of them. 'It must be hard having such a successful family,' a perfumed friend of her parents had said more than once at dinner parties, whispering as if in conspiracy over the snack bowls Rose had to pass around. The friend knew Rose was resisting her parents' wish for her to study beyond school, and thought her tone said *I'm on your side*. Rose heard it as a poorly veiled *It must be hard not being equal to the other Gregers*.

Her marriage to Robinson had been an escape from all that. She didn't have to be a Greger any more. Although she got married in a white lace mini-skirt and white fishnet tights, scandalous even to her 'arty' mother back in the late sixties, she happily dropped her surname for Robinson's: would not entirely understand the radical feminism to come in the seventies and eighties. She wanted the change of identity a married name implied, as if it could also bring a kind of oblivion, her past self forgotten even to herself. As Rose Marshall, now, new interests came to her like a vine putting out its first grape crop. Robinson loved the buzz of activity she generated, the paint pots, scraps of material, scent of massage oil, collapsing piles of yoga and gardening books, the way she flurried home after her day in admin at an accountant's, chattering and stealing kisses and squeezes as she dashed around him, getting ready to go out to night craft classes, committees, public talks.

She fuelled him: he took up Harriers, DIY, found work importing and selling cars, which still used his engineering degree a bit, but let him get outside: something he'd grown used to in the temporary job as a postie, and which he found he didn't want to give up. 'You'd be mad not to get real engineering work,' his mother had written from England, but in a country of hills and sea and creeks and rivers, Robinson had an itch to be out in it. Test drives on the open road. Around the harbour, along the beaches, or even way out to Central. There was something about a line-up of gleaming bonnets and windscreens in the sales forecourt that made him feel satisfied. He'd made sure they all ticked over: he loved to think of the wide country and big skies as he tinkered on the engines, planning the test drive route, anticipating the curves and hills, his body sometimes unconsciously moving to take the bends in the road while he was still doing his inspections. He liked to think he was helping other people to get places, you know, in their lives; liked to imagine them heading off on long journeys once they'd bought from him. Making changes.

Oh sure, he worried about environmental effects, even back then, before the children got on his back about it when they were teenagers: but he'd needed the job fast, and things just have a way of settling in. And his getting morose about the entire planet wasn't going to help anyone, certainly not once the twins were born. You wanted a better world for your kids — the seventies' oil crises were a sharp reminder of it all — but the car was here to stay, and the simple fact was, he had to earn money. And actually, if you really want to know, one of his little weekend projects in those days had been working on a design at home for an electrical car. Ironic thing being, he'd had less time to spend reading up in magazines and manuals and journals and library books, and experimenting away, when the children were born. The very kids who would hassle him later — although funny they never seemed to mention the environment when he was driving them to their sports practices or beach picnics. Kids. No, there was no point in him getting the glooms on, especially after the twins first arrived, when Rose had needed him more . . .

On the night Rose had come into Candy's room to see what Gram had said, Candy had nodded, to say *okay*, to stop Rose worrying. But she couldn't forget. It fitted in with the bad times, when Mum seemed to go away inside herself for long periods and think about things she couldn't talk about. It fitted in with too many other half-caught phrases: *No point getting the glooms on, when Rose had needed him more . . . But Rose did that before the twins were born . . . Twice the work? Especially when the twins first arrived . . . The condition has to be more widely recognised . . . Actually more common in the mothers of multiples.* Although Candy hadn't wanted to hear it, Gram's story had slid into place, like a bolt run into position with a heavy, definitive measure.

When Rose had gone back into the living room Candy lay silently, book poised in her hands, breath held, trying to sound as if she were asleep. But soon a delicate tap came at her door. It was pushed open slowly and Jeffrey stole in. She had guessed he would be listening through the thin wall that divided their rooms, straining to hear what was going on, wanting to push in on the conversation. Like the two of them side by side before birth, in separate amniotic sacs, competing for and sharing space and nutrients. With ultrasound (as Candy discovered, watching TV as an adult), twins can be seen punching each other. They can also be seen to kiss. Jeffrey came to stand close by.

'What's going on?' he whispered.

'Nothing.'

His expression didn't alter. 'What's everybody talking to you about?'

'It's nothing.'

'Don't play games, Candy, I know there is something.'

She chewed her lip, considering. Then she lowered her book. 'It's not *about* boys' stuff.'

He studied her for a moment, one eyebrow buckling neatly and sceptically in the middle. Then he shrugged, with an indifference that was meant to sting, to say, *I don't need you either.* 'Suit yourself,' he said, and walked straight out again.

Candy stayed watching the smooth, undecorated plane of her bedroom door after he had pulled it shut behind him. Even though she had been the one to try to deflect him, she couldn't help feeling the smart of his exit. As so often with Jeffrey, the emotions tumbled and tangled so that she wasn't sure what was what. Her instinct was not to tell him — but was she protecting him from the story? Knowing how a look of grave inwardness would appear on his face, a sense of him studying his failings too astutely, a habit she always took on the role of pulling him away from. Like the time they were eight years old, when he stood too close to the turf-lined, overhanging lip of the cliffs at Tunnel Beach, beneath which surged and boiled dark green waters. Or was she stocking up a secret, some form of future advantage? One more thing that separated them: this time, a piece of evidence she had, that he didn't.

She turned out her light but was sure she could feel Jeffrey through the wall, still glowering into himself, giving off a hurt heat. It took Candy ages to ignore it enough to be able to sleep.

The next morning in the kitchen, as she helped to set the table for breakfast, Candy found herself involuntarily tiptoeing, setting down plates and spoons as delicately as possible, prepared for any loud noise to set off a chain reaction, like lit Guy Fawkes bangers. The conviction that they were all angry with her only seemed reinforced by Dad's falsely cheery, hand-rubbing good morning, Mum's little frown as she waited for the pancakes to brown, Gram's series of questions directed too loudly at Jeffrey, Jeffrey's slinky walk to the table as he failed to help Candy bring the golden syrup, the brown sugar, the cream, to the dining room.

At the table, as everyone drew up their chairs, Candy swore she could feel the undercurrents sparking from knee to knee. As Gram chattered about general things, eyes bright on Jeff, Candy's parents were quiet. And when Gram asked, 'Did you sleep well, Robin-my-son?' Dad said, 'Yeah?' in a way that meant 'Okay,' or 'Not too badly,' but that really left everything still hanging in mid-air, questioned: said he didn't want to satisfy her with an answer. Gram's smiles at Jeffrey grew warmer, her little pats at his shoulders and hair more fluttery. He seemed to be enjoying it, his wide grin not in the least bit trimmed.

'Can I have the golden syrup, please, sweetheart?' said Dad to Mum, even though the tin was closest to Gram.

Mum's gesture as she reached for it was exaggerated. It told

Gram she was invisible, or at least not really there in any important way. And Dad's long smile at Mum said a lot more than thank you for passing the topping. He and Mum both set to cutting their pancakes, and just right then Gram asked Jeffrey to say grace. It was pointed, and it did embarrass them; they'd forgotten again, as they had at every meal she had been there for.

Jeffrey looked a choir boy on leave: fresh white T-shirt tucked in tightly, hair uncombed, one cheek still rosy from where it had been pressed against the pillow. Gram liked everyone to join hands so he put out a hand on either side: one for Gram, one for Candy. Candy waited for the offended spite from last night to travel from his hand into hers, but his grip was firm, dry, and he gave three quick milkmaid squeezes. It made Candy lift her head a little, filch a chance to glimpse at everyone — what had he noticed? But they were all bowed and waiting. Jeffrey cleared his throat.

'Yum, yum, pig's bum. Stuff yer mouth and fill yer tum.'

A hog's snort escaped from Candy's nose and then she and Jeffrey were off, falling about laughing, faces turning red with lack of breath. Robinson and Rose didn't look too stern, but both said, settle down, sit up straight, come on, you two. When everybody had picked up their forks again, Gram's eyes were still cast down over her plate. Her cheeks too had taken on two high points of cranberry.

'Gram? What's the matter?' asked Jeffrey. 'Is something wrong with your breakfast?'

Robinson frowned at him. 'Now, Jeff, enough's enough. Let your Gram finish her grace on her own at least.'

Gram's eyes butterfly-darted open; she had an air of just having arrived back at the table — from a higher place. Her lips pursed a bit as she examined her first forkful. 'Pancakes are a terribly fatty meal to have too often, don't you think?'

Jeffrey chewed, head cocked to the side. 'You just lied to God then, didn't you?'

'I beg your pardon?'

'Grace is meant to be when you're grateful for the food you've been given.'

Rose coughed terribly, had to slap her serviette up to her mouth and go to the kitchen, the tears from choking making her eyes oddly merry, Candy thought.

After breakfast Robinson said, 'You two go and wash faces and hands.' They knew from conversations overheard in the last week that he meant in order to be ready to go with Gram to church again, but he didn't say so directly now. Only one of the sermons so far had been interesting: the one where they heard the story of Jacob and Esau. It was strange: one of the Bible twins apparently got born looking like he was covered in a red hairy garment. Fur? Feathers? Was he really a human boy? Candy had asked Gram to explain it to her several times, though only a few things really came clear: scarlet, anger. Candy wasn't quite sure if she liked the story or not, though it stayed with her, like the mood of a dream, or a stubborn stain on a white cloth, long after you've forgotten what spilt there.

Candy and Jeffrey exchanged another look. In the hallway Jeffrey beckoned to her urgently. They went quickly towards his room, which was near the back entrance. As he reached it Candy opened the hallway cupboard and pulled out coats and scarves for them both: autumn seemed to have arrived overnight. He turned and saw, said nothing, but immediately changed tack and went to the back door. They slipped out, dashed around the side of the house, the garage, and pelted along the path that cut beside a neighbour's house and led a back way to the main road, rather than out the front to their own little suburban cul-de-sac.

'Here.' Candy passed Jeffrey his coat and scarf as they jogged alongside each other.

'Where shall we go?'

'Not that way, that's the way to the church, they might pass us. This way.'

'The creek!'

'Yeah, the creek!'

It wasn't far, and the creek bent through a local sports field, over which spanned two small white wooden bridges and a large concrete water pipe, which they could hide underneath, watching for eels and water rats and frogs, or at least a duck or two, as they built dams with rocks or tried to make fishing rods out of lancewood and string or strands of hair. A few other people trailed across the playing field: one or two joggers, a woman walking a small dog, a mum and dad teaching a little kid how to ride a bicycle.

They ran along to the bridge farthest from home. Near it, there were rough steps in the low but steep banks that dropped from the grass to the water: steps worked in by the number of local children who came down here to play. Today the creek was an ugly lurid colour, full of the strange green dye that now and then was used for some scientific reason: a test of water purity, or perhaps to kill a particular organism. It was also fuller than it was in summer; at water level there was only a small scoop of dirt and shingle, but just enough to offer a place for Candy and Jeffrey to sit down on their spread-out coats. Candy wrinkled her nose up at the poisonous-looking current, fearing the creek had been ruined forever by somebody, because how do you wash dye out of water?

'They've spoilt the creek, Jeff. Do you think the fish might be suffocated?'

Jeffrey eyed it too, but gave a resigned shrug. 'What do you want to do down here?'

'Let's skim stones.'

'From squatting only — they might see us otherwise.'

'I don't reckon they'll come this way.'

'But in case.'

'Okay. In case.' Jeffrey sifted through the stones at his side. 'Skimming and duck's farts, okay?'

'What's duck's farts?'

'When you chuck the rock up high in the air, and get it to come straight back down into the water without a splash, and it makes this funny "ploff" sound.'

Candy grinned at him. 'Yum, yum, duck's bum.'

Jeffrey wahk-wahked like a duck. Then his stone gave four skips. 'Aww, sucks,' he said. 'Need a flatter one.' His fingers hunted around again, and then he sat for a bit, thinking. 'Hey, Can-do?'

That was their father's nickname for her. 'Tell me, really. What did Gram say?'

Candy was shocked by the adult gentleness in his voice. She reacted like a crystal glass struck with a fork: helpless to stop what came from her. She pushed the heels of both hands into her eyes, but tears still leaked out.

She felt Jeffrey's touch steal across her back. He drew an awkward series of half circles and pats there for a while. Then Candy heard the rattle of shingle, the musical *plip*, *plip* of stones skidding on water, bumping into bedrock. She sniffed, then squinted into the grey, overcast light again, rubbed the rough woollen cuff of her jersey into her eyes.

'Gram said Mum left us — or maybe just one of us — in a shop once, when we were babies. And Mum walked away. For hours and miles. She didn't want us and she tried to run away, then the police found her, but . . .' There was a sick unwinding in Candy's stomach, as when she hurt something unintentionally and there was no repair: a praying mantis injured by the slam of a lid back on a jar, a ladybird picked up clumsily between finger and thumb, black underwing drooping like a torn satin slip. She lifted a fist, curled up in her cuff, and waved it briefly in front of her, wanting to smudge out the words from the air. 'But Mum says Gram told it wrong, that Mum was sick and she and Dad don't really even remember it properly any more, it's not important.'

Jeffrey had stopped skimming rocks but held a stone in his fingers, thumb working over it, feeling for roughness in its surface. 'Twins is meant to be harder. People always say.'

When Candy swallowed, it felt as if she were catching cold — throat hot and sore — because now she needed to rescue him. 'But Mum's all right now, eh, Jeff? She's been good for a long time. She seems happy to me. She will be when Gram goes, anyway!'

Jeffrey's fingers still examined the rock. Then he turned to Candy. 'Why didn't Gram come out to help Mum and Dad when we were babies? If twins was so hard? Remember the stories about how Granny Greger did? She made it so she didn't have to teach for a term, Dad said. That must have been after.'

'After?'

'Leaving the babies in the shop.'

Candy gave him a hard, startled look.

'Stupid old bag. She wasn't even here — what would she know? You listen to Mum, Candy, she's the one who can tell best.'

The babies, that's what had stunned her: his ability to stand back from it. They were eleven years old, and for the first time were in different classes at school. Candy hadn't wanted to be separated, had felt jumpy for the first week: sudden movements and noises startled her, as if all her nerve endings had lost a protective layer. She kept looking behind her, thinking she'd heard someone say her name, until the teacher noticed and told her off for talking, though Candy hadn't said a thing. But even if Jeffrey hadn't wanted separation either, he wouldn't let himself say so: it was sissy. And already his usual brooding on things had turned. Candy, hearing him, had her tears cut off as if a circuit had broken. The day felt lighter. The strange green dye in the creek didn't seem so oppressive, so science-fiction. The thing with Gram had tangled Jeffrey up momentarily, but like a boy walking through early morning cobwebs strung across a hiking track, he barely had to press against the resistance before he was free again.

Before, when things were hard or sad, he used to go quiet, right inside himself, and Candy would fight then, do anything to draw him out, even if she had been the one to drive him there in the first place. She'd sing to him, use his drawn-up knees as drums, tickle him, offer to play his favourite games (Monopoly, Yahtzee — games that bored her), read to the blanket-covered hillock of him as he hid under his quilts — from *The Bumper Book of 1000 Jokes*, *The Jumbo Edition of 1000 Insults*. She'd even crawl in too, and whisper, 'I don't care how mean or miserable or mad you are, Jeffrey Martin Marshall, you're my brother.' And she'd press her forehead and nose into his spine, just wait there until he was ready. When he turned around to goose her under the armpits, or try out his own insults *(May the fleas of a thousand camels infest your ears! May the nose hairs of a million warthogs sprout from your chin!)* she'd submit. She'd take anything that meant he was back again, not frightening her like Mum had.

Usually it was their mum who had put him there, screwed up tight like a hard black rock — look into his eyes and you couldn't see where he'd gone, his energy dense and dark and rounded in on itself. The three or four times it had happened really badly were when Mum had cried and cried and had taken to her own bed, earlier and earlier. Sometimes she was even there when they got home from school and there was a note on the hall table that said snacks were in the kitchen, go and watch TV, do their homework, and don't wake her.

They were the times when they could ask Mum anything (Jeffrey, in the early days, stuttering as if in fear of her answer) — what time would dinner be ready, where were the clean towels, what did this word in a book mean, could they watch TV — and Rose would look at them with such crumpled pain that they were sure they'd committed some — perhaps irreversible — destruction. Candy would search the day wildly — search yesterday, the week before — what had they done? In silent consent she and Jeffrey went to their rooms and tidied them assiduously. Then they did the dishes, the dusting, the vacuuming, the washing — although there was the time the laundry and kitchen flooded because Jeff had left some socks in the outflow sink. When Mum had woken up, to stand ankle deep in the grey soapy water, she just rocked and made strange mouths, with her arms around herself. So afterwards Jeff had thought it was he who had made her sick. Even though Candy tried to say: remember, she was in bed for days already, Jeff, it wasn't you. And sometimes, when he went so quiet and packed down, compact like coal, Candy hated him. She wanted to save him and yet she hated him for being strange like Mum too. It's not that she stopped loving the sad mum: not at all, never. It's just that the love slipped and turned in on itself, like a part of the body used incorrectly, pressured, twisted.

Once, Jeffrey frightened Candy at night after he had crept into her bed when their parents were talking behind their own door. Knees drawn up and just touching, hands clutched together near their chins because Jeff had seized hers and pressed it to her mouth to say *sshh*, they faced each other closely enough to be able to catch each other's whispers. Jeffrey told Candy he'd overheard some talk. Their dad had said it might be a good idea if Mum went into the day ward during school hours, so that she wasn't left alone while he was at work. But Mum had said it didn't seem like a solution. She was too scared to go to hospital — if she made that step she might never get out. Wasn't there somewhere else she could go, a community drop-in centre? The library even? Dad had said, Rose, honey, be sensible. Those places hardly have people trained in your area, do they? Mum said, my area? You make it sound like I specialise in it. You're tired of this, aren't you, Robinson? But I can't make it stop. Dad said, I know, Rose. It just goes on and on, Mum said. Rose, honey, I know — come here, it's okay. Will you give me a hug? But Jeff said it sounded like Mum couldn't.

Candy pondered. 'She really doesn't seem like the same Mum sometimes. She doesn't even look the exact same as the usual Mum.' They were both quiet for a while, visualising the way Rose wore their dad's outsized jersey and the same pair of threadbare trackpants all the time — pants that left little blue pills of cotton everywhere. Her eyes and mouth drawn low as a beagle's, her shoulders cowed.

Then, what Jeffrey had said sat as plainly in the dark as a bone tree against moonlight. 'You know what, Candy? Maybe she's not our mum. Maybe there is someone else who comes, while the real mum goes away somewhere.'

He didn't say the word itself, perhaps hadn't even made the connection, but Candy knew who the someone would have to be. She peered through the dusk to scrutinise him, to see if he'd meant it the way she'd thought. As she watched him, the lines and shadows of his face seemed to change, as if the moonlight had been washed over by cloud. She broke her focus to look down at their hands entwined in the half-light, and the eeriest sensation slowly filtered into her. Of elevating, a little to the side of things. The knuckles, the pads, the nails, the pink and white of all the fingers; she couldn't tell which were hers and which were his. She tried to move her own so that she could *see*, but none of the fingers responded. The numbness travelled from their joints and into her heart, her lips. Up so close to Jeffrey still, sliding into his eyes, where was she, here or there? The shade around her brother's eyes and lips turned unequivocally frightening now: she barely recognised him. He was the Jeffrey who wasn't Jeffrey, taking her away from herself . . . She squeezed her eyes shut, wrenched her arms free with all her might, hissed *Don't!* treading and oaring wildly with all four limbs: he was deep water and she was drowning.

He tumbled out of her bed, landed with a considerable thud on the carpet. His voice was furious. 'What's wrong with *you*?'

'Get out of my room.'

'Candy, ssshh! What's the *matter* with you?'

'You say horrible things. Horrible things.'

'Candy, shut up, they'll hear us. I didn't *mean* it.' But his voice hit a whine, sounded as if he were imitating her. He must have heard it too because he waited, then whispered 'I said I'm sorry.' But when Candy pulled the covers over her head, burrowed to the middle of the mattress, thinking to herself *I must turn invisible, turn invisible NOW*, defeat made him sigh and pad out of the room.

Really, that was the first time Candy could remember openly fighting against him. All the other times — the occasions when she wasn't sharing with him, or rescuing him — had been silent. Little nicks and slights that carved out a sore feeling you could forget about for a long time, until another snip came. Listening to him say, 'I was born first', 'But I'm the oldest', while she watched him, wondering how different it was, to be the first. So different that he had to say it whenever he could? She pondered over why he had to say it, when she loved him, and a lot of the time they did share.

That day at the creek, though, the way Jeffrey seemed apart from her wasn't frightening, nor did it make her feel brushed aside. Instead she felt relieved, felt the expansion of pride, as if this time it was his strength, not hers, that they could both lean on. It seemed that since they had been sent to separate classes Jeff was already changing in ways Candy was only just noticing. Things were good. Mum was well now, and had been for a while. She and Robinson had found a new American doctor who believed in what he called 'neurochem *and* neurochat'; Rose found him funny, which in itself was a huge improvement. She'd imitate his accent when she popped her pill each morning, pretending to be like someone on a chocolate ad. 'Mmmmm, *neurochem.*' She'd started showing more and more interest in her garden: it was as if richer colour seeped back into their world as she brought more plants home, and more 'whirligigs' as she called them: windmills, weathervanes — bright wood and plastic daisies, cartoon characters, sunflowers, all of which spun in the wind and made the outside of their house seem as busy as the cogs of a giant clock. She'd taken to making them, too: had set up a little corner in her old sewing room for woodwork and painting, and was thinking of trying to find somewhere to sell them when she'd perfected her designs.

So when *that creep* from their own school, Phil Redshaw, turned up on the other side of the creek, with *that girl* Wairata Lawrence, from another local intermediate, Candy didn't run off straight away like she might have otherwise, because today she and Jeff would make an okay team. Today she and Jeff were what everybody called them: the twins.

PHIL REDSHAW AND Jeff had actually been sort of friends once. For two or three years, in fact, until this summer — though it had always been intermittent: intense contact for a week or so, then nothing for maybe a month or more. Candy had joined in now and then with their games, when they had tired of French cricket or rugby passes and had instead wanted an evil scientist in Superman, or a lady pioneer or wahine to kidnap in Land Wars. Inauspicious beginnings, perhaps, but they were fantastic games, where she could change identity at will. *And now I'm the doctor, and now I'm the sheriff, and now I'm the dragon, and now you have to pass the test by fire.*

There had been a last game, of course: otherwise, perhaps, they'd still be friends. A game they had started off calling Sorcerers for some reason (though there were none in it). It was held in a 'magic circle' of trees in a dense pine plantation that stood beside local native bush trails, and which separated a small sports field from a short run of farmland. The circle was really made by foxgloves weaving here and there between several trees, and by a textured, russet mat of fallen needles. Someone else had discovered it before them: there was a ring of stones at the centre, burnt-out cans, ash, the toffee-coloured shards of broken beer bottles. The children had to clean it all out before they could start — but they weren't timid about their own trespass, as there was something about the remnants of this other camp that had the air of after dark. They'd be home before then. Except three or four times they nearly weren't, because some link in the chain of narrative play had slid over to another dimension, a place thrilling and wrong, but the wrongness only discovered suddenly, when Phil had turned strange at school. The wrongness had been sitting between the twins and Phil ever since, in a pent-up, dread-filled way.

Despite the physical allure of the circle, they'd nearly forgone any game at all when they'd discovered the spot on their berry-picking hike up towards the farmland late one weekend afternoon.

'Isn't that kind of like kids' stuff?' asked Jeff, kicking at the base of a tree when Candy had suggested they use the spot. But the privacy, the only-distant calls from ball games in the park below which was obscured from view by the trees, the strips of sunlight over the needle carpet, held them all there, somehow drowsy and nerve-charged all at once. Dryness, warmth, softness, sap. Rich soil and pine scents, the lazy occasional hum of bees answered overhead by tiny private aircraft, the sweet-sour tang of the one bush of wild raspberry they'd found so far — a handful shared around the yoghurt pottles they'd brought for the purpose — leaned on the senses, opening them up as if they were gates onto another, unexpected field.

Phil's voice had been low, quiet. 'Doesn't have to be for long,' he said. He'd looked behind him, stepped outside the circle, walked off for a few paces, then come back, turned gradually on the spot. 'There's something really different in here,' he said. 'You try it.' Candy and Jeffrey followed suit. Outside the circle it was cooler, danker, and of an instant, howlingly lonely. Although Jeff and Candy had trailed away in opposite directions, quickly losing sight of each other among gorse and tree trunks, they plunged back into the circle at almost the same time, Candy greedy for the sensation of being cradled in the small isolated circle of sun and colour before it disappeared with the angle of daylight. How to explain the way well-being stole its arms around her as soon as she was inside the circle? She looked at the others.

'I think there might be spirits here.' The boys frowned at her, but their silence, a kind of concession, filled her with excited conviction. 'We should try to listen to them.' She sat down, cross-legged. Phil and Jeffrey, hesitant, diffident, hovered. She closed her eyes. The sun was so warm against one side of her face that she thought of it as a hand held there, pressing close. *Stay*, a voice said in her mind.

'Did you hear that?' she whispered urgently, opening her eyes. The boys shook their heads. She felt sadness, cold wavelets, lap at the edges of the circle.

'Perhaps you can hear them through me. Sit down and hold my hands.'

Both boys laughed. 'No way.'

Then she had one of the sudden switches of focus that often came to her when the three of them joined together. Only this time it wasn't in the possibilities of character, but of tactic. She rolled her eyes, as if the others were chicken. 'It's only a game.' She didn't really believe that. The atmosphere was so different it didn't feel like play in the usual sense of pretending, imagining; though it still wasn't a world that could sit on the ordinary plane of home, school, after-school classes, something to share with anyone else.

Giving noisy sighs of stretched patience, Jeff and Phil buckled their knees, sat down near her and accepted her held-out palms.

'Close your eyes.'

'What are the rules of this game?' asked Jeff.

Phil's voice, since he'd sat down, had relaxed again. Candy imagined the day's heat in the pine-needle carpet seeping up from the backs of his thighs, along his spine and into his chest cavity: a sweetness stealing backwards, the reverse of swallowing molasses. 'I guess we just listen to what the place has to tell us,' he said.

The place told them to do various things. Weave a wreath of

foxgloves and gorse for someone who had died here a hundred years ago: if they flinched at the pricks and stings of the gorse, the circle would become *badly* haunted, but a successful wreath would keep the air of benevolence there. Bring the sheep's skull they had seen near the farm boundary fence, set it in the middle of the circle, get a candle and light it each time they came back. Find more fruit and make an offering to say thank you for inviting them to the circle. If they did so, the spirits here would watch over them even when the three had left the plantation. Make a pact never to tell about this place: like blood brothers, sister. Only it turned out Phil Redshaw was extraordinarily squeamish about real blood — any more than a gorse prick could draw. In the potent boundary of the sun circle, and after the shock of seeing his reaction when Candy used Jeff's pocketknife to cut the skin of her palm, the twins found they couldn't tease him. The change in Phil was so physical, like something hard and tight put into boiling water: instantly loosening, blanching.

When Candy and Jeff shrugged, said, 'It doesn't matter, Phil, it's only a g—' his eyes widened with a seriousness that was nearly anger — wanting the challenge still, wanting the truth of the place.

'It has to be something else. Something equal.' He shut his eyes again, sitting back in the tailor pose in which they all received messages from the voice of the place.

Jeff and Candy held back, as if letting him be alone with it. His eyes danced open, lines in his narrow, bony face sombre. 'We might have to wait here tonight until dusk. But it will say by then, if we wait.'

Candy felt a lock of fear snap shut at her throat. By dusk they ought to be home. But Jeffrey had seemed unperturbed — began whittling at a piece of broken branch, starting yet another of the attempts at a miniature totem pole he'd first begun when they'd found the circle.

And at some stage, as they lolled quietly together, listening to the cicadas, birdsong, the rustling of a late afternoon breeze that swept through the plantation now and then, as if it were a corridor and a door somewhere had opened and closed, there was a shift. Candy thought later that maybe it had come because, changing her position at one point, she'd leaned against Jeff the way they did at picnics sometimes, when they used each other as a makeshift chair: back to back. When Jeff had wriggled, pretended to protest, she quickly shuffled over to lean against Phil instead, but only briefly, only as a joke, thinking he'd instantly shake her off, like a spider that had landed in the light blond hair of his arm. But when she pulled away he'd watched as if trying to draw something from her. Then he'd slowly gone back into the message posture, eyes shut. Silence swelled slowly between them all.

'It's told me,' Phil whispered. 'You have to follow everything I do or say.'

The twins exchanged a quick glance, neither one nodding agreement, just waiting. But when Phil said, 'Lie down and shut your eyes,' the steel certainty in his voice meant they each did, willingly. A short time passed, with Candy sensing Phil moving near her brother, and hearing small unidentifiable noises. Like lungs bursting for air, her will to keep her eyes shut nearly broke just as his shadow blocked out the wash of the sun against her eyelids. His finger pressed something against her lips. She resisted and he whispered, 'Take it. You've got to.' Soft and fleshy, it mumbled into her mouth: a wild raspberry. Its natural sugars and warmth were twice as surprising for the delay in recognition. Still absorbing the pleasure, she didn't pull away at the sensation that followed — of Phil slowly lifting up her T-shirt, letting it rest at her collarbone. He immediately lowered her shirt again and said, 'It's over.'

The ritual grew from there. Some version had to be repeated each time: a renewal of their oath, Phil said.

The next time, when it was Candy's turn, he placed wild raspberries in a line along her bare stomach. That was all. When he said, 'It's over,' she sat up: saw that she and Jeff had both been decorated. They caught the berries before they rolled off their torsos, and ate them, happily, ready to move on to the next thing: more voices, or heading back home, whatever. Another afternoon her blind lips met a berry, her shirt was raised, more berries divided her in a line from clavicle to navel, but this time Phil's hands gently crushed and flattened each fruit into her skin. When she sat up she saw that the berries on Jeff, whose eyes were still closed, remained whole. The next meeting the berries were crushed and Phil's hands, mixing the berries into her skin as into cream, slowly passed up to the soft pouches of her aureoles, her baby-indented nipples. She saw, when he announced again, 'It's over,' that this time, although Jeff's berries were crushed too, they were only around his stomach: no higher.

She dwelt on the sensation of berry skin and boy skin between meetings, like recalling the tingling, airborne mood of a flying dream, and was ready for it next time. When Phil again moved to her breasts she lifted her chest a little, pushing into his hand, trying to direct him when the feeling lost intensity. They were older, so much older, in this game than they had ever been before.

One day, she said, 'This time it's your turn,' and Phil had to lie down next to Jeff while she invented her own version: berries into his mouth, berries mouthed from his chest, tongue quick at him here and there, like catching the melt from an ice-cream, the pulse hard and fast in her throat. It wouldn't have taken much for Jeffrey to have sensed how the ritual had lengthened and intensified outside him. He made the most terrible trespass at their next meeting, when Phil was in charge of the oath ceremony again. He turned his head, opened his eyes and watched. The others only knew it when, coldly, he announced, 'Either all of us or none.' This time the silence between them was an immense white sheet that could enfold, suffocate. Then, 'All right,' said Phil. 'But only if we all swear, *swear*, to keep our eyes closed.'

Candy felt she could hear time pass, a slow ticking in the branches of the trees and in the dirt and needles below her. But it can't have been long, as she then heard Phil say, 'I just can't.' And Jeff: 'If I'm the girl and you're the boy it doesn't matter, does it?' Said with the stolid logic, the stern belief of the most powerful of rituals. The day again rolled into a different dimension. And Phil must have made Jeffrey and Candy's oath-taking similar this time because afterwards Jeffrey's eyes seemed as if some darker juice had seeped into them through his skin. And it must have been similar, because that was the last time they'd ever played together. After that, Phil Redshaw had gone sour. He'd hurried away from the circle when dusk came that day: head down, not meeting their eyes, not talking to them. He ran, panicked, through the trees, leaving them behind. 'Wait up!' called Candy. But he didn't.

And here he was, now: something in him stiffening as soon as he caught sight of Candy and Jeffrey sitting on their coats. He and Wairata had been racing on bicycles: now they skidded to a stop.

'Rata!' he said. 'Look over here!'

Wairata, standing up on her pedals, pumped closer. She peered down the creek banks, then gave a disappointed 'So?'

Candy hoped Wairata's boredom would prevail, and tried to reinforce it by wearing a bland expression and sitting as still as possible as she tried to melt back into the stones. But Phil's face moved into a gentle sneer. 'Do you reckon one's a boy and one's a girl, or do you reckon they're both girls?'

Wairata shrugged.

Phil ignored this. His voice was somehow both cruel and infantile: not like the slow, older Phil of the game at all. 'Looks like they're both girls to me. Don't want to get your botty wet, do ya, Jeff-errina, pretty ball-er-rina? *Jeff*-ress the *Ack*-tress?'

So Phil had found out. Candy's lungs stretched with rage, elastic about to spring and snap. How did kids from school know? The theatre and dance classes were in another suburb. They weren't even real ballet, they were mainly acting, but there had been one term with half an hour each lesson of 'movement classes'. And there had been all kinds of dance: jazz, African, Polynesian, modern, and only some ballet, just the basics, because it could be useful in any kind of performance — there was no harm in knowing, their tutor had said.

But here was harm, all right. Phil Redshaw and the brooding sense of damage done. One day, right after that last time in the circle, Candy had tried to ask him at school if he'd be back at the pines that weekend. He'd come straight up, hissed at her, spit flying accidentally in her eye. 'I've found out. My cousin told me. What happened was wrong, really wrong. He said to keep away from your sort. He said someone will show you one day that kind of game is sick. You're sick. The both of you.' Candy was bewildered, could only remember drowsiness, variations in temperature, a spinning, excited sensitivity, and the reflection of all this in the glowing skin of Phil's face. Phil who'd started it all.

If she and Jeff happened to cross his path together after that he had a kind of hounded look but his insults still rained on them: childish, and somehow more rankling and harder to defy for that. The jibes were stupid, so bloody stupid, but fighting them would be like charging a soap bubble with a baseball bat. He called the twins *Siamese*. That was a favourite from other kids, ages ago, before Candy had known what it meant. Phil must have remembered how it used to make her kick and flail at their tormentors when she was just eight or nine. He yelled out *Green eyes, piss eyes, green eyes, bogey eyes*. He said *You look like a boy* and *You look like a girl* to the wrong one. *Si-a-mese, stink like wees* . . . inane, and yet somehow sinister.

Phil now dropped his bike on the grass. He walked to the edge of the clay bank, stooped down and picked up a handful of small dirt clods. He hiffed a series of them at Candy.

Jeffrey scrambled to his feet. Ever since Phil's insults had first started he had tried to pretend he had nothing to do with Candy whenever the other boy turned up: Jeff got that hounded look too. But Phil actually threatening to injure her: this was different.

'Don't you bloody throw stuff at my sister.'

Phil mimicked him, high-pitched. Then said, 'Too hard to tell you two sooky bubbas apart.'

Rounding towards the bridge from one end of the sports field, two joggers came into Candy's view. Phil couldn't do anything while people were watching, so Candy saw the chance to make a break for it. 'Come on, Jeff, let's just get out of here.' She grabbed up her coat, tied it around her waist and hurled the best insult she'd ever heard — caught in a supermarket once, as it was passed between a young couple — '*Grow up*, Phil.' Then she started to climb the clay steps. A dirt clod stung the back of her leg. She didn't react, though Phil whooped and laughed.

At the top of the bank Candy turned and saw him scoop up more dirt, then fire the clods at Jeffrey. Wairata dangled over her bike's handlebars, annoyed, it seemed. She called out to him, rang her bike bell like someone waiting too long in a shop. The joggers were getting closer. Jeffrey's head bucked back as a clod whacked him in the side of the throat. And then Candy snapped. She hurtled across the bridge, ran towards Phil's bicycle. She wanted to hurl herself against him, pummel his face. Instead she yelled, she bellowed, she used her gut muscles the way they'd learned in theatre class. 'You leave my brother alone!' The mocking echo came back. She belted over towards the bike. As a hunk of dirt split and scattered over her, she found the valves on the tyres. Nerves doing jitterbugs, she tugged off the protective rubber caps, and Phil's bicycle's tyres hissed angrily. She ran to the grass edge, dropping the little black nubs into the creek, staying there just long enough to see them hit a patch of mud and roll side to side, just staying out of reach of the water. *Shit.*

The two joggers had put on a burst of speed. 'Hey!' one of them called. Candy started guiltily, shooting a glance over her shoulder — then realised they were heading for Phil and Wairata. She walked quickly towards the adults, first seeing that Jeffrey had climbed up the bank, his oilskin coat smeared with peanut butter-coloured clay. As the joggers drew alongside her, the hard tang of their sweat on the air, one of them asked, 'You okay?' Candy nodded. 'Yeah, guess so.' When the men reached Phil and Wairata they stopped, hands on their hips, feet planted out wide, ribcages rising and falling. Phil and Wairata walked past them, shoulders doing a cocky swagger, but they kept their eyes on the ground and didn't give back any lip. The men stretched calf muscles a little, bounced on the spot, then headed off. Candy, running backwards, heard a voice drift across the field, 'We're keeping an eye on you, my son.'

She turned and hurried to catch up with Jeffrey. They were safe enough: Wairata was crouched down at both bikes, undoing her pump from the crossbar, while Phil, stumbling down an even cruder series of steps on his side of the creek, made his way down the bank to hunt for the valve caps.

Jeff had left at a fast clip over the damp grass marked in white lines that set out ball game boundaries, and had drawn well ahead of Candy. She ran in bursts, getting unexpectedly hot on the overcast day, and called and called to him, but he never seemed to hear. She cast a look over her shoulder and saw that the figures of Phil and Wairata were on the move. She gasped and her feet tangled up on themselves. Once she had righted her step again she found herself needing to say things under her breath to keep her legs going. *Don't look back, keep on track, don't turn around, make some ground.* She trained her eyes on Jeff. He had pulled up his hood, which beaked over his forehead, but left his coat unzipped, so that it flapped open around his hips. With his shoulders sloped, as he checked for traffic before diagonally crossing the road, he had the sideways look of a sad, grey, flightless heron. She called his name again and it came out with a raw sound like a sob, but he didn't even flinch. She fought against the dragging feeling in her lungs.

Somehow, the picture of Jeffrey worked into the rhythms of Candy's efforts to catch up: maybe, she thought later, it was even her first song; she'd always remembered it, short as it was . . .

sad grey gravity bird
your wings won't lift or beat
tall blue earth boy
flying on your feet

That was all: but her legs could run to it, keep up with it, and the words said over and over in variations helped to turn her mind ahead, kept her from checking to see if Phil and Wairata were gaining on her. When she swung through home's front gate, just behind Jeff as he tramped up the doorstep, adrenaline flipped her fear over into hyper-excited relief.

'Hey!' she called to Jeff. 'Sad blue earth bird!'

He halted mid-step, then stalked back towards her. His shove pushed the breath out of her in a *huh* that he took for laughter. 'What did you call me?'

Winded and furious, she could only shake her head.

'What do you think is so funny? You think it's funny?'

'It was just a rhyme I made up. I was saying it to make me run faster.'

His face had whitened in odd patches, as if the bones were trying to knuckle up under his face. 'I don't need to hear your nursery rhymes.'

'I only wanted to catch up with you after what Phil and Wairata did! I saw them hit you.'

'Yeah, well, I don't *need* some stupid little girl sticking up for me, all right?'

She clenched at his coat hem. 'Little? I'm the same age as you, drongo!'

He dragged away and slammed the front door behind him before Candy could follow. She whispered *Jeffrey you moron,* under her breath, but gave him time to get down the hallway so he wouldn't lunge at her again. She doubted Phil and Wairata would follow them this far, but when she let herself into the house, she locked the door behind her, just in case.

IN THE KITCHEN, Rose was drying plates methodically, listening to the radio news with all the concentration of someone peering closely at fine print. The Springboks were on tour, and that year Rose and Robinson wanted the news in all its forms, as often as possible — radio, TV, and even though they subscribed to the morning paper, Dad would often bring home an evening one from a downtown newsagent that sold papers from up north, too. Once, when they were driving home after something, he had pulled over to listen properly to a broadcast about the demonstrations. He and Rose exchanged anxious looks, even letting the kids overhear 'Ssshee-it, Rose,' and their mum saying, 'Perhaps we better not even go through town, love. There might be upset down here, too. We don't want a mob rocking the car with little kids in here.' Robinson rubbed her cheekbone with the back of his thumb. 'You'd take the rugger buggers on otherwise, wouldn't you?' She smiled a little, then turned away from him. 'Might do,' she said. 'The runty ones, at least.'

The weather report came on as Jeffrey was getting himself a glass of water from the sink. When Candy entered he drank in large gulps and started to leave, but Rose held her palm up. 'Uh-uh, stop right there. I want a word with you both.'

Candy leaned against the chopping bench, discomfort trickling down her back.

'Where do you think you've been?' Her eyes had caught the dirt smears on Jeff's coat and the wet patches on Candy's knees from her scramble up the bank.

Candy saw Jeff's anger defuse: it was clear as the light diminishing from a screen, shrinking into a last capsule of blue before it slid into the dark's mouth. Candy crossed her arms to show him her displeasure, and little begging lines lifted at his eyebrows. Honestly, his loyalties seemed to dance back and forth as erratically as a bee over a garden crammed with lavender.

Rose clutched her teatowel in a fist that rested on her hip. 'You know that your dad wanted you to go to church with your Gram today. Where did you sneak off to?'

Jeffrey pushed his jaw forward — in Marshall pig-headedness, as Rose would say. 'Why should we go to church with her when she's such a cow to us?'

Candy swallowed. He'd land it now.

Rose sighed, but her eyes glittered with a smile that both children could tell was hard to suppress. 'I know it's not been easy, kids, but she's been generous to us in lots of ways.' Probably she meant how Gram had helped to buy a new heater, a new toastie-pie machine, and new plants for Rose's busy garden. Candy no longer thought much of the sweets, tin toys. 'And she's not here for much longer. Think about your dad first, hey? It's awkward for him. He wants to feel proud of us all, to feel that he's done his best.'

'But even when he tries she just picks on him.'

It was true. First of all, Gram had been happy and amazed about how 'picturesque' New Zealand was, how 'tidy, naturally friendly'. She'd even liked the local newspaper, defending it against Robinson's mourning for London dailies; she said it was *nice* to see people with their prize lambs and dahlias on the front page, it was *nice* to read about pleasant, ordinary things. But when their dad said, bluntly, 'never again' to England — 'No, not ever, Mum,' — something in Gram had dug its heels in. They'd ask her what she wanted to do for the weekend, or on the days Robinson took off work, and she'd say, in a helpless voice, 'Oh, don't mind me . . .' And then if Robinson did try to choose something he thought she'd enjoy — a museum, historic home, pottery shops, the Botanic Gardens — something was always slightly wrong. The museum wasn't old enough: there weren't any *names* connected with it. The pottery was too difficult to take home in a suitcase. The duck and goose mess at the gardens was disease-carrying: tuberculosis at best, she said, and I don't suppose you've bothered to give those children their shots . . .

There was the sound of voices at the front door. For a moment Candy felt fear flare up in her stomach. Phil and Wairata? She cocked her head. No, it was Dad and Gram. When they came into the kitchen even Rose looked a bit shifty. It felt as if their conversation was still hanging in the air, a legible banner above their heads that instead of *Welcome Home!* or *Surprise!* said *Get Lost*.

'Oh! Look at these little ruffians,' said Gram. 'Sunday best, I see. And where might you have got to?'

'We went for a walk to the creek,' said Candy.

Robinson tweaked their noses in turn. 'Sermons in stones, eh, kids?'

They each gave him a *huh?* look.

'Shakespeare,' he said.

'A marvellous English playwright and poet,' Gram explained. 'I gather they don't teach the greats in this country?'

Rose folded her teatowel with uncharacteristic care. 'Of course they've heard of Shakespeare, Edith. But the children are only eleven.'

Candy pushed herself away from the bench. 'We've acted some of *A Midsummer Night's Dream* in theatre class. And at school we've done Wordsworth. The daffodil man.'

'*Done*,' said Gram, looking at Robinson and Rose for agreement about her grand-daughter's poor expression.

Candy shrugged. 'He's all right. Bit soppy.' She had actually liked the two poems they'd looked at in her advanced reading group, the words lilting and tapping like music: easy stuff, and things they could see from their own school playing field — clouds and daffodils — even though poetry was supposed to be difficult. But she wasn't going to share any of that with Gram.

When she and Jeff were told to go and clean up, in the hallway he silently held out his hand for *gimme five*. Then they did *up high, down low*, and instead of the tease *too slow*, Jeff gripped her hand in a sideways shake. 'Way to go,' he whispered. So they made up, just like that.

For the rest of Gram's visit, which was about another fortnight, Jeffrey and Candy stuck together at home. It was as if Gram had driven them together — though not at school still, no, not there. For Phil might see them then, so Jeff usually steered clear of Candy in the playground. At school, in fact, although they had never talked about *the game* — hadn't needed to, they both *knew* — they were both anxiously relieved not to see Redshaw for a couple of days; he must have been off sick, they thought. But when he reappeared there was a scene in the A Block corridor as the intermediate classes headed to the manual prefab building for woodwork, sewing, metalwork or cooking lessons. Though Candy tried to look away before he saw her watching him, Phil spied her, and swung out from the stream of pupils moving in his direction. He forced her up against the coat hooks outside one of the classrooms, and, pressing his plastic ruler like a fencing sword into her chest, held her at half-arm's distance. 'Don't look at me or I'll thrash the pants off of you, Marshall-mellow.'

Candy pushed forward and his ruler snapped in two. The group of girls who had hovered near her, ready to defend her if she'd needed it, laughed at the expression on his face and herded Candy away, pushing their tongues into their lower lips to make monkey jaws at him, the bravest adding a 'Mmm-*muhh*' sound for *Mental*, a word Candy hated, but this time she let it slide. ('Has your Mum been mental?' one skinny, bug-eyed girl from school had asked, after they bumped into her at A&E once, when Rose had been admitted after a severe reaction to new medication. The bug-eyed girl had a broken wrist. She'd come up to Candy at school later that week. 'No,' Candy had said. 'She's just had a depressive episode a couple of times, and an allergic response to medication, that's all.' The girl's eyeballs looked even more boggled by the number of syllables Candy had tripped out.)

'Bitches!' Phil hurled the remaining half of his ruler at their backs. It clattered to the floorboards and the girls pushed their laughter all the higher, loving the way the pitch bounced over the high-stud ceiling.

The whole episode was overheard by the metalwork teacher and Phil was given a two-week detention. Candy and Jeff didn't talk about it with their mum and dad: later, Candy wondered why. She decided that probably, in a peculiar way, she was protecting her parents. A Phil Redshaw would be yet another piece of ammunition in Gram's sniping comparisons about standards, choice of school, rules, curfews. And subconsciously both children had begun to hide difficult or upsetting things from their parents some time ago: hadn't wanted to trip up the family's walk along the thin tension wire of happiness.

Over that fortnight the children huddled on Candy's bed because it was farthest from the sunporch that had been converted into Gram's room for the duration of her visit. They'd say they had homework to finish. And they did do a little, but stayed away longer than was necessary, even forgoing TV, because they knew Gram would sit down behind them, knitting and telling them the local programmes were amateur and the accents grated.

After homework Jeff liked to flick through the scarlet hard-backed copy of *The Guinness Book of World Records* that he had been given for last Christmas, 1980. They searched for material about New Zealand: to return it to the foreground, no doubt, after Gram had started her withering assessments. They took a knock-back when Baldwin Street, the steepest street in the world, wasn't even listed. It was the street their dad had run up before they were born, when he'd wanted to wow and woo their mum. Rose had said that actually, she had been more impressed by the way he lay on the footpath and rolled all the way back down again. She had laughed and laughed at the way it had seemed to flatten out all the rectitude and sobriety that swelled the air of the street, the town's reputation back then for tight lips and twitching net curtains. Picturing their dad as he was in a photo from those years, in his zip-up gingerbread-coloured cardigan and brown slacks, his hair neatly combed to one side, nothing like the student and hippy contingent at all, it seemed to Candy and Jeff that some other marvellous record had been set. How extraordinary for the clean-cut, toothpaste-ad-style man that was their olden-day-dad, to frolic and gambol that way. How much more extraordinary than it would have been for one of the long-haired, be-flared and beaded people to tumble down the street, bright tie-dye and Indian cottons whizzing like the surface of a spinning top. Such tricks were in their nature: but their dad's was magical, like a horse breaking into song.

Disappointed by Baldwin Street's absence from the book, they scanned avidly for other records held by New Zealanders. The greatest number of pool balls pocketed in 24 hours! Records in brick-throwing and sheep-shearing! Longest non-stop run! Fastest backwards 100-yard run! The world's southernmost capital city! Deepest flexible dress dive salvage! (What?) Greatest number of consecutive ballet turns! Most consecutive ballroom dance titles! Usually New Zealand couldn't have the oldest anything, but they discovered that Whangarei had the oldest practising doctor!

Inevitably Jeffrey and Candy got sidetracked by other wonders, and they scoured the columns of small type, trying to be first to find new things to disgust, scare or amaze each other with. Descriptions of the fattest man, who couldn't be carried through local hospital doors in Texas because they were too narrow for him. Descriptions of the surgery that had uncovered the greatest number of metal objects inside a person's stomach, of the longest attack of hiccups, of the longest coma, of the rarest fully described illness so far: 100% fatal laughing disease, which a tribe in New Guinea could get from eating human brains. *Ohhh, yuck*. But it became a favourite saying of Jeff's when Candy told a bad joke. 'Oh you're so funny. You give me 100% fatal laughing disease.' Of the world's largest menu item, occasionally served at Bedouin wedding feasts: a roasted camel. Cooked eggs are stuffed in fish, the fish are stuffed in cooked chickens, the chickens are stuffed in roasted sheep, and the sheep are stuffed into a camel. And there were photos: of the longest beard, the longest hair, the man with the longest fingernails. There was the first moonwalk by a twin, a couple of years after the Marshalls' birth: 1972. And, of course, there were the grainy nineteenth-century studio portraits of Chang and Eng, the Siamese twins. When the children had first seen them Candy had felt that a place in her chest would split under the heat of delayed knowledge: the surface of it broken open like the tight husk of grain.

'*Jeffrey*,' she'd said, finger raising in a slow point at the black and white photo, the smart, side-by-side men in dark suits and white shirts, their hair slick and groomed as their dad's used to be, before it began to lift into the wiry frizz of age. Jeff looked at her, open-mouthed, a PT Barnum and Bailey fairground shy. 'It's them,' he said. He ran a finger down the photo, along the cloth that covered the join between the men. The children read the small biography silently together, Jeff nodding when Candy signalled that she wanted to turn the page. They re-read it, returned to the photo. They gazed into the men's eyes, trying to dip down into their grace, the physical image of hard-won balance between self-containment and reciprocity. At once awestruck, personally humbled, yet also, paradoxically, irrationally proud: the children grinned at each other with a sweet triumph, like the knowingly unsporting patriots of a private country who witness the effort of a supreme athlete. The photo and biography had sapped the old taunt of a little of its power, though Candy would still — outer composure mauled inwardly by frustration — want to root for Chang and Eng when Phil Redshaw tried it now: *Si-a-mese, smells like wees . . .*

In a strange kind of tribute at home (a ritual which, had they tried it at school, might have proved an effective antidote to the playground jibes) they appeared in the living room that Sunday afternoon sharing a single buttoned-up shirt and suit jacket of Robinson's, Jeffrey's left arm and Candy's right through the sleeves. They knelt side by side on the couch, reading carefully chosen separate books. Jeffrey's snack plate was stacked with cheese and crackers, Candy's with apple slices and raisins; a glass of cordial by him, a glass of milk by her. The buttons strained, and they had to sit pressed in closely together. They waited for Rose and Robinson to find them. They wanted to hear the delighted cry of 'What on *earth* are you doing?' It came, all right. And the children simply answered, 'Playing Chang and Eng.' They'd worked out the answer first, and a signal to show when to start it, each of them saying a word in turn. They were mischievously pleased with themselves, but then Rose had stumped them.

'Which is which?'

They had to lean back their heads a bit to look at each other. That was when Rose turned to Robinson and bit into his soft cotton sweatshirt to stifle herself. Dead-pan, Robinson said, 'Can't you tell, Rose? It's obvious. I didn't even realise they were twins at first. Chang is the one who looks more used to wearing a suit.' And Robinson had sucked his back teeth, as if pondering, but Candy suspected he was trying to hold his mouth shut to keep out Rose's infectious laugh. Their mum finally cleared her throat. 'These two gentlemen seem to be having some afternoon tea. Would you like a coffee, dear?'

'Good idea.' They ambled out casually, but the children caught the upwards trickle of their mother's laughter before the kitchen door shut. Her lovely laugh that said everything was all right.

'What's so funny?' said Candy.

'No idea,' answered Jeffrey.

They glugged their drinks in unison.

Ever since, reading *The Guinness Book of World Records* had been a favourite shared activity. They even brought home old editions from the school library now and then, hoping that there would be different photos of the world's marvels each time. (The world's heaviest twins always seemed to be photographed on baby-sized motorbikes — which Jeff didn't get. Once he said, 'Man, those fat twins really like their little bikes. They're *always* on them.' Candy had to explain. 'Duh-brain. The bikes are normal size: they use them to show how big those guys are.' 'Oh.')

When the small type began to hurt their eyes during Gram's stay they moved on to other things. They designed a code of scratches and knocks to use on the wall between their rooms: meaning *Come in here*, or *Let's go outside*, or *Say yes*, or *Say no*, which they thought would be useful when they were being asked separately if they wanted to go somewhere with Gram. On fine afternoons they discovered a new interest in the swing-ball they'd had for years. It was perfect because only two could play, and it was set up in the middle of a boggy patch of mud which you needed gumboots for, so none of the adults were likely to ask to join in. When the ball swooped in an even arc and rhythm it was as if something else passed between her and Jeff. As an adult, if she thought back to those afternoons, Candy recalled them as a time of feeling wholly present, her body a joint moving fluently in its socket of light and air.

The conversations they had then moved similarly; they passed ideas between them with a seriousness that also formed a defence against the atmosphere in the house, against the pettiness and barely disguised dislike of *Can't you get such-and-such a brand of baking powder here? Why is the school day so short? Well, I'm surprised, the way Robinson slaves, that there's not enough money even for a trip overseas, frankly.* The words seeped out from the kitchen, their mother and grandmother still partially veiled behind the skim of steam the boiling pots left over the window, even though it had been propped open for air. Candy and Jeff would try to shoulder off what they heard.

'If you had to be disabled, say either blind or deaf, which would it be?'

'Blind would be scary. But deaf would be so sad — what about music?'

'If you had to choose?'

'I'd choose to have no legs instead.'

'Well, if it were me, it would be deaf.'

'Really?'

'Because you can still have sign language. And you could remember music, maybe.'

'Like Beethoven.'

'Yeah. And there's music in *your* head all the time, you said.'

'What about colours? Do you see colours in your head?'

'Well, if you dream in colour it's supposed to mean you have a higher intelligence.'

'How could you prove it? You might remember you had a dream about apples and just think they were red.'

'But if you remembered one night you had a dream about green apples and the next night you had a dream about red apples, and it mattered in the dream that they were red or green . . .'

'Do you dream in colour?'

'I had a dream about a fire once. It was weird. There were a whole lot of scientists in a huge glass room with lots of steel benches and they were all in white coats, and the fire was red, it was definitely red and orange, and I had to run from it, and it was strange because I could *see* it all ahead of me, but really I was running away from it behind me. It wasn't really in front of me but it was definitely red.'

'Do you have dreams about being able to take things back into the real world from the dream?'

'How do you mean?'

'I dreamed that a man in a shop gave me a guitar and I didn't have to pay for it and he said, "When you wake up, you can take the guitar with you even then." I knew exactly which corner of the bedroom it was going to be in, but when I woke up it wasn't there. I thought he'd cheated so I tried to go back to sleep so I could ask why he lied to me.'

'I didn't know you wanted a guitar.'

'I might ask for one for my birthday.'

'For *our* birthday.'

Arc, contact, arc, contact.

'If you get it, can I have a go on it sometimes?'

On such afternoons there was no hesitation. 'Of course. It's our birthday.'

Candy began to take the phase of closeness at home as a given, although at break, lunch, and on the bike ride after school Jeff still kept his cautious, Phil-wary distance from her. Once home, though, if it were overcast, and their interest in *The Guinness Book of World Records* had tapered out, they played Monopoly or Five Hundred, throwing Candy's spare satin-edged blanket over the board or cards if anyone tapped at the door — in case they were told, *That's a good family game. Why don't we all play with Gram in the living room?*

One day, they got to talking in between moves, sprawled on the bed, each idly holding one of the red, partially translucent dice that looked like fruit jubes. Jeff drew Candy's pillow behind his neck; as he did so, a corner brushed over her face. When she was sure he had it in place behind his head she grabbed it back and folded one side up over his mouth briefly, saying, 'Watch it.' He whipped it back from her, pinned her down, buried her face with it three times in quick succession. 'Watch what?' Then he made innocent googly eyes at her. She flipped up the extra blanket folded into a roll at the foot of the bed, knelt beside him and boinked him four times on the forehead. 'Watch that, that's what.' He snorted and honked the words back at her, as if that were the way she'd sounded. Play drunk, Candy boffed him with the blanket again. He wrestled it from her and the Monopoly board skidded to the floor, paper money ticker-taping everywhere. In the tussle the blanket unrolled and they kicked and tugged until eventually they were both under it, all four feet elevated, making a private tent that filled with a woolly blue light. Jeff faced Candy, pushing his nose into a pug dog snub with an index finger, dragging down his bottom eyelids with the first and middle fingers of the other hand so the pinks showed. He woofed and panted, tongue lolling. Candy upped the ante, popping her upper eyelids inside out the way he hated — the way he'd said could catch flies like sticky paper, to try to get her to stop — and rolled her eyeballs up as far as they could go, pretending to drool. When they both came out of their horror faces they were laughing so hard there was no breath left, just their two small ribcages, soundless pneumatic drills, shuddering side by side.

They did hear the door open, and Gram's voice, unprefaced by a knock, but the drills juddered on — there was no off switch. In fact the very sound of Gram sent out another surge of laughter. They looked at their legs: peculiarly criss-crossed now, like the poles holding up a '*Wigwam!*' Candy managed to say, gesturing, which made the laughter hurt her stomach, and brought them both close to choking.

In one movement the blanket was jerked off them, leaving their hair tousled.

Gram's hands clutched the cover up to her chest as if someone had just walked in on her while she was changing. Consternation seemed to stall her. Then she said, 'Jeffrey. Out of there, please. And straight away.'

'What?'

A hop-bush pink stole into her cheeks and her eyes flicked from side to side. 'You had both better come to the table.'

That was it, then. Someone had been trying to call them to dinner and they hadn't heard.

'Hoe-kay doe-kay,' said Jeffrey in a mock posh accent. Candy tried to roll her eyes at him in warning, but he simply blew at his fringe to lift it off his forehead.

When they got out to the dining room the table wasn't set, Dad wasn't back from work yet, and Mum had only just started shucking the outer leaves from some corn cobs.

But: 'Sit down,' Gram said. Then she went into the kitchen and began chopping onions and tomatoes for the pasta sauce. Jeffrey and Candy darted frowns at each other. They shifted in place. They waited. Patiently. And some more. Then, elbows up on the table, Candy leaned her cheek on her hand, blew out a sigh, as if boredom were a dust that could be puffed away. Jeff jiggled his knee, whistled tunelessly at the ceiling. Rose turned around in surprise.

'Oh, hello there, you two. Have you finished your homework?'

'Yup,' said Candy.

'Do you want a job to do?'

'If you like. Are you ready for us to set the table? Gram said we had to come out.'

Rose raised an eyebrow, turned to Gram. 'Oh?'

Gram's chopping movements slowed. She set down the knife, then wiped her palms on her apron. Without turning, head still bowed to her work, she said, 'I really do feel that too much time together and . . . certain sorts of behaviour, at this age — a brother and a sister — there comes a point, I'm sure you'll agree, when some . . . lines have to be drawn.'

The house steamed with silence.

'Edith?'

'Jeffrey will know exactly what I mean, Rose. But it's quite possible, these days, that he hasn't been warned before. It's quite possible some sinful things are done almost in innocence. I'd say we shouldn't make any great fuss about it.'

Candy felt alarm bristle and fan out over her neck, like a peacock tail of shame. An image of pine trunks, pine needles, Phil Redshaw's berry-stained mouth, materialised so precisely she feared Gram could see it.

'Robinson will no doubt want to have a discussion — it's best for the father to do so. But let's leave it for him, shall we? Now.' A word that sounded as if a door had been locked. 'What else would you like in the sauce apart from what I've done so far?'

There was a sharp sensation in Candy's body, hard to locate precisely, like a fibre tearing. When she looked at Jeffrey his eyes shot away from hers, but she saw that they were at once wounded and savage.

Rose snatched up a broad, flat knife from the open cutlery drawer, and, leaning on it with both palms to cut the corn into pieces small enough to boil, she said brightly, clownishly, 'Quite frankly, Edith, I think this holiday has left you with too much time on your hands! You're inventing nonsense.'

Jeffrey pushed himself away from the table and went to his room. Candy swung herself out the back door and sat on the steps, where she examined all the life in the cracks in the pavement. She didn't go inside when Gram called her name. The way she used it, it was as if it belonged to someone else: a girl Candy didn't know.

ON THE MONDAY morning that Gram left, the children were told they'd have to skip a few hours of school so they could say goodbye. After their half day Candy waited for Jeff, wanting to talk to him about how strange it had been at the airport that morning, how all the adults had seemed uncomfortable, shifting in place, sitting in a line on the plastic seats, which made it difficult to talk — yet when they tried sitting in facing rows the aisle was too wide, and everyone around them had begun to listen in. So they had moved back, eyes in a middle-distance, not-looking-anywhere stare. When the boarding was announced, it seemed to catch them all off guard, even though the waiting had been so awkward, and the announcement was exactly what they were there for, wasn't it? Candy wanted to ask Jeff if he'd noticed how when Gram had held her arms out to Dad she had seemed suddenly wobbly, even lost her footing a bit. And even after all she had said, she and Dad had such a long hug that Candy felt her own face must have looked rude with surprise. And how Dad's eyes were teary as they all stood to watch Gram walk unsteadily up the corridor on low-heeled grey shoes that pinched even though they were Dr Scholl's, her tan-stockinged feet pushing against their edges like scones rising above the edge of a baking tray. And how Mum put her arm around Dad's waist, and leaned her head against him, so that he turned her around a bit and kissed her on the forehead, as if she were the one who was upset that Gram was leaving. All the spaces between people had altered, had filled with unexpected fogs and temperatures. Candy felt as if she'd missed something, as if perhaps there had been some news nobody had told her. She wanted to find out if Jeff knew about it.

After the school bell rang she and Jeff arrived at the bike racks simultaneously and for the first time in ages — Jeff thrown off his cautious habits, perhaps, by the break in rhythm to their usual day — headed out the gate together. Past the bus terminus, as Candy pumped hard to fall into a parallel rhythm with her brother, there was a yell from behind.

'Jeff-ress the ack-tress! Can't you go any faster than a girl?'

Phil Redshaw drew alongside Candy on his bike. Was she right in thinking he looked afraid, hunted, before he started up? 'Ooooh, sorry, my mistake, it's Candy-cane-shit-for-brains!'

They both ignored him at first. Along the main road Jeffrey kerb-hopped and headed along the footpath towards the sports field — even though that was the scene of their last confrontation — maybe because he knew it detoured slightly from Phil's route home. Candy followed when there was a break in the kerbing. A hot, queasy anger flashed when she heard a deep *Baa-aaa-aaaa* behind her.

'You're the bloody sheep!' she flung back over her shoulder. 'Why don't you go home your own way?'

She tried to pull ahead, but Phil effortlessly stayed parallel. His fear seemed imagined now. 'What did you say to me? Did you call me a bloody sheep? Did you?'

Just like last time, Jeffrey had drawn a considerable distance ahead. Candy wanted to mirror the power in his legs so that she could escape the frightening sensation of being pulled back towards Phil, his presence dragging her like a cold rip-tide. She called out, 'Jeff, wait up!' She knew he had been angry with her last time, but that was when she sang the rhyme . . . Then Phil aimed his front wheel for Candy's. She swerved just as he pulled back. Phil laughed and cycled around her, his blond hair catching the late afternoon light like a toetoe, his lean, dark-clothed form hawk-like. She took off again, and this time when Phil drew even he reached out and put his hand on her neck.

'Don't touch me!' She struggled to shrug and twist herself free while still trying to maintain her centre of equipoise and keep pedalling. Ragged sobs fought to be released from deep down. He unclamped his hand from the tendons around her neck, but then he fingered down under her shirt collar, moving from her top vertebra and around to her shoulder. And this time it was rough, pinching, ugly. No game at all. One of the sobs ruptured, shattering into a yell instead of tears.

'*Jeffrey*!'

Jeff cast a look back. He braked, swung his bike around in a skid, tyres cutting a muddy sickle mark into the field. He started pedalling towards them, his expression tight with anger visible even from a distance. Candy gave a backwards rolling movement with her shoulders, ducked her head, tried to twist away again and lost her balance. Phil stopped too, and kept his hand where it was, as if he wanted Jeffrey to see.

When he reached them Jeffrey raised a fist. 'Get your hands off my sister.'

'I haven't got my *hands* on her.' He showed one empty palm.

'Stop groping her, then.'

He already had his grip back on both handlebars. '*Groping*? Shows what *you* know. You think I want to grope something that's ugly as you lot?'

Jeffrey swung himself off his bike and held it aside with one hand, feet square and body undefended, his face so clouded that his eyes seemed to drain of green. He spoke with his lower teeth jutting forward in a pose Candy had never seen him in before.

'Don't try to hide what you did, Redshaw. I know, Candy knows, and you know it. You better back off.'

'Yeah? Says you and whose army?'

Candy pushed the hair away from her eyes. 'You're pathetic. Count up your own friends, Redshaw, you loser. Jeez, the park's full of them.' Far off in one corner, an elderly woman walked slowly behind a dog in a hurry. At a broken soccer goal a tallish, slim man practised footwork on his own, waterproof jacket billowing like the chute on a racing car.

Sternly, Jeffrey told Candy to get back on her bike. 'We'll be late,' he said, 'and they'll be out looking this way.' There wasn't really a 'they' at this time of day, but Candy got it. She nodded, hoping Phil would be deterred from tailing them. The siblings set off into a head wind that seemed to start up just as they began cycling again. Candy's nose began to run and her eyes to tear as she leaned into it.

'The wind is real strong, eh, Jeff?'

He didn't respond. Candy, studying his profile as he bore down into the wind, thought the angles of his face seemed as if the weather had worn closer to the bone. She wanted to ask what was wrong, but now the breeze was strong enough for her to realise that any speech would just catch like a kite and be dragged off behind her, over the field. She put her own head down and worked hard at her pedals, telling herself not to look behind, that if she were strong enough not to look, Phil would disappear.

The grass blurred under her wheels and the tread pattern on her tyres disappeared, blending with the speed. The words she'd heard in her head last time were no use, but even more now she needed something like a spell to keep her from staring over her shoulder. Half-nonsense whirled to the rhythms of her cycling.

wheels spin and I won't turn
wheels web and cripple Phil
wheels race and lose his face

Maybe they worked, Candy thought. Because braking at the driveway at home, and flinging a desperate glance over her shoulder, she could no longer see the tilting sprint of a boy standing up on his pedals to chase something. She and Jeff both ran into the garage with their bikes, leaned them side by side and tromp-tromped into the house, dropping their schoolbags in the hallway. Relief and the over-exertion of pumping their bikes for all they were worth drove them both to the fridge for something cold to drink. Candy said she was starving, too, but Rose hauled her back from the pantry.

'Save room!' she said. It was a Friday night; she said that she and Robinson both needed a rest after all the disruption of 'visitors' — as if Gram had been a horde, despite her family nickname, diminutive indeed. So: 'Fish and chips or a restaurant, kids?' '*Restaurant!*' they yelled. You could get greasies just about any weekend, but going to a restaurant was a rare event, saved for birthdays or wedding anniversaries.

'We'd better go crew level,' Robinson said to Rose when he came to pick them up after work. 'I don't think these kids could handle linen napkins and finger bowls after their politeness marathon with poor old Mum.' So they all went out that night to the Goldminer's Kitchen, a family restaurant with a children's menu that had its own drink list: Green Grasshopper, Sally Spider, Shirley Sherbet, Orange Rush, Fruit Fist. All the food had odd names too. Fish 'n' chips was the Old Salt's Favourite. Chicken and chips was Canary in a Cage. Lamb chops and fries were Little Mary's Special. A hamburger and fries was a Hungry G'rilla, which Jeff said was the dumbest thing he'd ever heard because there'd never been any gorillas in New Zealand, let alone at any *goldmines*, and besides, gorillas themselves were vegetarian. He told the waitress too, and Candy sank down on the red vinyl booth seat in embarrassment, but the waitress, dressed pioneer style, just said, 'Clever clogs. You think of a better name and we'll change the menu.' Which kept the children busy until their orders came.

Rose and Robinson had a carafe of house wine — it frothed on the top, which made Robinson say, 'Oh, terrific. They charge that price and it's been watered down, but what could you expect from a place that thought gorillas ate mince?' and Rose said it tasted like licking the outside of unripe kiwifruit — it left the same sour prickly feeling — and she pulled a stretched face which made Robinson's wine go down the wrong way, and the waitress, passing at the time, looked a bit peeved. 'Is everything all right with your meals?' she asked.

'Mmm,' Robinson said, and in a quiet voice just as she turned away, 'The wine flavour added to the jug of water was a very nice touch.' Candy sank down even lower in her seat, but she was giggling now, full fork held aloft like a hand above water to say *Help!*

'What's wrong with your dinner, Can-do?' asked Dad. 'Is your lamb chop all right? Nice and fresh?'

'Still bleating?' said Jeff.

'We-e-e-ll, I know the lamb followed Mary to school one day, but this chop tastes like she was about to start university.'

Rose began flapping her paper napkin in the air, then dabbing it at her eyes. Robinson chortled, and at one point took her napkin from her to dab at his own eyes, which made Jeffrey and Candy cry out, 'You're drunk!'

'On spiked Ribena!' said Rose. Jeff's laugh gurgled like a sink, and that set them all off again. They hadn't felt so free and easy for weeks. Candy wondered if she should feel guilty about not missing Gram, but the thought didn't lodge for long. Not when she remembered Gram's story.

After dinner Dad looked up at the evening sky, and though they were all hurried along through the empty carpark by the cool night air he said, 'Shall we go for a drive?' And they headed way out, towards the peninsula, music on the radio turned right up for the children to hear, and even Dad singing along. Candy leaned forward and put her hand on his shoulder to see if the deep buzz of his voice reverberated there.

'We've got ourselves a great couple of kids, haven't we, Rose?' said Robinson.

'We certainly do.'

Even Jeff seemed to have forgotten the nettle-words from Gram, and Redshaw's obsession. He gave Candy's knee a quick couple of Charley horses. So she gave him a mock Chinese-burn back: a squeeze in disguise, really. They grinned at each other, then returned to staring out their back-seat windows, both singing the radio choruses under their breath, stopping now and then to listen to Rose and Robinson on the harder-to-remember verses. Candy gazed up at the clear night sky, feeling her body fill with warmth, as if deep in her red-black blood she carried the flinty shards of microscopic stars.

All of which was maybe why, when Dad woke them both — and abruptly — the next morning, it was so much more of a shock.

Candy heard him at her brother's door first. 'Jeffrey. Get up, please, son, and come out here. Put your dressing gown on and wear something on your feet.'

It was too early for a Saturday. The flat, direct tone wasn't usual for Robinson. It gave Candy the beginnings of the cold-water sensation from the night they'd been woken by paramedics at the door two or three years ago. When their mum had been bundled up, Robinson trying to sound calm, saying here we go, my two kidlets, let's take coats and shoes and mittens and a couple of books to read, and your own pillows, too, while we're at it. We're following your mum to hospital just to check she'll be okay.

Is Mummy sick?

She is a bit sick right now, love. It's the medicine she's been given. It seems it's not quite right for her.

Why is she in the ambulance? Is she going to die? Why can't we go in the ambulance too? Who's holding her hand?

She's in the ambulance to get her breathing right, Candy. She's not going to die. We can't all fit in, Jeff. There'll be someone to hold her hand, it's all right.

Their mum had been able to come home the same night but she had her head in her hands for the drive home and kept saying, sorry, I'm so sorry, I'm a terrible mum. Candy had said, no you're not, you're the best. And Robinson said, they liked the drinking fountain and the little paper cups and they found a child-sized wheelchair, trust them, the monkeys. They were fine, Rose, there's absolutely nothing to say sorry for, it's hardly your fault, is it? We're just glad you're all right. And Jeffrey said, excited, hyped up, drumming on Rose's shoulder, Mum, Mum, what's it *like* inside an ambulance, Mum? Is it lots of tubes and needles and those heart-shocker things and can you see how they turn the siren on? Then he held his nose and moaned *Whaa*-wha, *whaa*-wha, *whaa*-wha. And somehow that worked. His questions gave the mood an unexpected flip, like the trick he taught Rose during a bad phase once when, frowning, tired and despairing — disproportionately, the children knew — at the triviality of her task, she verged on tears as she struggled to turn her washing-up gloves inside out. 'Here, I'll do it,' Jeff had said, taking one and putting its cuff to his lips as if it were a balloon or a trumpet. He blew, and, like banana-coloured cuckoos, or the plastic flag that popped out of the Christmas turkey to show it was cooked, the yellow fingers of the gloves shot up, splayed. It was magic. Mum's tears turned into a sense of how hilariously stupid — instead of how grindingly, crushingly, pointless — everything was: she and Jeff stood there together turning the gloves inside out just so that they could puff them back the right way again, hearing the satisfying *pphhlock*. On the hospital night Jeffrey's eager questions about the ambulance somehow managed to turn that emergency, too, into something bizarre, funny, a ludicrous adventure.

In the end the ambulance night *had* been fine and all right, of course. But the first confusion of being woken up, of seeing strange men in uniform either side of Rose, and just a glimpse of her back as she was helped into the ambulance, tunnelled into Candy's mind, sat in the dark corners, legs and arms wrapped around itself. It stayed, a latent dread, which meant that her heart instantly sprang in fear at her father's voice in the hallway. She was fetching her dressing gown and slippers before Robinson had reached her door. When he knocked and came in she said straight away, 'Is it Mum?'

'Pardon? Oh, no. No, it's not. I'm afraid someone's been arsing about, Candy. It's not very pleasant.'

Jeff stood in the corridor, looking almost fluey with sleepiness. His eyes were puffy, his hair bed-scrunched, face scored with pillow creases. Candy was relieved to see Rose in the hallway too, in her white satin bathrobe and the black karate-style shoes embroidered with orange dragons that she used as slippers — glad to see her despite the fact that her hands were fast and furious as she re-tied the sash of her bathrobe. As Candy closed her bedroom door, hopping on one foot to pull on her own slippers, Rose said, 'I think we should do this properly and call the police.'

'You might be right,' Robinson answered. 'We'll see what Candy and Jeffrey have to tell us first.'

Fear started up its hot scuttle in Candy's stomach. Police? Candy and Jeffrey? Absurdly, she found herself rewinding memory through to the previous day. Hadn't they put their bikes away properly? Had the bikes been stolen? Would the police be called because of burglars or because of Candy's and Jeffrey's carelessness?

'What's happened?' said Jeffrey, and his question seemed to be directed at her: he too had been thrown by their father's answer, recognising they had both been implicated.

'Come outside,' said Rose. Jeffrey and Candy followed behind their parents. And Candy would always remember that before they passed through the back door she and her brother put an arm around each other's waists — frank and unteasing. Like another time in the wilds of the South Island, when they stood on a bridge over a river gorge, gazing into the drop below to the immense volume of green, glacial water. They had held on to each other instinctively then, feeling precariously airborne.

Rose and Robinson unlocked the back door and began to lead the children out to the front of the house.

'Actually, just a minute,' Robinson said. They all halted on the spot, Rose clutching her arms tightly to herself against the fresh morning air. Robinson touched his children's shoulders. 'You might get a bit of a startle. Someone's made a real mess out here. But don't worry, all right? Whoever these hoons are they won't get away with it. They've got their own bloody surprise coming.'

A clot of nausea rose into Candy's throat. Their dad turned, and Rose ushered them on. At the front of the house, as Robinson began to drum on his thigh with the rolled-up morning newspaper, Candy then realised that he must have seen the damage when he went out to fetch the *ODT*.

And the strangest thing was that at first Candy almost laughed. In the tidy suburban cul-de-sac, for a brief, inverted moment, it looked to her as if they had been fêted. The two tall birches were laced in long ribbons of white, their trunks zigzagged over with vivid 3D squiggles. The large bay windows at the front of the house, and the closely clipped grass on the front lawn, had them too: great, looping abstract shapes, a vibrant riot of what Candy gradually realised was fluorescent, spray-on Silly String and white shaving cream. She gazed around in wonder. She saw their novelty, hen-shaped mailbox, which their mum had bought at last year's school fair to add to her collection of quirky garden decorations, now tilted drunkenly on its wooden post and smeared with broken eggs — a joke, Candy supposed. Which — when she saw that the innards had also been crammed with rubbish that someone had tried to light — seemed to say how stupid, how crass, how corny such a mailbox was.

At the sight of the singed rubbish in the mailbox Candy's comprehension skimmed back over the lawn. Oddly, none of Rose's miniature windmills or weathervanes had been snapped off or trampled, but pebbles and bark chips from one of the front garden beds had been kicked all over the lawn and driveway. The tree was hung with toilet paper. For a second she puzzled over how anyone could reach that high, then her mind flipped up an answer: a crowd shot on TV, a rugby game up north, angry fists punching the air at a referee's decision. And arcing out over the terraces: toilet rolls tossed up in the air, the trails of white drawn overhead before they trickled limply to the pitch.

Tracking back over the house she took in something she should have, must have, seen straight away, but it was as if disbelief had enlarged the optical blind spot, cancelled out the scene. There was the worst of it: the spray paint all over the smooth white sweep of their concrete driveway, which would be visible from the street. You could paint over a house. If they'd had to write things, couldn't they have done it on the walls? Their dad still had a tub of paint left in their shed, a tub in the colour of their house . . . but in black, the graffiti said *Candy is a fucken slut*, *Jeffrey looks like a fucken girl*, and in a gash of red, *The Marshalls Fucken Wank*.

In a way the last was the worst. Candy saw her whole family — standing there in the soft, foolish fabrics of their nightclothes — as misfits, natural victims. Why had Dad got them out here like this? Instantaneously she was repulsed by the bony ankles and sliver of shin exposed above his tartan slippers and below his half-mast pyjama pants. His old-man pyjamas, brown and white plaid, with trim brown piping on the edges, and his white bathrobe with its dumb monogrammed RM on the pocket (how *embarrassing* that he wore his initials on his dressing gown, as if anyone else in the family would mistake the bathrobe for theirs, *oh duh, Dad*, like they needed to be reminded who it was boiling the kettle for their mum in the morning) . . . and Rose was just as bad. She was the one who'd bought the stupid bathrobe anyway. She looked too fragile out there, in her white imitation satin: a thin flower that shivers on tussock grass, seems as if it'll never survive even a rumour of wind.

Candy heard Jeffrey whistle through his teeth, a sliding high to low, the way he and his friends had been obsessed with at the start of last year: a sound they used for imagining space rockets re-entering the earth's atmosphere, someone parapenting off a cliff, a bomb falling from an aeroplane. And at the sound, loathing for him, too, came in a rush, as if it had been capped down tightly all along, just needing the pressure released. Right now she hated the way he refused haircuts, so that his hair was too long by the standards of most of the other boys at school, too near her own length. She hated the fact that they were the same height, that her own body stayed almost as boyish as his, unlike the girls at school who talked about how they were going shopping for bras with their mum that Friday night. Jeffrey stood there, in the same brand of shapeless, two-for-the-price-of-one, royal-blue towelling bathrobe that Rose had insisted on buying for Candy even though she had begged for a shiny crocus-lavender quilted one with pearly buttons.

Candy saw herself beside Jeffrey as clearly as if they were reflected in one of the bay windows at the front of the house. Two dark matching forms, like deep, shadowed angel prints in the snow, or a shape made in ink by closing the two sides of a blank notebook together. Two shadows cast by a single body: joined at the feet, unable to move anywhere without sight of the other. Her heart kicked as she reread the graffiti. How ugly-dumb-stupid-weird for a boy and girl to match.

'What do you know about all this, you two?' said Robinson, his eyebrows pushed forward into an angry overhang. 'It's obviously been done by children.'

'. . . Who can't spell,' said Rose, quiet, wry humour trying to smooth the abrasive grain of Robinson's voice, which she just knew would make the children monosyllabic, silence drawn up like defensive battle-shields. Candy noticed the way Rose tried to parry Robinson's clumsy lunges, and shot her an ashamed, grateful look. Feelings travelled her with the rapidity of light along a wire, flickering, changing. She saw, now, Rose's quick perceptions, not her vulnerability.

Robinson was red-eyed, as if from lack of sleep. Perhaps he had woken on and off in the night: had caught the shuffling and hissing that he groggily dismissed as nocturnal life scuttling under the hedge beside the bedroom window. Perhaps, too tired now to be attuned to nuance, he missed the gentle mocking in their mum's voice altogether; he seemed to take what she said as ballast to his stern enquiry. 'Yes, well. And it makes me want to ask exactly what sort of crowd you've been hanging around with lately. I mean,' he swept an arm out, 'what on hell's earth brought this on?'

'Hell's earth?' muttered Jeffrey, pulling a loose thread on the stitching on his robe.

'What did you say?'

'Nothing.'

Robinson stood with one fist on his hip. 'Listen, Jeff. Are you taking this seriously? Do you realise how serious this *is*? Do either of you have any idea who did this?'

Candy couldn't believe it. After warning that they might be shocked, now he actually seemed furious with them. Rose stepped closer to her children, took them both under her arms, though they stood awkwardly, all stiff shoulders and elbows, bones jutting like another spiny defence.

'Go easy, eh, Robinson?' said Rose.

'Can't you *read*, Dad?' Like Jeffrey, Candy was barely audible, but her pout was obvious.

Robinson pointed his rolled-up newspaper at her. 'What tone are you taking, Candy?'

And Candy felt her voice box open, like a cactus giving out the bold red star of a stinging flower. 'How would *you* like it? It's our names there, Dad, if you hadn't noticed.'

'Very clearly it's because I don't like it that I'm trying to find out if you know anything.'

Of course, it seemed ignorant and slow of them, but right then, the scene was so out of proportion to anything they had witnessed before that truly neither of them could fathom where it all could have come from. Each time Candy looked over at the graffiti, horror rose to her skin like a thin layer of sharp, clinging bubbles. It came from seeing their names attached to words she had really only just fully understood a year or so ago — recently enough that they still carried a primal force, like the words in spells for the medieval, the witch-shy. Here, the words — even *slut*, which now apparently named Candy — meant that someone loathed you. They meant sex, but sounded more like spit, fists and hatred.

'Think hard,' their father was saying, his expression like a definition of the grim concentration required. 'Are you absolutely sure you have no idea who might have done this?'

Candy had to look to Jeffrey for help. He stood with his hands balled and pushed deep into his dressing-gown pockets, pulling the fabric tight and flat over his chest. His demeanour matched:

stretched into a deliberate blankness, as if he'd forcibly plunged his thoughts away, too. She could sense that anger was packed down somewhere in there. He and Candy had passed the mood between them the way they'd played swing-ball — yet she wasn't sure if the anger was directed at their father, at the ruin and detritus on the front lawn, or even at Candy herself, for being linked to him by the scrawled words.

When neither of the children gave Robinson any kind of answer, Rose scanned the scene again. She caught at a loose curl and fetched it up in an efficient tuck, her hennaed hair wound in on itself in a smart, pretty twist. Before she did so, Candy saw fear flutter over her face. Even that quick glimpse of her anxiety gave Candy her own electrified feeling. Would whoever did this come back? Were they watching the house even now? Why had they been singled out? Was worse to come? Panic hit as the sound of a car funnelled down their street. People would see. Everyone would see the shame dripped over their house like the thick globs of the broken eggs.

'We should clean this up, Dad,' she said, 'shouldn't we? Shouldn't we clean this up?'

The car turned at the cul-de-sac's dead end, strangers' faces looming at the windscreen before they slowly drove away again, apparently in the wrong street. But their prowling style seemed to put Robinson on edge too. He raised a hand to Rose's back, ready to shepherd everyone inside. 'No. We're going to work hard at finding out who did this, and *they're* going to clean it up. Don't you touch a thing, Candy.'

But as they all made towards the front door Candy had noticed something lying on the shallow concrete steps that went from midway down the driveway to their front door. A couple of pebbles placed neatly side by side, weighing down a piece of paper. She'd thought it was more litter at first, but now, as she picked it up, she saw it had careful folds. She untucked these and braced herself for something worse than the graffitied insults.

The message had been scratched with a piece of russet-coloured bark chip: an improvised pen that twice had torn through the paper. Although the process must have been clumsy and the spelling was bad, the printing was neat and clear, like that of a child fascinated by the design more than the meaning of the words. The 'i's weren't dotted, but — even in what must have been a hasty, furtive job done in torchlight, or under the weak pool of a streetlamp — had been topped with wide spirals. The paper felt gritty under Candy's fingers as she read:

Phil Redshaw and his friend done this.
We said stop but he woudnt listin.
Sined from Wairata Lawrence and Donna Cole

Donna Cole — who was that? But Wairata she knew. Candy felt a spring of gratitude: recalled how Wairata had irritably thumbed at her bike bell to try to return Phil Redshaw's attention to their cycle ride, whatever their destination had been that day out on the playing fields.

'It's from Wairata,' she said to Jeffrey. He leaned in to read over her shoulder.

'Wairata?' repeated Robinson. 'A girl did this? Wairata who? Does she go to your school? Or is she older than you? How do you know her?'

'Let me see that,' said Rose.

Candy tried to catch up with her father's misunderstanding, pull it back. 'No, no, not her, it wasn't her.'

'She wrote the note,' Jeffrey said. 'She knows who did it.'

Candy handed over the piece of paper reluctantly, wanting to hang on to the evidence that the damage to the house wasn't the way everybody thought you should treat twins so alike. Too alike for boy and girl, their bodies and faces confusing, repulsing people like Redshaw, making them spiteful because — why? Because twins were weird. Because of what happened in the pines. Because of Candy's willingness, then Jeff's too, for the same. But, but. Phil had started it, hadn't he? Yet that simple question set up a pulling in Candy's stomach, as if a rope were tied there that she was walking against.

Back inside the house Robinson told the children he was calling both the principal of their school and the police; the principal first because he would have access to the school records and could give them details of how to track down Redshaw over the weekend. And the police because, 'Make no mistake, this isn't just a tease or a prank. It's vandalism. It's wilful damage and violation of private property. Do you understand?' Nobody hugged Candy or Jeff. Nobody comforted them. And the blunted words, the line of Rose's mouth, as if she too were waiting to hear the children were clear on this, sent desperation through Candy, racing, lifting.

'Yes!' she shouted at her parents. 'Of course I bloody understand!' Then, in an appeal to Jeffrey, 'But it wasn't our fault, was it?' His eyes seemed to skulk under their lids before he threw a look of prepared indifference out to no one in particular. Candy was left so utterly lost among her own family that she was sent blindly running to her room — as unable to think herself out of the sobs as a leaf could resist being bowled along the ground by a gust.

Howling, she flung the door shut behind her, flung herself onto her bed, and flung the covers up over her head — but somewhere in the turmoil, she was aware it was no real escape. One of the others would be tapping on her door soon, wanting to talk her out of her distress, telling her not to behave like this, like an eight-year-old — she was almost twelve for goodness sake and it would all be all right . . . When the point was, Dad was not only thoughtless and insensitive but plain *wrong*, unjust and, from the look of cool, gritted annoyance that had been on his face all morning, unlikely ever to apologise.

To Candy, engulfed by her emotions, her father became an immense, unbudgeable thing, a wall like the wall of gospel song: so wide, so high, so low, you can't go around, over, under, or through it. In her mind's eye now even the plaid and stripes of his pyjamas grew big as the sky: never-ending ladders without rungs. Feelings of insignificance, smallness, wrongness, seemed all that were left to her. They became animal, instinctive. As if she had no choice but to burrow into them, pull them up close around her . . . She had to hide, run away to somewhere safe: *now, now, go, go, go*.

Some time later Candy heard her brother's voice.

'Found her, Mum. It's all right.' A light passed into her face, flinched back, startled at the sight of her.

Far off, Rose's voice. 'Jeffrey? Where?'

The torchlight pressed onto paint pots, tarpaulin, cobwebs, dirt bank, rusty nails, an old cracked bucket. It seemed to light up the musty smell too: a smell Candy found oddly comforting. She wanted to nuzzle back into it.

'Round the back, Mum, down here. Under the house.'

Jeffrey came closer. 'Candy-cane? You got them worried. Mum's given Dad a bit of a telling off, but you have to come out now. The police are still here. They want to make sure you didn't hear anything last night. We all thought you were still in your room.'

Candy's neck and ribs on one side were stiff, though she'd been curled up on an old toddler-sized mattress, stored under the house in swathes of plastic sheeting.

'You're a mess,' Jeffrey said. 'You've got dirt all over your face.'

She rubbed half-heartedly but Jeffrey, crouched at the small door that bolted shut from the outside and led to the house foundations, said, 'It's from your hands, I think.'

The dirt tracks were a mix of tears and grime from when Candy had crawled under the house, something she had only as much memory of as a woken sleeper has of how many times they've tossed and turned at night. She remembered a sensation of burrowing, burying, wanting to dig herself deep into hiding, but that was all. Her head was stuffed with the aftermath of crying, the pads of her fingers and under her nails were raw, caked with muck, a few of the nails split. She wanted to wash them but Jeffrey led her into the dining room, where two policemen were sitting at the table with a clipboard and vinyl-covered notebook. Candy realised everyone else had changed out of their pyjamas: she was still in her dressing gown and nightie, felt foolish, grubby, a runaway the police might give the third degree. Robinson's head perched forward on his neck — he looked as if he were trying to swallow a fragment of bone that had caught in his throat. She could tell, then, that he was embarrassed and sorry, and she almost didn't need him to squeeze her and send his big paw stroking down her tangled hair.

'It's thrown us all out of sorts, this thing, hasn't it, Candy?' He looked apologetically at the police officer with the bristly grey crew cut, grey moustache and pink roll of fat at the back of his neck, like the small triangular pillow Gram had sewn for herself, saying she should have patented it because it was essential for long-distance travel. It gave the impression that the officer was comfortable anywhere; was prepared to sit out any long haul.

The police were from the Youth Aid division, they said, and, assuming the two letter-writers were correct, of course, had agreed to have a chat to Redshaw and his parents. The language of law and circular documents came off the older policeman's tongue with a slow, easy drawl. 'If the alleged offender's under fourteen, as you say, our course of action is quite clear cut, Mr and Mrs Marshall. A home visit and official warning is what he'll get at this stage, assuming it's his first offence. But his isn't a name that's come to our notice before, is it, Don?'

Don thought, chin gripped between his thumb and forefinger. He took a breath, then paused. 'Not to my knowledge.'

Robinson leaned forward on an elbow. 'And what about the clear-up?'

'Victims don't always feel happy about that, of course.' The older officer with the buzz-cut looked over quickly to Rose. 'Some old dears get pretty shaken up when their post box is kicked over or their milk bottles are smashed up, and the last thing they want is anything to do with the kiddies who've wrecked it.'

Kiddies. Candy couldn't believe he was using that word about Redshaw. She wondered how Phil would take it, imagined him in his blue-and-black checked bush shirt, jeans with the hems chewed by his bicycle chain, his hollow cheeks and thin-boned nose, beside his parents on a couch as the officer said, 'I'm afraid to say this kiddy here's been making a bit of trouble.'

The officer turned his pen in one hand, tapping it end to end on the tabletop. 'When a kiddie's play goes a bit far like this it's usually symptomatic of other issues, we find.'

'Play?' said Robinson. 'You don't call this play. You call this play and it belittles the effect it's had on my family. Look at my daughter,' he said. 'She's a sensible, grown-up girl, and just look at her.'

Candy wanted her dad to calm down in case he got arrested. 'I'll go and clean up,' she said. Rose shook her head.

The Youth Aid officer gave a preparatory chew at his moustache. 'The situation out there is not pleasant, I'll agree with you on that. The boy needs to take responsibility for his actions. Needs a bit of wind put up him, I'd say. But the law's quite certain about how we treat a child of this age, sir, and I'd ask you to think about how you'd want your own son dealt to in a situation like this.'

Robinson glared at Jeffrey. Rose touched her husband's arm and he gave a little start. 'Yes, yes. Of course.'

When the officer came back that afternoon, with Phil Redshaw, another man, and a boy Candy didn't know, the boys were made to knock on the door and speak to the family first. Through the windows the Marshalls could see that the boys were holding buckets, sponges, scrubbing brushes, black bin-liners. In the driveway there was a little engine contraption, like an exposed motor on wheels.

'What on earth have they got out there?' asked Rose.

'Water-blaster. That'll be to get the spray paint off. Bloody hope for nothing less.'

When Robinson answered the door the boys both turned saucer-eyed with alarm, as if up until now they'd not really thought about having to confront anyone but Candy and Jeffrey. They hung their heads; Phil mumbled an apology. He shifted on his feet, bucket swung back, ready to turn, but Robinson would have none of it.

'If you've got something to say to us, I want to hear it clearly.' Candy saw how tall her father was, how his arms and shoulders, broad with the circuit training he did at a fitness parlour at lunch breaks, almost filled the doorway, so the best view she got of the group on the front step was through the foyer windows beside the door. She almost wondered if Robinson had chosen the black turtle neck he called his beatnik top (which he usually only wore out to the movies) because the material hugged tight to his muscles. His height and strength filled her with righteousness now; if she was still dwarfed by him, it was with the sensation of swinging gleefully from a giant jungle gym, of leaping from the wide, flexible trampoline of dadness. She thought she'd have to fight back the impulse to shout at Redshaw, *Up ya bum ya little dickhead think you're so great well you're not now are ya!* but the presence of the police, the overcast day and the sight of Redshaw sniffling with the cold made the occasion too solemn. It also didn't take much insight to see the fear and regret on the boys' faces.

Phil spoke up, but it still wasn't enough.

'Do you think I can believe you if you won't meet my eye, boy?'

The police officer and the other man waited. Bravely, Phil tipped back his head, said each word clearly.

'Right. Now I think you owe both Jeffrey and Candy their own apology.' Robinson gestured for his son and daughter to shuffle nearer the door.

Phil faltered, so his friend took the lead. 'It was pretty dumb and irresponsible what we did. It just seemed kind of like a buzz, but I didn't really think, didn't really mean it. I'm sorry, eh.'

Phil swallowed and nodded. 'I was . . . real angry about a bunch of stuff. I'm sorry I did it too.'

Candy was startled by Jeffrey's voice right beside her. 'Why don't we just forget everything that happened? It was just a game. Just . . . a game. And you played too, eh? So.' The adults' expressions were first perplexed, then coming to some realisation, about to ask, 'Ahh, what happened? What game?' Candy butted in. 'Yeah. We should all just say sorry and forget it. Everything.'

Phil's mouth twisted sideways, as if to bite back an automatic response. The man behind him cleared his throat, leaned past the boys and held out his hand to Robinson. 'Barry Webber, Phil's foster father.' He gestured to the other boy. 'And this is Kim Apiata, Phil's half-brother.'

Candy shot a hard look at the other boy. 'But you don't go to our school.'

'Kim's just with us for a few weeks while his mum sorts a few things out, aren't you, Kim? Why don't you boys get to work, then? Do the tree first while I have a quick word and set up the water-blaster.'

'Aw, man, but how do we get up there?'

Webber's arm jack-knifed out, thick index finger pointing into Phil's face. 'Are you whining at me? Are you *whining* at me?'

Officer Knowles motioned with his notebook. 'That's why we've got the ladder, Phil. I'll hold the base while one of you nips up there. Right?' He rounded the boys up and sent them off down the steps, saying evenly over his shoulder, 'Calm example, mate.'

Webber settled down. 'Right.' Lower teeth resting against his upper lip, he whistled out. 'Had it up to here with those boys, right now, I'll let you know. They're good lads, they really are. But there's been all sorts of shenanigans since Phil's heard their mum's up before the courts again — for shoplifting, drunk and disorderly — and that Kim was coming to stay.' He ran a hand through his hair, looking embarrassed to have been so personal so quickly. 'Anyway, that's beside the point here, in a way. Haven't been able to get much out of him on this one, to tell you the truth.' He scrutinised Candy and Jeffrey briefly, as if the light from them was too bright. 'Seems to be something that's gone on, ah . . .' he floundered for the right words, eyes hunting them on the air. Candy offered them, firmly. 'In private.' A three-way look passed between Rose, Robinson and Barry Webber. Behind her back, Candy crossed her fingers hard, until the knuckles hurt, a sign to keep out further looks and questions. Then she slipped back into the depths of the house. She expected to be called to heel but for some reason (discomfort in front of their visitor, perhaps?) Rose and Robinson let it ride.

Candy's own head was tangled with all the new strands of circumstance. That was Redshaw's half-brother out there. They didn't look *anything* alike; she didn't even know he had a brother, or was a foster kid, or that his mum did shoplifting. She had been late-night arcade shopping with her mum and dad often enough, could imagine the kind of scene. She saw a woman with large, disco hoop plastic earrings, long, permed yellow hair, dark stripe along her roots. The black and blonde would unintentionally match her leopardskin leggings. She'd be too thin, and smell of cigarettes. She'd wobble on high-heeled little sandals, trip and crash into a rack of scarves or hats in a posh department store, a chocolate bar or pair of warmer leggings clutched up under her jacket. Phil's mum mustn't have much money. Candy found she wanted her to get away with it, the woman in her head — wanted the shop assistant to think she'd just dropped the purchase she was about to make, and not smell the wine or gin behind the three peppermints she'd chewed on the way out of the pub . . .

Yet Candy felt odd all afternoon, knowing that Redshaw was in her front yard: didn't feel quite at ease anywhere, as if he had X-ray eyes that could track her lazing about with a book and drinks of cordial whenever she wanted, while he stood out there in the chilly afternoon, hosing down the driveway, sweeping off the water, bark chips and pebbles in the heavy rhythm of punishment. And when he had to come inside to go to the toilet she sat frozen on the spot with her book in the living room, the very pores of her skin straining open to hear the click of the door again, the thunk of plumbing in action, the tread of his feet along the creaky floorboards under the hallway carpet, the front door thudding shut.

Rose must have noticed how Candy tensed on the couch. After Redshaw was outside again she brought through a tray laden with mugs, a milk jug, a sugar bowl and a neatly arranged fan of tiny sterling silver teaspoons, all with decorative crests declaring tourist spots: presents from Rose's mother, from her visits to academic conferences. Granny Greger had once said sometimes the pictures on the teaspoons were the most she got to actually see of the place: mostly it was looking at her own feet as she listened to seminar papers. 'It means I remember to keep my shoes polished,' she'd added, mouth puckered up into a little self-mocking walnut, which made Candy laugh. She and Jeff loved Granny Greger: couldn't quite believe that Rose had felt such intolerable pressure from her and the rest of her family. 'That's because they've backed off,' said Rose. 'They know I'm a lost cause.' But Rose, their granny said, one eyebrow lifted in amusement, was 'always rather prone to exciting flights of exaggeration'.

Usually the only hot drinks the twins were given were Milo, or milk stirred with honey and nutmeg before winter bedtime: they had always been told caffeinated drinks weren't for children. But in Candy's mug was strong, wood-dark tea. 'It's good for shock,' said Rose. 'If only I'd had the wits about me to give it to you this morning.' It was a granting of new privileges. As she sipped at the unfamiliar taste Candy felt a little nearer adulthood, as if shock and sweetness mixed to make wisdom.

When the clean-up was over, the tired, cold, drawn-looking boys knocked on the door again as they were leaving. Robinson inspected their work. 'You've done a good job of the front there, lads. I think you're both smart enough not to get into this sort of mess again, aren't you? Eh? Are you smart enough?' Through the window Candy saw the pair finally nod in desultory unison. When the sound of the police car had drawn away down the road Rose made more tea, and the whole family was summonsed to sit around the dining table.

'Now, what I want to know,' Rose sighed, 'is why neither of you told us this boy had been giving you trouble at school. The principal phoned back to check everything had kicked into action for the clean-up, and to tell us about the detention Phil got for harassing Candy last week. Something had been building up, hadn't it?'

Candy pressed the rim of her tea mug hard against her mouth as she gave a movement that was neither nod nor shrug, half wondering why people say *stiff upper lip* when her bottom one always seemed to be the first to betray her.

'Do you know what the problem was?' said Robinson.

Jeffrey blew into his tea. 'He just got upset in a game we'd invented.' Candy felt the top of her head prickle. 'Thought we'd broken the rules or something. Weren't playing fair.' There was enough truth in that for Candy to nod.

Robinson leaned forward. 'What kind of game?'

Candy felt her jaw jut out. 'It's secret.'

Robinson started another question, but, rubbing one of his shoulders, Rose said reflectively, 'Ah, that kind of game.' Something in her tone made Robinson sigh, and think, then change tack.

'So how long had this fight been going on?'

Jeff shrugged. 'Not long.'

Rose's thumb worked over a lacquered picture of a kowhai blossom on her coffee mug. 'Why didn't you talk to us about it?'

More half-shrugs, two children shifting in place.

Rose set her mug down carefully. 'You must tell us if anything is ever worrying or upsetting you. Both of you. We'd like to know, so that we can help.'

The children turned in a little to each other, side by side like the two shuttering covers of a private diary, and in tandem said yes, okay, they would. Words they used because they offered comfort, not because they could easily tell all when bad days dawned. The look they exchanged said they knew their parents needed more shielding than that.

PHIL REDSHAW WASN'T at school on Monday. Then he wasn't there for a whole week, and somehow — perhaps a teacher had finally given in to pestering — people found out that he and his whole foster family were moving up north, all the way to the Wairarapa, that supposedly they'd been planning it for ages, and it had nothing to do with what happened to the Marshall twins.

Candy wasn't too sure about that, but was fit to bust with the news by the end of that day. She bounded down the classroom steps, buoyant on her sneakers despite her backpack loaded down with school library books for a project on 'A Foreign People'. (She'd chosen the Roma, curious about how the wrong name, *gypsies*, could have lasted for so long, when they weren't really from Egypt, and she loved the pictures of house-trucks, Clydesdales. She liked the way Roma could sound like Rome or Romania or the roamers, people who could have a different view from their front window every day. If anyone littered the ground and trees outside their caravans they could just find another street or town, Candy thought, unaware, still, of how one town can harbour the blood relatives of another: the family of superstition marrying over the borders into the clan of fear.)

Outside school Candy sat happily on her unchained bike, rocking herself backwards and forwards a little, waiting for Jeff. She wanted to share a quiet sense of freedom, of the end-of-a-story: their toes dipped in the same subcurrent of the unspoken that meant she'd nodded to the version of the pines game he'd told their parents. Jeffrey appeared from his class in a gaggle of boys, all of them chattering and shouting and laughing, an air of excitement about them, as if they'd tasted the far-away summer holiday in the air: sun, fresh-mown grass, coconut oil, the sweat of running free in open spaces.

Candy called out. 'Hi, Jeff!'

He glanced over.

'Hi, Jeff!' one of his friends squeaked back at her, in a voice like Minnie Mouse, or the Chipmunk Punk ads on TV. Jeffrey hesitated, torn, but then laughed, turned his back as he unlocked his bike, joined in the jostling sprint and attempts to leave skid marks at the school gate. He turned off in the opposite direction to home and in a happy phalanx the boys made for someone else's place.

That was really when she realised Jeff had already stepped into two, she thought later. Even though Redshaw had left their school for good, even though none of the kids picked up his twins taunts and carried them on, he had left a legacy. At school, in front of others, Jeff withdrew from her even more fully. Later she thought it was as if that last afternoon in the pines, and all the harassment that followed, had revealed another secret he had to hide; and Redshaw's departure was the chance for him to do so with greater ease. He refused to go to the theatre and movement classes any more, though the tutor phoned home twice to say they needed more boys for the end-of-year production . . . Jeff joined hockey and football teams instead.

And so he and Candy started their waltz of near and far. For at home it was still okay between them: easy, light. Jeff sneaking into her room early in the weekends, hiding at the end of her bed as his hands danced in spontaneous, bizarrely funny puppet shows he'd put on just for her. Jeff doing silly stuff out of the blue, like draping himself in their mum's scarves, belly dancing in the kitchen, clashing pot lids together like cymbals. Jeff helping her with her homework, Candy helping him with his. Sometimes, watching TV, Jeff asking Candy if he could brush her hair: he told her one hundred strokes a day would keep it healthy. But it was different if any friends were watching. Like when their thirteenth birthday came along. Jeffrey blocked every suggestion Candy or their parents made for ways to celebrate.

'Do you kids want the works again this year? Pass the parcel, musical statues, pin the tail on the donkey?'

'Oh, *what*? That's baby stuff! We haven't done that for *years*.'

'Costume party?'

'That's a girl's idea.'

'Ghost theme?'

'Oh, yeah, *right*. So all of Candy's friends'd be screaming if any of us tried to tell a decent horror story.'

'Well, what suggestions do you have, Jeffrey?'

'Why do we have to share a party, anyway? Why can't I just go out with my friends to a movie or a video game parlour or ten-pin bowling or something?'

Rose and Robinson looked from child to child.

'Is that what you want?' asked Rose.

'Everyone else gets their own birthday.'

'But you've never had a problem sharing with your sister before.'

'Who asked?'

Candy sat very still and watched him. She thought of how at school, if his friends saw them together, he'd move away from her, as if she were a magnet pushing another magnet away — even when she called out his name, had something to tell him. As if her following him was exactly what made him flee. She remembered a birthday from when they were seven or eight. It had been just the four of them — something quiet because their mum had just come through one of her *bad patches*, and Robinson said it would be a good idea not to create extra work. Candy had very much wanted to make friends at the time with a new girl in her class, whose name was Cherie, and she had hoped they could have a party with a Wombles theme because she knew Cherie was mad on them. Robinson took her to the room she still shared with Jeff and told her he knew it must seem hard, but they could have a party next year. She couldn't stop crying. Then her heart was shunted out of place because her father said quietly, with a gravid disappointment that stoppered the tears in her mouth with a sour green bitterness, 'I never thought a child of mine could be so selfish. Jeff's not behaving this way. Why should you?'

For many nights following, she'd had frightening dreams: nightmares about a monstrous truck with hundreds of wheels coming to take her parents away because she had done some evil thing that nobody would explain to her. She had no chance to say sorry, and when she tried to speak, the words wouldn't form sound. One night, as she was pushed to the verge of a scream, she woke with a start to feel Jeffrey's warm hand on her shoulder. He slipped into bed beside her and hugged her for a moment before whispering, 'Go back to sleep, it's a bad nightmare, but still, only a dream.'

And on that birthday the family had gone on a long, long drive to a river and had a picnic down on the wide rocky shore. It was too cold for swimming but the children were given butterfly nets which they used in the river shallows, wading in with gumboots, promising not to go above their shins. Rose was bundled up in jerseys and blankets on a collapsible deckchair. Robinson sat on a rug and cushion, leaning against her legs as she ran her fingers over his hair now and then, and they passed each other the thermos, the cheese sandwiches. Candy knew they were watching, and a sense of what was required leaked into her from the dappled browns and greens of the water sliding over the weeds and stones. She breathed in the cold river smell, watched the tilting surface of the water. Then she jerked her knees and elbows in surprise.

'Hey, Jeff, over here!'
'What?'

'Look, there's an *enormous* fish!'

She stooped over the water, peering down to bedrock. He waded over to her side.

'Where?'

'Stay still!' she said. 'It's just hanging around right there, in the water.'

He leaned over, hushed. '*Where?*'

Candy could see her parents both sit up a little, interested; could feel their enjoyment like sun through leaves patterning her cheeks.

'Wait, wait. I got it, I got it.'

'What's it *look* like? I can't even see it.'

'There!' She swooped her butterfly net over his head, capping him like a pen, and danced around wildly in the water, crying out, 'Mum, Dad, help me land it! Help me land it! It's the Great White Jeffrey Fish!'

Jeffrey yelped, but then he started giggling, and taking it in his stride, pretended to flap his fins, crying, 'Blub, blub, blub,' the sound of drowning in air. And then the delight was reversed: the children screeched as Robinson came blundering over the stones on the shore, calling out, 'Hold on!' then pretending it took both hands to struggle with the weight of the catch. Even Rose stood up, laughing. 'Reel it in! Reel it in!'

With Robinson and the children staggering backwards towards the picnic, somehow all four of them ended up clutching one another and trying not to be sent sprawling over the shingle; instead they fell slowly in a tangled heap on the rug, breathless with laughter. Bubbles of it seemed to stay in their bloodstream for the rest of the afternoon. Even Rose hugged both the twins to her at one point, saying, 'My two goofy moon units. You know how to have a good time, don't you? It makes me so happy.'

'What's a moon unit?' said Jeff.

'It's an us,' answered Candy.

They both giggled, and Rose and Robinson shook their heads.

'What have you been teaching these kids of yours?' asked Robinson.

'That we need *ice-creams!*' yelled Jeff.

'Yeah, *ice-creams!*'

And on the way home in the car their dad stopped at a petrol station. When he'd filled up the car and paid, he came back with four double-scoop-chocolate-dip-with-a-chocolate-flake-bar-stuck-in-it-too ice-creams, propped up in a cardboard tray. He opened the driver's door and poked his head in. 'You kids didn't really want ice-creams, did you?'

'Yeah!'

'*Yeah!*'

'Thanks, Dad.'

'Thanks, Dad.'

'Thank your mother too — she's the one who said it *was* your birthday.'

'Thanks, Mum too.'

'Thanks, Mum too.'

'Do I hear an echo?'

'You do hear an echo.'

'All right, that's enough. Pipe down and eat up, you cheeky monkeys.'

'Oo-hoo-oo-hoo-ehh! Ehh! This is banana-chip flavour.'

'This is orange-chip flavour.'

Candy and Jeff eyed each other's cones, and halfway through, without speaking, swapped for the final scoop. And then, there was the centre of the memory. She had drowsed against Jeff's shoulders as the sun went down, the sky turning from dusky pink to dust orange, then fading to the colour of the words sung low on the radio: 'Afro-blue'. Jeff pressed his palm into her knee.

'Candy, look.'

Fleetingly, against the darkening sky on a hilly paddock, she saw three pale horses who wheeled and followed one another, movements flowing along a large slope and down, apparently gliding parallel to the car before it pulled ahead, drawing beyond them. She and Jeff looked at each other, and he let her nestle against his shoulder again, as he whispered, 'They were the night mares,

Candy. It's going to be all right tonight.'

Long after she'd forgotten what he gave her that birthday, or what she'd given him, she remembered the way he'd taken away her disturbed dreams. Sometimes, on the shimmering borderline of sleep, she still saw the three horses, pale and grey, against a sky soaked in black. The floating, free-falling sensation she felt was as if she followed them as they raced on; she rode the rising dark as they did. Examining the expression on Jeff's face now, she tucked this all back, hid it as best she could. In case he denied it, in case he took away what he'd given.

This year there was a fight just before the day of Jeffrey's party. He'd insisted his should be on their real birthday, a Saturday, and Candy's on the Sunday — or if hers had to be a Saturday, the following week — because, he'd said, with flat-toned logic, 'Born first, wasn't I?' Candy looked at him hard. When he acted this way it was as if he'd outgrown the other Jeff, kicked him off like a worn-out tennis shoe, and not given him another thought. She wondered if he even remembered the boy she used to cajole out of grief or the Sunday glums, tickling the soles of his feet, sitting on him, telling him bad jokes though he pretended not to hear.

When they began to discuss numbers for the booking at the bowling alley, Jeffrey said, 'Why ten? It's nine.'

Their mother listed the names.

Jeffrey's jaw pushed forward into its stubborn shovel expression. 'I'm not going to Candy's, so why's she coming to mine?'

'Jeffrey.'

'What?'

'Be reasonable.'

'*What*? The whole point of us having two parties is so we can get a chance just to be alone for once. Just to breathe.'

Words that meant Candy sucked the air from the room, copied his every move, and cramped him so people hardly knew him, he hardly knew himself. Which wasn't true. Usually it was Jeff who came to her door, tapping and saying, 'You busy?' Jeff who said, when they looked through the TV listings, 'I want to watch what you want to watch.' Jeff who tried on the new selection of hats she'd started to collect (which she liked to look at, more than to wear). In her floppy, blue velvet peaked cap, black Greek fisherman's cap, Turkish fez: he eyed himself in the mirror with a brooding curiosity. Jeff was the one who hung around when she had friends over for pikelets and games of Five Hundred, and who offered advice on how to whip the cream, or how to stockpile tricks, though he'd shove his own door shut if she tried to do the same when *he* had visitors. And it was Jeff who, when in a bad mood, would start his maddening mimicry, following her so closely all day that eventually she'd say something like, 'Can't you go and do your own thing?' Wounded, he'd set into it.

'Can't you go and do your own thing?'

She'd wait a few beats, try a slight change of tack.

'Just give me back the scissors, Jeff. I had them first.'

'Just give me back the scissors, I had them.'

'Stop copying me!'

'Stop copying me!'

'Leave me alone!'

'Leave me alone!'

Sometimes he could stretch it out for so long that she felt the claustrophobia of being boxed in a tiny but echoing cave. But the way his face reddened, it was almost as if he were trapped in it, too — the chanting a kind of self-hypnosis. Maybe they both needed someone to snap, or slap, them out of it. For Rose did once — slap Jeff — a quick, curt whack across the buttocks, though he was nearly a teenager. He *just wouldn't stop*, and it had driven everyone to breaking point.

And now, two-faced Janus in one boy, he was insisting on their separation. And how strange: in another kind of reversal Candy was hurt.

'All right, all right. If this one-at-a-time thing is so important to them all of a sudden,' said Robinson to Rose, when Candy hadn't even shed the single sigh of the *start* of a word. 'Only one of us will be able to go to the bowling alley, so that takes the numbers down to eight.'

89

'Doesn't matter,' Candy shrugged. 'I don't need someone to stay here and look after me.'

'I don't like the idea of leaving you here on your own, Candy.'

'I'll be fine. I won't get into any trouble.'

'It's not trouble I'm worried about. It just seems a little — *mean* to leave you behind.'

A shade of guilt lurked around Jeffrey's face.

'Don't worry.' Candy feigned lightness, nonchalance. 'I've got my guitar now. I've got plenty to do on my own.'

They asked a dozen times if she were sure, then arranged for someone to be home next door so she could pop over if she had any worries. On the day of Jeff's party Candy didn't even come out of her room to call goodbye when the others left. Two could play at disinterest, she thought: I'll show him *I* don't care. Her birthday guitar sat in the chair at her homework desk: placed there ceremoniously, out of harm's kick or bump. When struck accidentally it seemed to cry out like a wild animal in deep-throated, off-key pain: a noise that made Candy's joints seize. She'd already learnt to carry it around the house held close to her body, as in a waltz, so that it wouldn't knock against door-frames. Robinson had taken it from her when he first saw her do this; he'd crooned to it, then led it in the party polka around the living room, coins and keys jangling in his pockets, twirling the instrument out at arm's length, bowing a gracious *excuse me* to the living-room lamp. Candy found she involuntarily had her arms out, like a mother wanting her baby back, out of the clutch of a brash uncle whose game of toss and catch has begun to leave the catch a little too late.

She had been hoping for so long for a guitar and lessons that when she first saw it in the black case, its neck tied with ribbon, it felt as if she had been unconsciously holding her breath — the world turning blue — for weeks, and now air rushed in, her vision tingling with pink.

The desire to play guitar had taken seed over a year before, digging in deep enough to turn up even in sleep. It had started at an end-of-first-term party for the junior movement and theatre class students. Their teacher had asked a trio of musicians who had once studied in the senior music classes held at the small community arts centre to come and play dance numbers for the juniors. Based in a deconsecrated suburban church, the arts centre was also where some members of the Baha'i Faith ran one of the first local vegetarian cafés. Known for its platters of homemade bread and spreads, its unofficial name from the older theatre students was the Dippy Hippies. Candy saw the lithe, black-clad musicians doing a lot of business with electrical cords, mike stands and speakers before they burrowed away backstage for a while, and the juniors tucked in to the food laid out on the Formica-covered trestle tables. (Tables which, could they talk, could tell the real-people history of the district: they were used for everything from stands at Pacific arts and crafts fairs and Best Bride contests to scrutineers' workbenches on national election days.) As Candy gazed now and then at the musicians and their crew, little hands browsed over food that seemed to be a variation on just three themes: cheese, fish and sugar. There was a Party Cheese Roll and a Party Cheese Ball, there were cheese straws, cheese on crackers, cheese dip, Cheezles, Cheese *balls*; and salmon pâté, shrimp tartlets, tuna roulade, sardines on crackers; and chocolate truffles, lamingtons, coconut ice, jelly, ice-cream cake and softdrinks. (The Baha'is, next door, were amazed that people still *ate* that way.) The mums and dads would say afterwards that the tutors, Nanci and Wendi, had outdone themselves. More than one child would cry for the car to be stopped so they could be sick on the way home.

Candy would have been eating but she was still smarting over how one of the tutors, flustered and sweaty, had asked her to help move chairs off the dance floor, and had bloody well called her *Jeff* for Pete's sake: had confused her with a *boy*! ('It's Candy,' she'd corrected, so astonished it was nearly a shriek. Nanci's eyes took on an irritated glaze. 'Candy, Shelley, Nicky, Susie, whatever. *Marshall* twin,' she said, as if that clarified and settled it. 'Could you just get a move on and help?') But Candy had been told in classes that she had a natural sense of rhythm, that she had a strong stage presence.

They'd always told Jeff to listen harder, and not to fidget. How could anyone confuse them?

Distracted by these inner snarls, she hadn't noticed that there was a young woman amid the musicians until the group came back on stage in their performance get-up. The woman musician introduced the band. They were The Ferns, and they would take requests from the audience. She was Meremere; the men were Hone and Turoa. The guys wore matching shirts, green, printed with white flowers, a general South Pacific style. Meremere wore false eyelashes made of fine rainbow tinsel. She had short dark hair, in a flicked-up sixties bob, wore an almost white lavender lipstick that looked fluorescent against her dark skin, and a long halter-top dress that clung all the way to her ankles, shimmering with pink and silver lurex, the pink patterned into a lush flower matching the plastic hibiscus behind one ear. For some reason Candy imagined she would sing while the men played guitar and drums, but she had a guitar too, and the band members swapped over every now and then: everyone had a go on everything. Although it was unusual, then, for a woman to play drums, Candy couldn't see her properly when she was sitting down, so she became truly stuck on Meremere when she played guitar. She swayed side to side on the slower songs, undulating like a plant under water. On angry songs ('I See Red') you really wouldn't want to betray her; the guitar was like a rifle slung over her shoulder, the metallic chords slotted in place and aimed into the air, small bullets of jealousy and betrayal. On the peppy songs she made it look like the guitar was light as poi, as maracas, as a tambourine.

One of the tutors — Wendi, in her black scoop-neck leotard and flowing gathered skirt — set up a game of Snowball to get all the children onto the dance floor. Jeff turned a livid purple, a mix of pride and embarrassment, when a tall, smoky sort of girl called Virginia asked him to dance. Candy was asked by a flop-fringed boy called Darren, a fourteen-year-old just discovering the New Romantics. He smelled of liquorice and Blue Stratos, wore one of his dad's old white shirts open at the chest, and a pair of baggy jodhpurs with a trendy thin double belt, which had the effect of exaggerating his lankiness: it looked as if the belt had been wrapped around him twice and still didn't fit.

Not many of the boys — most were under fifteen — could cope with being made to dance with a partner. They tended to gyrate off and crash into one another like dodgem cars so they had an excuse to start pushing each other around instead. Oh well, never mind, thought Candy. The band gradually made her blind to them. The sound of Meremere's voice — somehow like honey and cream warmed in a pan — set off a response in Candy's bones: her spine tingling pleasantly, a tuning fork struck against the hand. Involuntarily, she sought Jeff's eyes, to see if she could read the same reaction in him. He was shuffling with Virginia, swallowing hard, eyes fixed on a crêpe-paper streamer with the look of someone awaiting a judgement. It made her feel strangely released — a fan unfolded and stretched, wind lapping at its skin — and it made her wonder, wonder. Soon she wore a suit of perspiration from dancing, singing, clapping, jumping on the spot. On the third-to-last song, Meremere said, 'This is a song you won't know: it's one I wrote with my friends here. We think of it as a musical raranga, or weaving. It's about a fairy woman called Niwareka.' Some of the boys blew raspberries. Meremere raised an eyebrow, Candy could *swear*, right at Candy herself. Meremere was saying, 'Niwareka taught the Maori people how to weave. She made the first ever cloak. So this is a song to wear when you're maybe tired and alone, or at night when it's dark and cold, and even the wind seems to have better things to do than keep you company.'

The boys moved on to trying to do bird calls with a complicated arrangement of palms and thumbs up to their puckers, or to trying to do what they called 'super-rasbs', squeezing hands into sweaty armpits: the wetter the reverberation, the ruder. Candy wrapped her arms around herself and swayed on the spot, trying to loosen her hips around the axis of her spine the way Meremere did. She grinned, and then, incredibly, Meremere beckoned to her with a tambourine. Candy glanced over her shoulders, then pointed at herself. 'Me?' she mouthed. Meremere nodded and when Candy reached the stage, reached out a hand to haul her up. 'Just keep a rhythm,' Meremere said. Candy scouted the hall for Wendi, the tutor who'd been so off-hand. When she could be sure Wendi had noticed, Candy tossed her hair, and began to follow Meremere's movements: now and then glancing over at Jeff's four left feet, something in the contrast making her feel the euphoria of the rise and fall of a playground swing.

It was hard to believe how the hall had been transformed by the musicians once the evening was over. Brimming with energy that had been poured into her from the stage, Candy tried to describe it all to Rose as they scrambled into the car.

'They were *soooo* professional, Mum. They put everything into it, even just for a little thing like an end-of-term party — didn't they, Jeff?'

'Yeah. Oh, shh-oot. There's Virginia. Pretend you haven't seen her.'

'Why? You liked her enough to dance with her.'

'Just don't look!'

Candy wound down their car window. 'Bye, Virginia!'

'Sshhii —'

'Jeffrey,' Rose eyed him in the rear-view mirror.

He'd slumped down as far as he could. 'That is *so*, so uncool, Candy. You are *so* uncool. And the way you dance is just totally embarrassing. I wanted to pretend you weren't my sister only Virginia laughed and said I'd never get away with it. She said it was like we're the boy and girl version of the same person.'

Something cold slid down the back of Candy's neck, making happiness retreat a little. 'At least I didn't look like a moving eggplant. He went purple, Mum, he really did.'

'You two, that's enough.'

And it was: Candy felt a heavy disappointment with herself for reverting to ordinary family bicker when she'd wanted to prolong the mood she'd been infused with by the music. In the silence again she could hear Meremere's guitar in her head, and tiny but tough roots of determination trailed down, already forming the light, furled nubs of concentration and focus, green coils that would eventually span out into hope and ambition.

The desire for a guitar, which came too late on the heels of her twelfth birthday, perhaps grew stronger for having to wait. Candy had to prove, too, to her parents that it was what she truly wanted: they were wary of covering the cost of continued theatre classes as well as music lessons if it was just a passing dalliance, even though Rose had gone back to part-time work — she was 'general dogsbody', she called it (but cheerfully enough) at the southern regional office of a children's charity. (Whenever they held fundraising fairs Rose got even busier at home, producing more and more of her garden whirligigs, always trying new sorts: Big Bird, dahlias, trotting cats . . .) So Candy had to promise to save up part of the cost of the overall instrument, trappings and lessons. Five dollars a week pocket money for her chores, plus the money from a paper round for the suburb's freebie news circular, meant that week by week, more and more of the acoustic guitar, metronome and music stand materialised as approaching fact. She imagined saving up for each part separately: starting with the sound hole, the gap in the middle like the centre in a doughnut — because in a way it was the bit she already had. As her savings accumulated she moved on to the neck, the tuning keys, the fingerboard, the body, the soundboard, the saddle, the bridge, and then, from the sixth string — silver or bronze — to the first: clear nylon, like heavy fishing line, the string that she imagined would pull the guitar in from wishing to reality.

And now, the week of their thirteenth birthday, it was here. It was full-sized, because her hands were already large for her age: seemed to have developed ahead of the rest of her, which she hoped was a sign that she was meant for music.

Since opening the present Candy had taken to just sitting in her room, doodling over the strings with idle, clumsy fingers, trying to work out the principles of the instrument by ear alone. When she tired of her own cacophony she simply looked at it a lot. It had a womanly shape, she thought. Its curved waist gave it hips and chest. Perhaps its human contours helped to make it feel like a companion: a replacement for her brother in some ways. At other times it looked like a steering paddle: an oar she would use to move herself away from the isolation Jeffrey's words and manner stirred in her now, away from the swift undercurrent of sadness his increasingly curt treatment of her in public set off. Much later the division between the two sides of Jeff reminded Candy of something else. For there was the private Jeff who still tried on her hats, who lay on her bed and awkwardly, round-aboutly, asked questions about her friends — 'girl stuff'. This was the Jeff who still now and then came to her when he was low: worried over rumours he'd heard about the boys' school he was being sent to in a few months, and what they did to 'turd formers' (hang them from bus straps, flush their heads in a piss-filled loo, force them to masturbate onto their own sandwiches). And then there was the Jeff who seemed to deny how he needed her. Yes: later, as an adult, she thought it was something like couples she knew who, in front of friends, habitually disagreed, or aired their most petty of arguments. Was it to make disagreement safe? (The temperature could only go so high in public.) To find allies? Or to persuade themselves of their own independence? It seemed such arguments were a sign of just the opposite: cabin fever, living excessively in each other's pockets, needing too much agreement or approval from the partner or spouse. ('Brian says I look frumpy in this coat! Brian says I have to give away two books for every new one I buy, because we just don't have the shelf space! Brian won't let me use maple syrup on my pancakes! Or have sugar in my coffee!' Candy wanted to ask, why *let* Brian not let you?) If they staked less on each other, knew themselves better as separate entities, perhaps the need to air — and assert — their differences would be less?

Her education in how two can at times uncomfortably make one, how one can be cramped by two, had begun long before the pub drinks and dinner parties where the Brians of her world were gently rebuked. At some level midway between conscious and unconscious Candy began to sense that the guitar was one thing that would truly be hers and hers only. She began to look forward to the Saturday when she'd be left alone, so that she could try to figure out some of the pages in her music book before her lessons officially began — and without Jeffrey passing sarcastic comment.

The feel of the strings under her fingers made her itch to know more, as if there were music budding on the back of her tongue. She pictured the hard, glossy black kernels of seeds, like quavers or semibreves, lodged deep in dark soil, still ignorant of heat and light, but somehow already rustling with heavy, saffron-coloured flower-heads. Impatiently she scanned the first pages of the lesson book she'd be using.

Her head swam with all the cross-hatchings, spiky lines, dots, and how to get two hands doing different things at the same time — like the trick Jeff brought home when they were six, of patting his head and rubbing his stomach. Her mind boggled when she looked ahead at the music. It was as disorienting as a hilltop view of an unfamiliar city: streets, buildings and parks reduced to blocks and circles, all networked with power lines and pylons. She remembered her father standing beside her on a trip to Wellington, arm around her shoulders as they all stood on Mount Victoria. 'That's the direction we're staying in. See the blue neon light over there?' He pointed, then cupped her chin in his hand briefly to guide her eyes in the right direction, but the lights swarmed, the streets tangled. 'I think so,' she said, because it was what he wanted to hear, and because she wanted to keep his arm around her a bit longer, for the warmth and the private space it drew: a sweet moment separate from Rose and Jeffrey.

Somehow this recollection and comparison fed back in to the craving for music. She slammed the book shut, pushed it away with her foot, let her fingers travel each string along the frets, from the soundboard to the neck, as she plucked, high to low, humming words to follow the mood on a hilltop in a town in the dark.

We stood on a hill at night
you showed me the city lights
and it was like we were underground
in a dark cave
where fire flies danced
and wrote our names
and it was like we were flying
high above the planet
looking down on other suns
and I thought when we walked over the stones
back to the car
the sound of our feet
was so sad . . .
If you ever go back to that electric city
and forget me
my name will burn like a spell on you
from the lights on its hills

She found herself looking up and around her room, half asking the walls where the words and melody had sprung from. She shivered. Then slowly she tried and tried to pluck the right notes from the guitar for each word: to reassure herself that they did at least exist somewhere beyond her mind's ear, and she'd get to them properly, eventually. But the fit of words and tune had dissolved as she'd sung them, spreading and separating like breath on a frosty morning. Crouched over the instrument, crooning at it in a voice she knew was off-key, she was totally absorbed when Jeff booted open her door. She leapt with surprise and the guitar slipped from her knees before she could catch it. Jeff stood there with a couple of his friends clustered behind him, grinning. He clutched his hands up under his collar-bone, batting cow eyes at the ceiling as he swayed in place and sang in a trembling, cracked falsetto, 'I will survive! I will survive now!'

His friends *heh-heh-hehed* behind him as they all moved into the room.

'Are you making up your own words to pop songs?' Jeff asked.

'And most of your own tune too?' one of the boys grinned.

'Why don't you *knock*? And who said you could all come in here anyway?' Her hands went out for the guitar as she readied herself to sit with it again, and make it seem she was unfazed by their teasing. Jeff shot over and grabbed it from her.

'Jeff!'

He bounced the neck on the air, strummed at the strings in a rapid crash of notes, windmilled his arm like Pete Townshend from The Who, then flipped the soundboard up so he could read the label inside the body. Made of green paper, and with the appearance of a tea coupon or a book plate, it said Yamaha C-310.

Jeff peered more closely and read the rest out loud. 'Made by YMMI Co Ltd in Indonesia, according to the specifications of the Yamaha Corporation. Yamaha!' He straddled it like a hobby horse and sang a mixed-up advertising jingle. 'Yamaha cars, Yamaha cars, better cars!'

Candy was white and shaking. White like the hottest kind of heat. Through clenched teeth, and as slowly as her galloping heart would let, she said, 'Put it down. Right now. Give it back.'

The boys snickered. 'Rev that bike, man!' one of them said. The other leaned over and cranked one of the tuning keys while — puffing out the sides of his cheeks — making the sound of someone opening the throttle on a motorbike.

'I said, *put it down.*'

They laughed, and Jeff said, 'Chuck us that dish on the desk.' One of the friends tipped out the drawing pins, felt pens, and paperclips Candy kept in an old ceramic mixing bowl and pushed it to Jeff. He put it on his head. 'Erik Estrada, man, from *CHiPs*!'

'Put it down!'

'Yehk, yehk, yehk, cool, man.'

'Choice.'

Candy picked up a handful of felt pens, paperclips and, ignoring the stabs, drawing pins — then threw it all into Jeffrey's face. 'Put my bloody guitar down, Jeffrey! Right now!' Blotches of fury shot over her vision.

'Ooooooh . . .'

'Oooo-*whooooh*,' said the friends.

Jeffrey clapped a palm over his eye. 'Shit! You little bitch! That *hurt*!' He tried to take the hand away but the eye flickered shut and streamed with water.

Robinson appeared at the door to see what appeared to be both his children crying. 'What's going on? What's this language I can hear?'

Pain shortened Jeffrey's fuse. '*She* threw a whole lot of stuff at me and it hit me in the bloody face!'

'Candy?'

'*He's* been treating my guitar really badly. It cost us heaps of money and he just grabbed it from me and started using it like a motorbike and *he* —' she pointed at the friend, 'yanked on the tuning keys. But it's not a bloody toy, it's an expensive musical instrument! I never said they could even touch it!'

Eye still pouring water, Jeffrey made a show of gently resting the guitar against Candy's chair. 'God, Dad,' he said, voice calm now, despite his crippled eye, 'I didn't know she was going to be so *sensitive*. I was only joking.'

'Can't you two get along? It's your birthday, for Pete's sake.'

'Could have fooled me,' Candy said. 'Everyone around here's acting like it's just *Jeffrey's* birthday. Well, excuse me for being born too.'

Robinson pulled both hands out of his pockets and pushed up his sweater cuffs. 'Right. That's enough feeling sorry for yourself. We all agreed you'd have separate parties this year so I don't see what the problem is. I don't want to hear any more about what's been going on here. But I do want to hear an apology from you both. To each other. All right? All right? Now. *Both of you.*'

But Candy wouldn't come out of her room at dinner time: she said she wasn't hungry. When Robinson said, 'But it's *pizza*, Candy-girl,' she answered, 'So? That's Jeffrey's favourite, not mine.'

As she had hoped, Rose eventually came in on her own. She brought what was known in the family as a Mosaic Meal: a plate of snack food the children had often been served when their mother had been 'in a bad patch'. It was a guilty pleasure: a favourite dinner, but one they knew was associated with the blank or weepy Rose, as she prepared it partly out of guilt, to make them happy, and partly out of sheer lack of energy or interest in anything else. Candy gave her mother a startled look when she saw the array of cheese and pineapple chunks on toothpicks, the bread and relish, crackers and pâté, boiled egg, carrot sticks, tomato wedges, the handful of nuts and raisins and chocolate chips. But Rose's expression was lively, full of colour and warmth from the kitchen.

'Sure you're not hungry?' she asked.

'Oh — okay,' Candy conceded.

'Can you tell me what's wrong?' Rose curled up on Candy's bed and helped herself to one of the sticks of celery filled with cottage cheese. 'You know it would be nicer for your brother if you came and joined us,' she said.

Candy's mouth quirked up in doubt. 'Jeffrey's what's wrong.'

'What about him exactly? He did say sorry about the guitar.'

Candy sighed. 'But why'd he have to do it in the first place? He's weird these days, Mum. I mean, he used to be my real friend as well as my brother. He's gone all . . . funny. He's so often *at* me.'

Rose watched a moth bump at Candy's window, legs and feelers skating on the spot. It seemed to turn her dreamy.

'Hmmmm. Thirteen. It's one of those in-between ages, I think, Candy. You're not a child any more, and yet you're not used to being a teenager. It must be twice as hard for you two.'

Candy eyed her suspiciously. Rose was always the one who'd insisted they were just like a 'normal' brother and sister: nothing mystic or special about their twinship at all.

'What do you mean?'

'Going through the same age at the same time, but not the same stage.'

'What?'

'Oh, well. I guess I mean . . . the old cliché. Girls mature faster than boys. I can't help thinking that must be hard on Jeffrey.

Perhaps he feels he's being left behind.'

Right. Feeling sorry for Jeffrey. He was the focus. *As always*, Candy thought, and a surge of hurt gave a moment's resentment all the force of incontrovertible fact. 'I don't understand.'

'He's not . . . showing the same signs as you. That he's growing up.'

Candy felt a scattering of confusion. 'What signs . . . am I showing?'

'Oh, well. Little curves and so on.'

'I am?'

'Of course.'

'Where am I?' she leapt up from her bed and pulled her shirt down tight. 'Where?'

'In all the right places, Candy, don't you worry! And of course anyone in a family notices that sort of thing.'

Candy was still staring at her chest. 'That's *curves*? Looks more like . . . pikelets!'

Rose reddened, trying not to laugh. 'The beginnings of curves.'

Candy puffed out her chest. 'Will I need a bra soon?'

Rose raised an eyebrow. 'Well, eventually.' (Candy wouldn't, really, for a few more years, though she'd insist on buying one, to be like all the other girls at school.)

She sat back down to munch happily on a cracker topped with pâté. 'Do *you* think Jeffrey's changed lately?'

Rose pressed the pad of a finger onto the salt left behind by Candy's cracker. 'What sort of changes?'

Candy shrugged. 'He's just — different.'

Rose's body curled deeper into the blankets and eiderdown on Candy's bed, settling in to her subject. 'You've always had your differences. That's been one of the most fascinating things to watch. I suppose I imagined you'd always want the same things at the same time. But it was almost like you both knew — like you worked as a team. Even took it in turns to learn how to feed, to get colds, to teethe.'

Candy chewed her lip, catching the echoes of other overheard stories. 'But didn't that make it harder? If one of us was always giving trouble?'

'Oh, trouble's not the word I'd use, Candy.'

Candy could feel the look of scepticism creep over her face.

'I don't mean to dismiss how hard it was sometimes,' Rose said. 'But your children — our children — they don't, I mean, you didn't *cause* the trouble. You didn't mean it, that's what I'm trying to say.'

Candy's mind locked on the stumbles. There was trouble. The twins didn't mean it — how could they, they were only babies, then only toddlers, then only little kids — but still, trouble. Double Trouble. She'd seen a pair of adult women twins wearing customised T-shirts that said that, once: tight red T-shirts, the lettering done in minute, fake stick-on diamonds. They wore matching white jeans, both had long platinum hair, almost geisha-like make-up, matching handbags. They seemed to make street theatre of their relationship: swung along the footpath in a synchronised walk, blew a simultaneous kiss at an old man who staggered to a stop to stare at them, his whole torso turning because his neck was stiff with age. 'Is this a stunt?' a Samoan businessman asked his friend, briefcases between their ankles as they leaned against a lamp-post, munching filled rolls in the sunshine. 'This is the *real* thing,' one of the women shot back, and the sisters leaned in together, laughing as they walked on, hips swivelling. The businessman's friend whistled, 'Imagine a threesome with that.' Candy thought he meant imagine triplets who looked like that, and thought he was just plain stupid. But she was also oddly embarrassed at the way the twin women called attention to themselves: as if their behaviour implicated her. Now the thought, Double Trouble, meant something else. Trouble sounded like mix and tangle itself. There was a glitch, a halt, a trip up in the middle of the word, and then the rest of it tumbled on.

Jack and Jill went up the hill
to fetch a pail of water
Jack fell down and broke his crown
and Jill came tumbling after.

One mistake, then another. Rose chucked at Candy's bottom lip with the edge of her index finger. 'Hey, what's this? What's this pout? You're still bothered by something, aren't you?'

Her mother knew her too well for her to say airily, 'Oh, nothing . . .' so Candy tried to swallow the gravel in her throat, the stone and stumble of trouble. 'You know you've said Jeffrey and I have always been different. How, exactly?'

Rose examined her nails and began to push down at the cuticles with the blunt, bitten-off end of a toothpick. 'I suppose Jeffrey is the more light-hearted. You're the more — thoughtful. And maybe Jeffrey tends to lead, and you to follow . . .' Rose frowned. 'Though not all the time. That's the wonder of it, having you both. It's unpredictable.'

'Mum?'

'Yes?'

'Is unpredictable a good thing or a bad thing?'

Rose's expression struggled with something. She swung her legs off the bed and dusted her hands off on her knees. 'Come on, Candy, enough brooding. It's supposed to be a happy day. Bring the rest of your dinner out to the table.'

But Candy felt that Rose had avoided the questions. Memories of Jeff burying himself in his misery in his room, Candy being the one to lead him out of that cold crevasse again, fought against the description Rose gave of her children. Candy felt her bottom lip involuntarily edge back into its sulky pout. 'No, it's okay. I'll stay in here.'

Rose's fingers pushed into the hair at her temples, holding it back like side combs, pressing into her head; Candy's voice seemed to be chalk running the wrong way over a blackboard.

'Candy, be reasonable. Be reasonable. This is exactly what we're talking about. Jeffrey wouldn't brood and sulk like this, would he? He asked where you were at dinner. I won't have a prolonged argument on your birthday. I can't take it.'

Whenever it looked as if Rose were going to be pushed too far, dread wheeled up from Candy's mind like a disturbed falcon. With the colour pressed from her cheeks, she nodded, unfolded her legs, and took her half-empty plate out to the living room without having to be asked again.

When he saw Candy slink out with Rose behind her, their mother's agitation still just visible from her tousled hair, Jeffrey shot his sister a slightly guilty half smile. As she sat down next to him he raised the wine glass their dad had filled with freshly squeezed orange juice for the occasion.

'H'ppy b'thd'y,' he mumbled.

Robinson poured Candy a glass from the old willow-pattern jug too, and the family — and Jeff's friends who'd been asked to come back to the house after the larger party at the bowling alley — settled into a watchful approximation of Having a Good Time. Candy, too, did her best, though her sense of herself felt shaken up, was still sifting down again, the same components shifting, rearranging, the colours mingling, realigning. Like a tacky mantelpiece decoration she would see in her first flat in years to come: coloured sand sealed inside a thin, clear, plastic rectangle, the dimensions of a paperback. The rectangle rotated on a Perspex stand — the hourglass principle turned into a decorative object in which the layers of coloured sand vaguely gave the effect of landscapes that rearranged themselves each time it tipped over. It almost annoyed her that she was attracted to the object: it was an ugly executive-stress toy that didn't quite have the sense of humour of something like a lava lamp. But the drifting coloured sands made a kind of sense. They seemed to reflect something in her, when she looked back on her childhood, or even on the months leading up to her arrival at that flat. Layers always rearranging and merging — and sometimes it felt she was only composed of a million shattered fragments of something larger: tiny, glinting, hard-edged pieces of the expectations of Jeff, Rose, Robinson.

MIDWAY THROUGH CANDY and Jeff's final year before high school, a letter had come for the family from a medical institute in the United States. When the twins had turned ten their mother and father had been tracked down through hospital birth records and asked to sign a consent form that said they would be willing for their children to be included on an international register of multiple births. Their medical records were to be accessed by research professionals for the compilation of global statistics on the growth, weight and general health of twins, triplets, quadruplets and what their dad called (to Rose's dismay), 'don't-even-mention-ets'. Rose hadn't been particularly keen at first, was worried about any extra fuss and attention, but let Robinson persuade her with the argument that only research professionals would use the register, and any personal information compiled would be anonymous, reduced to numbers. The institute had also, every two years since, asked Jeff and Candy to sit IQ tests, which were conducted under the supervision of the local university psychology department. Usually such tests were done on identical twins, but the institute wanted control groups of fraternals and ordinary siblings. (There wasn't, their family GP surely would have been disappointed to know, a separate group tagged 'Third-Type-of-Twins'.)

The latest letter this year said that Candy and Jeffrey would be asked to sit an extra series of tests, and the whole family would be asked to fill out further forms that covered much the same ground as the initial papers Rose and Robinson had completed when they first agreed to the project: nationality, social background, race, income, age, health, height, weight. All because last time Jeffrey had performed in the top three percent of all twins examined.

Robinson read the letter over a whisky and soda after work while Jeffrey was — *show-offy, greasy, bum-licky*, Candy thought — leafing through the 'A' volume of the *Encyclopaedia Britannica* in the living room.

'General knowledge doesn't mean you're brainy,' said Candy, whacking the cover of the volume with her fingernails.

'What's the capital of Antarctica?'

'What? But a capital's a city.'

'It's the letter A, thicko.'

'Oh, ha *ha*.'

Robinson looked up from the forms. 'Is this right? What percentile is Candy in?'

'It doesn't actually say. They've only specified if your child is in the top three percent — so Candy could be in the top four, ten, fifty . . .'

Robinson tugged at his earlobe, an irritated scowl on his face as if some bug was nipping at his ear. 'Well, I can't believe the kids would be too far apart. Can't see there'd be any significant division at all, really. Maybe we should ask for a recount, or a retest, or something.'

Rose briefly ran a hand up and down his back. 'I don't see why. Candy has to sit all the same tests anyway — they're examining all co-twins of those at the top.'

Robinson's scowl stayed put. 'How does separating them out like this help anyone?'

Rose looked over the pages again. 'Well, like you said at first, I guess it helps science. Might help other people in the long run. Somehow. And as long as we handle it properly . . .'

Half-sceptical, half-concealing, Robinson shrugged and nodded.

'And still, Jeff has a right to be proud, don't you think?' Rose had lowered her voice but both children heard clearly enough. A long silence followed, in which Candy broke her pretence of reading the TV pages in the latest *Listener* and sneaked a glance at her parents. Robinson was looking from child to child, expression complicated by dozens of little frown lines as if they were guy ropes pulling him in as many different directions. A puzzled pride, a tender confusion, an almost disappointed love. She could just about hear what he'd be thinking. My little dittos! Yep, my two pearls! My spitting images, two chips off the one block — where had they gone? What *was* so special about twins if they weren't marvels of similarity? Boy, girl, fast, slow, bright, dull, left, right, forward, backwards, loud, quiet, top, bottom, dark, light: how ordinary, ordinary.

Candy felt her very cells had reneged on some deal her dad had thought was sealed and delivered. She wanted Robinson's pride: but what did his pride mean if it was just because she was neck and neck with Jeff?

Robinson fingered the pages of the letter again, sighed. 'So I guess we'll go ahead.'

'Might as well.'

Robinson, walking past Jeffrey on his way through the open-plan dining and living rooms to track down the evening paper, rumpled his son's hair, sounding a slightly forced cheer. 'How are ya, Superbrain?'

Jeff pinked with pleasure.

'Bit of light reading, eh? What entry are you looking at there? Antibiotics.' He gave a short laugh and wandered back to the dining room. 'Trying to impress these medical institute folks, are you? Good on you.'

Candy waited for Robinson to come over and rumple her hair the same. Beside the letter on the dining-room table was her Roma project: the one that pupils were supposed to pursue in their own time for two whole school terms the year before. They'd had the marks long ago, but their teacher had been away on extended sick leave and the projects themselves had only just been returned, more than six months and a whole form year later. Candy's had been given 72 percent for content, with an A for research effort but a C- for presentation. 'You *must* neaten your handwriting,' the teacher had written. 'And what a wasted opportunity for interesting pictures!' But it wasn't Candy's fault that her family didn't subscribe to *National Geographic* so she couldn't cut out the photos like Kitty Richards did; it wasn't her fault her school didn't even have a photocopier in 1982, let alone a colour one: luxuries undreamt of by local school PTAs then; it wasn't her fault she couldn't draw. Just because you had a hundred double-tipped (thick and thin) felt pens and had ruled neat coloured frames on the edges of all your pages didn't mean you knew any more about the Roma or the Inca or the Nepali Sherpa people. That's what Rose had said.

To Candy the presence of her project on the table was like a huge white candle burning off an unmissable heat and light. What was her father *doing*?

He flicked through the forms the science institute had sent. 'This is the parents' section, is it?'

Rose leaned over his shoulder and they read silently together for a while. 'Huh. See, there's a question about mental health.'

'Where?' Robinson frowned.

'In the same section as whether you've ever divorced or separated or had a criminal conviction.'

'What's that got to do with twins?' Jeff piped up.

'Is there a before or after option?' Rose scanned the forms.

'Eh?' Robinson squinted.

'I mean do they want to know if you divorced or were ill or whatever before or after having a multiple birth?'

Robinson looked up and sideways at Rose, to clarify what her tone implied. Then, one arm around her waist, he squeezed her to him the way he often did: a kind of Heimlich manoeuvre for the soul. He threw his chin back to let out a bluff, braying laugh at the ceiling light. 'If you weren't crazy before, you will be soon after!'

The grim colour that had threatened to steal over Rose's face vanished. Jeff rolled his eyes at Candy, then buried his nose back in the encyclopaedia.

'Are you *studying* for these next twin tests, Jeff?' Candy asked, warmed by the shred of attention he'd just given, and wanting to show interest in return, to see if she could draw him out again. But he took it the wrong way, was put on the defensive.

'No, y'dimwit!'

She sniped back. 'So why are you reading a nerd's book?'

'It's not nerdy to want to know things. What about you and your *Roma* project?' He pitched the word high, as if Candy had been putting on airs. 'You read books for that, didn't you?'

'Yeah, but that was for a *project*. I had to.'

Robinson's eye finally caught Candy's assignment. 'Ah, the Roma project's back at long last, is it?'

Now she hoped he'd ask her questions about all the facts she'd found out so she could show off what she'd learned — though she just knew that now Jeff would hiss *Nerd!* — and also because when she talked about it, pictures from the library books came back vividly into her head. Particularly of a woman whose dark, glinting eyes had made it feel she could really see you, had sensed that you would find that photo plate. She was performing for the camera, showing a flash of gold molar as she bit down on a bottle cap to open a beer. She stood outside a horse-drawn, red-painted caravan that was pulled up on a small grass traffic island in the middle of a huge motorway: you could see the fast blurs of cars passing. 'One of the last Roma to travel by traditional means,' the caption had said, and the article had explained that 'Many now opt for sedentary family businesses in their choice of host towns, and the car has all but driven out the horse-drawn home.' Which sounded as if the cars had snapped at the caravans' hooves, mustering them off to some field. 'Stereotypically associated with freedom, the truth is actually quite different, as the Roma have suffered centuries of persecution.' Which made the woman biting the beer bottle cap seem all the more defiant, strong, not least of all for doing something Candy distinctly remembered being warned against in a junior school assembly once, in a talk from the dental nurse. Candy nearly boiled over with information.

Robinson flicked straight to the last page of the assignment, looking for the marks.

'Ah, that's right. Seventy-two percent! A for effort! Two bright cookies in the family, eh? Hmmm. *That's* more like it.' His voice seemed plumper, happier again.

'Do you know about the Roma, Dad?'

'They roam-a around-a, don't they? You'll have to tell me more about them some day.' He took a swig of his drink, then came over to Candy and stroked her cheek. 'Bet you're in the top three-point-one percent, eh? Stupid tests, really.' But then he and Rose settled in to reading over the material forwarded by the institute, and checking dates in Robinson's diary. Candy had to fight back the odd misplaced rejection that pummelled its small fists against the walls of her head, the lurch between jealousy of Jeff and a sense of who-cares defiance. Don't be stupid, she told herself. It's just nothing, don't be stupid. But the only thing for it was to take herself out of sight before they ribbed her for being over-sensitive. She went straight to her guitar and took it into the small odds-and-ends room, which held two trestles and planks of wood that acted as Rose's work bench for her windmills and whirligigs, piles of magazines, an old second-hand couch that had white foam stuffing bursting through its seams as if it intended to send off seeds for new sofas, a quarter-finished 5000-piece jigsaw of a map of the Ancient World on the floor, an exercycle, a stack of old photo albums and a second-hand set of golf clubs.

Candy set her music stand up in a corner and took the guitar out of its case. She made herself practise until the pads of her fingers were almost sliced from pressure on the strings and she had cricks in both shoulders and her right elbow, although her teacher had said never to push it, and to rest if she started getting cramps as it was counter-productive in the long run. But Candy drove her feelings of hurt rejection (*top three percent, top three percent, they can't be that much apart*) and channelled them into the guitar. And it worked: music helped her to say, well, we *are* far apart, that's just the way it is. She freed herself from the vortex, the suck and force of Jeff; travelling on the light wooden coracle of her guitar off onto an island of self.

Over the next year or so she looked forward to Wednesdays after school almost as much as to Fridays and the weekend: not just for each inching step, each new string played, each new finger position on the frets, but for the whole adventure — which incorporated catching a bus into town on her own, watching the other passengers, the city fanning all its sights past the bus window.

The city was a cinema reeling out scenes from a hundred stories: a fruiterer helping a woman choose pears from a pyramid in the shop window — putting them in a paper bag that he held in both hands and twirled so it ended up with two little brown paper ears. A girl walking down the street with two white rats perched on her shoulder. A poor man in shorts and women's sandals and floral jersey, his beard down to his ribs, half a dozen shopping bags in each hand — out of which spilled more plastic shopping bags as he scurried back and forth on the same small stretch of pavement, head down, talking to himself furiously.

After that year or so of lessons Candy felt the city and its strangers seep into her music. One bitter day she got off the bus on the way home, even though it would mean having to wait in the cold for another bus, perhaps one so crowded with office workers she wouldn't be able to sit down. With nervous breath tight in her lungs she approached the little rushing man she'd watched for so many months. 'Excuse me?' He stopped, eyes rolling up at her, bright with fear. She rummaged in her bag, the guitar shifting on her back, and handed him some extra sandwiches she'd made and taken to school that day, a chocolate bar, and a pair of men's gloves she'd stolen from her father's bureau drawers, which she'd never seen him wear. The man did stop his harried pacing, but his distress took another form: he fossicked through his empty shopping bags, muttering, confused, holding them each up to the light, looking inside them. 'You could eat the food now,' Candy said, shifting the strap of her guitar nervously, 'and wear the gloves now too.' His hands were reddened from withstanding all weathers, even split in some places into open sores.

A young man with starkly dyed platinum hair, one pierced ear and wearing baggy black trousers and black shirt draped with decorative silver chains, darted out of a shop and veered near Candy. 'Don't encourage him,' he said. 'He'll never get a job if you give him hand-outs.' Then he took off again, leaving Candy stunned. The pacer man slipped the food and gloves into a bag at last, bundled all the others up, and scurried through the people on the footpath on an erratic course.

Candy stood at her bus stop as the dusk deepened, roughly pressing the heel of her hand into her eyes now and then, mind whirling over the shock of deprivation and victimisation veering so close, side by side. She'd thought about that man when picking out the simple melody of an American folk song on the guitar later that week, his image somehow directing the tempo, slide and fall between each note. Her dad, passing the room where she played, stopped to listen and, surprising Candy with his enthusiasm, said, 'It's really coming along, isn't it?' She mulled over that.

But there were glimpses of beauty in the city too, which sometimes made her want to hit the bell on the bus, leap off before it had stopped properly, and track through the crowd, follow the sight like a disciple. It could be anything. An African man playing large acorn-shaped drums on the pavement, while a white woman dressed in the same fabrics danced and collected money in a peakless red, yellow and green striped cap. It could be a tall woman with hip-length white hair who unloaded a large painting from her car, and who was dressed entirely in red velvet — right down to her watch strap. It could be the punk girl with green mohawk whose spike-studded collar matched her dog's exactly. Rapid frames that, more and more over the years, Candy wanted to slow down so she could find the sounds that matched.

After the bus ride Candy slung her guitar over her shoulder and walked past the smells of fried beef, shoe leather, incense, fresh baking, chemists, car exhaust, beer, smoke, fresh newspapers tied with string and dumped outside a newsagents. She had expected the guitar to weigh her down — to make manoeuvring through town a difficult exercise. But with the broad strap over her shoulder (if she carried it briefcase-style, it caught the wind the way one of Rose's weather-vanes would), it reminded her of a detachable sail: the leather case, the timber and cords inside, like something built from sketches which she'd seen of Leonardo da Vinci's early designs for flight in Jeff's books on aeroplanes.

At the building where she had her lessons she had to swing through double glass doors, over polished wooden floorboards, past a dance studio, then swing up a grand curving wooden staircase, with steps that creaked and sank a little under her weight. The staircase wound between walls painted fresco style in a pale pink, so it felt as if the interior were curved in on itself like a giant conch shell, the building echoing now and then with a sea of human sounds.

Candy's teacher was an overly tanned, craggy-looking man who had a deep vertical line scored in each cheek; she guessed they must be his real smile lines, though even after several months she'd never actually seen them in use. She would only see the smaller fingernail dents right at the side of his lips show up now and then, which made her wonder how the others had grown so marked. It gave him the air of someone who'd once embraced life, laughed all the time, but who had since been roughly sobered. It made her curious. It made her want to make him laugh. Later she'd think that early impulse helped to shape the way she worked on stage: the loopy, clownish gestures she'd spin off into even when the lyrics were muted and melancholic.

When Candy had first entered his studio she'd barely been able to concentrate on what he said to her. All she'd had to learn on the first lesson was how to sit and hold the guitar for classical musicianship, and how to do the rest stroke on the sixth string, because, he said, even if you're in a band one day — *especially* if you're in a band one day — you'll need to know how these things are done properly so you'll have a common language. When she went home she couldn't remember a thing she'd been told and had to carefully comb over the lessons in her booklet again. She'd been transfixed by his room.

One wall was lined with books and folders of sheet music, crammed into an elaborate bookcase made of recycled rimu, so hefty it seemed it must have been built in the studio. At the top edge the wood was carved into a decorative shape that could have been a whale fluke rising from, or a sea bird diving into, the layers of books below. One corner of the room was stocked with various guitars sitting on their own stands and a selection of black speakers and amps. The other two walls were almost completely covered with black and white pictures: not a splash of colour anywhere. Postcards, posters, framed prints, a couple of paintings, clippings from newspapers and magazines, cards people had sent: all was monochrome. Sometimes he even seemed to have deliberately tracked down black and white reproductions of works usually noticed for their rich or luminous use of colour (Miro, Kandinksy, Chagall). Over the years she'd come to recognise more and more of the images: Charlie Chaplin, Ella Fitzgerald, Dame Whina Cooper, Gertrude Stein, Martin Luther King, Jean Batten, Little Richard, Greta Garbo, Edmund Hillary, Marilyn Monroe, Clark Gable, Beethoven, Count Basie, Louis Armstrong, Katherine Mansfield, Nelson Mandela, Django Reinhardt, Jimi Hendrix, Che Guevara, work by Frida Kahlo, Ralph Hotere, Henri Cartier Bresson. It was initially dizzying: a thousand different faces, many different decades and fields — a huge mosaic of the nineteenth and twentieth centuries that shifted in detail as time went on, as her tutor added more, altered the positions of things, took away the clippings that had faded or torn.

The mosaic was more than a means to decorate the old water-stained walls. Julian often used particular images as a teaching tool, if Candy got stuck, blocked, slapped her palm on the belly of the guitar, said, 'I can't do it. I just can't.' He'd point to a picture. 'Clear your head and look at that for a couple of seconds.' He'd stay calm, brown eyes cool as creek water, unmoved by the frustration mottling her face, or the angry boxer's set to her jaw. 'Right. Play the top line again.' Or, 'Jesus, put some Marilyn into it, girl! Where's the smoke?'

But that was many months down the track and the reverse of what had happened after her first few lessons. Lifting her head from weekend practice, going for a walk to stretch out the kinks in her back, catching the bus home again during the week after a lesson, Candy was startled to find not that images led to music, but that music overlaid everything else. The white paint marking out a rugby field with slur marks and staves; the pegs strung out like a melody along the clotheslines in back yards; the contours of the hills that rose and fell beyond her suburb in chromatic scales; the triangular roof gables — tipped-over crescendos and diminuendos — on houses along a particular street; a rest-shaped hat sitting on an elderly man's lap on a park bench; pilasters that like repeat bars bordered a door on a building, a visual pun on entrances and exits; raindrops leaping back up from a small pool of water, jumping like the hammers inside a piano. Everything suddenly seemed to have its musical notation parallel: everything wanted to be played.

At school when gripping a pen or compass, at home watching TV or holding her knife and fork at dinner, her fingers involuntarily danced and raced, hunting down rhythms and phrases, a dumb show of melodies in her head.

Now and then she came to notice Jeff watching her fingerwork closely, and sometimes she'd realise he'd taken up a duet: drumming on the tabletop in matching rhythm, or, entranced concentration on his face, trying to keep up with the way she moved her left hand on an imaginary fret board on the air.

'You really love it, don't you?' he asked once, when she'd wandered out to their sundeck after half an hour's practice and, lying on her back with her eyes closed, had found that her arms — as if the muscles were used to sitting in one place — had drifted back to their guitar-playing position, trying to get a tricky transition right. She'd shielded her eyes from the light and grinned at him. 'It's brilliant.' He seemed to want more. 'Sometimes just a couple of bars can sound like . . .' she groped for a description '. . . like you could listen to them again and again, and never want to go anywhere or do anything else.' If she'd been older she might have put it differently. A certain phrase or melody could sound like both definition and formula for happiness, passion, grief, rage . . . like another facet in her had found its fit — tongue and groove.

'You're lucky,' he said, a turn in his voice that made her roll onto her side and take a good look at him. Until now she'd often found the compliments he'd paid her music, and even his duplicating intrigue as he followed her hand movements, a little false, contrived. She was suspicious of it as their public worlds had more noticeably divided: he at an all-boys' secondary school now, she at an all-girls', and his academic bent growing more obvious since his top twin register results. As he brought home better and better marks, dazzling both parents, she couldn't help but believe that everyone was disappointed in her. She'd go to her music for comfort — and it felt as if Jeff's praise had the patronising edge of someone who still felt they were superior saying, *but at least you've done your best*. Or else, now that there was this more tangible divide between them, it felt as if some element of guilt drove it. Asking about her music was a way of apologising for stepping outside the vision of twinship that their dad had savoured; perhaps, even, the vision Jeff had still held of how he and Candy operated in private, as a pair. '*That sounds really good, Candy, keep it up! You're doing really well!*' As if *he* was her dad or something. Gross. It made her more possessive of her music, wanting to block him out completely. Not wanting him anywhere near it, even with his words.

She drew herself up into a sitting position, cradling her knees. 'Well, you're lucky too. You've got your maths and science, haven't you? And practically every other bloody subject besides.'

He chewed hard at the inside of his lip, not answering.

A couple of days afterwards she'd caught a later bus than usual home from school, having hung around the Octagon with friends and their boyfriends, pretending not to be interested in a guy called Tractor who they'd said had his eye on her. She came home through the front door and called out for her mother, who usually got back from work just a few minutes after Candy and Jeff arrived from school. Rose was in the kitchen, already wearing the bright scarlet smock she used when painting her garden decorations or 'Outdoor Fun-iture', as her new freelance business cards called it. She kissed Candy on the forehead and automatically presented her with a freshly rinsed apple, and a box of chocolate milk powder. Candy gave her a squeeze around the waist, mixed them both a drink and cut the apple in half, holding a piece out to Rose. 'Want some?' Rose, making the horse lips that had the twins in stitches when they were little, took a bite from it in mid-air. Candy headed off to her room, calling over her shoulder, 'Okay if I practise in the den?'

'Yep. No woodwork to do tonight, just a few pieces to get painted.'

The first thing Candy thought when she entered her room was that they'd been burgled. The breath was punched from her and tendrils of alarm snaked from her heart out along all four limbs. A scramble of manuscript paper lay over the floor, as if a great white bird had lost a fight with a predator, its feathers torn out at the roots. Her music stand had been knocked over, its brass struts awkwardly and partially folded up: another wounded bird, trying to hold its wings akimbo. Her guitar case lay open on the floor, the empty pelt of a skinned animal — the guitar was gone. The hat tree her mother had built and painted — every other 'branch' hung with a glossy, painted green leaf — had been partially stripped of its hats.

She just stood for several seconds. Then she heard it. Jangle, twang, pluck, scrape, a scale that sounded as if the guitar were a young boy whose voice was breaking: no note quite on pitch. She felt anger draw back, bow and arrow. She burst into his room.

'*Jeffrey*! What do you think you're doing?'

He sat on his bed, guitar on his lap, her Greek fisherman's cap on his head, her fez and beret hooked over his toes like makeshift slippers, and the first lesson booklet she'd ever used — which she'd moved well beyond now — open beside him on a pile of pillows.

'What?' Defensive, injured innocence, before he shrugged. 'Borrowing your guitar. I'd have asked, but you weren't home.'

'Well, you should have waited. And who said you could trash my bloody room?'

'I didn't trash your room.'

With a strength she was almost frightened of herself she hauled Jeff off the bed — jerking the guitar from him as she did so — and drove him next door, the unlikeliness of her attack catching him off guard so he was easier to push around.

'What the hell do you call that then?'

'Jesus, calm down! It must have all fallen over. It wasn't like that when I came in here.'

'No, it bloody wasn't. It was like that after you'd been snooping around. *Who do you think you are?*'

Indignance drained colour from his face. Rose appeared in the doorway, turps-smelling rag and brushes in her hands.

'What's going on?'

'Jeff's bloody nicked off with my guitar and left my room in a total bloody mess.'

He thrust a fist at her in the air. 'I haven't nicked off with it. It's in your bloody hands.'

Candy could feel the tendons in her neck stand out, as if her own body was straining to rope her back from lunging at him. 'He didn't ask, he just took it. And he left all my music gear looking like *this*!'

Rose wrapped the bristles of the dirty brushes in the rag, tucked the set under her arm and began to gather up the manuscript paper littered on the floor. 'When you borrow other people's things, Jeffrey, you should treat them with twice as much respect as you do your own. Get the music stand, please.'

Still pale, Jeff brought the stand upright. Candy scanned the guitar, checking for scratches or dents. 'That's not the point. He shouldn't even be using it in the first place. He didn't ask.'

Rose straightened up. 'Jeff asked me when you weren't home and I thought you wouldn't mind. You two . . . were always so good about sharing.'

There were photos in the family albums of them helping each other into gumboots, holding hands in the shallows at the beach; there were stories about them judiciously trimming their own pieces of birthday cake to make the servings fair.

'Yeah, well, we're not three, now, Mum. The guitar is something I've worked for on my own.'

Rose pondered that. 'We should have asked. You're right. Perhaps there'll be some favour Jeff will be able to do you in turn. But your father — well, really *and* I, I suppose — thought you might actually enjoy having a shared hobby. Something in common.'

Candy felt a tension headache start. 'What?'

Their mother turned to Jeff, waiting for him to answer, but, eyes on the floor, he took off Candy's cap and hung it on the back of the hat tree.

'Jeff asked us last night about music lessons, didn't you, Jeff? And we all figured for a start the guitar made the best sense, really, financially. Jeff could use your books, and you could share the one guitar, at least at first, until he saves up for his own, or maybe even decides on another instrument. You know Julian Tyler offers a discount if more than one family member enrols with him.'

Candy dropped down onto her bed. 'Can you both get out of my room.' Intonation flat.

Worry beetled its way over Rose's face. 'We didn't think you'd mind.'

Candy closed her eyes for several seconds. 'Now.'

Jeff left, then came back immediately with the two other hats, which he hung back on the hat tree before he walked out again.

'I don't think you should be talking to me in that tone of voice,' Rose said, but with an air of uncertainty that meant Candy kept her eyes trained on her own white knuckles, clenched around the arm of the guitar, and simply waited for her to leave. 'I'll give you some time to cool off,' Rose said.

Alone in her room, Candy began talking to herself, the words tasting of wet, warm salt, as if her mouth would cry itself out until it ran dry too. *It's not fair. I thought the guitar was mine. He's already got everything else. Everyone says how clever he is, why can't I have just one thing, just one thing, for me? Why can't I just be me? I don't understand him. What's wrong with me? If he's good at it, what have I got, then? What am I, then? I thought the guitar was mine. Guitar was mine...*

It was as if she'd had no real idea of how much she'd already staked on her music until she'd seen her ransacked room. But what could she do? Her parents had paid for part of the guitar, they paid for her lessons. Sharing, having a lot in common: that was virtually a definition of twins, her dad would have said. She was surprised at Rose, who, of all the family, she would have thought, would know that this could be hard: *Right from the start, they've been different.* Candy weakly pummelled the pillow under her head. Robinson and Jeffrey must have talked Rose into it, using a logic which, when they worked on it together, always seemed to stack up in neat, unbudgeable walls. And Rose — Rose didn't like to fight, to 'cause trouble'. For her, an even keel was a thing to treasure after those early years; it was better and easier to say yes, yes, yes.

That night Candy had a slow, constantly mutating dream, that kept coming back to the same scene. She and Jeff were in a grove of pine trees rimmed by native bush, where the limbs of fuchsia trees glowed here and there: peachy and warm, like bare skin. They seemed to emanate contentment the way a flower would a scent, and Candy listened closely to the lilt and fall of birdsong. The bird was testing her, and if she guessed . . . but always, just as she was about to find out what would happen if she recognised the melody, Jeff reached out to touch her elbow. She'd realise then what he was trying to tell her: that they were like the fuchsia trees. Their skin began to dry and peel, to drop in strips like papery bark. Then she'd realise it wasn't like fuchsia skin at all, but that she and Jeff, whose hand was on her elbow still, were made of some sticky brown substance: clay, or thick, viscous glue, and the more she tried to draw away, the more she and Jeff became entangled, skin pulling on skin, clay picking up clay, the boundaries between them smeared and smudged. Some force was reducing them to formless indistinction. She finally woke with a rush of breath and a weight lifted from her chest, as if she'd been held under her own subconscious like someone pushed under muddy water.

FOR A MONTH or so after Jeff started lessons, Candy didn't feel like eating much, or even like talking much, either.

Robinson had said to her that first night, with a jolliness out of sync with his words, 'Seems uncharacteristically selfish of you not to want to help Jeff, eh, Candy-cane?' But even when he took her shoulders in a big warm arm, the citrusy scent of his aftershave still detectable after a day's work, and said, out of everyone's hearing, 'You're a good kid, hey, Candy? It just makes us so happy when we see you two having fun together. And you're quite a way ahead in music already, aren't you? You can still be proud?' — even then, there was a deep slump in Candy. As if the earth of her had given way, baring a long, dark cave. She was both in it and contained it, and here in the dropped-out dark nothing really tasted right, nothing really interested her very much any more, apart from music: sad music. She was peripherally aware — around the edges of the breakfast plates, dinner table — that her parents were growing ruffled, concerned, but she'd just say, 'Maybe I'll be hungry later. I think maybe I just feel like being quiet.'

One night, over this arid month or so, Robinson tried to pep

Candy up. He and Rose thought maybe there was a bit of boy trouble she wasn't talking about; perhaps she just needed to feel loved and wanted at home. Or else her drop in appetite — a typical teen phase, a lot of people said — was itself making her run down; perhaps, again, she just needed a big dose of TLC. So Robinson worked with Rose in the kitchen, making peppered carpet-bag steaks (which Candy loved), fresh baby potatoes, crisp green beans, stuffed tomatoes cut into crown shapes, a chocolate soufflé for dessert. He mixed a beaker of rich eggnog, thinking a little dose of alcohol might just give Candy a shot of bonhomie, help to relax her, sharpen her hunger. And, at dinner, he made a point of saying — rare treat indeed — 'Dessert in front of telly, twinlets! There's a documentary I think we'd all like to watch.'

Family togetherness — what else could the TV show be about but, surprise, surprise, twins? Well, everyone else enjoyed it. Small bursts of comment came from chair to chair — over the scrape of spoon bowls against china — 'That's incredible,' 'Far *out*.' 'God, think of that!' — while Candy just felt a slow uncoiling in her stomach. It was the uncoiling of some emotion she was almost afraid to look at, as if an innocuous shape, before her very vision, were stretching, lengthening, rolling over to show its glistening belly, flickering eyes.

The story that most fascinated the others was an account of what the voice-over called the Jim Twin Phenomenon. The Jim Twins were identical, raised apart by adoptive families but coincidentally given the same first name. They finally met again in 1979 — the same year Jeff and Candy had been asked to take part in the international study of multiple-birth siblings. Maybe the Jims' meeting was even the reason Candy and Jeff were tracked down, she thought: the TV programme said the brothers' reunion had triggered a surge in interest in 'genes versus environment' research. Upon their reconciliation Jim and Jim themselves were rushed to Minneapolis for a week of psychological and medical study: a fact that gave Candy a bizarre image of the two heavy-jowled, wry-smiling men — they both had mouths that quirked up at the sides

— playing with coloured building blocks and jigsaws, and matching up tables of pictures, just as she and Jeff had in their first ever test at the university.

The Jim Twins were eagerly sought after by newspapers, academics and talkback shows because of how closely their separated lives had unconsciously dovetailed. The details left Robinson, Jeff, and even Rose, enthralled.

Although they'd had absolutely no contact for over forty years and had no idea of each other's existence, when they met, the two Jims discovered each had been married twice, and each time their wives had the same name.

Both Jims, as boys, had a dog called Toy.

Both Jims smoked the same cigarette brand, and drank the same brand of beer.

Both Jims chewed their fingernails.

Both Jims suffered a kind of migraine.

Both Jims were six foot tall and weighed a hundred and eighty pounds.

Both Jims had given their sons almost identical names: James Allan and James Alan: only the spelling differed.

Both Jims had been part-time sheriffs.

Candy watched Jeff lean forward on the edge of his chair, cushion clutched to his stomach now he'd finished his chocolate soufflé, the excitement and tension in him like the posture of a sports fan watching his team canter to victory. It baffled her. She heard echoes in her head of his little-boy cockiness: 'I was born first. I'm the oldest.' She saw the impish, gleeful, teasing face he wore on occasions like the birthday when he'd snatched the guitar from her in front of his friends. Then, with a revolution of focus, whirligig-headed as one of Rose's contraptions, she remembered the constant welling-up feeling of tears, from when she and Jeff were separated before intermediate school, as if sadness could burst out of you any second, beyond your control, just like a sneeze. It seemed they always swapped stance: dark to each other's light, light to each other's dark.

Candy set aside her helping of soufflé and excused herself in an ad break, avoiding everyone's eyes.

Yet, an odd thing was that it did turn out to be easier, in a practical sense, to share the guitar with Jeff than she'd expected. He usually forgot to practise until the night before his lesson, and seemed to get frustrated quickly, so the guitar was actually only out of her possession for about an hour each week. When it was gone she'd listen through her walls, despite herself. Jeff seemed stuck on the same two pages: 'The Ash Grove' and 'Good King Wenceslas', the notes blurred and blighted, both melodies halting and so out of tune that each sounded like a protesting wail. She wondered how he and Julian got on: which pictures from the studio mosaic Julian tried to use to orientate and prime Jeff in his playing. She tried to picture her tutor's face as he watched Jeff's hesitant hands — imagined those deeply scored, unused smile lines actually fading altogether with disappointment, and let herself give a huff of nothing's-very-funny laughter.

Unbeknown to Candy at the time, Rose and Robinson had decided to make a family appointment with her school guidance counsellor. ('It's like . . . it's like there's something wrong with her *mouth*,' Rose admitted she'd found herself wanting to say. 'She won't eat, she won't talk, we don't even hear her singing so much any more.') But — just in time — Jeff dropped a casual comment that about-faced everything. Slouched in front of TV, wearing a Greek fisherman's cap he'd finally bought for himself after Candy had repeatedly gone into his room to retrieve hers, he was munching red-skinned roasted peanuts when Rose popped her head around the door-frame.

'Shouldn't you be at guitar lesson right now, Jeff?'

Jaws working at the nuts, he shook his head.

'You've changed times?'

'Not going any more.'

Rose stepped fully into the living room. 'Why not?'

'Gave up.' His eyes stayed fixed on the TV screen.

'You didn't enjoy it?'

Why was Rose so bothered? thought Candy. It'd save them money, it'd, it'd . . . she felt something warm begin to creep up gently under her skin.

Jeff shrugged. 'Didn't enjoy it, didn't get it.'

Perching on the arm of the sofa farthest from him, Rose said, 'So do you think you would like to pick up some other instrument?'

Jeff brushed his hands free of salt, frowned at the TV, said irritably, 'What did that reporter just say?' After they'd both stared at him good and hard, Candy and Rose exchanged a what's-got-into-*him*? look. It was so unlike Jeff to be terse with Rose. Candy eased herself out of the chair where she'd been leafing through a copy of *NME*, and she and Rose both moved out of the room with the slippered stealth of people trying not to wake a cantankerous dog. By the time they'd reached the kitchen the warm tide had reached Candy's ribcage.

'Do you need help cooking dinner, Mum?'

As she tasted samples throughout the recipe steps, flavours burst on her tongue with a clarity that just about made her eyes water. After dinner she was back in the kitchen, concocting waffles for a decadent dessert, thinking the relieved, grateful looks that passed between Robinson and Rose were because they'd had their sweet teeth activated, too.

Candy practised guitar that night with an intensity that left her exhausted and slightly spacey: as she fell into bed she knew her body was the bones of a song lying down on white manuscript paper, and if she could just hold still, stop the notes from fizzing off her skin like foam from a wave, someone would come to hum her soon . . .

And after all this: 'You're obsessed,' Jeffrey said when she wanted to switch TV channels to music chart shows or the Young Musician of the Year finals; when she failed to answer a question because she was drumming out a rhythm on her mat at the dinner table, trying to imprint it in her memory so her fingers would follow it faster when she got back to the guitar.

'Why do you have to be so *critical* of me all the time?' Candy asked him.

'Jeff, are you bugging your sister?'

'No! All I said was she was so focused on her guitar.'

'You did not. You said I was obsessed.'

'You misheard me.'

'I did not!' But she wasn't genuinely angry; more relieved he'd really let music go. She swore later she didn't know where her life could have gone if he hadn't.

Swore, sore, see-saw: up and down, she and Jeff sparring partners in the family ring. Usually it seemed he was the problem; sometimes it seemed he was the only one who really understood. Like the time there was a fight about Candy wearing the guitar strapped to her back at the dinner table, which meant she had to sit right on the edge of her chair, the instrument's neck visible over her shoulder, perched there at a piratical, parrot angle.

'You're not bringing that guitar to the table, love.'

'Why not?'

'You have to sit up properly. Like a lady.' Rose puckered her lips and fluttered her eyelids to make light of it.

'Why?'

'It just . . . looks ungainly. Plus you'll hurt your back.'

'My back's fine. And looking ungainly doesn't hurt anyone else, does it?'

'Well, yes it does.' Robinson's eyes did seem bewildered. 'It looks like you're ready to fly off your seat any second. Can't you bear to sit with us for more than a few minutes?'

Candy bent her head forward, concentrated on buttering some bread.

Robinson stood up. 'Take the guitar off and give it to me. I'll just lean it against the wall.'

She tucked her chin into her neck: a snail retreating, the guitar her shell.

Robinson sighed and reached out to start detaching the strap. 'Less guitar, more respect, and more study at your *school* subjects would favour us all, Candy, yourself included. I'm all for hobbies but you've got to get your priorities right.'

Jeffrey ducked his head too, and under his breath said, 'Play for me after dinner?' The smattering of kindness prickled in her nose like pepper. That was the Jeff she loved. But without him to compare herself to, her priorities might never have seemed wrong. Without her brilliant twin Candy might even have striven harder at school. Ever since the hullabaloo about Jeffrey scoring in the Top Three Percent of Twins Candy had felt: and *he's* not *me*.

More and more, school became his territory, music hers. Robinson couldn't quite understand it. He offered to pay for extra tuition for Candy, and even to find another music tutor for Jeff, as if their dissimilarities were a set of scales he wanted righted into balance again. Yet over the three years before when they turned sixteen, Candy's marks had slipped, a barometer of self-esteem, until the only subjects she could concentrate in were English and, strangely enough, Chemistry. English because the words often reformed in her head as music, or prompted her back to the guitar to try to net the mood of a phrase, a chapter. Chemistry because the patterns and equations were so clear and precise, and the diagrams for molecular structure slotted into her memory with little effort. And also, she supposed, because all the chains and hoops of carbons, hydrogens, oxygens and chlorine somehow reminded her of notes in a scale, swapping and interchanging, making whole new entities.

Throughout the rest of her subjects she tended to dally, daydream, doodle — song lyrics of her own and quotations from favourite bands — or the name of her first ever boyfriend, Shane, which she'd then disguise as music. The capital S was a G clef, the other letters hitting and falling all over the stave, a notation of erratic feeling. Distress or excitement? Often just a dark, knotted, indistinct scrawl — the name, the musical phrase, almost entirely crossed out.

She'd met Shane because he had wanted to meet her. He'd seen her watching one of Jeff's weekend hockey matches — had been there to support the opposite team. He'd worked his way to her by asking friends how she was connected to the other side, what school she went to, who they might know in common. Then he persuaded a mutual acquaintance to have a party, invite the Marshall twins and introduce him to Candy. Jeff hadn't come to the party: said he wasn't really part of that crowd, despite most of them being involved in secondary hockey teams. It made Candy think about how his friends from intermediate school seemed to have drifted away, Jeff on his own more now. At hockey he moved almost silently among the players when they were going on and off field: head down, or gaze fixed on some distant tree as if nutting out some removed, cerebral puzzle. Other boys were greeted with deep foghorn nickname cries: 'Bah-ruiser!', 'Skull-ah!', clapped on the back, subjected to mock air punches. Jeff took in their glances. That was all. Candy couldn't tell if it was a form of isolation or of respect. At least they didn't snatch his kit bag, dump it into mud in the middle of the field or carry him like a battering ram into the changing rooms to shove his head under a cold shower: things he'd reported happening to other guys, the school pariahs.

Candy couldn't tell, either, if Shane mightn't be the kind to participate in that sort of bullying. When she heard about how he'd tracked her it gave her a sick, hunted feeling which, to her own shame, flip-flopped over into feeling flattered: a kind of preening, despite herself. As if the adrenaline of being pursued became mixed with the adrenaline of attraction: panic and momentum driving the fox to continue the chase past the first obvious safe haven. But although it was animal, primal, that made it sound too much like victim and hunter. It was always less clear cut than that. Because something in her recognised the force of the sexual, separate from Shane himself: became fascinated by what he brought, and confused it with the bearer . . .

The funny thing was, in a way it was she who made the first move. He'd talked to her — and only her — at that first party: passed her potato chips, poured her new drinks, even said no to beer when she did.

'Oooo-whooo,' said his mates, gathering in a temporary horse-shoe around the couch, their faces red with booze and the thrill of an easy goad. 'Trying to make a flash impression, eh, Shane?' 'Never trust first impressions, Candy, he's a *baaaaaaad* boy.' 'Hey, leave her alone, Shane, mate, she looks all right.'

Shane had stoically ignored them — hadn't blushed or blinked — but he'd swallowed visibly. It was a moth fluttering, a small sign of nervousness that probably did more to lower Candy's guard than all the attentiveness, the offer to drive her home, the rose — which she saw in the porch light was half tea-coloured and crawling with aphids — that he'd yanked from a bush in the front yard to give her when she'd declined the lift. But in the awkwardness that came after all that, as they stood at a dark bus stop — Shane insisting he couldn't let her wait alone — Candy sensed there was already a question he wanted to ask, waiting with them, between them. She couldn't work out why he didn't confront it, after all his attentions at the party: why the long minutes out on the windy street kept stacking up between them. So that was why she did it, really: made the first move. To get it over with, to pull him out of himself, to help him do what he seemed to want but was too diffident to try. As her bus pulled up she put both hands on his shoulders and kissed him, high on the cheekbone. He looked so startled: a baby lowered backwards into bathwater. But then he nodded at her.

'Call you.' Matter of fact.

'Yeah,' she said, equally so.

He told her later he'd thought she'd be the sort to need harder work than that. Which seemed to lead to other expectations from him. Expectations he'd try to make her feel guilty about. For he could be a little cruel: gently hassled her, criticised her in a way that felt familiar. Looking back, she realised the familiarity meant she'd had unconscious expectations of her own. When Shane sulked, got low, she thought it was her job to fix his mood — to clown him out of it, to persist and pester, to tenderly provoke him back to himself. But Shane you left alone; Shane you let draw himself out of a slump. Getting in there with jokes, prods, games, cranked his mood over into anger. 'Just piss off!' he'd lash out at her in the street after school, over some disagreement: all six foot of his sixteen-year-old frame rigid with disbelief before he stormed away (but waited for her, usually, at crossing lights or intersection) — his man's height making his school uniform seem more like a suit.

One weekend night, when they were alone at a house where Shane was babysitting his much younger cousins, he persuaded Candy to let him hold her on the sunroom bed, with their tops off — 'Just tops, Candy, I promise. Nothing more.' She'd been unfussed — hadn't needed the promise — stripped off casually. But she was as stunned by his bare torso as he was by hers. She'd somehow expected a thin, boyish hull and the flat coffee-coloured aureoles, the hairlessness of her own skin. Had expected the male mirror of her own body. Shane's solid muscularity, the pinkness of him beneath the generous, mature kiss-curls of body hair — it bewildered her, made her feel suddenly out of her depth. Her nipples responded of their own will to the slow brush of his palm, but underneath the astonishing physical flurry she was afraid, disoriented, unsure what to think now she'd discovered her own hidden assumptions. When she crossed her arms over her chest, drew away and hunched her shirt back on, his voice on the air stung like a slap. '*Cock*-teaser.'

He was backtracking before she'd even got to the sunroom door but her thoughts and hearing were scrambled. She couldn't string together a proper fight, force a real apology. She just needed to get out. She slammed the door of his uncle's house and ran down the path, leaving Shane tied to the responsibilities of having to mind his cousins.

He had to work hard to mend things between them after that. He came around, uninvited, with records for her to borrow, with the latest rock magazines bought from his babysitting money, even with flowers and a silver charm bracelet — started off with a pair of silver quavers, then her star sign and a tiny guitar — for her seventeenth birthday. And he held off touching her.

It was the silhouette in her head of her brother — a sensation like leaning down over a lake and expecting to see her own reflection (expecting any intimacy to be recognised territory: a shifting image of twinship) — that had helped to send her stumbling from Shane's embrace. Yet in a sense it was Jeff himself who drove her back.

Whenever Shane came around Jeff was such a prick that home became a kind of no-go zone for their encounters. When they went into Candy's room with cups of tea and cassettes Shane had made for her, Jeff would knock on her door, then walk straight in without waiting for a response. He'd plonk himself on the bed beside them, or straddle a chair opposite, eyeballing them.

'What are you guys doing in here?'

'Talking.'

'Yeah? What about?'

'Private things.'

'Oh yeah?' And he'd just sit there, and wait. Or pull some prank, like tuck up Candy's hair into one of her hats, saying, 'Do you think she looks good like that?' Putting his own face beside hers, tilting their caps in the same direction.

Shane responded by trying to use Jeff against himself. 'Yeah, so what, you guys look alike. Your mum had a litter, like a cat.' Or 'Did you know in West Africa they used to kill twins and exile their mothers?' Little abuses that included Candy too, though he'd have said not.

'He's kind of kooky, your brother,' Shane said once. 'Don't you think he's a bit — off?'

'Soft?' Candy asked, wondering if she'd misheard.

'Yeah, that too. Is he . . . ?' His face was pulled up into an offensive 'bad odour' expression.

'Let's not talk about him.' Which she said as if bored, but partially it was to protect Jeff. From whatever name Shane was going to come up with.

Yet when Shane was gone, Jeff asked endless questions about him. 'What subjects is he doing? Where's he live? Why do you like him? What do you really talk about? What's it feel like, you know, when you . . .' Until, exasperated, Candy said, 'Why don't *you* find someone to go around with, and work it out for yourself!'

Jeff shrugged. 'Too busy.'

'Doing what? Bugging me about my private life?'

'Studying.'

He made it sound like a moral choice.

'It doesn't have to be either–or, Jeff.'

He shrugged again. 'Maybe not.' And then, when Candy turned back to her own books, or her guitar, he'd still loiter, watching her. She let her hands drop into her lap.

'I thought you were busy studying.'

'Yeah. I'll bring my notes in here; we can work together.'

She'd want to say no, just leave me alone, but there was something adrift, anchorless about him, which made her feel obscurely guilty for having spent the hours with Shane, despite all Jeff's historical signals that she wasn't to share *his* friends. So she'd relent: take care of him. Something that also, in the end, made her claustrophobic — the heat of Jeff pressing into her lungs, over her mouth, unwanted insulation.

One Saturday Shane called and asked her over to his uncle's again, to keep him company that night while he was babysitting. Candy had initially said she'd have to see: her parents weren't home right then, and she'd wanted to practise guitar, then watch a TV show about Yehudi Menuhin.

'He's not a guitarist,' Shane had said, piqued.

'No, but he's a fantastic musician.'

'But all that's totally *old* music.'

'I'm still interested.'

'Well, why can't you watch it at my uncle's?'

She could have said, because we won't exactly *be* watching it, will we? But she hedged. 'Well, I'll see what Mum and Dad say.' Convenient, sometimes, parents. You could say they'd said no, fabricate ogre identikits for them ('I'll get into such deep shit if I sneak out!') and even Shane had to respect that. He was already pretty jumpy around Robinson, though he'd pissed off Candy with his comments about Rose's garden weather-vanes and windmills. ('This is *beyond* kitsch! I thought your family was brown bread and alfalfa sprouts middle-middle class. But this is a riot! Totally fantastically crass!' And so on.)

After she hung up from Shane she went to lie down next to the stereo, to listen to a Velvet Underground album and closely read the sleeve-notes. She day-dreamed idly about being in a band called Jacket, releasing albums called *Zip*, *Pocket*, *Collar*, *Up*. Jeff wandered in, chewing a pen, thumb-marking his place in a fat maths textbook. He started chattering to her just as Lou Reed reached a line she'd never been able to decipher. She ignored Jeff, put the track on repeat. He paused while she adjusted the play sequence, but started talking again as soon as the elusive phrase came up. It happened twice more, so Candy viciously flicked his bare arm. 'Get lost, Jeff.' She flinched from the upset in his eyes before he'd even grabbed a pinch of her bare arm, and twisted.

'Jesus, you little bitch, why don't you chill out? I was only being friendly. I thought you'd been talking to *Shane* on the phone. Isn't what you two get up to supposed to relax you? How does he handle such an uptight . . .'

She slammed shut the double-spread album cover. 'God, if anything makes me uptight it's you!' She sprang up from the floor. 'Maybe I do need Shane to help me relax. It's bloody impossible around here.'

What was wrong with him? Now he looked even more crestfallen. Guiltily ignoring it, she went to her room, packed up her guitar and music, grabbed her wallet, left a note for Rose and Robinson, who were out shopping, and stalked to the front door. As she loped down the steps Jeff appeared at the door.

'He's a jerk!' he called after her. Then, more desperately, when she didn't fight back, 'He's not even very good-*looking*!'

She yelled back over her shoulder, her guitar. 'Yeah? By whose standards?'

'*Ours!*' He did. He actually stamped a foot and hit a fist against his thigh, apparently close to tears.

She wasn't even really sure where she'd been intending to go. She'd half thought about heading to the building where Julian Tyler held his lessons during the week, just sitting in the corridor and practising there — nobody would be around, and there was a music stand set up outside his room for any waiting students. Or, if the weather held, she could sit in a park somewhere, play to the birds. But Jeff's odd doorstep panic sent her straight to where he'd already assumed she'd go.

She recalled his face as it tried to hold back from crumpling. God, was she really that mean to him? Did he really want her company that much? Why couldn't she just stay and listen to him, give him some time? He was her brother, for Christ's sake. But when she thought of turning back now, she could only think *Ours! Ours! Ours!*

No.

She altered direction slightly, began to cut through side streets to get to Shane's place, guitar bumping against her hip. They could bus to his uncle's together. There was a sensation low down in her, dragging, and in her head a lightness and expansion, as if she'd skipped meals on a day of burning up extra energy. She didn't really understand it until she and Shane had put his cousins to bed and the Yehudi Menuhin special reached an ad break. Shane put his arm around her, tilted her chin and kissed her, deeply and surprisingly hard. Usually she drew back a bit, and they'd fall into a rhythm like the two actions of one wave — he'd advance, she'd soften like sand and then retreat. She wasn't ignorant, but she hadn't had her head properly turned; she liked what they did enough, and knew she was happy with just that. But tonight her body felt like a sea anemone, pores starved, opening. She wanted to plunge far away from herself, far away from what she knew. So she pushed aside all the little niggling doubts that clustered around her knowledge of Shane: closed an inner eye to them.

Shirtless this time, he was a new land. Texture, colour, dips, planes, a map of possibility, a dozen routes out of constriction. In her head she was Alice falling through the looking glass entirely, leaving all familiar images behind.

Shane breathed and gasped, a pot approaching boil. His mouth on her breast reminded her of a painting she'd seen — a naked woman wearing giant pale honeysuckle cupped over her nipples. She felt beautiful for once: wished he could see how well she wore him. He tried to shift positions but she cradled his head in place, which he seemed to read as another decision. Face anxious, almost sad, she thought, he struggled with the zips on both their jeans. Trousers ludicrously shackled around their knees, they rolled and rocked on the wide TV room couch, which began to make a regular sound like a small guard dog barking. Incongruously, at the same time, Candy could feel a sweet, taut swelling of a quality like heat, which she suddenly knew — recalling magazines, school gossip, novels on her parents' shelves — would soon peak and scatter. The absurd, angry, yipping of the couch helped fuel a quick sense of alarm. If she let this happen, let her mind break apart like a globe of thistledown against its own hot blue — who would she be afterwards? She instantaneously knew that what was about to happen was too . . . astonishing for now, for here. A switch in her body flicked off. The ruff, ruff, yap, yap of the couch suddenly made her guffaw. A big snort.

Shane lurched back, face a bit puffy and red. *Yuk*, thought Candy.

'What's wrong?' he said, breathless.

She started to laugh, nervous.

'What?'

She shook her head, ribcage hiccupping.

'*What?*' Annoyance was rearing up in him, and Candy felt a small dart of fear. She shifted her weight, which forced Shane to roll off. She hauled up her jeans, hands shaky. He sat there, disbelieving, his own jeans still half mast, a small spill of dampness on his underwear. God, that was close, she thought — mind racing to all the letters from fifteen, sixteen, seventeen-year-olds to the problem pages in magazines . . .

'Look, I'm sorry, Shane. I'm really sorry. It just all suddenly seemed so . . . stupid. Funny. The couch . . . didn't you feel . . . ?' She watched him frown at his hands. 'Sort of . . . silly. Do you know what I mean?'

He wouldn't look at her. She reached out to touch his knee and he pushed her hand away.

'Shane,' she pleaded, too late recognising the cajoling tone that worked at home, but not here.

He hauled up his jeans roughly. 'I think you'd better go before my uncle and aunt get home.'

'You don't think we should talk about . . .'

'About *what*?' Meaning, go away. Now.

This time there was no insistence that she needed someone to stand with her at the bus stop. Candy slipped out into the dark, shivering in her denim jacket, gripping the strap of her guitar case like a supportive hand-rail. The cold, straight, empty street amplified the peculiarity of the scene she'd just walked from. It felt as if she'd just left a movie theatre, or stepped back from a parallel plane: a world, a mood that ran alongside her but was usually hidden. As bus lights rounded the corner of Shane's uncle's street, she had a sudden recollection of foxgloves, sunlight sinking down in broad strokes on a pine-needle bed, the tang of wild raspberry. She swallowed back on an odd lift of self-doubt, self-dislike, and signalled to the bus driver.

She wasn't too surprised when Shane didn't phone her during the week — she didn't feel inclined to call him either. By the next weekend she was still surfacing from their last encounter, and felt like hanging out with girlfriends rather than trying to see him.

As they waited for a TV movie to start, the girls Candy had invited around for Friday night chattered about families, their weekend homework, their favourite subjects, the naff things teachers had said. Candy began to argue with someone, saying she understood what the new English teacher had meant when she told them about the Elizabethan notion of the music of the spheres, didn't think it was odd that a physical body like a planet, or a crystal sphere encasing the earth, or a carbon atom, could — maybe not emit its own note, but encompass a sound — be attributed with a sound . . .

'You're such a psycho, Candy,' Jeff said, and gave her an affectionate thwack on the head with a cushion. Even by age seventeen, he was clearly startled to hear her, of all people, talking ideas.

'Eff off, Jeff,' she answered, and fired a piece of popcorn at him. It stuck to his hair like a dry, buttery clump of snow.

Anna, one of Candy's friends who tried to dress and wear her hair like Adam and the Ants, twirled the lace-thin side braid tied with a strip of red leather — it looked as if her hairdresser had missed a final snip — around her finger. 'If you guys had totally different faces, and hair and eye colour and stuff, you'd, like, *never* know you were even related.' Various girls fell about laughing, grabbing cushions and pillows like life saving rings that might stop them drowning in hysteria.

'Anna, are you *stoned*? What are you on about?'

'*You* know. They are just *sooooo* different.'

Jeffrey's face squashed up into an American-sitcom *Say what?*, and as Robinson passed through the TV room he said, 'Stick around, Dad, please? You'll help me lift the intelligence level to something approximating current civilisation.'

Candy flipped him the fingers once Robinson had left. 'FU, Mr IQ.'

'Did your twin swallow a library or something?'

'He's not *mine*. Anyone else can take him.'

Anna's mouth was still a little agape as she idly twiddled the braid. 'Did you guys ever get confused about boys and girls when you were little?'

Popcorn-crammed guffaws travelled around the room.

'No, *seriously*. You just look *so* the same, but you're totally different *sexes*. That still just freaks me out sometimes.'

'You are stoned. Where'd you get it? Quit holding out on us, Anna.'

'Have you seen that graffiti on the bus poster? You know, the one that has a cartoon of standing passengers bunched up near the driver? And it says, 'Space out — please pass to the back of the bus.' And someone's written in "the joint".'

'I don't get it.'

'*Anna!*'

'God, Anna, read my lips. Space out — please pass *the joint* to the back of the bus.'

'Oh, right.'

'So where is it, Anna?'

'Stop *picking* on me!'

Jeffrey snorted. 'Oh, now I can see why you and Candy are friends.'

'Well, if you don't like it here, why don't you just piss off?'

'Temper, temper.' He sassed his hips, but left.

'You know, they're not that different,' someone said. 'Sometimes he moves like a chick.'

'He's still pretty skinny, eh?'

'Don't say that when he's around, honest. He'll eat your liver.'

The girls laughed, postures slackening, stomach muscles relaxing, hair falling back from where they'd tucked it neatly behind their ears: all the small readjustments that meant their only half-unconscious performances for The Boy in the room could be dropped. They all settled down to watching the movie.

Later the next day, when the girls who'd slept over had gone home, and Candy was on her way to the laundry tub with the sheets and pillowcases her friends had used, she heard her parents talking.

'They're just so extreme.'

'I know. I heard Candy drive him off last night — and so what does he do? He doesn't go out with his own friends, just heads off to his room to study. He'll burn out. It can't be good for him. He should be out with his mates, with other lads. This isn't the way he used to be. Sometimes I've got doubts about the pressure from that school after all. It's changed him. And meanwhile his sister's either gadding about with that Shane character, or hanging out with that . . . *airhead* Anna, and watching the intellectual equivalent of sugar.'

'Oh, Robinson, that's dreadful.' But really Rose seemed to find him funny. 'Anna's a perfectly harmless girl. And there's nothing wrong with Candy relaxing. It's the weekend.'

'I know, I know. But her whole *week's* a weekend, if you ask me. It's always social life or guitar first, books last. Don't you wish she'd buckle down more, and let Jeff cut loose with her if he wants to?'

'Well, she buckles down to her music hard enough. I'm proud of that.'

'I know, I know. She is very focused, you're right. It's just . . . I worry, Rose. How will she survive in the real world if that ends up being the only thing she has any attention span for?'

'Robinson, love, they're only seventeen. They've got a few years up their sleeves. They'll probably spend the next *ten years* changing their minds. I mean, look at you. You've got an engineering degree you don't even really use the way you'd intended.'

'But I had the choice, didn't I? And what about the kids and money?'

'There are all kinds of ways to get money.' From her tone of voice Candy could picture Rose rubbing Robinson's shoulders, the way she did when he was disgruntled for no particular reason.

'Now why don't I find that in the least bit comforting? No education, no good grades — what does Candy do, pour beers for sleazy businessmen?'

Rose teased. 'Like the ones who own car sales yards, you mean?'

He must have fought back in some way, as she gave a half-amused yelp. 'All right, I'm sorry. I didn't mean it. I just meant . . . you're creating worry out of air. Candy gets by just fine at school. It's hardly "no education".'

He grumbled, conceding her point.

'The world's not all evil, Robinson. You were the one who taught me that. You were the one who always told me not to fret, that the worst might never come. And their happiness is the main thing, isn't it? Candy just needs space to work it all out for herself.'

'But she's only a little girl. What she needs is us to direct her. To protect her.'

'Well, what about Jeffrey? There's plenty to protect him from too. In fact sometimes I worry about him more.'

'You hardly have to protect a son the same way. Unless maybe you're worried about paternity suits . . .'

'Robinson.'

Candy heard the steely percussion of cutlery sliding into a drawer. It accented the pause that followed, before her mother spoke again, her voice tentative now, and, despite what she said, worried. 'We especially wouldn't have to worry about that with Jeffrey. That's what I mean.'

Candy's fingers, clutching the sheets and pillowcases, had grown colder as she tried not to move or breathe in the freezing corridor. There was a long silence, which for Candy filled with the sense of her father's stillness.

'You must know, Robinson. He's not shown any real interest — I mean, there was that little girl Virginia at theatre classes, but that was *years* ago now. Look at Candy, how much she's changing, opening out socially. He's had friends who are girls, but surely there'd have been more fascination by now if he . . .'

Candy buried her knuckles deep into the cotton sheets, burrowing fruitlessly for warmth.

Her dad's voice sounded small, a lost, midway thing, like a pre-adolescent's. 'Of course I've wondered. But like you say — they're only seventeen, right?' There was another pause. 'Oh, Rosey. Hug me? Please.'

Confused by the broken sound, Candy slammed into the laundry, slammed out, tramped heavily to the shared practice and woodcraft room. Her heart was working fast, as if it was going over and over the same two notes, trying to get them right. So weird, so bizarre, but she'd never really bothered to think about it properly before, despite trying to fob off Jeff by telling him to meet someone of his own. She'd only just had her first real boyfriend herself — the topic hadn't been relevant until now. Maybe that's why Rose and Robinson were discussing it — somehow believing she and Jeff had both been in neutral until this point. Until this conversation. So what upset her? She tried to swallow down the tightening in her throat. It was the way her father had talked about it. The anxious tone. Surprised by the hot lick of a tear down one cheek, thinking *he's got no right to be sad, he's got no right, Jeffrey is Jeffrey, that's all*, she scrubbed it away furiously, ripped open the zip on her guitar case and rammed the instrument into her lap like a parent on the edge of losing control, seizing a small child to wrestle with it over what it must or must not do. She fell into thrashing out chords *furioso, agitato*, building up a loud wall of anger around her.

Yet when Jeff opened the door she stopped almost immediately. He wore a wary, puzzled look, as if — as her dad had said — he thought Candy would drive him away. She set aside the guitar.

'Hi, Jeff.'

The small muscles in his face lifted with a pleasure he quickly guarded again. 'Hey.'

'Could you come here?'

He stepped forward, hands in his pockets, shoulders sloped. 'What?'

Candy stood up and hugged him. When she released him, he shifted inside his clothes with a startled look, a bird shaking out and folding back in its feathers.

'What's up with you? I heard what you were doing to that poor sucker of a guitar.'

But she wouldn't say anything unless he did. She had to hear his version. So she covered and deflected.

'Was I horrible to you last night?'

'What? Last night? Uhhh . . .' He looked up, then gave her a sly, cat's-eye grin. 'Any worse than usual?'

She prodded him in the stomach.

He doubled up, exaggerating, and fell onto the collapsing sofa. 'Any worse than *that*?'

She plumped herself down next to him, watched his green eyes. 'We don't really hang out together any more, do we? I got rid of you last night. I'm sorry if it upset you.'

'What made you think I was upset?'

'I heard Mum and Dad say . . . something.'

'Something?'

She decided to lie — and to push. 'Kind of in the context of me going out with Shane last weekend.'

His eyes shied away. 'Those two.' He turned up his palms with a *what can you do?* shrug. 'They're scared they've bred a super-nerd. A raving queer boy.'

Heat trickled down inside Candy's throat, as if she was swallowing liquid tension. 'You think so?'

'I got the hard word last night.' He pointed a shaking finger and half closed his eyes in an imitation of an old fogy. 'It's not healthy for a boy your age to isolate himself so much. It's feeble. I feel I'm harbouring a . . . *peculiar recluse!*' He slapped his hand over his mouth and jerked up his knees to his chest, like an ad showing the audience for the latest *Phobia!* film.

Candy laughed, relieved as a sense of companionship folded around them. It was the mood that, Candy thought, twins were *supposed* to have as the bass note to their relationship, but which in reality had so often been shunted back: by circumstance (Top Three Percent); by the constant comparison (are they the same, are they different?); by Jeff himself; by the push and pull they became caught up in like internal weather.

'Do you want a hot chocolate?'

'Okay.' They agreed to bring it back to Candy's practice room for a game of Risk — which, apart from hockey, was now Jeff's only hobby. He played it nearly every other weekend with a group of three boys who worried Rose because they wore so much khaki ('Are they militants?' 'No, Mum, they think they're kind of like Mods.' 'There are *still* Mods? Good heavens. But they must be Retro Mods by now. How strange!') For some reason they didn't feature as friends in Robinson's parental landscape, maybe because they all looked like 'peculiar recluses' too.

Candy wanted to prolong the mood between herself and Jeff, to fatten it up so it would last and last. So it could protect them — or him. In the kitchen she took over making the hot chocolate and broached a subject they might share, so they could get on to other things . . .

'Hey, Jeff? Do you remember much from when we were really little?'

'Yeah, a bit.' He sifted through the jumble of fruit in the fruit bowl. 'Why?'

'I was just remembering the first time I really thought about being twins.'

Their mother wandered in just then with a couple of empty coffee cups in her paint-streaked hands. She'd caught what Candy had said; started rustling through the freezer and then the pantry. 'How old were you then?' she asked.

Candy, not really wanting her mother to muscle in on the conversation — this was about her and Jeff — dismissed her with a terse 'Dunno. Pretty small.' She turned back to her brother. 'It's funny, but I just remember — I think it must have been the first time we were ever really apart. Or else why would I remember it so clearly? But I know I was in the front seat of a car, and you were standing at the end of a long driveway made of small — hundreds of small — white pebbles. Somewhere in the country. I can remember thinking when we first arrived that if we were allowed to wander about on our own we could use those stones like Hansel and Gretel. I don't know why we were there. But I know it was the countryside, because I'd been told that you were going to be able to feed some chickens and some cows because you were staying behind at the house, and for some reason I wasn't allowed. And I looked from side to side in the car, wanting to see the cows and chickens, but I could only see rolling green. And some sheep that bolted at the sound of car. I looked back at you, at the end of the driveway, and the car started reversing. As I watched you, you just stood there, with such a serious face. Your eyes were all scrunched up. It was one of those really bright, cold, frosty winter days: the sky is clear but looks — frozen. Blue ice. And you had one shoulder hunched up, right close to your ear, you know, the way some kids stand when they're shy? You didn't wave or run after the car or even cry — just stared, all hunched up. I can see it so clearly. And I don't know how I remember this, either, but you had those little red gumboots on, and we were both wearing those blue woollen mittens that had a kitten design on the back, and a string we had to wear up each coat sleeve and around our necks so we wouldn't lose them. We both hated them.'

Jeffrey made a gesture as if to speak, but Candy couldn't stop the expanse of memory now, detail revealing detail: snow cover receding as spring works down to its centre.

'And anyway, in the car, I suddenly had this weird feeling that we were the ones sitting still, and you were the one rushing away from us at a huge speed. And it felt like you got littler and littler. And it's silly, the way kids think, really, but I remember getting confused, and thinking that if you were getting smaller, maybe, when I came back, we — well — you wouldn't be my twin any more. Does that make any sense? That perhaps you'd have changed — no, grown away from me.' Candy shivered. 'And I was . . . so hollow. Lonely. That's the main thing I remember. I remember straining against the seatbelt,' she rubbed her chest, 'trying to lean forward to touch the windscreen. Wanting to get back to you. I imagined flying through the glass like an arrow. And I kept saying, *my Jeff, my Jeff*, over and over.'

Jeffrey was shaking his head.

Awkwardness made her mumble. 'I guess it doesn't sound like much. I haven't put it very well.' And perhaps she did go on to falsify an acuteness of recall, slightly. Yet it was only in the sense that all memories of their subsequent — involuntary, to her — segregations (which she'd had to endure as if they hadn't mattered, because Jeffrey seemed to, and because they Mustn't Upset Their Mother) — like separate classes at intermediate, Jeffrey's rejection of her towards the end of those years, being sent off to single-sex highschools — surged up and sought outlet while they had the chance. 'But it felt like — when you hurt some part of your body and suddenly you realise how much else uses it. You know? You sit, you walk, you talk to someone else and hope they'll help you forget, but it just seems you touch on the same nerve, again and again.'

She couldn't explain to Jeff why she had to tell him this now. Her tone was steeped in a kind of anger that was really for the Rose and Robinson she'd overhead from the corridor. The Rose and Robinson who praised Jeff's high achievements but still found reason to criticise him, who'd agreed at some point that keeping the twins apart at school would do them good; who maybe, maybe, hadn't at first wanted twins at all . . .

Their mother leaned with both hands against the kitchen bench. 'You really remember all that?'

Candy nodded.

Jeff was frowning and rolling one of the toggles on his cotton sweatshirt between finger and thumb in a distracted gaze.

Rose pressed herself back from the bench. 'That house was my cousin's — or actually my father's cousin's. April. Do you remember her? Really, the only relative I had who didn't seem to think I was a black sheep. We had to leave you there when you were both three or four . . .'

Candy felt a deep itch of irritation as her mother seemed to edge her brother out of the conversation. She butted in with a 'Jeff? Do you . . .' and at the same time he pulled the sweatshirt's hood ties taut, the way someone would quickly pull up a venetian blind to let in a flood of daylight. 'No, no, I remember that. I'm sure. Wasn't it Candy who . . .'

Rose was already nodding, knowing what her son was going to say. 'It was because Candy had an ear infection, and we wanted to keep her warm, not running around too much. We were taking Jeff to the mountains. We were all staying in April's tent and caravan park near Wanaka. Her house was just a few minutes' drive from our cabin — we were renting one of the caravans they had set up there permanently. April just charged us a tiny amount for electricity.'

Jeff jittered on the spot with impatience. 'I'd wanted to be with Candy in the snow. It was going to be our first snow and we had a plastic sled big enough for two. You'd promised we could "dub" each other, taking turns at the front. We'd been practising on a little grassy slope in the campground, which had been covered with heavy frost.'

'But then we had to keep Candy inside. We just didn't want the cold and wet to exacerbate her ear infection, and she wouldn't have enjoyed the trip anyway. April offered to look after her so the rest of us could still go.'

Jeff frowned at Candy. 'It was me in the car. We had one of those cars with a single long front seat. I was between Mum and Dad. I watched you on the pebble path, and I was concerned that when we came back you wouldn't know what snow was. Because we'd always done and known the same things. And it was me —

I was the one who worried, would we still understand each other when we got back?'

Candy stared at them both. 'That's not true.' She waited for their expressions to alter: with suppressed laughter or fake innocence. But they matched each other's perplexity. 'Don't do that. You're giving me the creeps. You're just having me on.'

Rose blinked. 'We're not. And I remember — you can ask your father about this — when we got out into the snow, to play around on a beginners' slope with Jeff, he kept turning around, watching another group of small children, and asking, "My Candy? My Candy?"'

'But I can . . . see him. I can see Jeff, standing on the path. Against those white pebbles. His hair seems to have a shine like coal. His gumboots, the mittens . . .'

'You must be confusing stories you've heard.'

Anger flashed along some switchboard in her. 'But I *haven't* heard anything! We've never talked about it before.'

Turning pinched at Candy's outburst, Rose said, 'Be sensible, Candy, you must have. You just don't recall.'

'But I *do*!'

Jeffrey was staring at his sneaker toes. 'I don't think we have ever talked about it before. I could just . . . feel it creeping up on me again when you got it all wrong. Huh. Weird.'

Fear flapped around Candy's mind: when she thought, whose thoughts were they? When she looked back, whose eyes was she using?

'Do you still want to go and play Risk?' Jeff said.

She felt a shudder race down her shoulderblades, with the small, cold claws of something reptilian.

'I never said I wanted to play in the first place.'

'You did. *You* asked *me* if I wanted a game.'

'No I didn't. You asked me.' Setting her mouth in a *don't talk to me* sickle she walked gingerly — careful not to spill the prepared hot chocolate — out the door. She retrieved her guitar and took it with the drink to her bedroom. She heard Jeff ask, 'What's *up* with her? Why is she always so bloody moody?' And Rose answering, conspiratorially, 'Lord only knows, Jeff love. Typical teenage girl, I guess.' As if Jeff didn't give her any of the same worries. Liar. Traitor.

In bed that night Candy heard words unreel in a dream. She stood on an empty grey shore where a piece of broken reflective glass sat against a rock. A figure walked towards it, walked behind it, and didn't reappear. A tune slowly trailed along the sand, wound around the words.

> *You've put your pictures and pebbles*
> *inside my mind's warm pockets.*
> *I take them out, they lose their light,*
> *I lose my way.*
> *You've stolen all my memories.*
> *You've stolen all my memories.*
> *In every mirror*
> *I find white circles*
> *where you write your lines on me.*
> *You've stolen all my memories*
> *put your night times in my head.*

She woke with one hand grasping the bed covers, wanting to stop the voice from receding. She flicked on her lamp, which sent a butter moon over her bed. Somehow the dream had beaten back the angry fear, the strange lost-balance sensation that the scene in the kitchen had given her, where she had felt that she was made of glass, filled with glitter, and that all the substance of her was being tipped out. She fetched her guitar from where it sat near her door, its shape carved like a black keyhole where the light dimmed at the far reaches of the room. As quietly as possible — just touching, not plucking or strumming the strings — she fingered over the melody, then scratched chord progressions down onto her pad of music manuscript paper. When it was all written down she plunged into sleep like a stone dropped from a bridge.

AGAINST ALL THE confusions of Shane, and Jeff, Candy felt herself need to turn decisively into the place music offered: an animal curling itself more tightly into a ball, a defence against cold and disturbance. She took the dreamed song to her tutor that week, wanting to know if it really worked. Just before she started to play she felt a wave of dismay, and stalled. 'It's probably rubbish,' she said. He quirked an eyebrow at her, stretched out a leg, and, with his heel hooked around it, drew the metal wastepaper basket — covered in band and ski gear advertising stickers — closer to them. 'No problem. If it's rubbish, we file it under R and start again.'

The leap of laughter she caught in his eye made her sudden diffidence wobble enough for her to try the first couple of chord progressions. Julian didn't say anything about her finger positions, or the way she sat over the guitar: it wasn't like an ordinary lesson. She stumbled, went back, took a deep breath, and started again. The way he sat there — arms folded, stomach thrust forward a little in his chair, the frown trained on her hands only broken when he seemed to try to swallow a yawn — made embarrassment snake up under her clothes. *Why did I try, why did I try, stupid, stupid, stupid.*

Age seventeen, beginning to wear black, buy eyeliner, trying to grow her hair like Siouxsie from Siouxsie and the Banshees, testing out second-hand women's Korean army boots with small square heels, debating for ages in front of the mirror about whether a black beret made her look French or just dicky, and suddenly she felt as if she was in white knee socks and button-up cardy all over again — too afraid to take her eyes off the scrap of manuscript paper. She sat with her head bowed, a pup in the midst of a telling-off. Julian lunged forward to pick up his own guitar, peered at her scribbles, began to follow the chord progressions, faltered on the words. Then she felt a slow skid of surprise as — instead of sarcastically repeating one of her phrases as if she'd spoken his language with an appalling accent — he gave her the biggest compliment she could have hoped for.

'Can you teach it to me?' he said.

They practised it for some time, and then Julian nodded, chewing his lip. 'I don't suppose you've heard about the local rock contest coming up, for new young bands, have you?' Candy frowned, wanting to say she had, though she hadn't. 'It's being sponsored by a radio station and some new softdrink brand — Popz or something or other. What about auditioning for a band, or forming your own? You're definitely ready for something like that now.'

Candy's embarrassment retreated. 'Really? Really?'

Julian's one-sided grin almost, almost seemed to work on those old, disused ravine smile-lines of his. '*Really* really. If you want, I can ask around for you. Or you can check out the classifieds, and noticeboards at the music stores in town.'

She beamed at him, his praise giving her a surge of invincibility. 'I'll look into it myself. That's great. Thanks. Thank you. Really. Thank you a lot.'

At the end of her lesson Candy searched his walls for a picture to focus on before she left. It was a small habit she'd developed, a kind of private good-luck ritual. She liked to carry an image in her head from the studio into her week of solo practice, and sometimes into other situations: exam weeks, school dances, her recent dates with Shane. It was like tossing a coin into an internal wishing well. She found a picture of Gene Kelly, carrying an umbrella, leaping in the air and clicking his heels. She mentally tipped her hat at him before she left, and went down the building's stairs two by two, heart swinging between her ribs' branches, a red, fist-sized nest hatching plans.

Forming a band, composing songs. Something definitely her own: no mistaking who the experience belonged to; no way she could be compared to Jeff over this. At home, regular Family Discussions had moved on to who would get A Bursaries, or who would sit Scholarship . . . The heat of expectations and constant comparisons smelted Candy's enthusiasm for setting up a band into a huge all-consuming need: even boyfriend trouble nearly forgotten. (Things between her and Shane still just bubbled. They had moved into a less intense phase, by virtue of cautious mutual avoidance: although they still talked on the phone every week they actually saw each other less and less.)

As a start Candy put up carefully lettered posters with a fringe cut along the bottom edge, her phone number printed on each thin tongue of paper, so anyone interested could tear one off and take it with them. She managed to get a tiny box of text about the auditions — a free ad — in the weekly Youth Beat section of the local newspaper.

She also reached an agreement with Julian that she could use one of the old electric guitars and amplifiers he wanted to sell off if she went on postering rounds for him too — putting up ads about the music school he'd set up with two other musicians, and paying him in small monthly instalments from her newspaper round money.

As she waited for the phone calls from people wanting to try out for the band she began to build up visions of who she might choose. There'd be another girl — an older girl, who Candy visualised was something like Meremere from The Ferns, her first real idol (*yeah*), who would become like a kind of sister to her: a sister in hazily imagined wickedness (the point being, because Candy *was* hazy on such details, she needed someone else to supply them for her). And there'd be maybe two or three guys — to deal with the ugly punters at the kind of bar gigs all new bands had to start with, according to interviews in *Trash It, The Face, NME, Rolling Stone, In De Swim*. The guys would be very tall, very broad, very sussed, very smooth, very professional, with very, very mean steel-tough jaws, steel-capped boots and cold steel-plated stares. Which, of course, would soften and lighten up for Candy backstage.

In bed, in the dark, trying to get off to sleep, she tucked into the molasses of fantasy. Maybe all of them could be attracted to her. They'd talk about who would have the best chance of going out with her. But never in a jealous way that would ruin the band dynamics on stage. She snorted, pulled the blankets up over her head as a muffler, then sighed. As *if*.

She tried not to remember her date with Shane that bad weekend. Recalling it despite herself, she did an about turn in her mind from memory back to fantasy. Much simpler than the real boy–girl thing, and it sent her off to sleep — when she hadn't expected to get any at all, she was so wound up about how to run the auditions.

She'd never been in any kind of *real* band before. There were end-of-year concerts run by Julian, with various duets, trios, quartets, and so on: she'd played in plenty of those. Still, she felt odd setting herself up as a sort-of-leader when she'd only written a few — okay, maybe five or six — finished songs. Yet if she didn't look organised, it would all start off too slack. She didn't want people in the band who'd just . . . goof off, talk about TV, or clothes, or their Friday nights at McDonald's, the malls, the movies. And she didn't want people whose parents thought the band was a good idea — like it was a babysitting option. She wanted people with ideas, passion. People who could push her own music further.

It had even irritated her when Rose — after Candy had fielded about ten phone calls over the week and arranged different time slots for people to come over on the following Saturday — tried to offer help. 'Would you like me to set up drinks and a tray of snacks for your music get-together today?'

'It's not a party, Mum. They're *auditions*. This is serious.'

Behind Rose, Jeff grimaced, which told Candy clearly that she was being a bitch. It only made her defensive. She knew you were supposed to look out for Mum, but sometimes it just got too tiring.

'I mean it! If I don't treat this seriously now, how am I ever going to do anything with my life? You and Dad are always on at me about getting a career, having a sense of direction, but when I do something that really matters to me, everyone acts like it's just some sort of game.'

Rose, looking stretched to the limit, said, 'Well, you might want a kettle and some coffee in the shed if you're going to be in there all day.' Then she moved out of the room as if on hidden castors, the careful glide meant to conceal her sense of injury.

Jeff groaned. 'Would you like it any better if she wasn't even interested? At least she's noticed.'

He was right of course, but that only made things worse: it just poked with another hot stick at the little demon that flexed and prowled in Candy these days, and would have flung itself at her family, flaying and hissing, when she felt any small slight, if she hadn't fought it down with sheer strength of will. They thought she'd grown difficult but they had no idea how difficult she really could have been if another, splintered-off part of her weren't aware of her temper.

She didn't know where the snarling had come from, hated the way the moods flared up while another part of her watched astonished and only gradually snapped out of it to try to get back control. Often it just seemed to . . . happen to her. Jeffrey's even, lake-in-summer manner these days, and the way he still managed to watch out for their mum, despite the little peckings and proddings both parents gave him too — over his need to get out more — made her envious. Which — vicious circle indeed — just turned her back to snide and spite again.

Straight. Square, she whispered under her breath, and the way he feigned deafness and tolerance put her on the boil — which eventually gave her a formidable air as audition-mistress. Everyone who actually managed to turn up to the right address took it as a given — Candy having maintained the week-long sulk that made her green eyes crackle like cheap wood on a fire — that it was going to be *her* band, and her motivation that pushed them towards the contest date in eight months. No matter what she said about wanting a group who were into teamwork: no big egos but plenty of good listeners.

Most of the hopefuls who showed up couldn't quite tell how old she was — an effect that was probably helped along by the fact that she'd put on heavy Cleopatra-style kohl eyeliner and green eye shadow, and borrowed knee-length black boots and a red paisley wrap-around skirt from her mother. (Without asking: but Rose never wore them, and Candy managed to slip out the back door to the shed without being sprung.) She also wore a black woollen jersey of her dad's that looked — well — unusual next to all the stonewashed jeans, pink, white and blue sweaters that most of the others turned up in.

Back then she'd have argued with anyone who suggested she was shallow enough to judge the final four on the basis of their choice of *image* — the whole point about people who wore black or looked *alternative* was that they were *deeper* than that. Their clothes said they questioned society, you know? (Jeff and Robinson were both disparaging about this. 'And does weird dress sense also give us any of the answers?' 'Dad, you just don't *understand*!' 'Well, Candy-girl, I'd agree with you on that. I just don't see how dyeing your hair the colour of a blueberry leads us closer to annihilating poverty.' 'But at least they're making some kind of — I don't know — statement.' Jeff's smirk was uncontained. 'The statement being: "I have blue hair."' 'God, you're both so frustrating!' Which put a glimmer in their eyes as if a goal had been most *satisfyingly* achieved.)

But the thing was, she just kind of had a feeling about the band members. Candy got her Meremere — or as close to it as she could hope for, out of the people who turned up. Grace had long, red, teased hair, and was in a Cyndi Lauper stage (which, if Candy were to bump into her in London fifteen years later would be almost impossible to replay: as a shaven-headed lawyer working for a local borough council she'd look as neat, natty and eerily hairless as a shop mannequin). At the audition she wore black lace fingerless gloves, lots of chunky plastic costume jewellery, a black apron over an immense, gathered, red-and-black-tartan-print skirt, which was hitched up and pinned here and there with safety pins, and a piece of black netting tied in her teased-up hair. The overall effect was somehow like a twentieth-century punk and a Victorian scullery maid had met and raised a child.

There was another girl too, so Candy's fantasy ratios hadn't quite worked out. She was a ratty-tatty little blonde, who'd coloured several streaks of her hair black and blue with felt pen. She wore soft vinyl boots with multi-coloured beads made from Fimo strung on the laces, electric blue tights, a second-hand, tight-fitting black lace dress with a stiff, high, ruffled collar, and cuffs to match on sleeves that came right down past the base of her thumbs — which made the dress seem like widow's weeds. She was one of the first to turn up: a keyboardist. She brought along a tiny electronic synthesiser only just bigger than her lap, which actually made Candy immensely embarrassed: when she'd written on the poster 'must bring own instruments' she hadn't quite thought through how some people would manage to lug along full-scale synths on buses and so on. No wonder Lucy was only one of three keyboardists to even show. (Of the other two, one brought an accordion. The other skinny, spidery possible dragged up a full-on Roland synthesiser. But when he saw Candy he said, actually, he was more interested in a group of older musos he'd been jamming with the weekend before.)

Zane, the bass player (another moody blond) and Tip, the drummer (whose name seemed to suit his quick, darting energy), were boys. Or rather, guys: both were eighteen and had left school already. Zane was at polytech, doing a drafting course; Tip worked in a music store and said he was saving up to go to polytech too, to do a course in catering.

'Why not music?' asked Candy, partly wanting to lavish him with praise because his dad — who'd seemed pretty cool: wore a leather jacket and a Velvet Underground T-shirt — had to help him heave along the huge black cases that held an impressive sparkly red drum kit, *and* helped him set it up. The two men's slow, bumping progress along the drive of Candy's house made her grateful they'd even showed — and gave her a sinking premonition of how few teenage drummers would be turning up, despite the number of callers she'd spoken to during the week.

Tip bounced on the little portable chrome and vinyl swivel-seat he'd brought — which looked like a disabled unicycle, the wheel replaced by three retractable legs. 'I'd thought about a music course at polytech, yeah. But Dad's a muso, and he reckons I'm good enough now to just learn through getting into bands and maybe carrying on at master classes and that kind of thing, you know? And he reckons it's also a good idea to have another trade, because our society is, like, so crap about artists. You know? I mean, he's earned his living through the music business but he says he's always been glad he's had building skills too, for when you fall on hard times or you need extra cash fast or even if you just fall out of love with your craft for a while.'

It felt as if a wind had rushed through Candy's head. 'Fall out of love with your craft?'

'Yeah.' Tip twirled a drumstick between the fingers of one hand, dropped it, blushed, then tried to save face by grinning and repeating the whole thing in self-mockery. 'Dad says he's had times when he felt building was more honest, and more appreciated.'

'Wow. It must be *so* hard to be a real artist, eh.'

Tip nodded matter-of-factly, holding her gaze. 'But you have to try, don't you?'

Astonishing heat radiated from Candy's solar plexus — shooting comets and sparks and circular bands of energy, which perhaps gave that part of the body its name, she thought. Microscopic suns came into being there. She'd met people who took her own ambitions seriously, who shared them, who spoke the same dialect (raw hope, vague plans) as she did. It actually made her more generous with her family after she returned to the house as night fell: it wasn't their fault they just didn't *know* how things really were for her.

Robinson patted her shoulder, saying he was glad the auditions went well — how enterprising of her — but 'I trust this band isn't going to take up too much of your study time. You know you've got Bursary this year . . .'

Candy breathed in, very deeply and very slowly, through her nostrils, concentrating on using the cool air to douse the urge to lash out at him. 'No, Dad,' she said. 'Not too much time at all.'

She reasoned that when the competition was over there would still be time to swot up for the exams — though in a way she felt they didn't matter so much anyway, now that she had UE. But she flung herself into after-school practice like someone bordering on a hectic fever, so that the promise to Robinson came to seem a vow of straw that the wolf of her need for music flattened, no trouble. Candy continued her lessons, attended rehearsals in studio rooms made available by Tip's dad, and at first practised for only an hour a day. But her appetite for practice grew and grew, sometimes forcing her awake before dawn, pushing her out of bed and down to the cold end of the house, far away from her still-sleeping family, where she could play without disturbing them. And more and more she ignored the tired, aching sensation her body gave her after these long sessions, censoring out the memory of Julian Tyler saying, never push it to the point where you feel stiffness or cramps, always make sure your posture is correct . . .

When she wasn't able to play — obliged to go out with family, assignments and tests exerting demands she couldn't postpone, or even when she had agreed to go to a film with friends — some combination of corkscrew and clamp wrung her through a gamut of moods, black and blue: ill at ease, bored, distracted, frustrated, low, even panicky. As if one day without music could breed, and there Candy would find herself: at the end of the long corridor of years, deserted by music, emptiness wrapping itself around her, unhappiness and dissatisfaction buckling her spine, a degenerative disease. Her perspective always leapt from one lost day to endless years of the same. And so, like the industrious ant, she tried to build and build her store of notes, of bars, of phrases, of verse, chorus, verse, drilling and drilling herself: music the harvest that would bring iron to her blood, water to her cells.

As the date of the contest approached, her practice hours crescendoed. Julian said at one lesson, 'Leaps and bounds, Candy. You're just surging away there.'

He scrutinised the way she absently rubbed her hands and forearms. 'You do give yourself some time off, though, don't you?'

'Yes,' she lied.

'Are you sure? You look pretty . . . washed out. Are you sleeping okay?'

'Not too bad.' Only a half-lie. Songs would sometimes push her out of bed in the small hours, or just before dawn, their voices urgent as a child that needs soothing after a nightmare. But she attended to them, scribbling down fragments of words and chord sequences in such a twilight daze, it was almost like another version of sleep.

She wished she had what seemed like the natural gifts of Tip, Zane and Lucy. Only Grace really shared her sense of time compression, of urgency to get it all right. Sure, the others were determined, but they thrived on it, collectively saw the band as an extra, not the centre. It was time off their other commitments. In fact, if there was anxiety from Zane and Lucy it was usually about how the band itself took up one to two weeknights a week, and their Sundays. They were the two who most often called up to say they'd be late, or would have to leave it until next week. Balancing course work and part-time job was getting to Zane; while Lucy, at seventeen, was in a melodramatic relationship with a first-year teachers' college student who kept alternately proposing marriage, and sleeping with other girls. Sorting it all out seemed to involve an awful lot of driving or bussing around to distant suburbs. 'Hi, it's Luce-unit, here,' she'd say on the phone, self-deprecating, voice unusually pitched, about to high-dive into tears. 'Look, I'm way out in the wap-waps, Newgrove or Highcliff or something or other.' 'Where?' 'Yeah, that's what I mean. The wap-waps. I'm not gonna make it in time. Dave and I have had a really bad fight, he's driven off without me and there are no buses for half an hour . . .'

As the performance date got closer and closer Candy couldn't help a strangled note of Highly Pissed Off in her voice when the others failed to get it together. But what could she do? Practise and practise, in case she had to carry them on the night, in case they all dissolved into the nervous wreck of the poorly prepared: a school orchestra of children with ears made of tinfoil, forced to perform in the face of their own debilitating self-consciousness.

Whenever a rehearsal fell apart, though she was feeling the steady erosion of broken nights and hard graft — her body forming twinges and tingling not helped by fractured sleep — she forced herself to practise longer and longer on her own the next day. Or she'd focus on new ways to tighten up the short dashes of choreography she and Grace were working on: simultaneous leaps, half turns, grapevines and twirls, bouncing the necks of their guitars on the air in rhythm downstage — what Grace called 'the visuals' — for the judges' elusive category 'Stage Presence': that thing Candy was once supposed to have had — but did the whole band?

Tip's dad tried to tell them — when he asked if he could listen in on a rehearsal — that some musicians 'just have it'. He didn't seem bothered by the worried frowns that shot back and forth between them all. 'They exude it. You can tell something's going on before they even hit a note. It's like when you see a couple in a café, sitting opposite each other over the coffee cups. They're not even touching, they might not even be looking at each other: one's reading the paper, the other's flicking through magazines. But you can just tell how much they want each other.'

Tip had quickly busied himself with examining biro marks on his hands. Which surprised Candy: she hadn't realised you could be embarrassed by your family even when you shared as many personality traits as Tip and Graham seemed to.

At their next session Candy asked Tip, 'So do you really think we can't work on stage presence?'

He shrugged. 'I'm a backroom man, myself. 'Sup to you three at the front, I reckon.'

Zane just nodded. 'When my parents threw for charisma, I got a really low score.'

'What?'

Tip translated for him. 'Dungeons and Dragons. You use dice to work out aspects of your character.'

'Hey, you've played? We should start a game,' said Zane.

Candy fidgeted. 'Okay. We're getting off the subject here. So, maybe we three girls will have to work on a bit of stage stuff on our own, but I think we all need to look the part, right?'

Grace repetitively flicked the nails of her index fingers off the pad of her thumbs — a habit that was a barometer of her excitement. 'Yip. Yip, that's it. Costumes. Get-up. Glad rags. That'll do it. Just sort of . . . *harmonising* what we wear will make it seem like we've got some kind of co-ordination.'

Zane's shoulders drooped. 'Costumes? Nothing too wacky though, right?' Dressed all in black himself — black stovepipe jeans, black shirt buttoned up to the Adam's apple, blond hair newly dyed black, black onyx ring on his left pinky, black winklepicker boots (Nick Cave style), black stud in one earlobe — he was the sort of skinny, quiet guy who got picked on by aunts and uncles at family Christmases. 'That suicide cult in America, they all wore black, did you hear? You're not going to do anything funny, are you? So what's the message here? "Oh I'm so depressed, life's so hard?" You young folk don't know you're born. *Look* at this lovely tea you're about to eat. Black indeed. You need to cheer up, that's what you need to do.'

But he eyed Grace's head. A dozen hairdresser's clips, butterfly style, yellow and red, pinched her hair into little sections over her scalp. She wore a tight-fitting orange lace top and a matching red and yellow checked full-circle skirt, held out by a many-ruffled red petticoat. He gave her the kind of look a vegetarian might give a Christmas ham presented with pineapple and maraschino cherries stuck on toothpicks.

Grace, catching his glance, speed-read its subtext. 'But it will have to be vibrant, right? We're not all wearing *black*; we'll disappear. We'll look like stagehands. We have to make an impact.' Her fingers flick-flicked.

So another of Candy's preoccupations, when rehearsals became enfeebled because the guys were hung-over and Lucy was late, was to fill page after page of blank refill with coloured sketches of potential costumes. She figured that Tip's glittering red drum kit was a starting point, but their look also had to fit in with the name they finally chose. Arguments about this took up an inordinate amount of time.

'What's unusual about us?' Lucy asked during one discussion, throwing her arms wide. 'What's going to give people some kind of clue about what we do?' She'd arrived late again; was trying to compensate by cranking up her enthusiasm.

Candy wasn't kindly disposed. 'What about . . . The Fart Arounds. Or The Sorry My Watch Must be Slows.'

'Lighten up, Candy,' Zane said, grouchiness all over him like the crumples of his unironed shirt; he was gagging for a cigarette but there was no smoking in the borrowed practise room.

'Well, Candy started off this whole group. So what about something like Candy Floss?' said Grace.

'Too poppy. Too girly.'

'So, no Candy Canes or Candy Stripes either?'

'Look, if we're a team, we can't just name it after me.'

Tip surveyed the ceiling. 'It's all we've got to hook a name on, though.' He pressed a drumstick against his lips, then, with a start, waved it like a windscreen wiper in front of him. 'Hey, hey, okay, what about — I mean, if we're talking about *unusual*, what about The Twin? I mean, that'd be *awesome*; it's like, so weird to think of just one twin. People will be going, *whaaa*? Where's the other one? Which one's *the twin*?' The face he pulled was too much. Candy's mood flung shut like a trap.

'That's it. I'm off. If you're not going to take this seriously, I'm calling it quits for today. I've had enough.'

Tip flinched in bewilderment. 'Hey, I *was* serious! What's the problem?'

But Candy was unplugging the guitar she'd bought from Julian, winding up the cord, packing it all away. After she drew the door shut behind her she eavesdropped on their reaction.

'Jeez, she's just so intense these days.'

'She's a live one, all right.'

'Come on, you guys. She's put a lot of time into all this.'

'So? We practise too. It's her choice.'

'Yeah, but she writes the material, she's the one organising the entry forms, trying to design what we wear, *and* she's trying to set up those gigs at some girls' party and those colleges . . .'

'Why's she bothering if it gets her so stressed?'

'We need to try it out in front of an audience.'

'But I've already *said*, there are probably bands at those colleges who are going for the same contest and they'll just nick all our ideas!'

Sometimes the endless bickering — her own included — pushed Candy to the threshold of quitting altogether. But it never took long (sometimes only the bus trip home) for the nagging sensation to start: that there was something amiss, somewhere she should be.

Her dad's urging that 'Mightn't you want to pull your grades up to match Jeff's? You'd be a natural match for him if you tried' (*A scholarship candidate, no question*, his teachers were saying, getting him to take extra tuition to push him through the additional exams), amplified the sensation that the air around her was thinning. The guitar held close to her body was like a flask that mainlined oxygen. Arranging her sitting posture, striking the first note, then the deep breath that caught the sail of the song and sent it skimming, all slotted her back into her rightful place. The days and minutes slid around her skin and fitted her again, cool hand in warm glove.

She'd return to rehearsals full of beans, jumping around with new ideas, and although their set was getting slicker and slicker they squabbled on, about most things, but particularly about the name and stage image, right up to the entry deadline. They tried new angles: Teebeeay (for To Be Advised), Incandescence ('That's just setting us up for failure. If we're not completely brilliant, think of all the bad jokes about "more like rising damp" or "more like wet fizzle". . .'). But they circled back to the same take on the Candy theme: The Cottons, The Jubes, The K Bars, The Sparkles, The Aeroplanes, The Gum Drops, The Minties, The Pineapple Lumps, the Tangy Fruits ('Who are you calling a fruit, Zane, mate?' 'Nobody, nobody.')

They stayed at an impasse until one day Jeffrey turned up to a jam session. They still needed to rehearse in front of an audience, and had agreed to invite along friends or family. Most of the audience drifted away after the first run-through but Jeffrey stayed on, his eyes gleaming black with excitement released, for once in a rare moon, from his book-work, the swotting that was as obsessive as Candy's musicianship, only it seemed to get less comment at home because it conformed to the school's — and Robinson's — model of success.

Jeff was so energised that Candy was a little concerned that he didn't know how to 'do cool', to hold back. Would the others think he was a freak? But they, in turn, seemed to thrive on his presence, laughing and chatting with him, occasionally shooting Candy glances that were clearly astonished, filled with *Wow, they're so the same, they're so different*. She knew she should be used to it by now but it made her feel awkward, territorial, bolshy, confused. Proud of Jeff in a funny way: jealous too. *Don't steal my friends!* Immaturity that she had to bite back, hard.

Tip told Jeff about the band name dilemma. 'It's really Candy's whole idea, yeah, so it's got to be named after her.'

Lucy chewed on a strand of felt-tipped hair. 'But you know what she's like.'

Candy slouched one hip out, fist on the waistband of a tie-dyed skirt she'd bought from a market stall. 'I can hear you.'

Jeff flattened his lips together, thinking. Then he snapped his fingers. 'Got it.' They all waited.

'The Raggedies.' He held Candy's gaze, giving her a thin paring of a smile.

'Why?'

'Because of that book we had, that you used to love. Remember? You used to read it to me all the time.'

It dawned on her, slowly, with a mixture of pleasure and envy: why hadn't she thought of it? The Raggedies: because they had a pop-up book, when they were very small, about two rag dolls, Raggedy Ann and Raggedy Andy, who made toffee and held a candy pull that turned into a comic tug of war. But the name hid the child's story, could mean anything. When Jeff explained it to the others ('Just a sort of private joke, connected to Candy still, but the audience doesn't have to get it,') Grace's fingers flickered on the air, dancing with eagerness.

The name simplified the costume design too. For the girls: red woollen pigtail wigs, big round rouge circles and stylised eyelashes drawn in kohl right down to their cheekbones, red and white striped tights, simple pinafore dresses. For the boys: red and white striped braces holding up their baggy (*'Yes, Zane, black's okay'*) trousers, the same dramatic but simple makeup. It all seemed to click: paradoxically, even the slightly iffy choreography sharpened up when Lucy, Candy and Grace realised it should flop and loosen to fit the rag doll theme.

The others warmed to Jeff so much after that particular rehearsal that they told Candy to bring him along again so he could offer more feedback. They shone at her, as if Jeff were of her own making, and she had to agree: somehow he'd just managed to come up with exactly the right fit of name, image and character for the group. His fresh enthusiasm, along with his calm temperament, massaged away the stale tension between them all. Candy mulled it all over.

Here was her love for her brother: a beautifully carved, capacious wooden bowl, the colour of honey. But underneath, if you turned it up, the unexpected shock of rot, a patch that mouldered, jealous green. Which was truer?

IT WAS WHEN the band was three weeks off the competition that Candy could no longer ignore the burning sensation in her fingers, forearms and even up into her armpits, which had become more and more persistent since she'd formed the band. Though Julian was always on at her about posture, moderation, she'd somehow been convinced that the burning would go away if her playing improved, if her fingers became more fluent. She'd thought it was a sign that she needed to push harder, get more limber, increase her endurance.

The group had been put through automatically to the contest's final round, because of the low number of eligible entries. Lucy said that gave things a slightly grey, drizzly, what's-the-point feel, although Tip countered, 'It's great for promos. I mean, who's to know, in a year or so, that only ten bands entered in the first place? Come on, guys, get positive.'

Candy had carried on practising like a maniac since hearing they were through to the finals — and since she and Shane had finally officially broken up. He'd said she was selfish, too preoccupied with the band, and besides, another girl had come along . . . She refused to think too hard about the day she'd found out, calling him from a public phone box, wondering where he was when they'd arranged . . . no. Music. Concentrate on that. Not getting a decent ranking when so few bands had entered in the first place would be untenable. She imagined her father's face, stern and trained in on her like a close-up camera: *What did I tell you, Candy, love? You've given too much time to something that won't really repay in the long run. You've got to think ahead. Like Jeff does.* A voice that just made her want to try harder and harder so that one day the look on his face would break open with respect, and he'd say: *Well done, Candy. I'm proud of you.*

But also because, in a peculiar, contrary way, his criticism was a form of validation. It singled her out. It made her not just one of two. Candy almost sought his disapproval: if it was the only way she could slip out from under his notion that she and Jeff should always be *neck and neck, a matching set*, she would provoke him, a kid riling an animal, for the excitement of the response, a silly sense of power. *Look what I can do, see how big I am!* But it was all so mixed up: upside down, back to front. Just because she provoked Robinson's responses didn't mean they were painless. A notion of your identity as oddball was a distorted kind of reward for distinguishing yourself.

The unexpected consequences of all her hard work hit late one afternoon, when she was doodling with chord changes in the practice room. Finding she could no longer ignore the hot, stretched tension in her arms, she looked for a momentary distraction, her eye roving the room — and her gaze lit upon a box stored up high in a cupboard, whose swollen door never fully closed. She'd seen the box a hundred times before and had a vague memory that it held some of her mother's old clothes. Maybe useful for a costume? Some instinct told her she should stop practising for a bit, should maybe make her muscles do the opposite of the detailed, cramped stitch-and-knit work that music needed. So, pushing the thud of alarm to the back of her mind, she got up on a chair and lifted down the carton from the shelf. It contained a crotcheted burgundy poncho, a few Simplicity sewing patterns, a tangle of old belts — one made from plastic disks painted gold and embossed with a clumsy lion rampant — a few old matchbox cars of Jeff's, and a sight that released a warm rush of unanticipated recognition, along with a prickling of the uncanny.

Her old Hide-me Find-me doll. How could she have so completely forgotten about it? Pulling it out of the box she raised its sheet-white arms with the sides of her fingers, then let them drop again, and imitated its limp, lifeless slump, the way its head fell forward from its thin cloth neck. She smiled, imagining all the band members doing this simultaneously when their final song ended and the lights went out. Candy ran a fingertip over the red silk thread that made the doll's mouth. The texture unlocked a response that mingled memory and mood but wasn't quite either. There was the heady hit of fresh-mown grass; a child's looping, expansive joy at the sight of a plane; the smell of Jeff's hair and his jersey close to the heater as she hunkered down next to him on the rug, sharing a book or board game.

As a small girl she'd always been intrigued by that toy. Granny Greger had given it to her — called it the Topsy-Turvy doll because when you lifted the woman's skirt and pulled it up over her shoulders as if to undress her, the reversed skirt became the long, swishing riding cape of another doll that had been concealed. The underside rim of the woman's bonnet now just poked out from the hem of the cape and was painted to look like the tips of shoes. The other doll was a man, with smart sideburns, trim moustache and a mouth stitched of rougher pink cotton. As a child Candy had usually kept the doll in a toy box in her wardrobe but there were particular times that it sat on her bedside table. Hard times. When Jeff was first sent off to a separate class at intermediate, and she'd only brought the doll out after her light was out, in case she was discovered and called a *baby* by Rose or Robinson. Or when they were small, and in quick succession Jeff was sick with tonsillitis and appendicitis and had to go into hospital; then even when he was home he couldn't play for ages. She'd find herself drawn back to the doll after periods of not being interested in it at all. She'd pull it out, search its expression, the surfaces of all its fabric, the way someone much older might scan a text for hidden messages. When she was little the action of concealing and revealing each alternative doll would fascinate her again, offer inexplicable comfort and reassurance.

Usually it was the woman doll that Candy would leave upright, but when Jeff was sent away, or made to stay shut up in his room, Candy would let the man doll free. A guardian, a kind of shamanistic effigy, like the figurines she would see much later — the little South American Worry Dolls that you were supposed to put under your pillow so they could absorb and spirit away anxieties overnight. As an adult Candy hadn't needed them explained to her once she'd heard their name, thinking children everywhere reinvented these comforts for themselves, year on year.

Humming lines from one of The Raggedies' songs — *When a mirror looks into a mirror/what does it see?/When I look at you/what will you find in me?/Through your stolen spyglass/I've found your looking-glass/so now fill my shot glass/before I remember what will be* . . . Candy fingered the material of the male doll's riding cape. A searing pain, like the fibres in miniature knots were being yanked on and tightened all along her forearms, hauled on further strings that ran through under her shoulderblades. It pinned her to the spot and she felt an accompanying stab of realisation.

'Oh no,' she said out loud, staring into the doll's opaque, nowhere stare. 'No. Oh no.' She turned her hands over, looked at her palms, then gingerly pushed up her sleeves. She gazed at the blue S bends of the large arteries that curved through the soft, untanned muscle of her forearms.

When she stared at them it was as if they mapped the damage in the structures beneath her skin. Already half guessing what could come, she nudged the doll and box aside with her legs and retrieved her guitar. Trying to swallow down the thick taste of hopelessness and disappointment she started to launch into a number that — easy words with easy chords to match — started off with her voice on its own, a cappella, before the full band came driving in on the fifth line. It was one she'd written after storming off from a rehearsal, then snapping at Jeff at home when he'd said, in front of their dad, 'Excuse me, but are you my sister? Hardly see you these days. That band's taking up all your time. How's it going?'

Her shitty outburst had been followed by anger at herself; she'd written the song late at night, feeling the cold body of the guitar through her nightgown, like a compress that helped to staunch a fever, allowing her to see how irrational she'd been. She'd played it to Jeff the next day, to say sorry, and he'd greeted it with a wry grin, saying, 'Yeah, too true.'

Hot head

You let flip
you let slip

your remarks
aren't half heart

they're word bombs
that torch the

paper they're
written on

So, like
to like

I've lit out
I've gone off

oh yes
hot head
we're getting on
like a house on

fire

a place all the
small creatures

scuttle from
(hot head)

the taste of coal
in my mouth

says burn off
burn out

I'm burnt out
by you
hot head . . .

She couldn't finish. She let the guitar fall loose from where it was still buckled to the strap that draped over her shoulder. Her fingers were curled up like tapers, consumed by the music that had flared through them. Bolts bore through odd places — the outsides of her elbows, under one shoulderblade, below the knuckle of her left hand.

My hands!

Who could she tell? Even when she was this distraught, part of her held back from calling *Mum*, always a little scared that a problem shared with Rose could mean the great oppressive hills of sadness might close in on their mother again. So, *see-saw, Margery Daw*: half paralysed in the sewing-cum-music room, Candy's heart flew to Jeff. Envy gone like cloud into blue.

There was a creak and scuffle in the corridor. When Candy went to grip the door handle the jabs shot up again, as if the doorknob itself had pierced electrified spikes into all her knuckles and the pads of her palms. There was a scratching at the door, then it opened on Jeff, his face puzzled.

'Hey, Can-do. I've been looking for you but I didn't think you were in here, 'cause I couldn't hear you studying your twangology.' His joke fell flat.

'My arms,' she said to him. He lifted the strap from her shoulder, propped the guitar against a wall. 'What is it?'

She looked down at her hands as if they were covered in something unfamiliar.

'They hurt? Okay. Okay, look, Dad's home already,' he said. 'He and Mum are in the kitchen. Come and show them.'

When Rose and Robinson saw their children's stricken faces neither of them could tell which one was in trouble, though it was clear that there was bad news . . .

'What is it?' Rose was anchored to the linoleum, as if believing that were she still enough, the bad things in this world might lose the scent and sound of their quarry.

'Candy's hands,' answered Jeff.

'My whole arms.'

Rose held her daughter's elbows, turned her hands and forearms over. 'What is it?'

'I can't use them. They're — broken.'

Robinson's concern made him terse. 'What do you mean, broken? Broken bones look nothing like that.' He moved in on Candy and Rose, took Candy's fingers, carefully bent them up towards the palm. 'See? You can bend them.' He did the same to her forearms. 'Not broken.'

The movement made Candy hiss in over her teeth but she blocked him out.

'I think I might need to go to the doctor, Mum.'

'Doctor?'

Jeffrey answered him. 'She can't play guitar.'

Robinson leaned back on his heels, for a moment trying to make light of it, josh them along. 'I don't follow. First of all it's throw yourself into this band like nothing else exists, then it's "I can't play guitar."'

'Robinson.' Rose cut him off. 'She's serious.' Rose examined her daughter's arms again, perhaps expecting the problem to come to the surface like a rash. 'Find my car keys, please, Jeff. If it's bad enough for tears, I think we should probably get to the surgery today, just in case.'

Jeff nodded. 'Have we still got time before it shuts?'

'Dr McClelland works till six. Otherwise we could go to the urgent clinic.'

Robinson was still floundering to catch up with the rapid switch in dynamics. '*Is* it that important?'

Rose gave his five o'clock stubble a quick rub with her thumb. 'Best we find out, yes?'

Eyes filled with worry now, Robinson conceded. As Jeff dashed out to hunt down Rose's car keys, Robinson pushed his daughter's hair away from her flushed face. 'What do you think it is?'

'I don't know.'

Rose asked, 'What could we do for muscle strain?'

'Well, I don't . . .'

'For sports injuries, when you were in Harriers, what did you do?'

He stared at Candy's cramped-up hands and the way pain skewed her face. He rubbed his temples. 'There was a word. A mnemonic. RICE. Rest, Ice, Compression, Elevation. I'm just not sure if this is the same. I mean, what's she done?'

When Jeff hurried in, car keys hooked over his thumb, which he held up, jingling, Rose answered, 'I don't think she knows. Let's just get her to the doctor. We probably don't all need to go.'

But Jeff followed Candy and Rose out, as Rose said over her shoulder, 'If we're going to be longer than an hour, we'll call you.'

The only other patients in the doctor's waiting room were a mother with a placid toddler, and a rudely healthy looking man with a whistle on a cord around his neck, who looked as if he were about to dash off to referee some sports match. These other patients were quickly in and out of the consulting room. When the Marshalls went in — all together, Jeff evidently so worried about Candy he couldn't bear the wait on his own — Dr McClelland's face lifted into a smile.

He'd been their GP for years and had a good memory for his patients: if you bumped into him at the grocery store he'd always nod and greet you by name before sweeping on his way. He'd never lost the sense that Jeffrey and Candy were a kind of pet project of his: they'd always seemed such striking evidence of the Third Type of Twin hypothesis, and he'd often had to provide medical certificates for the international study they were taking part in.

He, too, looked from face to face as brother and sister stood before him. 'Now, what can I do for you? Who are we seeing today?'

Disgruntled, Jeff indicated Candy.

She explained what had happened. That yes, the symptoms had been building up for a while, maybe even a year or so, even before the band, but she thought they had just meant she wasn't agile enough, needed to train harder. Yes, she'd been pretty tired lately, no, not really sleeping all that well, actually, if she was honest. But that was partly worry. About doing well enough in the contest. Oh, a music contest coming up. In case she . . . disappointed mostly herself but — ummm, everyone. In case her family, or really *mumble mumble* ('Sorry, Candy? I didn't catch that'), in case *Dad* was disappointed in her. She knew he really would be, now. Even looking down at her hands roosting in her lap she felt Jeff and Rose stare at her, and the spaces between them all alter. What she'd said was only a shard of the truth, of course — and like a shard, it seemed to lodge in her gullet.

Dr McClelland, sitting back in his chair, pen up to his mouth as they talked, nodded slowly. Said he had an idea about what this could be, as he'd seen it a couple of times before, but he'd have to do a few tests. He manipulated her joints, asked her to lift and clutch objects, asked her to turn, bow and lift her head, asked if she could feel pinpricks in the pads of her fingers, palms of her hands, even her toes and the soles of her feet, asked her to walk in a straight line, heel to toe, across the room, asked her to squeeze his hand, try to hold it tight without flinching.

Then he sat down opposite her again, leaning forward with his hands between his knees.

'Well, my guess is that this is something I've started to see in office workers.' He turned to Rose. 'It's still a vague term, but you'll have heard of RSI?'

Rose frowned. 'A little.'

'Repetitive Strain Injury. A lot of medics say they want more scientific evidence before they accept it's a bona fide syndrome. A few say they don't believe it exists at all — say it's a phantom of the eighties. Call it "compensationitis", after the surge in ACC payments in Australia.' He focused on Candy again. 'But I've actually seen it close to home. Our son suffered almost exactly the same thing when he finished his MA thesis — all that typing.' He smiled, but Candy couldn't respond.

Syndrome. Suffering. Was she ill? A small stone of fear sank through her. 'What does it mean?'

'We're just not built for hours and hours of tiny movements. We don't know much about it yet, but actually it's probably been around for centuries. Leonardo da Vinci had something like it, you know. Eighteenth-century clerks, seamstresses, lace-makers — they all reported very similar symptoms. It means you've probably been overdoing your practice.'

The words leapt out, close to a wail. 'But how am I supposed to get any *good* at things? And will my hands ever get better?'

Dr McClelland shuffled in place. 'I think the answer to both those things is bit by bit, over time. Time and yet more time.'

He handed her a box of tissues that stood on his desk — she pulled out a whole string of them, managed a stuttering *oops* through the tears she still hadn't really noticed until he offered her the box.

Rose leaned over her handbag, which she held clutched to her stomach. 'Is there something she can take to help?'

'She'll need to rest, first, I think. Learn how to take breaks, Candy. But there isn't any sure-fire way of treating it. No drugs, that is — because we still don't fully understand it. I can recommend . . .'

Candy had stopped listening. Rest? She waited until her mother's and the doctor's mouths finished moving. 'So when can I play guitar again?'

'Gig's in three weeks,' Jeff added.

Dr McClelland lowered his eyes in apology, and shook his head. 'You'll have to judge that on the basis of how you feel, I'd say.' He drew a pad of paper towards him. 'I do know of a physiotherapist in town who's trying to work out treatment ideas, and who can help you to keep track of things.' His pen hovered over the pad. 'But you'll have to start to think of the pain as your body's telegraph system. A Morse code. You'll have to learn how to translate that for yourself into when to relax, when to work.'

He began to write down contact details for a massage and physiotherapy centre in town, people who'd even been proactive, he said, in setting up the first local RSI support group . . .

Candy let Rose take over all the remaining practical details, the nods and thank yous. Numbness filled her head. Through it, she heard him tell Rose to watch out for signs. Often people who have their main focus taken away, and who have to deal with chronic pain where there's no visible evidence of injury can slip quite low . . . Rose turned brisk, efficient. 'Yes, of course. We'll keep an eye on that.' She escorted Jeff and Candy from the clinic. Outside, by the car, she cupped Candy's chin in her hand, tilting her head to watch her reaction closely. 'Okay, love? I'll talk to Dad, if you like.'

Candy swallowed. 'About?'

'All of it, if you want me to. That he's been too hard on you?'

She shrugged. 'I don't know. If you think it will change anything. But I guarantee he'll still think I've failed.'

Before she could regret what she'd said, she climbed onto the car's back seat, slumped down and slammed the door.

ONCE CANDY HAD spoken to all the members of the band, and a letter had gone with her to school to explain why she wouldn't be able to take notes for a while, she retreated into herself. Her parents wanted to talk things through more, Robinson trying to build a bridge by rumpling her hair, pinching her nose, the way he used to when she was about ten, and then saying, 'Your mother's had a word with me. And I think we probably need to have a dad-to-daughter chat, what do you reckon?' But Candy kept saying really, she was all right, *please*, she just wanted to rest, lie on her bed, read, listen to music.

Jeff shuffled into her bedroom one afternoon, bringing her a cup of tea and a saucer of oatmeal cookies. 'Doesn't listening to music make you sad?' he asked as she took off her walkman headphones.

Candy scratched up a half smile for him but said, 'No, not sad. It's good thinking time. In a way I can concentrate more clearly if I'm not jumping to get my own ideas written up as fast as possible.'

He nodded, eyes downcast. 'I think Mum and Dad would appreciate it if you could tell them that sort of thing. They kind of need reassurance.'

'Yeah, well. I don't think it matters what I say right now. They're going to worry anyway. Could you tell them I'm fine? I just don't feel like talking, that's all.'

He hung on. They both watched the silence build.

'They want you to come out of your room more, to be with all of us.'

She sighed. 'Okay.' But even so, she still buried herself in a book, or the lyric sheets of her favourite albums, as the stereo sang on, soundtrack to the slow, wrenching hours of fully absorbing what had happened; flinching with increased realisation when she tried to turn a sheet of paper and even that registered with spasms in her arms. The smiles and the 'I'm fines' she gave to her family after she'd started her trips to the physiotherapist were an act she worked hard at, to fob off the probing, the worrying.

Underneath the fake cheer was glum, and underneath the glum she did register the phone calls coming in, mainly from the band, and girls from school, although there were other well-wishers: relations, family friends. She was surprised and grateful at how supportive people were being — yet at the same time it all seemed to emphasise the situation. Sometimes the sinking feeling could have taken her right through the floorboards. She tried to keep her attention trained on something neutral: her book, her stereo, the TV. Still, not fooled, her heart jolted when she heard that Julian was on the phone.

At first he was teasing, jovial, in a way that seemed not at all in character. 'Didn't I *tell* you to watch your posture? Didn't I *tell* you not to try "Stairway to Heaven" until you were twenty-five? Didn't I tell you not to try that Spanish Flamenco stuff? Flamenco is like being a Jedi, Candy. You need years of apprenticeship. You need Yoda. You need the Force behind you.'

What a stupid-arse joke. A silence, as he registered her mood. 'Hey, I know. I know. I was just . . .'

Stroppy, mouthy, as if her screwed-up hands had screwed with her head and tongue, except that she couldn't keep out the sound of tears, fussing underneath like an off-key bass: 'I thought you'd be the one who would really understand. I thought you'd wonder what it would have been like if it was you, so you'd know what to say.' She'd so wanted him to repeat something like he had in a recent dream, in which she was wondering why he hadn't called, and then she'd found him busking in a glass-strewn demolition site. He'd not looked up at her but said, 'This is nothing, it happens to all the best students. In fact, you can't call yourself a musician unless you've lost your hands at least once.' Then she'd realised his fingertips were transparent, invisible, though all six strings of his dark guitar moved beneath his hands.

She'd wanted him to know about some miracle ointment, or technical exercises, or some vitamin that all musicians used at times like these. Instead, he'd said, 'Hey, look. I've written out a cheque for a refund on your lessons for the rest of the semester. I'll post it to you, and you'll call me, won't you, when you're ready to start up again?'

It didn't really help that the cheque arrived with a card saying, 'Get better soon,' and 'Bank this towards your future musical career.' She started refusing phone calls after that.

When a few days had passed she heard Jeff talking to Tip, and Grace again, and she was surprised that he still protected her, didn't bring her to the phone. But he came into the living room, flumped himself down beside her. He brimmed with an unfamiliar energy that made her scan his expression.

'What's up, Jeff?'

He startled her by giving her a quick, dry kiss on the cheek.

'The others want to know if you'll still head along to the finals night. They're all going, said they hope you'll be there.'

Candy winced as she picked up a glass of fruit juice from the coffee table. 'I don't know. I'd just want to be *up* there.'

His eyes were big, worried. 'The others are thinking of entering still. They think they could still have a chance at the composition category. And I mean, they're *your* songs they're performing. They all said the lyricist should hear her own debut. Grace and Tip also said they know there's no way they'll get anywhere for performance or best band now, but that after . . .' he gave a deep whistle out over his bottom teeth. 'After all the practice . . .'

'They don't want it to go to waste.'

He nodded. Candy set her glass back down, hugged her stupid cotton-stuffed arms to herself to hold back the rush of misery.

Jeff took a sip of air, like someone fortifying himself with a strong drink, but it was a while before he built up the impetus to talk again.

'Say they go ahead and perform, well, even though it's such a shit that you can't be up there with them, you wouldn't want to miss it, would you? Wouldn't there always be a part of you that wondered how your songs — and the band — went?' He pushed his long curls away from his face. 'And you might pick up some useful stuff for later. When you can play again.'

She knew he was only trying to help, but advice from him about music came so close to patronising that she could have bitten him. Instead, she gave him the cold shoulder, burying herself back in the lyric sheets of one of their mum's old records, Joni Mitchell, *The Hissing of Summer Lawns*. 'Maybe.'

But what made it more galling was that his suggestion wouldn't be shaken. She probably *would* feel worse being left out so entirely that she didn't even get to see the other competitors, let alone hear how her songs fared when out on their own. The thought ticked away. Maybe, just maybe, this was a way of getting a fresh perspective, hearing them as if they were a stranger's work, wares someone else had to sell. Maybe she could tell what they were really like, or how they'd have to be changed, if she went along.

A few days later she sidled up to Jeff at the kitchen bench, where he'd been chivvied into grating cheese for a lasagne Rose was making.

'You going to help?' he asked. 'You could do the onions.'

'If you think you're up to it,' Rose added.

Jeff visibly quenched a face that said *drama queens*. Candy had been brooding long enough, though, to be sick of her own mood, so she rolled a papery sheathed onion towards her. 'I'll give it a go.'

Rose sent her a questioning look, which Candy answered: 'The physio guy says I should start to try to do more, in little bits, anyhow.'

They all worked companionably for a while, Candy clamping down on her disbelief and the sense of affront at how ridiculous it was that, actually, something as bloody basic as slicing a bloody onion still bloody hurt . . .

'Hey, Jeff?' She had to turn around to see if he was listening, so was glad of the excuse to rest for a bit.

'Yup.'

'I've been thinking. Maybe I will go to the rock quest night.'

'Really?'

'Do you want to come? It'd be good to have someone else there when The Raggedies are on.'

Rose interjected. 'Can parents go along too?'

Candy and Jeff shared a quick glance, reminding Candy herself vividly of a little toy she'd seen once: the carved figurines of two ice-skaters, set on a small round mirror. Their bases were fitted with magnets so that when another magnet moved below the mirror, the figures slid over the glassy ice, kissed abruptly, then shot away again as if stung.

Rose laughed out loud. 'I get the message. No go, folks.'

Jeff and Candy both looked at their feet. 'Sorry, Mum. You could come, but . . .'

'I'd have to stand at the back and pretend I didn't know you? Well, I could . . .' she laughed again. 'Don't look so appalled! Goodness, sometimes you two act like I'm from outer space. But I'm your mother!'

Jeff held up two carrots beside his head. 'My mother was an alien.'

'Great name for a band,' said Candy.

Rose shook off excess water from the lettuce she was rinsing at the sink. 'Seriously. Your dad and I would still really like to come along, even though Candy's not playing. It'd be a chance to get some idea of all the hard work that's gone into this.'

Candy battled with herself, managing somehow not to say, funny how Dad wasn't really all that interested earlier, isn't it? Funny how it's taken having useless hands for me to get through to him, isn't it?

Rose put her hand over her heart. 'And we promise to get there under our own steam. And to stand at the back. And not to even *talk* to you there.'

'Well, I guess we can't stop them,' said Jeff to Candy, sighing.

She copied, nodding. 'You're right. They're adults now, after all.'

They both patted Rose on the shoulder. 'You can come.'

'But only because you've promised not to embarrass us.'

Rose pressed her fingertips to her temples, chanting, 'Remember not to embarrass the children, remember not to embarrass the children.'

Jeff clicked his fingers in a way that reminded Candy of Grace. 'Hey, Can-do, will you call everyone and tell them you're going along?'

'Yeah, sure. It's time I talked to them, anyway.'

When she did phone the others, and was nearing the end of her final call, hopping from foot to foot, saying, 'Yeah, yeah, hey, look, Luce-unit, I'm busting, really busting, can I call you back later?' Jeff sloped through the hallway.

'Can I have a word?' he said, and she was so preoccupied with getting to the bathroom that she just said, 'Yeah, yeah, hurry, here,' and quickly passed the phone to him like a relay baton, no time to wonder, and no reason at all to recall that moment, until Friday night, the third of September.

AS CANDY STEPPED into the beery light of the rock quest venue, some of her raw disappointment about not being able to take part in all the musos' hubbub was alleviated by curiosity and excitement about being in a pub without having to worry about being turfed out for looking too young. Although the publican must have realised that several of the musicians were under the decade's drinking age, Candy, Jeff and The Raggedies hovered together with plastic pint mugs of lager in the dim light, shifting nervously, excitedly, scanning the room for people they knew, or to assess the mood, making small talk that seemed to skid over the surface of everything. The conversation lunged at serious matters — Candy's hands, how she felt about being here, how the others had managed with one fewer band member, how they were all feeling about the thinner sound, the makeshift outfit, now that they were actually faced with judge and audience. But each time a topic like this was raised they all seemed to scuttle away from it again, each almost as easily startled as the next, though Tip looked particularly alarmed. At one point he thrust his drink at Candy, saying, 'Shit, I think I'm gonna be sick, 'scuse me,' although he came back quickly, looking just as hounded.

'Relax, Tip,' Grace said. 'You know it's not like the real gig would've been.' But Candy actually envied their nervousness, their awareness of being at the centre of it all. She thought Grace, too, seemed on edge, the knuckles of both hands white around her beer, and she wondered if she had reassured Tip just for Candy's benefit, as she kept clocking her out of the corner of her eyes.

In the milling and shuffling, bumping and passing that went on among the crowd as the bar filled up, the noise built while the technicians checked the sound system. When they had left a Cure album playing, Candy somehow became separated from the others. She caught a glimpse of Jeff at one point — as if his were a swimmer's head surfacing — but just as she decided to make her way towards him a wash of newcomers arrived and there was a surge of pressing and jostling as the room readjusted.

'Crowded, eh?' said someone next to her: a guy in his early twenties, perhaps, in leather jacket and red checked shirt. He held his beer up over his head so that it wouldn't get spilt as others tried to make their way to the bar.

'Yeah, really good turn-out,' she said, and was struck as she realised there seemed to be a mix of curiosity, hopefulness and uncertainty in the way he watched her. She felt a jolt of attraction, and as they fell into a tentative banter she was hyper-aware (as never before — not even when being held and too hungrily kissed by Shane) of how her body moved. It was in the way he watched her: she noticed her hips in their sockets, how her spine helped her dip and pivot and bend. When she thought she saw her parents arrive she had a brief instant of wondering if it was incautious to stay alongside a stranger, but soon she was throughly distracted.

Involved in the kind of half-shouted, half-intimate conversation that noisy bars required — liking the way the guy had to tilt his head down low to hear her, the way she had to go slightly on tiptoe, and lean in to him as he told her he was Lewis, doing an Honours degree at uni, in Pols and Economics, and she told him that she'd been in one of the bands, had to pull out at the last minute — she lost track of where the others were. Perhaps her enjoyment of

Lewis's company left her more off guard when The Raggedies came on. She was unprepared: had no time to wonder where they were, or get anxious about not having Jeff beside her for moral support.

The MC looked relieved after a horribly chaotic, thrashy, unrehearsed mess of a punk band left the stage: a band Candy knew was made up of prefects from a private boys' school in a leafy, quiet suburb — the sons of backbench MPs and agricultural money. Huh. The Sex Pistols would have spat on them. (Though, come to that, they probably would have spat on her too.) Plenty of teenage boys had pogoed along to the one-line song, 'Eat my bollocks, eat my bo-o-o-ollocks' but the band had blown an amp, and afterwards the lead singer could be heard squealing in a tantrum when the bar's double glass doors swung open onto the stairwell. After that, the fans had tried to melt into the crowd.

The muscular, Maori, Marley T-shirt-wearing MC shoe-skated to the mike. 'Okay. Right. Yeah. That was Glandular Fever. Right. Yeah. And now, the next entry. They hail from here, they're new as the news, please welcome — The Raggedies' Tribute Band.'

What? Tribute band?

The lights came up. The band rose from a heads-slumped, arms-dangling position. Five of them. What? Candy's head felt swollen with drink. Who . . . She looked away to clear her vision. A voice said *one, two, three, four* and they launched into a number she had written when she was furious with Shane, at the end of their brief-lived relationship. (That day she didn't want to remember. One of their long-deferred dates after the scene at his uncle's house. She'd called Shane from a payphone after he'd stood her up for a Sunday matinée and he'd announced that at a party the night before he'd met a new girl who was willing to 'put it out' for him if she wasn't. With no stomach for the movie any more, she'd had to walk all the way home: no buses for an hour on a Sunday.) As Lucy's keyboard gave the first run at the melody, Candy felt the wheels of that hurt pride get turning again.

dirt

Days the dirt looks kinder than you
ways the ground holds steadier than you;
at least asphalt and tar
with their white crows' feet
keep their intentions clear . . .

Days I could lie down in the road
to hear the gravel's voice
lie down in the street to feel its rough cheeks
'cause it's warm, and it's warm,
and it's steady, and it's warm . . .

And in the morning when I wake
to step outside the door
it's waiting, it greets me,
sun at its side,
its arms spill with trees and sky

and it's warm and it's steady
and it's warm and it's true
and the only time it's cheated
is when it led me straight to you

but dirt can't take the blame

you'd walk over anyone
you'd walk over anything
that was warm
that was steady

till it was worn.

The Raggedies looked amazing, partly because no one else had bothered with stage image. One or two had worn glittery lurex tops, Glandular Fever had ripped their black T-shirts and army surplus trousers, but the rest of the bands had just worn ordinary jeans and shirts. Most of the boy bands had played guitar sealed to one spot, crouched with bent knees, body of the instrument pressed against their crotches, pelvis thrust forward as if the guitar was some kind of extension of their cocks, which actually looked pretty funny — and wishful — on all those stick-insect teenagers. Zane, though, moved lithely in the background with the guitar, twisting, ducking, craning, deliberately puppet-like: a physical dance in dialogue with the others, whose movements, too, were consciously managed, turning each song into a small piece of theatre. But that wasn't what left Candy's throat coated thick with speechlessness when Lewis leaned in to her and said, 'They really wouldn't be bad with a bit more work, eh?'

The beers she'd gulped nervously over the build-up to the performance seemed to have induced a weird ghosting effect to her vision. Like hope projecting a hologram? No, there were definitely five of them on stage. There she was, in her costume, someone else's guitar strapped to her, which she wasn't playing; carrying out movements that were a cross between a rag doll's and a marionette's, she treated the instrument as a prop. Sometimes she was lip-synching, sometimes singing. The Candy on the ground swayed, verged on losing her balance completely.

Of course the band was a bit rough around the edges. They didn't have the slick patina, the relaxed demeanour of experience; they had to keep a constant eye on one another, giving and taking cues, the nervous tension sometimes just about glinting between them like the silver wires that hold a pantomime aerialist hovering above a stage. But that very sense of how seriously they all took it, their keenness, their absolute focus on their short set, came spinning off them like a spray of brilliant photons. Lewis was right: with a few adjustments, The Raggedies could be very, very good.

The pints of beer sent more of their dry-ice fog barrelling into her head.

Lewis gestured at her with his empty glass. 'You okay?'

She tilted on her feet again. 'Yeah.'

He peered at her doubtfully.

'That's them. The band I was — am in. *Whazam. Shazam.* Ha.'

Surprise lifted across his face. 'No bull?' He turned to watch them make their way off stage, slipped his empty beer glass under his arm so he could clap along with the rest of the crowd.

'That girl? Really I was that boy. The one dressed as a girl. With a boy's voice on. That should have been me.' She swayed, the mast of a small skiff finding deep trouble.

'Eh?'

'Ooopsmedaisy.'

He caught her by the elbow. 'Hey, how much have you had to drink?'

'Yess-uhh.' Her eyes brimmed.

Lewis turned around. 'Look, there're a couple of stools back there. I think you might need to sit down.'

'No, I need to be — see my brother. My brother? He was me tonight. And that's not fair. Don't you think? He's not music. He's everything else, not me. Everything.'

One layer of consciousness grew belatedly aware that her muttering had not only been going on in her head, and that Lewis — a complete stranger — would have no idea what she was talking about. So once on a stool at the back, she held a beer mat up to her face to hide.

Lewis's smile was lopsided. 'Hey, kid. You're here with other people, right?' He brushed her jaw briefly with the back of his hand: a gesture ambiguously between flirtation and something paternal.

'Kid?' she said.

'I'll sit it out with you just to make sure they get you home safely.' He pulled back from her slightly. 'You're looking kind of green. Do you need the Ladies'?'

She was already nodding, teetering to a standing position, lifting an elbow with a pleading look so he would guide her there.

''Scuse me, emergency exit here,' he kept saying to the people he steered her past. 'Emergency for the young lady? Cheers, mate.'

The toilet cubicle was so ugly — the concrete walls a lurid yellow and textured like cottage cheese, everything secured by chains embedded in the concrete, as if people would steal even a plastic cistern (or perhaps try to hurl it in a bar brawl) — that it seemed to say there was no hope of fighting the fast, shallow breathing and the dreadful clenching that preceded being sick. Candy's mind filled with just one thought, which pounded like an accelerated heartbeat. *How could he, how could he, how could he.* Meaning Jeff. Meaning how could he step over those unspoken boundaries, the territory mapped out as clearly — albeit silently — as a line drawn down the middle of a shared room. Seeing him on stage cross-dressing in the costume she'd helped to design, dancing his own version of the steps she'd helped to choreograph, accompanying Grace and Lucy on the songs she'd written, even knowing it was supposed to be a joke, a *tribute*, she felt . . . robbed. Disembodied.

The colour behind her eyes was scarlet, shot through with orange as if flying with long-floating tendrils. The angry colours were suddenly very important. They meant something. Yeah, they were the colours of that strange fable, in the sermon they'd heard when Gram was here; Candy had read it at home, over and over, because it said: *and there were twins in her womb, and the first came out red, all over like an hairy garment; and they called his name Esau; and after that, his brother came out, and his hand took hold on Esau's heel; and his name was called Jacob and* . . . (something, something, something) . . . *Jacob said, sell me thy birthright* . . . She saw an image of herself, stretching after Jeff, grabbing his ankle to send him sprawling, only to find herself lurching forward and turning around as Jeff clutched at her heel . . .

Was it the alcohol or the staged reversal that had induced the sensation that the ground was tipping and she was lifting above it? Like the experience she'd had as a small child, of flying up to the ceiling at night and hovering there as she watched the expression on the sleeping face of the girl below, which seemed to be following the words of a distant conversation. And back then — as tonight, when

Jeff appeared on stage — the hovering, disconnected self had thought, which is Candy? Which is she? But also, now, hunched over in a dismal public toilet cubicle, as physically as her body was drained, her heart was filled with a sense of morose failure. Of her own ... pointlessness. Why was she? Why was there a Candy, when Jeff could pretend to be one and the same? *Right from the start they've been different.* But he reneged on that deal. A song their mother used to sing pranced around behind her temples, the words squeezing the tender parts of her head. *Anything you can do, I can do better, I can do anything better than you. No you can't. Yes I can. No you can't...*

Familiar voices whispered out near the handbasin. 'Oh, grody. Someone's being sick in there.'

'What a waster.'

Lucy and Grace giggled, then said something she couldn't catch, and the main door swung shut again.

Her stomach was empty, tongue and throat hot with acid burn; a headache was already thumping at the panels of her skull. But her thoughts actually felt slightly clearer now. She couldn't stay in here forever: perhaps Luce and Grace had even been looking for her. She'd have to go out, congratulate them all, laugh and say, 'Oh boy, you sure fooled me, ha ha.' And that guy — Lewis — he'd been so nice. More than nice. He'd said he'd wait — she needed to show him that she was pretty sober now, pretty *onto* it. But man, oh man, how to make an impression in this state? Both on him, and on the others. Already a salvaging instinct was working away, trying to find those scraps of herself still left and knit them back together again. She wanted the others to see her with him. A way of saying, *look, someone is interested in me. Just me.* Already, in those torn, random seconds, she wanted to fasten onto Lewis, a man she didn't know: to anchor herself. He'd shown an interest before she'd even said she wrote songs, played guitar. He must have — known, found — some quality in her. Seen something she, too, needed to know about, if she were to find out what a music-less Candy really was.

She inched over to the sink, wanting to rinse out her mouth, get rid of the clotted, acrid taste. She was dismayed at the sight of herself. Puffy eyes, clammy hairline, pale as a freak. A woman came into the toilets, slid her a cool look, brought out a flat, folding hairbrush and a lipstick from the inside pocket of her denim jacket. Damn. Candy had always thought that people who preened or put on makeup in public were vain, pea-brained. But now she wished she'd had the foresight. Steeling herself against another supercilious look from the woman, she splashed cold water on her face, then rubbed hard at her skin with the coarse beige paper towels from the metal dispenser, to try to scrub some colour back into her cheeks.

The icy woman regarded her, slipped her hand back into her jacket pocket, then withdrew a foil-coated tube of mints. 'You need one of these?'

Candy, taken aback, stood there. Then a shaky hand accepted.
'Hard night, eh?'
She nodded, smile watery. 'I look awful.'
'Honey, you look under twenty-five. Be grateful.' The woman popped one of her own mints, raised an eyebrow and sashayed into one of the cubicles.

Candy took a shuddery breath and prepared herself for the exit.

Outside, the final band were gearing up for their set: an all-woman group, with double bass, flute, electric guitar, drums, and a separate trio of singers. They were nearly all shaven-headed, and all wore red silk shifts: dresses that looked vaguely like ministers' robes or the get-up of a gospel choir. They were the only other band to have put much obvious effort into presentation, but there was a moment of half-embarrassed hush as they swished to and fro in their silk, adjusting cables and mike-tripod height even though the stagehands had done just the same. The women didn't really look very — rock. Or even very Independent Label. You could see those parts of the crowd who were there for the thrash, the hard core, the pogo, the body dive, the stage surf, the deep pound low pump, the heave, the hype, the mosh pit sweat-fest, weren't quite sure where to look or how to stand. So they headed to the bar, refuelled, huddled into conversational knots and turned up the volume on their voice boxes, one section of the crowd announcing to the other that as far as they could see, the contest was as good as over.

Lewis was standing just where she'd left him — or rather, just where he launched her off. He raised his eyebrows at her. 'Hey there,' he said. 'You've been a while.'

'Sorry, Lewis.' She was still moving gingerly.

'Lose your lollies in there, did you?'

It was the first time she'd heard the term, but his tone, half sympathetic, half mocking, said enough.

'Do you want to find your friends and see if we can get you home?'

'No, that's okay.' Avoiding the fact that her entire family was here too. 'They'll just want to stay on for the announcements.'

'Oh, of course. They're in one of the bands.'

'Yeah.' How to keep him interested, keep him talking? 'Hey, look. Thanks for . . .' she shrugged, empty handed.

'It was nothing. You're looking a bit better,' he said. 'Can I get you a softdrink, or a water?'

A craving for the childhood comfort for upset stomachs came on strong. 'Actually, ginger beer or L & P would be great.'

'Okay. You hang around here and I'll grab you one.'

The way his eyes worked on her reminded her of touching someone briefly on the elbow, while saying something bland, banal, like 'Excuse me', only to find a static electric slam has both people leaping back. Lewis sped off into the crowd and Candy abruptly crossed her arms and legs, drawn into herself as if in self-defence. Except really she was lying in wait for the next such contact. She held her breath for a moment: an attempt to take stock. What with her still pretty much useless hands, Jeff's sister-ventriloquism, and now this weird sorcery starting, it felt as if the reliable metal struts and canvas canopy of her heart had been flipped inside out: red umbrella tugged kitewise in a gust of wind. Breathe now, breathe.

Lewis made his way back through the crowd again, precariously carrying three glasses. 'What have you got there?' Candy asked.

'L & P for the young lady, with stingo and a whisky chaser for . . .'

'The gentleman,' Candy interrupted, accepting her glass, and eyeing him with a sparkle. 'What's stingo?'

He took a slow drink from the glass. 'It's a word my uncles used for strong ale — they always had a stingo after they'd been out hunting in the bush. It was just called beer the rest of the time. That always struck me. Like a hunt somehow changed ordinary things.'

'So you've been out hunting today?'

He paused, eyeing her over the rim of his pint glass. 'I don't know. Have I?'

She picked up his suggestive tone, but her own innuendo had been so totally unintended that she had to blink at him wordlessly as she tried to figure out how they had got to this point. She jumped when she felt a hand on her back.

'Hey, Candy, we've been looking everywhere for you!'

She turned to see all The Raggedies — and Jeff — each still in costume. Although they had taken off their makeup, each face was still slicked with happy sweat from their hard work under the bank of temporary stage lights.

'We wanted to find you before the judges came on.'

She only then became fully aware that the band in red silk had finished, and that the MC was announcing that there'd be a half-hour break before the results were presented.

The satisfied, vibrant look on all the band members' faces made her swallow hard. She knew she should say, well done, you were great, and — to Jeff — what a *surprise*! The fingers of one hand involuntarily began to do up the buttons on her denim jacket in a protective gesture. The twinges in the underside of her forearm — which felt as if the tendons were crossing over, twisting — were like a part of her body saying *fuck you, oh fuck you*. All the bitter disappointment flew back up, a flock of confusion, thoughts scattered and disoriented.

To stall, and to focus on something else, she said, 'Hey, guys, I should introduce you to Lewis. He's been looking after me since you guys took off.' Resentment sliced the last sentence but nobody else seemed to notice. Thankfully, Lewis began to say all the right things: fantastic set, you must be thrilled, how do you feel; so that Candy could dissemble: nod and smile as if she agreed, when all the while she bit back the juvenile wish to beat her fists on Jeffrey's chest and say, *Give it back! Give it back! It's mine!*

She could tell, from the way Jeff's smile kept alternating with an anxious, grazing glance sent her way, that he'd picked up on her mood. So many times she'd have seen it as her job to comfort him, to ease him back into happiness, fearful he'd go the way of Rose. But now her tongue was paralysed. As the others chattered she became hyper-sensitive to the way she and Jeff moved. It seemed to her that her actions always unconsciously followed his. He brushed his fringe away from his eyes a millisecond before her hand moved to do the same. He adjusted his jacket collar just fractionally before she felt an uncomfortable rubbing at the skin on her neck and had to shift her clothing slightly. He turned to search the crowd just as she'd thought, I wonder if Mum and Dad are still here? The more heightened that conviction became, the more she began to lose immediate sensation in her body. The word *shadow* washed into her mind, as if a hill were rising into the light, darkening a valley. Jeff was real, and she just the shape cast by him — an insubstantial, inferior copy. She watched the way coloured spots from the ancient disco ball overhead danced over his face, and now she felt a strange weightlessness, a tingling in her lips, as if she were filling with a sad helium and could drift away completely. And maybe she would have: lost it entirely, started shallow-breathing and babbling as thoughts about the intangible, mercurial nature of identity overtook all the little logical, orderly cells and habits in her brain, if Lewis hadn't said the most ordinary, most startling thing.

'So how do you guys all know each other?' He neatly downed his whisky chaser.

Glances whizzed to and fro between all the others: quick couriers of amusement and expectation. They looked at Lewis again, waiting for the obviousness of at least one of the connections to hit him, while Candy braced herself for the usual, *Oh, my God, you two are so alike. You've got to be twins. Oh, you are twins! I knew it!* And then something from the rest of the irritating, repeated (doubled and redoubled: oh how merry) repertoire: *Do you both feel it when one of you is hurt? Do you always know what the other one is thinking? Do you know where the other one is, even if nobody's told you?* Or even, like one little jerk at primary school, all those years ago, 'So do you both know what it's like to have a dick and tits?' And Redshaw's relentless, babyish teasing: 'Twin-pins, twin-pins, shitty little thin-shins!'

Grace, raising her eyebrows at the others, responded, 'Well, most of us know each other through the auditions for the band.'

'And the rest?'

Tip grinned. 'I guess you could say that Candy and Jeff, here, have known each other for a lifetime.'

Lewis seemed to have to work out which one was Jeff from everyone else's sightlines. 'Oh, okay. So you're related?'

Jeff gave a quizzical half smile, and Tip rolled his eyes. 'Brother and sister, you could say.'

'You could,' nodded Zane.

'Pretty close brother and sister, actually,' said Lucy.

'Twins, practically.'

'Practically and totally.' Tip grinned, proud as a father.

'Really?' Lewis was momentarily distracted by someone in the crowd jostling to get past. 'And — uh — so what place do you think you guys are aiming for? One of the top three?'

Candy felt newly awake. Returned to her body: red thought fog gone. Lewis had barely even noticed what she and Jeff were. No double vision, no double up with laughter. It gave her a delicious swell in energy, enough to joke again with the others. 'If you got first place, you wouldn't forget me, would you guys?'

Just then, she caught sight of her parents struggling through the crowd as they made their way over to their group. Her dad was beaming.

'Hey, kids! Your mother tried to stop me coming over! She said it would embarrass you. But you're not ashamed of your dear old dad, are you?' He pulled a monkey face, and Rose slapped him on the arm, though her cheeks were hot with laughter. 'Robinson, you *promised*.'

He gave Candy a nudge with his shoulder. 'Did your brother give you a bit of a turn? Canny bastard, eh, Jeff? Well,' he said to the surrounding Raggedies, 'it's an obvious one, but you wouldn't think it'd work with a boy and girl, eh? They've never pulled it on us before, and I have to tell you, for a few seconds they really had me going!'

Rose was nodding, the sentiment *lovely old fool* legible on her face. 'He was in a state for a moment there. "What about her hands! What about her hands!" he kept saying. "If she does real damage she might never play again!" I had to take hold of him' — she demonstrated, fitting the V of both palms to his cheeks, then gently turning his head towards Jeff — 'and say, have a proper look, love.' Everybody laughed, Jeff especially, though he still sent Candy pointed glances, puzzled by her long non-response. A comet of distress hurtled through her head. Even their own father had confused them. Then he thought Jeff was so funny, so clever, so fine and shiny in the limelight. But he'd feared for Candy's music: wasn't that good? Something positive about Candy had finally sunk in, past the sicko-father-son, or my-little-twinlets thing. So why did the night still feel so twisted around?

She looked from person to person like a foreigner trying to catch words everyone else understood. Lewis's gaze said he too was slightly removed from the family-and-friends banter. He seemed to be using their conversation as a kind of screen, behind which he tried to conceal his intensity as he watched her.

Like a change in season pulling at the senses of a migratory bird, this minute shift between them drove Candy towards him. Instincts teaching her, instantaneously, how to turn, smile, when to bestow attention, when to withdraw it slightly, provocatively, how to behave so that her body drew him nearer: river to sea, salt to tongue.

Instinct engineered her away from friends and family during the break in proceedings. It engineered her away from offering Jeff the reassurance she'd once have willingly given. His face was now scribbled with hurt and confusion in a way that made her realise — even as she shouldered it off and slipped away — that the performance, the changed group's name (Raggedies Tribute Band) really was meant to have been an elaborately staged compliment, or gift, a well-meant in-joke: only good bands have lookalikes, imitators.

Instinct pushed her away from her brother, engineered her and Lewis outside, into the street, down an alley lined with small shops that ended in a tiny curved public garden with a central white stone sculpture, of a man curled over a woman, curled over a child, curled over a bird; a small row of native ferns and hebes and an alcove with a wooden park bench set with a brass plaque that said, 'In memory of Ethel Gilkinson: for how she loved this place.' It engineered her to make the first real move again, although this time it was to answer a question in herself, and even though Lewis was facing away from her. He was gazing at the sculpture, which seemed to pool and reflect the city's light, while he said that her family seemed like good people, and was she sure she wouldn't rather be inside? Hadn't she said the songs she'd written were up for appraisal as much as the band's performance? The break before the announcement would be over soon. Her folks would probably be wondering where she was again, could get pretty suspicious of this strange guy who seemed to prompt vanishing acts in their only daughter . . .

She answered by slipping her hand into one of his jacket pockets, waiting. He turned slowly to her, small frown on his face gathering the shadows of the miniature park into a knot behind his eyes, filling him with something inscrutable, inaccessible, which yet made the desire budding along her skin all the more urgent, determined to find some kind of access. So instinct carried on, engineered — or helped her know how to engineer — the moment where, instead of backing away into some kind of polite normality, she framed his chin in one of her hands (an unknowing echo of what she'd just seen between Rose and Robinson) and drew his mouth towards hers.

The first contact was warm, dry, papery: as if she'd kissed a letter she'd just written to him, rather than the man himself. And then that letter held over a heat source, caught and torched. The smoke and peat and spice of whisky breathed into her. Her veins swirled, the kiss channelling a thin stream of another almost-alcohol into her blood. Time stole away for a while.

Lewis was the first to pull back. 'Hey — hey. Wait a minute. Shouldn't we think this through? We need to rewind here.'

'Why?'

He looked over his shoulder: perhaps a noise had alerted him to some other presence. 'What we should do is take this inside somewhere.' She watched him, thinking about how that made it sound as if it were related to a fight — no, the opposite of a fight. He held her shoulders. 'But another time. With clear heads, right? I mean, I hardly know anything about you. More to the point, at your age, you hardly know anything about me.'

Her heart sped up with unfamiliar determination. 'My age? Age hasn't got anything to do with it.' She found the words streaming off her tongue, drink-fuelled, despite the fact that she'd probably lost most of the alcohol when she was sick. 'If it did, you wouldn't have started talking to a total stranger. You wouldn't have *stayed* talking to her. What you've just said about thinking things through — well, doesn't that show this isn't normal for you? So something's made you step outside normal. You must have picked up on something else. Something that can't have had anything to do with my *age*.'

She could feel he was swaying on some fulcrum, on the verge of pulling away even more, but that there was also enough confusion to keep him teetering. So, with a calculation that astonished another part of her, she ran a hand under his jacket, along his back, up to where his shoulderblades perched under thick cotton.

'How often do you do this?' he said.

'Do what?'

'Find older guys in bars and sweet-talk them in dark alleyways? You're taking a hell of a risk for a young thing.'

With one hand still in his jacket pocket she tried to draw him a little nearer, and he had to quickstep to keep his balance. He was right: there was a sensation of danger here, of closing her eyes as she let her body drop through the air towards someone who might not put their arms out in time. But the sensation was so close to flying: how could she resist? How could she tell the difference unless she gave in to it? And it came not only from the sexual source he might have thought, but from the dark, floundering place of not really knowing, tonight, who she was, and the urge to confide that in someone else as a way of learning. The feeling of tenderness and nausea in her throat came not from some kind of residual primal fear (as there had been with Shane), of what happened, body to body, when you followed this kind of scene through, but from fear of how he'd react when she said, 'But what does older and younger really mean? You know what? When I try to write songs, I feel really old inside. Like I've seen everything in some other life, and music brings it back.'

His frown set. 'You've really got no idea what you're getting yourself into, do you?'

'Into you?'

He looked at her as if she'd just stepped into brighter light, yet he still couldn't be sure he recognised her. 'Look. I could be a madman. An axe murderer. Have all sorts of . . .' he hesitated '. . . issues. Or unexpected habits.' He gave a short, barking laugh, but when she merely blinked at him, he sighed a little. 'Okay, here. Let's just say, at the most, I would like to see you again, but another time. Sober. Maybe for a coffee. And maybe we can . . . discuss a couple of things.'

'Somewhere in town?'

'Yeah. Or maybe we could go to a movie, head out for a coffee, meet at one our flats first, whatever suits.'

They went back into the pub, just in time to hear that the red silk crew had won best overall band, and The Raggedies had won a prize for best composition. Everyone in the band — and even Lewis — was jubilant for her, but Candy only half let herself register the news: afraid to start hoping too soon. She didn't want to freshen her recent disappointment, which surely would happen if she flung herself right back into her passion before her hands were fully healed, even if she were only writing songs. For how would it feel not to be able to play any new material? And there was something else conveniently in the foreground right now, to help distract her. That single vague arrangement with Lewis, a hazy maybe in a night of grand confusion, was all it took for Candy to be propelled into a manic, rash, headlong change. *One of our flats*: a fleeting assumption that worked away like a flash flood at the expectations that family — and Candy — had for the path her next year or so had been going to follow.

LEWIS BECAME THE unwitting filter for everything she did next. The encounter with him had been about stepping outside girlhood boundaries. It was about shaking off family like shattered chips of shell; trying to race ahead of the feeling that she was a shadow.

She phoned Lewis soon after the band quest night, only to have him say he was heading up north to see relations for a fortnight, and that he then had a set of exams for his economics papers, so would have to take a rain check on that coffee until things had settled down for him. Her heart and stomach had clenched up tight, snails jabbed in their softest quarters. She tried to effect his own blasé tone, even as she said, 'I don't get to see you for a whole fortnight plus? That sucks.'

'Yeah, sorry, but I'm really stressed out about these exams. I barely made terms on two of the papers — had a shitty semester, all kinds of drama.'

The silence on the telephone wire almost singed with her wish to know more. What did *shitty* and *drama* mean? Her mind angled and tiptoed to try to find a way to snooker herself back into his immediate future. 'Hey, Lewis? You know what this whole bad hands thing has taught me, though?'

'Oh, yeah, sorry, your hands: how are they, first?'

'Oh — better, I think. The physio I'm going to helps. He's doing research into this kind of problem, and it's good that someone takes it seriously. Plus not playing so intensively for a while is probably helping. But I can still feel it all kick in when I do stupid little things — you know, play with a pen, twiddle my hair. That's honestly the main thing I have to watch out for right now.'

Remotely, she realised she was babbling but she couldn't find the brakes. 'You know, I'll be watching TV or reading a book and somewhere deep down I guess I'm still super-super restless. I find my head's wandered off onto a series of chords, or how some words fit together, like I might hear someone say, 'shed any light', and I'm imagining a glasshouse, you know a shed that's all light, and wondering how I could get that into a song, and *bam*, I discover I've been twisting my hair into little nodules all over my scalp, so it looks like I'm bristling with tuning keys, and my forearms and knuckles *really* hurt again. It's so trivial, such a dumb mundane little daily thing, I mean, it's not like I'm ferrying water from a village pump for my sick, starving children, is it? But it means I can't do what I really want to do. And how can I change something so unconscious — shave my head? I could have a really ugly skull.'

How long had she prattled on for? She felt like an FBI plant in a movie, saying any old crap that came to mind, keeping some culprit, some kidnapper, on the line so the call could be traced. Lewis the safe-thief, the heart-felon. But what was that? The sound of him laughing. Was what she said funny? Who cared? The sound of his voice, right up close, was a breakthrough.

'Anyway, I was saying. This bad arm thing?'

'Yeah?'

'Well, it's taught me that you have to take time out. That is, *you* have to take time out. You can't go at it hard all the time.'

'You said you were seventeen, right? Sure you didn't get that wrong? You sound more like thirty-seven, forty-seven.'

'You're not saying I sound like your mother, are you?'

He laughed again. 'Hell no. My mother would be afraid of you.'

She savoured that: like a pig in a mud bath laced with food scraps.

'So . . .'

'So, shall we say I'll call you when I get back from seeing my folks?'

'Okay. And if you don't, I'll be on to you. Dragging you out to something hideously time-consuming, like a movie or something.'

He gave another startled laugh, which told Candy he had no idea what to make of her — but at least he was still intrigued.

After he had hung up, at first she felt a creeping, egotistical disappointment that could have grown into full-blown dismay. First, rejection from Shane — and even though she'd been unsure of him it had still hurt, somehow. Selfish, but it had. And now, another guy — who wasn't *dying* to see her. Wasn't cancelling his trip home, flunking his exams, or asking her to go *with* him to see his family, or at least asking her to drill him on his study notes: like all the big-toothed, clean-haired, high school and university students in TV sitcoms did, kissing over the textbooks. Before she fell asleep each night she churned out version after version of how she'd meet up with him again, what it would be like, what he'd say, she'd say, he'd say, she'd say (*he'd* say, *he'd* say, *he'd* say). After watching countless episodes of her own private soap she gradually lit on the fact that his absence could be the ideal opportunity to hatch a new Candy: the one their first encounter had seemed to make possible. Time to hustle up a job, a flat — because, quite bluntly, she simply couldn't imagine taking Lewis home, to her family house, and there — in its ordinary, habitual spaces — managing to find the mystery he'd held in a tiny city park one whisky-tinted night.

All the new reactions competing in her seemed so tangible sometimes, it felt as if she would split the very air around her, as physically as a child outgrowing shoes and clothes. She was moving out, she said. Getting a job, getting a small room in a cheap flat, delaying university for a year. She and her parents argued bitterly about the sudden-sprung plans.

'Where has all this come from?' asked Rose. 'You've had a pretty rough time recently, and you've still got exams, Candy. Do you really think you should be leaping into such big changes before you've got yourself back on your feet again?'

'This *is* getting back on my feet again.'

'No, it's not. It's rushing into things, love.'

Candy lashed out with a tongue that felt alien to her own mouth: cruel to be kind, in order that her family, too, would want to be done with her, so that when she did leave they'd be relieved. She said some things she was shocked and ashamed of later, but at the time all she thought was that they would work.

Robinson tried to help Rose lead Candy back. 'You're too young, Candy, too inexperienced.'

'What better way to get experience?'

'I'm just not sure a year off before university is such a good idea.'

'But at least I'll be getting all that extra experience, right?'

'How can you be sure you'll find work?'

'Because I've done it already. Music store part time.'

She relished the stunned blank on his face. 'That won't be enough to live off, will it?'

'And doing hostessing at a restaurant, three nights a week as well. Why don't you ever give me credit for having some intelligence?'

'*Hostessing*? That sounds like . . . like . . . an escort service!'

Candy felt a rush of new indignation. 'I meet people at the door, check to see whether we have tables available, then show them in. So I don't have to worry about carrying plates and stuff while my hands are still dodgy. And in the record shop I'm working with someone else on the counter. They've said they'll try to minimise what I have to do manually there too. It'll mainly be answering queries and showing people around the different sections.'

'But . . . but what if you lose interest in going to university altogether?'

'Yeah, how will that reflect on you, Dad? What will you tell your friends?'

'That's enough. That's not why I want you to go to university.'

'Isn't the point whether or not *I* want to go to university?'

'Look. Have you sat down and talked to your brother about this? He's taking a sensible route. He could advise you. The thing is, Candy, at your age, you don't really know what you want.'

Jeff looked torn, but said, 'You know, you could wait till I start university. We could flat-hunt together.'

Robinson nodded. 'We'd be more than happy to help you out financially if you decided to share. It seems a great idea, striking out together. Side by side in it all: a great support.'

Candy talked over him. 'If Jeff can know what he wants, so can I. And I *do* know what I want! I want to get away from people who keep ordering me around, who think that their choices should be the ones everyone else makes. Who think Jeff and I are some kind of two-headed oddity, or that their daughters aren't half as good as their sons.'

She could see Robinson's arm was rigid as he pointed at her, while Rose watched her with an expression not unlike that of someone eyeing a prodigiously large spider edging its legs around a door-frame.

'Now, look. We treat you children equally. We've given you everything. When have I ever implied those comparisons with your brother? You name one single date.'

'August 1, 1970. August 2, 1970. August 3, 1970 . . .'

Her parents' anger didn't frighten her, because underneath all this she could see they were hurt and, at some level, knew it meant they loved her. And that gave her a sense of mission, of power: at once euphoric and guilt-ridden. It was like a bruise some peculiar part of her wanted to keep pressing, to confirm it, to measure and remeasure the injury she could do.

Robinson was ready to boil over but must have been wise to the way she was feeding off his mood, stoking the coals of her own self-righteousness, as he briefly tried another tack, asking calmly, 'And how will you choose a flat?'

'Look in the paper.'

Even Rose couldn't last. 'But . . . with strangers? Honestly, love. Why don't you wait until your brother or a friend or two are ready to set up with you? Otherwise you won't know what kind of people you could end up living with.'

'I didn't have much choice here either, did I?'

'It's *you* we're thinking of, Candy. You don't know how people can hurt a young girl.'

'Don't I?'

The heavy implication a lie. Or worse, a half-lie, but there was enough slanted fact in the bridling outburst to make it sound like a home truth. Her whole family stood there, mouths agape, as if she were a tidal wave they'd only just seen coming, and it was take a breath now or go right under: founder, flounder.

While other seventh-formers were isolating themselves in their studies for Bursary or Scholarship, Candy was flat-hunting. Jeffrey and her friends at school had became increasingly preoccupied with Attic vases, Shakespeare, Roman politics, calculus, quadratics, cellular biology, Sylvia Plath or organic chemistry; Candy felt suspended in a separate, distant bubble. They all seemed to think that the difference between 65 percent and 85 percent would be the difference between swimming in the real world and plummeting through it like an anvil dropped in water. Candy felt she had much more difficult things to master. The logistics of working out income and expenditure worried her far more than the thought of whether or not she'd recognise the reproduction of a Dürer print in her art history exam. And in fact, for the first time, study actually felt like leisure and pleasure: an escape from nagging doubts. The knowledge that she had taken this moonleap into self-sufficiency gave her more focus than parental nudgings ('Should you really be watching TV?') or fraternal wind-ups ('Aren't you stressing about Bursary? I'm so stressed out about Bursary. I don't know how you can't be stressing about Bursary!') ever had.

In those initial weeks of juggling her two new jobs, fitting last-minute swot into spare corners of the day or night, quietly assessing how her hands were mending (she had special dispensation to sit her exams in a private room at school, where she was going to dictate her answers to an official amanuensis), Candy felt on a constant high. As if she'd won the lottery, or fallen for the world all over again. Every night she slipped into bed with a small internal cheer: *I did it. I did it.*

The flat she chose was about the sixth she'd looked at. As soon as she saw it she wanted to move in. Outside, over the ground-floor veranda, a line of green, powder blue and yellow Chinese paper lanterns swung in the wind. They made the house, which was set on a hill with a clear view of the city and harbour, seem only briefly anchored there: a great wooden ship, its masts rigged out with lights. She found out that the only room available was the turret room at the top. When she said, 'No kidding? But why hasn't anyone already taken it?' she was warned that the roof was sometimes home to wildlife — birds, possums, rodents — that made the easy migration from the town's green belt, which backed right onto the ramshackle building's chaotic rear garden: wildlife the landlord was often slow to do anything about. Also, in winter it got bitterly cold up there — it wasn't insulated, and the sash windows were rotting, gappy, rattled in the slightest wind. She could tell that the cramped, hexagonal space was going to be a headache to fit even her sparse furniture into (the gear from her childhood bedroom, taken on extended loan from her now exhausted and resigned parents, on the promise that she'd return it all as soon as she could afford to buy her own). But the view from the turret room — of rooftops, pedestrians and, in the distance, more hills and the sea — along with the feeling of seclusion, had seduced her instantly.

At the interview she sat on the edge of the living-room couch, wanting her performance to call on the same kind of bouncing, sequined energy she might have summoned for a Raggedies gig, if she'd been able to play.

There seemed to be four other current flatmates and a number of hangers-on: passing a joint, drinking coffee, reading the newspaper or the album notes from second-hand Bob Dylan records someone pulled out from a plastic bag printed with the logo *Vinyl*

Offer. Hmmmm. There was a back-cataloguist in their midst: someone into more than the latest top ten. Candy felt something like a trill start at the back of her throat. As she breathed in, to quieten herself down, she caught a full swipe of the flat's lingering, sweetish smell: marijuana, old beer, and the large rubbish bags in the corridor, which brimmed with bottles, cans, crushed paper plates and a few soaked, torn paper lanterns like the ones outside.

Seeing her glance at the black polythene sacks, one of the flatmates explained, 'House-warming'. It was the petite woman — Jayshri — who, underneath the grey woollen coat she still wore inside, was dressed in various shades of green, her swing shirt glinting with tiny oval mirrors sewn into the fabric. She seemed to be some kind of unofficial spokesperson for everyone gathered there. 'We've had a party for each flatmate who's moved in.'

'Oh, right. Wow!'

Everyone blinked at Candy with the same slow measure. She immediately felt too loud, too big. She'd already found out all there was to know about rent and bills, so waited for the others to start asking questions. There was a silence in which she was able to take in the posters that were sellotaped and pinned all over the walls like a community noticeboard at a library or café: Vote Green, various New Zealand bands she had in her own record collection, ads for theatre and dance productions, protest marches calling for education reform, homosexual law reform, anti-vivisection, Reclaim the Night, anti-nuclear causes, free higher education, anti-Apartheid, cannabis law reform, and in the corner, an undressed shop mannequin, painted silver, wearing a plastic tiara and carrying a handmade cardboard sign that said 'Depicted at Half Natural Size'.

The walls were practically a job description: advertising some of the basic qualities you'd need to fit in. Compared with other flats she'd seen — the one where two sisters collected the kinds of rotating musical dolls in hats and crinolines that Candy had stopped thinking were beautiful when she was about twelve, or the flat where a chef and a paint salesman had *Penthouse* and *Playgirl* pin-ups in the toilet, commando posters in the living room, and showed her their shared train set project in the garage, or the flat where the overweight, gloomy older couple had expected her to sit down to a full roast meal at two o'clock as part of the interview, and told her she'd not be allowed men in her room, nor be let into the house if she ever came home after eleven pm without her keys — this flat offered a little slice of a lively-minded utopia: or at least a sub-set of people idealistic enough to believe in trying to build one. They were all watching her take in the setting.

'Great selection of posters,' she said, and could see a layer of guardedness dissolve on some of the faces around her.

Jayshri's constant animation had her shifting restlessly on the chair opposite Candy, the coat falling open to show hand mending: a tangle of bright, multi-coloured threads along the inside bottom hem, and a similar scrawl of stitches behind each button: red, yellow, green, white, blue. It looked as complicated as the wires in an old switchboard. And as Jayshri blurted questions, nodded vigorously at Candy's answers, all the while fiddling with cigarette papers, a tin of reddish tobacco and a metal tool that helped to streamline roll-your-owns, it did seem as if a high-voltage energy — barely contained in her small frame — were constantly being channelled around and through her.

'So you say this is the first time you've gone flatting?'

'Yes, it is, I —'

'You at university?'

'No, no I've just got Bursary exams to go, and I'm also working part time.' Candy nodded to Jayshri's nod. 'University next year.'

The whole room nodded with them.

'Are you into arts or sciences?'

'Arts?' The rising inflection gave away the hope that her answer would still get her the place in the flat.

'They haven't got you on youth rates at your job, have they?'

'I —'

'Look into it, make sure. Kick up a stink if they have, yeah? Equal pay for equal work.' A few of the others nodded again, earnestly mumbled yeses.

209

'So,' Jayshri frowned with — Candy thought — a diagnostic eye, 'is your family from here?'

Dispirited, wishing she could claim *I have Romany blood, I have Spanish blood, I have Cherokee in me* . . . she said, 'My dad's English, actually. But he's lived here since the sixties.'

'But I mean, they live in town?'

Candy blushed. She'd thought because Jayshri seemed perhaps part Indian — although her accent was as Kiwi as Candy's . . . she stared into her coffee mug, thinking maybe she shouldn't have said yes to the fifth or sixth coffee at her fourth interview that afternoon: she had a racing heart and could feel her face flush not just with a sensation of heat but of building pressure. She imagined it, red as a stop light at a railway crossing, telling the assorted flatmates *Danger! Nice but dim! Do not pass go, do not collect $200 bond!*

'Yeah, they are. They actually just live a half-hour bus ride away.' The shame.

'Oh, right, right. Big family?'

'No, there's just me, Mum and Dad, and my brother.'

'Older or younger?'

'My brother?' So many questions, Candy wondered if she'd given the right — or 'right-on' — answer to any of them. Were only people from big families wanted here? Is that why the lounge seemed to be so crowded?

She swallowed some more coffee, despite herself, to score some time. 'Same age, actually. We're twins.'

Sigh. There it was. The frisson of interest, of livening around the room, and, in Jayshri's case, an odd, sudden stillness. Candy gave a sulky glare at her feet. Before they'd found out anything else about her they thought her claim to uniqueness was doubleness: her relationship to Jeff, which seemed to question the very idea of uniqueness. She was a curiosity only because she was one of two.

Jayshri's fingers rested on the cigarette-rolling device but her eyes snapped so visibly it seemed they reflected fire, though the room was lit only by pigeon-grey, late afternoon daylight. 'Twins,' she said. Then, across the small portion of carpet between the sofa and chair, a hand darted out and tapped Candy's wrist. 'That's *lucky*.'

'I guess so,' she replied, awkwardly, not wanting to contradict when she was up for selection, and already succumbing to the force of Jayshri's personality.

Her first impressions of Jaysh would endure. She always seemed to be on the way somewhere else, her mind crackling, sparking, five leaps ahead of you. Everyone admired and adored her, because 'She's a little crazy, and very ballsy,' as another new flatmate, Nash, would say. He told Candy — with an air of secrecy, of having himself felt bestowed with an honour in being told — that on one side she came from a third-generation Indian family who'd done extremely well in property investment and ran a chain of shops around the country and in Australia, which sold saris, sari petticoats, kurtas, incense, jewellery, Bollywood videos, ornaments, rolls of bright silks, satins, cottons. And that some of the overseas extended family disapproved of Jaysh's father not insisting she went into an arranged marriage, but that her dad — who wanted her to go to university — agreed to let her find her own husband, as he'd married a Kiwi woman himself. Unreal things were always happening to Jaysh, said Nash. But Candy felt that it was more that she carried the aura that just by being around her, you'd experience some stir, sooner or later. The cluster of followers Candy caught sight of that day at the interview trailed after Jaysh with a slightly hungry, questing look that at first made Candy think maybe they were all a little in love with her. Which they probably were. Men and women alike waited to be selected from the crowd, and sometimes Jaysh's own attentions were ambiguous enough for Candy to wonder how she'd manage telling her parents that she didn't want to find any particular man for any kind of marriage at all.

It turned out that it wasn't just sexual attraction that drew people to Jaysh: she was also almost a kind of political leader to them all. The group of people that hovered around her weren't really members of anything specific, though many of them drifted around the fringes of already very fringy eco-anarcho-socialist fusions. But — at least when they were drunk or hung-over — they wanted to believe themselves to be the start of a movement, a new political will. They talked about their present conditions — paying nominal rents in condemned warehouses or substandard houses, using the university clubrooms for meetings, sneaking use of the photocopiers at work or in their university departments for the production of fliers or leaflets — the way musicians joked, when drunk, about how maybe if they hit big time, their dingy rehearsal rooms could be turned into a tourist spot in fifty years; or the way aspiring artists and writers joked, when also drunk, that their little fist of friends knuckled together in the snug of a bar was a future southern version of the Blue Mountain group, or, if they were bouncing overseas and back, the Lost Generation . . .

Initially Candy took it all very seriously, reading the leaflets and photocopied newsletters strewn around the living room, joining the shopworkers' union, listening in on conversations, buying a copy of the *Communist Manifesto* and reading it in her room with a bike light under the blankets in case anyone knocked on the door because she'd have been ashamed to admit she'd only just learned the tract even existed. But then, perhaps just six weeks into her time at the flat, there would be an incident with a man.

He'd come down from Hamilton with his girlfriend for what Jaysh and her crowd called a 'sit-sesh': a weekend of sitting and brainstorming at the student union, smoking, sucking on endless cups of coffee, talking, swapping photocopied material that argued the pros and cons of different party political positions, and always with the same thin, long-haired, bearded, bespectacled American PhD student who would fidget in his chair, then rocket up, arms pushing away the air on certain words, as he reddened and yelled, 'How can anyone still *believe* in communism after Khrushchev, and the Twentieth Congress, and the revelations about Stalin? This is the *1980s*, for Christ's sake! Is this *brain*-forsaken country really so *stuck* in the *1950s*? Wake up!' But instead of provoking fury, he made everyone rally: people who'd been slumped in their chairs sat up, butted in on each other, gabbled and grinned. Once people were back at the flat the talks carried on late into the night, over big pots of vegetarian chilli or pasta bakes, casks of cheap wine.

It was at one of these communal dinners that Candy stood with the Hamilton man, listening to him, asking him questions, and he said to her, 'Yeah, I'd bear arms. You can't have political power without bearing arms. You can't win food for the poor from the rich without bearing arms. The bloody revolution has to come. The night of long knives won't be turned back.' And she, a little drunk, believed in his passion for freedom and justice, felt it soar in her too, on the throb of cheap alcohol — although weapons, war, killing, were so far removed from her experience that fear made her mind contract, turn to shelter in something anodyne, everyday: the snapped-off element dial on the gas cooker, the black and red stripes on a box of Beehive matches. She felt the man's fingers touch at her waist, then rest on her hip as he stressed his points about apartheid, the British working class, the people of Latin America and what the European had raped of their lives centuries ago, how the drug barons were raping the people still. All the while his hands, choosing just which words to touch her on, were gently, expertly printing out a subtext: *she* was weak, ineffectual, naïve, all the things he'd despise. Then the man's girlfriend appeared beside them and his hands moved unselfconsciously from Candy's body to pour himself more wine.

Late that night she'd had to make her way to the downstairs toilet. Some drugged-out git had blocked the one upstairs by trying to flush the crumpled-up pages of the daily paper, which, they'd shouted, was 'Juss another part of the capitalist plop!' (Jaysh dragging on his arm and saying, 'I don't call blocking your friends' bog a very effective protest effort, y'dipshit.') On her way through the corridor downstairs Candy had heard voices from the bedroom the Hamilton man was borrowing from one of her absent flatmates. A woman's voice, quiet, even-toned. And his: strident. Light from the room they were in lay neatly — incongruously — in the shape of a geometry set-square over the corridor. Candy looked through the half-open door, already mumbling a brief, 'Gidday' so they'd know she was there, not see her only after she'd flitted by and imagine she'd been eavesdropping.

'How can you be such a cunt?' she heard. 'I know how you talked to him. *Slut.*' And she saw the back of his hand, up and across, while at his mouth sat the same mild irritation of someone who'd batted away a stinging insect. Only, the woman's head had sprung back and now she held her cheekbone, expression dazed and anxious. She turned and caught sight of Candy, then tried to step out of view. The man saw Candy then too, and came up, ready to close the door.

'I'm sorry,' he said. Though not to the girlfriend: not to her. 'A mistake. I'm sorry.' Then he drew the door shut. By the time Candy got up the next morning — after what seemed like a full night of lying in bed with her heart catapulting, wondering what she should have done — they were gone. So too were the roasted and ground Trade Aid coffee beans Candy had bought for Jaysh's birthday, the last of the strawberry jam Nash's mother had given the flat, and two whole French loaves bought with the last of that week's household grocery money.

'Pricks,' said Jaysh when she found out: although it sounded admiring, mildly amused.

Candy still listened to the ideas of Jayshri's crowd after that, even sometimes felt the same uprush of conviction for what they believed in. But the disciple's fervour, the craving for blueprints, unbending solutions, which she'd felt in the first six weeks of flatting there, could never ignite after that night. She bluffly told Jaysh she'd stopped attending the Students for Socialism meetings because she was still defining her beliefs, so couldn't come down hard for any political group. 'But that's why we debate these things, Candy,' Jaysh said. 'Everything's open to redefinition.'

'Yeah,' Candy said, 'I know, but I'm just not ready to be part of any . . . faction just yet.' She said it was because she was trying out, for the first time, what it was like just to be 'one'. She'd always been seen as part of a unit, a member of something greater in number than herself: only not by choice. And knowing Candy meant because she'd always been a twin, Jaysh sucked her bottom lip thoughtfully, brown eyes shimmering, and let Candy be. Even though Nash, who'd overheard, had coughed on his Bell Tea until it came out his nose, and said, 'That's worse than pop psychology, Candy. That's . . . *muzak* psychology.'

Yet the only real embarrassment she felt was in using the twins excuse with Jaysh. Twins were Jayshri's kryptonite. On the afternoon of Candy's flat interview, Jayshri had said, 'I should show you up to the room one more time before you go.' Candy had already hoped, from the silent exchange of smiles that sifted through the room, that she had a chance. And being allowed to look over the room again implied the choice was really hers now.

Upstairs, the flat seemed to be the reverse of the Tardis. Outside, it had appeared huge, ramshackle: perhaps it had once been a small, respectable boarding house for ladies of independent means, or a grand family home at the start of the twentieth century. Now it was well known, among a certain social group, as a transition zone for students, or other young singles on low incomes. Although there were high-stud ceilings for the four ground-floor rooms, somehow the top level — which contained a small lounge, the kitchen, one of the bathrooms and two bedrooms — was narrow, cramped and dark. People turned sideways to give each other room, even before they got to the etiolated stairwell that led to the turret. As Candy and Jaysh stood in the elevated hexagonal box, looking out at the distant, still harbour, its grey hue tinted with the yellow sunset as if it were soaking up the spillage, they both went quiet and just gazed for a while. Gradually the reflection of the interior of the room, their two faces side by side, began to fill up the windows, blotting out the harbour. When Jaysh spoke, her voice seemed to cause ripples over the image.

'So do you think you'll miss your brother?'

The question seemed so out of context that Candy had to consciously rewind what had been said and listen to it again. Then she felt a pinch of annoyance that it had been asked. It was something she hadn't let herself dwell on at all, thinking that now she was ready to make the break herself, it would be different: the tension between them as teenagers meaning their separation wouldn't be at all like the gnawing dismay Jeff's absence had left when they were small.

She shrugged. 'He's not far away.'

Jayshri was still turned to the window opposite, as if watching the harbour, but Candy could feel her stare trained on their reflections.

'I think I'd miss him,' said Jayshri, 'if I were you.'

It sounded like an instruction.

And Jaysh did turn businesslike after that, one hand out to show Candy to the door as she said, 'It's getting pretty cold in here. I guess you must have other places to look at.'

Candy followed her lead, cooling off a little. 'Yeah, I do. Shall I call you, or do you want to call me?'

'Oh, well.' Both hands in her pockets, she opened out her coat a little, showing the scrambled mending threads, the pink satin of its lining, like a flash of vulnerable underbelly. 'See who gets in first, I guess.'

Jaysh did: phoning Candy the following night, saying, yeah, everyone liked her, thought she'd fit in pretty well: better than the neo-fascisto rugby head and the Young Nat marketing student they'd just had through, that was for sure! Candy went limp with relief, but also felt an odd gallop of stage fright. To Jaysh's set, everyone seemed to come with a label: to declare themselves as blatantly as a pair of jeans hoisted its tiny red bum-flag. *Neo-fascisto; Young Nat* . . . Could you give yourself away even if you weren't too sure what that self was? Then again, maybe these people who seemed so sure of how to name and place others would help her sort out the tangle in her that already wore the label Candy Marshall.

So she moved her gear in, with the help of a gnarled, tree stump of a man who was half her height but five times her strength. When she apologised for how little she could do because of her still-mending forearms, and for the number of stairs, he told her not to worry, he'd done far worse, and you could carry just about any amount of weight on your back. He'd taken a grand piano up a spiral staircase that way, on his own. 'It's all in the strapping on, love,' he said. 'If you've strapped it right, *you'll* be right.' Though he was bowed under a chest of drawers at the time, peering out from under it like a canny turtle, the angle of knees and elbows gave the impression of wink and nudge. Candy felt she'd been entrusted with a trade secret, and that — though she didn't plan to spend her life hoisting heavy furniture on her back — she probably ought to tip him for letting her in on it. When she refused to take her change, he looked confused. 'No, it's forty dollars, love. Like the ad says: one man, one truck, forty bucks. That's the deal. You'll never get on in life if you go throwing it around like that.' He folded his bills meticulously, lining them up edge to edge, corner to corner, readjusting the central fold when the ends didn't quite match. 'You've got to be *careful* with money.' He touched the squared bills to his forehead, then held them towards her. 'Good fortune,' he said, and trundled himself off to his truck.

Something about his permanently furniture-stooped posture, his deeply tanned, lined face, and his role of ferryman — helping her cross over from the suburban sticks to this central other-world — made it seem like the wisdom of a monk. It was a message. She vowed to get herself a 3B4 notebook, draw up columns and write entries in religiously: all the dollars and cents for chewing gum, cassette tapes, new socks, electricity, two weeks of rent in advance, lipstick, bath towel, new guitar strings, music manuscript paper . . . God, the little man was right: you had to be *careful.* She folded up the change he gave her, edge to edge, touched it to her forehead, and saluted the room. 'Good fortune,' she said, grinning.

Once she had all the boxes and furniture in her room — her body aching already and still all the unpacking to do — Jaysh tapped on the door, bringing in two mugs of coffee. She was in her trademark colour: emerald green glass nose-stud, forest green velvet shirt that came down mid-thigh to her grass-green leggings. On anyone else as thin as Jayshri the colour would have looked froggy, insectile. Instead, she seemed to bring the word *willowy* into the room as clearly as a nineteenth-century painting of an allegory announces its subject. 'Thought you might like a break,' she said. ''Cause I seem to remember from your interview that there's something up with your arms and — ' she raised a cup — 'that you take it strong and white.' She set the coffee down on the floor and wedged herself in, cross-legged, between two boxes, one eyebrow arched mischievously. 'Like your men?'

Candy turned her surprised laugh into a puff to cool down her drink. 'Not really sure how I take my men.'

'So no boyfriend at the moment? I'm assuming you're het.'

'Errr, no, I'm not too bothered.'

'You're bi?'

'What?'

'You said you're not het.'

Candy frowned at her. 'Not too angry, no.'

Jaysh pulled her chin in, reminding Candy of the little guy from childhood TV: *Different Strokes*. 'What're you talking about?'

'You mean het up, right? So no, I'm not too het up about it.'

Jaysh sealed her lips, but the pulses of laughter moved through her small frame like an egg swallowed by a cartoon snake.

Candy looked from side to side of the room. 'What?'

'Het. As in hetero*sexual*. You know, attracted to the opposite sex.'

'Oh, *that* het.'

The corners of Jaysh's smile tweaked. 'So, no guys on the scene?' But Candy had drifted away slightly: the thought of Lewis had already expanded the fabric of her heart like a breeze in a sail, or perhaps the air in an accordion, as she couldn't trust what note her voice would hit even with a word as short as 'no'. The two sat in a slightly uncertain silence for a while, coffee sips measuring it out audibly.

'How about you?' Candy said, eventually. 'Are you seeing someone?'

'Just casually. Might call it off, though. Won't have much time for it next year — I've got lots of extra study plans and so on.' Jaysh's unsmiling nod left Candy glad she hadn't even hinted anything about Lewis: although the mere thought of him — after only one encounter and one phone call — left her feeling raw and overturned. It was the stuff of schoolgirl crushes next to Jaysh's unmoved detachment.

She covered these thoughts by peeling up the packing tape from one of her boxes and beginning to unload some of the items: fiction, photo albums, trinkets, sheet music: resting between each object, doing wrist twirls and hand stretches, which made Jayshri's eyebrows lift slowly, like two sleek, groomed, miniature cats wondering whether to pounce on something that's roused their skittishness. Before she could tease, though, Candy explained, 'This is going to be a tedious job. Like I said, I've sort of injured my hands from too much guitar playing.'

'Yeah, you mentioned it.'

'It's not going to be a problem — around the flat, I mean. It's not going to be permanent.' She twirled her wrists again, and Jayshri imitated it, built on it: a flourishing, curlicued dance, her head, neck and shoulders turning, lifting in accompaniment. She laughed at Candy's wonderment.

'You're really good at that,' Candy said.

'Nuh-uh, little honky girl, I'm not. My aunt — *she's* good. I just fake it.' She shuffled onto her knees. 'So've you asked anyone to help you unpack?'

'Oh — my family wanted to, but I said I'd be okay. I can just take it slowly.'

'I'll help for a while if you like. I've got a Pols essay I should be doing, but I'd rather talk it than write it, you know? Which means right now even cockroach eradication would seem like a majorly attractive option.'

Candy picked up a painted papier mâché hen-shaped container from the bottom of her crate, opened it, shook it out. 'No bugs in here, sorry.'

Jaysh's self-contained smile was one that Candy didn't quite know how to decipher. Her thin fingers, with their nails varnished iridescent green, ran over the imitation gold that stated *Photo Album* on the spine of one of Candy's books. 'Mind if I have a look?' she said. But while Candy was still bobbing forward, saying, 'Ummm,' wondering what embarrassments were between its red covers (some of the albums held photos, and others her own handwritten song lyrics, clippings from magazines about her favourite musicians, or the copied-out words of admired songs), Jaysh had flipped it open and turned through some of the heavy, plastic-coated leaves. And there were all the old family photos: Jeff and Candy so often side by side, dressed in similar, genderless clothing up until they were fifteen or so: muted blues, jeans and jerseys, Bata Bullet sneakers. Candy felt a squirming embarrassment at the haircuts, the hand-knitted woollens Rose had so lovingly, laboriously made, the goofy smiles, the primary-coloured ordinariness, the poses at tourist spots (Rotorua, Taupo, Mansfield's birthplace, the Punakaiki Rocks, Moeraki Boulders) that probably replicated thousands of other family albums around the country, north and south. Part of her wished, now, that Jaysh had stumbled on the song-writing files instead: the sheaves of secret dreams, the life that both translated and leapt beyond the pictures framed in the family albums. She could hear one of them in her head already, as if the album were like a trick greeting card that played a tune as soon as it was opened. It was one the other Raggedies had hated, saying it was fruity nonsense.

When we were small
our thoughts were tall
with stories
and we believed
belief alone could make them swing
in the open loft of the piney tree
that simmered in summer
with the coo-coo of birds,
the frou-frou of their feathers;
the sound they made
pinned the sun to our backs
like a Pan-boy's shadow

and our plump hearts sat perched
in our ribs' ship masts
watching for where the days would land us

and what do you know
what do you know
we were already there
so longing ago

Oh Jesus, be it photos or song lyrics, hide the bloody thing, quick. But her embarrassment and dissatisfaction were halted by Jaysh's expression. Her head was bowed on her thin neck like a sunflower; something luminous seemed to come off the page and cover her face. Candy shuffled nearer, curiosity making her look at the photos as hard as Jaysh was, though she knew them better than her own face now: which surprised her in the mirrors in this flat, with the new angles that the day's excitement seemed to lend her.

With the tip of a finger Jaysh smoothed out a bubble in the protective plastic over one of the more recent pictures of Candy and Jeff. 'Your brother,' she said, with a tone of slow realisation. 'I guess you hear this all the time — but you're very alike, aren't you?'

'Not in personality.'

'Really?'

'Hope not.'

Jayshri stayed gazing at the picture. 'So what's he like, then? Is he the total opposite of you?'

'It's not that simple.' Candy pulled the album away from her, pretending it wasn't rudeness, but the wish to start filling the small, hip-level wooden bookcase she'd taken from home. When she turned back from her brisk arranging of books and objects on the bottom shelf, a small gate of surprise slid open to see Jaysh still sitting, cross-legged, arms around her knees, with one of the photos held up to the light. She must have slipped it out of the album. She examined it as if her vision were trying to distinguish between shades too subtle for the small scale. On her face was an expression that gave Candy the same dipping sense as plangent, baroque chords heard at a distance on a clear, wintry day.

'Are you okay?'

Jaysh slipped the photo back onto the pile of albums. 'Sort of.

Wait a mo?' She loped out of the room and Candy heard her trot down the stairs, and, through the hollowness of the upper storey's small chambers, heard a scuffle and clink in the kitchen on the second floor before her quick footsteps slowed down for the tread back up to Candy's room. She brought in a half-full vodka bottle, coated in a thin sheet of ice from the freezer, a half-full lemonade bottle, a small, puckered lemon, a knife and two thick brown Pyrex mugs. 'A drink will help us relax into this unpacking thing, eh?'

Candy shrugged, wiped her palms on her trousers. 'Sure.'

When Jaysh had poured them both vodka and lemonades, topped with thick lemon-slice hats — a drink she called Dancing Cossacks — she just leaned against one of the sash windows, watching as Candy opened further boxes and tried to focus on creating a logical order in which to tackle the contents. Candy was sure Jaysh had left something dangling and unspoken when she hurried down to get the spirit and mixer. First of all she felt at a loss in the seeping silence, then a little irritated that Jaysh was still hanging around if she wasn't genuinely going to help. But once her few possessions were unpacked, and the boxes folded, the drink fuzzled out her organisational mood. She was happy to relax into the Susie Jupiter tape Jaysh flipped into her tapedeck. Flushed and drowsy, both young women sat on the floor as Candy folded and sorted clothes, and leaned up against the single bed. Jaysh giggled.

'I read a review once that said the only thing that makes Susie Jupiter tolerable is that you just know her sincerity has to be an act, and she must go home after one of those acoustic gigs for S & M in a wild foursome.'

Candy found herself squeaking. 'I admire her! I admire what she does! A woman soloist, in the rock industry? I'd love to do that! How can you *laugh*? She's one of my sacred cows!' But the inelegant snort Jaysh gave was so incongruous that Candy knew she'd never be able to croon over Susie Jupiter alone in her room again. Suddenly all those teenage nights curled up next to a tapedeck, heart lonesome as a dog for the moon, felt easy to discard. She grinned at Jaysh. 'I guess I'm a bit of a sap underneath it all.'

'Underneath that serious, hardened exterior?'

'I have a serious, hardened exterior?'

Jaysh cackled, eyes bright with fun. 'Oh, impenetrable.'

Candy sighed. 'But I wouldn't mind being impenetrable. How do you get to be impenetrable?'

Jaysh shook her head. 'You don't really want to be. If you're impenetrable, nothing — no one — gets in. How boring would that be?'

The lines on her face were more pensive than her tone implied. When Candy glanced at her watch she was surprised to see that her first day in the new flat was almost over, though the shadow of a giant eucalyptus tree in the tangled back garden still washed over the floors, screening the early evening sunlight in branch patterns through the windows. But there was an odd lagging feeling now: that sense that Jaysh remained there — listlessly helping to shift piles of clothes onto the bed — because there was some topic still hovering in the margins of the room. Finally Candy decided to net it in: hunger made her want to get free to go downstairs and forage out some food from the stained, peeling kitchen cupboards. She chewed her lip and went over to her now fully stocked shelves, as if something there weren't quite fitting correctly. She moved her photo albums to another spot, knowing that the photo Jaysh had been transfixed by would slip loose, as she'd only rested it on the top of the pile.

Jaysh watched it drift to settle on the floor. Candy waited for her to feel her stare. When she looked up, Candy said directly, 'Was there something about that photo?'

Jaysh's eyelids flickered, her lips set in a small thread hole, like a child trying to whistle, to keep her courage up in an eerie passageway. Then she cleared her throat.

'The photo? Oh, yeah. I guess I was sort of interested in it. Or actually, interested, even when you came to the interview, in your, oh — I don't know.' Her eyes searched the small room, again giving an impression of fearfulness. She cleared her throat. 'It's just that it reminded me of something. I did this thing once — this stupid thing, superstitious mumbo jumbo stuff I guess, and first I was furious it had worked its way into my head.' She paused, so Candy nodded.

Jayshri ran a hand over her hair. 'Not sure why I'm telling you this. I must be drunk already.'

'I don't mind listening, if that's what you're worried about.'

Jayshri took another large swig of vodka. 'Anyway, I was having a really hard time — after a break-up with a guy, right? I probably wouldn't have done it otherwise: it was sort of just a time-filler, really. Maybe the whole episode wouldn't have bugged me if I'd been feeling normal.' She began to dig around in a small green velvet pouch which Candy only then realised was a cloth shoulder bag and not part of her shirt. She fished out her cigarette paraphernalia, which she toyed with as she spoke. 'But I was on holiday with some friends, travelling through Nelson on the way to the lakes. I couldn't really afford the break — I should have been looking for work, not taking a holiday. But the whole reason I was there was to try to get this man out of my head. Like that old fix-up for a broken heart — send someone away to help out on a farm, or to the seaside, or to another country. Which works, apparently: a guy I know in the Microbiology Department at uni, he says it's to do with pheromones. You get away from all the traces of those wicked seductive body chemicals that have permeated your clothes, your sheets, your cushions. Even your curtains, I guess, if the bastard was always the first one up, throwing them open until one morning he's saying, welcome to the day I dump your arse.'

Candy shifted on the spot, not sure what to say.

'Anyway, these friends and I had decided to have a rest stop at Tahuna Beach, and when we got there, there was a tiny travelling sort of . . . carnival thing set up on the grass. Not a circus, really — though there was a dancing monkey in a little tutu who did tricks on the back of an old white Shetland pony, two jugglers, and kids could go on donkey rides that were supervised by a couple of clowns. Real clowns, I mean: curly orange wigs, baggy pants, white faces, that sort of thing. There were candyfloss and hotdog stalls. And a few automated lucky-dip games: you know, where little kids get seduced to beg for fifty cents so they can try to control a metal claw inside a glass box full of teddy bears or baby dolls. And there was one gorgeous wooden gypsy caravan.'

Gypsy caravan. Candy's heart still swung on the description. It ran a film through her head of pictures she'd come across when researching her school project all those years ago: of red, green, yellow and blue lacquered wood, a little, worn step-ladder up to a door set with coloured leadlight panes, and inside — copper pots bubbling on the stove, armchair covered in embroidered fabric, gleaming eyes, pipe smoke, lavender. Childhood imagination already had her hooked on Jayshri's story.

'We were pretty cynical at first, of course. Gypsy schmipsy, like one guy in our group said — he was a Californian, a Jewish musicologist, here on teaching exchange. I'd sort of been hoping I'd hit it off with him — you know, imagined being whisked off to the US and being able to thumb my nose at ex-boyfriend from *Planet of the Apes*, with postcards from the Golden Gate bridge saying, "Having a wonderful life! So glad you're not here . . ." but, anyway. I digress.' She gave one of the elaborate hand flourishes she'd shown Candy before, who imitated it, to say, go on, I'm with you . . .

'There was a wooden sandwich board sign outside, advertising Palm Reading and Tarot Cards with Sweet Gypsy Rose.'

Candy felt expectation slump. 'Oh. So she *was* a fraud. That's just a Neil Diamond song.'

'Was she a fraud or was she giving people what they wanted? Is that fraudulent?'

Candy gazed at the ceiling, trying to read over the question, but Jayshri carried on.

'I think in the end I partly went in to the caravan as a protest against Yosef's sarcasm. He was going on at me about religion and superstition, opiate of the people, etcetera, etcetera, and I began to think, you bloody hypocrite. It hadn't taken me long to work out on that holiday that he'd be going back to California, Mom and Dad, finding himself a bride his own clan approved of. He said that was for family and culture, not for faith — which is fair enough, in itself, you know? But don't go on at me about the falseness of *other* people's creeds, that's all. Maybe she was a real Romany, maybe she'd built her whole life on trying to have a tradition miles from her own people. But how would we know unless we went in there?'

A rider in a saddle preparing for a long trip, Jayshri edged around to get more comfortable. 'Yosef said, "C'mon, a real gypsy in Nelson?" And I said, "C'mon, a real Indian in Nelson? A real Jewish boy? This is the *era* of Diaspora, man." And he went all tight on me, of course.' She pulled a face: pinched nostrils, pursed lips. 'Diaspora wasn't a word I was supposed to use lightly. Pissed me off. I mean, don't lecture a part-Indian woman in fucken Lamb-land about political correctness, right?'

Candy assented, though her thoughts had looped back on themselves and knotted up.

'Anyway, there was something about this woman. First of all she didn't seem to want to let me in. And then she seemed to think I'd be there to look over some display boards of jewellery — sterling silver rings, turquoise, amethyst, resin — which she had propped up on a little coffee table. But I couldn't afford any of it, and the sign outside said she'd tell your fortune for two dollars.'

Candy thought back to her Romany project: the laughing woman in the *National Geographic*, trying to remove a beer bottle cap with her teeth. 'What did she look like?'

'Long salt and pepper hair in a ponytail. Very worn and lined face, but heart-shaped, you know: pronounced chin and cheekbones still. Nothing like the sconey-looking old white ladies wandering around with their grandkids outside. Made me think of . . . rocks in the sea.'

'That's just how I imagined her.'

Jayshri scrutinised her. For a moment Candy felt it was because she'd been frivolous. Then an eerie sensation tightened under her skin: maybe Jayshri was giving her what *she* wanted: their dialogue a box within a box. Then Jaysh nodded. 'She so much looked the part that I was a bit spooked, actually. I kept peering behind her to catch a glimpse of something like a TV or a microwave, something to ruin the illusion, but I swear to God, the only thing I could see was one of those heavy old wooden radios from the thirties or so, with so many arches and decorations it looked like a miniature church.'

Candy swallowed. Why the nervous fibrillation in her chest?

'I told her that, sorry, I wasn't interested in the jewellery, but would like my palm read. And she said, "Why, when you don't believe?" It totally caught me off guard. But I tried to reply honestly: "Maybe because I want to believe." So then she took this bluish river stone, which had formed so it was piped with some kind of white quartz, like icing, from the caravan windowsill, where it had been sitting in the sun, and rubbed it between her palms. I said, "Is that some kind of talisman?" And she looked at me so angrily, and said, "Everything the gypsy does is magic?" Then she put the rock down and said she just wanted to feel the warmth. I reached for my bag, thinking, crabby old bitch, if she doesn't want me around I can do with keeping the two dollars, and she said, "You're looking for something you can't find." I stood up, and it was then that she literally *snatched* both my hands, ran her thumbs over the backs of the knuckles, stroked my palms. But what really startled me was that she pushed my hair back from my forehead and checked my hair line. She said, "A cow's lick." Then she asked what hand I wrote with, and I said, my left. She nodded, and said, "How old were you when your twin died?" "I don't have a twin," I said, and she said, "No, I know — how old were you?" And then it was all over, because Yosef and the others knocked on the door, said we had to get going if we didn't want to lose our deposit on the motorcamp cabin we were booked into out past Nelson. And I didn't want Yosef to know I'd been so unsettled, so I just thanked her. She said nothing, just gave me a hard, angry stare again. Like a magpie when it's threatened. And we left.'

'But if you never had a twin . . . ?'

The answer snapped out, Jayshri irritated at being interrupted. 'That's the thing. For some reason what she said really . . . bothered me. So when I came back home I went to see my mother, and I told her about it, wanting her to exorcise it, expecting her to laugh, say,

"How bizarre, so many charlatans out there, you keep your wits about you," but when I said it —' Jaysh unconsciously acted out how her mother must have appeared, pressing a hand to the left side of her torso, at the ghost of the sharp pain drilled there '— my mother actually cried out, and my father came in, thinking she'd cut herself, burnt herself, something. She repeated what I'd said, and he looked so bewildered, he said, "So you told her?"'

Jaysh reached out to Candy, the way she had in the flatmate interview, grasping her wrist, and Candy put a hand over her hand, as if she might need to pull Jaysh back on board, back onto the deck of the present. Jayshri withdrew a little, although the force of the story still insisted itself.

'And so it turns out — they never told me. Because they said they didn't want it to hurt me. But I did, I did have a twin. They adopted her out soon after I was born. Just a couple of hours, in fact. I've already got four brothers and sisters, you see, and they just decided — well, it was better for everyone, for some reason. Money, time, I'm not sure. Only they'd decided not to tell me, because . . . I don't know. Just decided it would be best for me not to know, until somehow, I guess, I caught them off guard.'

Candy had a vivid memory of how Jeff would have looked a few years before the photo that had initiated Jayshri's confession. The little gap between his front teeth, which for a while had been one of his claims to distinction, before it closed over. Candy had been fascinated by the way he could fit a drinking straw into it, and his assertion that he could feel the soda pop bubbles tickle the little strip of gum between them. She suddenly wished he could see her in this new life, wanted to bring him here, like boasting: see how rich and complex it all is outside our cul-de-sac? Yet at the same time some twinge, some catch of hurt she could see hook in Jayshri's face made her wonder at herself. How much did she really appreciate her own brother if the loss of an almost-phantom sibling could follow someone this far?

She chewed her lip again. 'So the gypsy wasn't a fraud.'

Jayshri shrugged. 'Dunno. There's a theory that a high

percentage of us start off as twins. One guy I read even said that all singleton left-handers must have lost a twin in the womb. So maybe Gypsy Rose had a pretty good statistical chance of making a successful random guess.' She swirled the lemon slice in the few centimetres of liquid left in her glass. 'It's not the so-called magic of it that shakes me, really. It's not how she knew . . . or whether she really knew. It's the fact that it made such sense, as soon as I found out it was true. It was like . . . that's why nothing's ever felt right. That's why I've always felt so — separate. Alone. You know?'

Candy hadn't wanted to turn on the light when Jayshri was still unfolding her story, and now the dimness in the room helped to increase the new, unexpected feeling of intimacy, as if the two were sheltering together under the grey tent of twilight. Candy felt filled with a sense of pride as physically as if she were a hollow beaker, Jaysh's confession poured into her from some warm natural spring. As she watched her toy with the hem of her shirt, Candy was quietly incredulous that someone as active, as sociable as Jaysh could have this melancholic tempo beneath the up-front vitality.

Didn't it say that Candy was the exception? That almost as soon as she stepped into the flatmate interview Jaysh had felt a potential link? Why else confide all this so quickly? An end to her separateness. The correspondence between them like a conjoining — a real twinning: of souls.

CANDY WOULD BE relieved, later, that she didn't try the 'twinning of souls' line on Jaysh that night. She was pretty soon to learn that the word 'soul' was bourgeois: like most things about her, apparently. She found that out in one of the just-past-midnight, couch-slouched, flatmate conversations they all had in the first weeks that she was there — Candy still wound up tight on the filter coffee she'd had to keep her peppy on her restaurant shift. Over-tiring herself was supposed to be something to avoid with her hands the way they were, but she figured that staggering the shifts at her two jobs, and avoiding too much manual work, was the best she could do.

That night the others were gossiping about a mutual acquaintance who'd sent out invitations to a farewell party before his travels overseas to India, where he was going 'to *find* himself', Jayshri said acerbically.

'Well, he's definitely *lost* something, so let's hope he gets lucky over there,' said Tricia, the usually-absent flatmate: a woman studying for an MA in social work, earning money by shelving at the university library until half-past eleven each night, even at the end of the undergrad term, as the summer break was used for a huge catalogue reorganisation.

'He reckons his soul needs healing. He's discovered through rebirthing classes that he's the reincarnation of some Brahmin from Himachal Pradesh — which just *happens* to be where he'd already planned to travel. So now he's going to "convert" to Hinduism. He says he needs to find out how he fell from grace to end up as a white guy, graduating with just a BA. He told me like I'd be really excited for him, like I'd say, "Oh, so you're one of us!" Ex*cuse* me? Either you're born into Hinduism or you're not.'

Tricia pulled a black crocheted shawl more tightly around her garage-sale 1950s ball dress: she looked like a brown paper package tied up in string. 'Funny how whenever anyone discovers they've been reincarnated their past lives are always kind of . . . dramatic. Or dream ideals.' She crossed her legs, kicked her ankle a little. 'Like, have you ever heard anyone admit they came out of rebirthing with the revelation they'd been a really, really good woodlouse in a past life, and that's why they've ascended to this existence as a Western hippy with a job in a health-food shop and his only problem a dairy product allergy?'

Their other flatmate, Nash, sucked on a thin, starved-looking joint until a red bead glowed at the end, like the LED light on a household appliance, announcing that the electrical circuits in his brain were still on — just. '*Man*. I'd be too afraid to do rebirthing in case I discovered I *was* a woodlouse.'

'Very Kafka,' said Jayshri.

'What?' asked Candy. But Jayshri turned her profile away. She hadn't spoken to Candy all that much since the first day of Candy's tenancy. Some days it felt that the tipsy, then mellow, then frank conversation in her room had never happened. Jaysh was busy with her hordes of followers, the weekly discussion groups, the big 'sit-sesh' they organised when the man from Hamilton came to stay. Tonight was an exception: usually, if she was in the flat on her own it seemed to be just to change clothes or drop off her bag before some party, some meeting, some coffee.

'Very LSD more like,' Nash exhaled smoke through his nose: a pale, unshaven dragon.

Candy settled in on the couch opposite him and he roused himself enough to motion that he could pass her the joint if she wanted. Candy laughed. 'You're offering me *drugs*, just after you talked about the possibility of believing you're a woodlouse? Nuh-uh, that's not good publicity, Nash.'

'It's not acid, Candy-cane.'

Jaysh smiled at him. 'It doesn't have to be for our little flat-pet, does it? When you're pure as the driven snow, even a glass of wine spreads a dramatic stain.'

Why the delicate sensation of tearing, like a flick-knife run down silk? Candy had perhaps misread something.

Nash leaned over and squeezed Candy's cheek between finger and thumb. 'Kootchie kootchie koo!'

She tried to laugh. They all made an issue about the fact that she was so young: pretended she needed protecting, tried to lecture her on the big bad world they'd had a whole three or four more years experience in than she . . .

She slumped down as low as the others in the couch, swung open her legs in the same who-cares attitude, and only at the last minute saved Nash from a flash of her underwear when she realised she was still in the black skirt she had to wear for work. Oops. She tried to compensate by narrowing her eyes into mean-and-hard mode.

'So you guys don't believe in any kind of spiritual journey? Or just not in this guy's?'

Jayshri straightened herself up, fist punctuating her words with the passion of a demagogue. 'The notion of the soul is a mere construction of historical forces! The so-called individual is merely a constellation of different and conflicting social discourses! The self, the soul, are ideological conveniences!'

Candy had already tried to cram down some of the photocopied book chapters Jaysh had left lying around the living room, the hallway table, even the washstand in the bathroom, from the sociology, political science and literary theory courses she'd been doing that year. Whenever the words *discourse* and *ideology* came up Candy knew that Jaysh and her friends would be animated into their fast-and-furious, competitive mental ping-pong. And although she'd thought she'd be wrung out after her own school exams, she'd found the energy to dig into the photocopies, prompted by the thought that she might not get so dizzy trying to keep up if she covertly swotted the dog-eared papers left to collect coffee rings and ash-scatter in the shared rooms of the flat. And tonight — for a minute — she felt she had almost grasped something. She could see chinks of light through the brickwork that had so far blocked her.

'But doesn't that kind of imply that we're all just . . . like robots? All sort of pre-programmed? And how could you guys have your revolution, how could we even have disagreement and change, if that was true?'

There was total silence. Thinking that meant there was room to say more, Candy added, 'And don't we sometimes need . . . I don't know, what would you call it? A shorthand.'

Nash was staring at his hands. 'Man. This is getting to sound like one of my Honours tutorials. But my fingers never felt this big in tutorials. My fingers . . . feel really *big*.'

'You're totally trashed, Nash.' Tricia watched him from under sultry, lowered eyelashes. 'Totally Nashed, Trash.' Was there something going on between these two?

Nash still stared at his palms. 'Don't confuse me.'

Candy waved a hand slowly on the air, a little like the dance Jayshri had shown her, a little like conducting an invisible orchestra. 'Maybe what it feels like to be in *this* body, to have *this* particular set of — what did you call it? — different conflicts or whatever, is still an individual. Or even a soul. I mean, is it so bad to have a convenient word? We've got to communicate somehow, don't we?'

She caught Jayshri rolling her eyes at Tricia: not too perceptive an observation, as she'd made no effort to disguise it. Jayshri drummed her knuckles on her knee. 'What*ever*.' Then she launched herself out of her chair. 'I'm hitting the hay.'

Candy was bewildered, and a little hurt. A puppy dog not

praised for fetching when it had learned the trick so *quickly* . . . Was it because she'd stepped out of her role as junior? Because she'd sounded critical? She was only trying to understand. Surely it couldn't have been just because she'd seemed to disagree with them? Could it?

The coldness she felt that night seemed to set in like a personal winter. Such a different climate to the mood of her first evening there, which surely had suggested so many companionable riches to come: long conversational lazy afternoons on green hillsides, skins soaking up ozone blue; riverside summer times, water golden brown like the glass of beer bottles, sun filling her head. The murmur of their voices, side by side, delving deep, lost twin to found. But no: Jaysh was terse, practical. Their conversations now extended only to facts about bills and phone calls. Candy pressed for more — even hovering outside Jayshri's bedroom door with fresh coffee, the mail, or once some home-made muesli early in the morning, for Jaysh to taste and approve. But whether Jasyh had a cluster of her followers with her in her room, smoking and chatting over newspapers or political circulars, pulling at the threads in their holey jerseys, or whether she was alone, Candy was never let in past the threshold. She realised, much later, that Jaysh always stood in the space between the part-way open door and the doorframe: a minor detail, but it gave the impression that even to glance casually past her was to pry, grubbily digging for private details.

Candy alternately told herself to shrug it all away, and fretted about what she could do to rewind things to the starting point her first night in the flat had suggested. What had she done or said to shunt things off course? Perhaps Jaysh just felt overexposed, that she'd said too much too soon. So Candy backed off a bit. Despite a slight reluctance, because of the whole question of her music, she tried to call Grace from The Raggedies, hoping they could hang out together more, and in a less stressed way, now that the rock quest was over. But she found out from Grace's brother that she'd left town for some holiday work, picking fruit up Central. Candy felt isolated, untethered, out of step.

It made her realise that she hadn't called home for ages: hadn't talked to someone who cared, basically. She'd wanted to prove how little she'd needed to. But sometimes at night on the edge of sleep, when she lay curled into herself in bed like a leaf unhatched, still so unclear of what dimensions her life should stretch to, she would imagine she heard a rhythmic, deliberate tapping through the wall. Jeff, softly scratching out the old Morse code they'd invented for when Gram stayed. During daylight she knew the sound was linked to the crosshatch shadows the tall trees outside sent into her room, the branches stirred by midnight winds. But equally, in the dark, semi-conscious, she was persuaded it was a connection to Jeff. She was back home again, as he thudded softly to and fro in the corridor, from bathroom to bedroom; went to bed with stereo headphones on, and maybe some study notes. Perhaps the tapping wasn't their old code at all, but the drumming of a pen or pencil against his bedside table. The beats were clear and steady. Sensing the mood and undercurrent of the music he was listening to, Candy found words winding themselves around the metre he tapped out, but when she woke in the morning they were gone, and she felt disproportionately bereft. Once, to her own bewilderment afterwards, she even found herself slipping over to the small beaten-copper-framed mirror she had propped up on her chest of drawers, and studying the reflection for echoes of her brother, trying to mimic his halfway smile–frown, for company.

Maybe Jayshri was right. It was impossible to walk away entirely from her twin, no matter the strains, the niggles, between them. Maybe it was time to invite him to the flat, try to start afresh with him somehow; as adults. Maybe, even, Jaysh would warm to her again if she introduced her to her brother: after all, he was what had triggered her initial fascination, even Candy's acceptance into this place.

She'd have to engineer an encounter: a barbeque, a potluck dinner maybe. There had initially been talk about another party specifically to mark Candy moving in, but juggling everyone's work shifts and weekends away had proved too complicated so far. As Christmas came closer, people would have more time off, surely? She could invite Lewis too: if it worked, it would be perfect.

Jayshri, Lewis, Jeffrey: all these people her mind constantly worked over. They were the stones and boulders shaping the course of a river, which also tried to smooth them to its own path. On the way to and from work, or in the lunchtime shopping crowds, Candy watched the faces of strangers, freshly aware of how in their heads there must be similar private populations: precious and complex cargo. Her own skull felt like a rat's nest of barbed rose vines: there was a slumbering happiness in there somewhere, which her thoughts were trying to fight their way to.

For alongside the chipping away at what it was about her that sat wrongly in the flat, Candy was increasingly preoccupied with her sort-of courtship with Lewis. And the old-fashioned word courtship seemed somehow appropriate. There were so many small shuffles, heel-to-toes and side-steps in this intricate choreography she just about wished for something as outdated as a chaperone, to instruct her in what to do or say next.

Lewis had said, for a week or two after he got back from his visit up north to see his family, that he was genuinely, seriously, too busy to do anything very social for the next couple of weeks: Honours research essay deadline still to go post exams, and he'd have to look for work at the same time. He'd really like to see her, but. *But but but.* And Candy did want to ram her head against the wall by the phone, to knock sense into herself: he's probably too old for you anyway, you don't really even *know* the guy, why are you letting it *do* this to you? Wise up, get hard, get real. (Not a chance.) The words to an entire Lewis song wrote and rewrote in her head each ludicrous time she swallowed her pride and phoned . . .

Boyoholic

Whisky kisses
make me heart sick
whisky kisses
make your tongue sly
whisky kisses

make my mind shy
from your upside
down your lowside
high your shadow hand
cast by bar light
your promises sworn
blue as cusses
your touch as tender
as money ill spent
your mind a kerbside
hard slide streetlife
trust turned out to fend there
with less wisdom
than a greenhorn
just grown up past hip high
you lend a strange kind of vision
a change in this ill wind
would blow so much more good
than your whisky kisses
your whisky kisses
your whisky kisses could

. . . but the thing was, the words came: not the melody, not the chord pattern. Although the lines set down their own path in the coils and crannies of her brain as clearly as the groove in a vinyl record, the silence surrounding them helped make her think maybe she'd lost her composing ear for good. She was right not to have let herself celebrate the rock quest prize: it was a fluke. An adolescent flash in the pan, that's all she was.

At the thought she rubbed her arms. She felt the tendons, muscles, nerves, whichever parts were damaged (the new theories the physiotherapist offered seemed to be changing all the time, so she'd given up trying to understand) were probably rested enough for her to at least test out how it felt to position her fingers again, to try small bursts of practice, lots of breaks along the way, as recommended by the physio. But her guitar languished in its case still. It looked like a single black skittle: precarious, vulnerable — one last hard hit from bad luck and it would be knocked out of her life for good. She'd moved it from side to side of her room, double-checked she still had Julian Tyler's phone number, set up a music stand, took the guitar out of its case. And then just looked at it all, before letting the phone, a craving for coffee, the sound of flatmates in the kitchen, distract her. She was afraid of it: afraid she'd have lost all musical ability completely, and of that old, taunting hope that could seduce you so high, only to slam you right back down again. The prize for her composition at the band quest didn't seem to amount to much if she couldn't play her own work.

Thinking about Lewis, thinking about music, thinking about the foreign country that her flat was, with its arcane communications and social interactions she couldn't entirely follow — sometimes it seemed her life was lived entirely in her head. But then: serendipity. Coincidence. Chance. The encounters a small city so often brings, and which, for Candy, in eighteen's tumultuous heaven, felt like fate, destiny, meant-to-be.

She was at the hairdresser, a place she'd chosen just because she was passing it when she realised she'd done all her messages, and still had an hour to fill in before work at the restaurant. She was sitting under a hairdryer, reading a magazine, was partially aware of other customers coming and going, but was absorbed in an article about Patti Smith's influence on the place of women in the music industry. When the hairdresser came back, and stood behind her to check how she was doing, she raised her head to smile at her in the mirror. The woman moved and, reflected there, was — she thought — one of her usual hallucinations, from thinking so much about Lewis that she often believed she'd caught a glimpse of him in a crowd, disappearing around a corner, passing her on a busy escalator: which usually turned out to be a heart-mirage. The swivel chair was just tilting back up, lifting his head from a washbasin. His hair was wet, a tight dark cap on the scalp. It made his face and throat, his collarbones just above the scoop neck of his T-shirt, seem naked, exposed: a visual shock, a sudden intimate sight. It hinted at how he would appear stepping fresh out of the shower, or rising to the surface of a swimming pool, shoulders, legs, arms, bare and wet in the summer. She was struck by his somehow unapologetic self-examination, looking straight into the mirror the way he would look through a door. Not admiring, not embarrassed, not critical, just frank, unmoved either way. At ease, she thought. And then beautifully alert when their eyes met in the mirror. The surprised smile too seemed unexpectedly naked: bare delight. He excused himself to his barber as he turned his chair around.

'Candy?' he said. 'Unreal! I was just thinking about you.'

'Oh, really?'

'Don't sound so sceptical. Yeah, really. Things have eased off a lot.'

As simply as that, their strange dance kick-started again. He asked if they could go somewhere when their appointments were finished: he'd shout her something at a café. She had to get to work — was secretly pleased to seem even slightly elusive — but they arranged to meet the next day, for the coffee he'd first mentioned on the night of the Raggedies gig: the invitation that had become legendary to her.

Then there were a couple of movies, a few dinners, a play, a party or two he invited her along to. Dropping her off in his car, at three or four in the morning, stillness filling its darkened interior as they talked in low voices — about their families, about abstracts such as the future, friendship, freedom, fidelity . . . When she coasted into the flat one night, still high on it all, guard down after a few glasses of wine, she tried to convey it to Jayshri and Tricia. 'I've never talked to anyone that way before.'

Jaysh repeated it back to her, mockingly. 'Families, futures, friendship, freedom, fidelity. And what about fucking?'

'It's not *like* that,' Candy said, trying too late to cover with a self-deprecating laugh.

'Well, poor you,' said Tricia.

'Yeah. Welcome to the life of the last twentieth-century virgin.'

Jaysh gave a swivel of her hips and glided out of the room.

Maybe their cynicism stung precisely because the unpredictable repel and attract that went on with Lewis *was* so chaste. In his car they talked about relationships: what each of them had experienced in the past. Candy said, 'Nobody has really appealed to me — I mean, *really* appealed to me — much before, to tell you the truth.' And Lewis said — in a tone of voice that made the shuttle of hope burn up as it plummeted back to earth — 'Yeah, I've still never really met anyone either. I've never met someone I could spend twenty-four hours with, you know? I always need to get away. And there's plenty about me I bet someone else would find hard to live with.'

Candy fiddled with the radio dial, cheeks burning. 'I find that hard to imagine.'

He laughed. 'You wouldn't say that if you had to share a house with me.'

Was he fishing? She met his eyes. 'So, what is it? You're a bit of a slob?'

He jiggled a knee with a nervous laugh. 'Oh, well. Let's just say I've got some quirky night-time habits.'

For a moment Candy had a vision of him wrapped in a dark cape, his toes curled around a door-frame as he hung upside down like a large vampire bat. 'Quirky?' The smile hovering in her voice perhaps deterred him.

'Oh, well, you don't want to hear about that now.' He glanced out the car window, thinking. 'And, you know what? The thing is, I'm not sure I really believe in this whole one-on-one scenario anyway. Sometimes I don't even know what . . . type of person I'm attracted to.'

Candy swallowed hard. 'I guess you'd just know, eventually, if you met them.' And though this conversation was perhaps the most they'd ever confessed to each other, she'd really thought that was it for her. Over. Kaput. Finito. So she was bold enough to lean over and kiss him goodbye, thinking it was probably the last time she'd see him — or at least the last time she'd see him with particular expectations. Then there was a tentative shift in the atmosphere: one he seemed reluctant about, yet he was the one who carried on . . . And they happened again: intermittent, fleeting kisses, hands cupped to chin, smoothing over hair, shoulder — although it all had something experimental, uncertain, about it. A deer mouthing the green shoots of a strange plant, unsure of the aniseed tang, or the bite of mint. Then startled off again: by the sweep of someone else's headlights, the sight of a silhouette under the street lamps, or a car backfiring somewhere out on the roads, gunshot startling them both from the dense, dark undergrowth of a forest of emotion barely ventured on. And next time the reverberations of that nervousness might dominate the entire evening. It seemed they frequently worked their way back to the courteous formality of hardly knowing each other. She wanted to ask someone about it: thought about phoning Grace again, or even Lucy, from The Raggedies — though she'd been out of touch for so long, so absorbed in all the changes that had come about recently. But maybe, with their greater experience, they'd be just as sarcastic, as patronising, as Tricia and Jaysh? Maybe she needed to talk to someone really familiar. There was only one choice, really.

Jeff was so thrilled to hear from her that she said, 'Well, now I really feel like a big yellow calloused heel. I should have called sooner.'

'No, no. I understand. You've been settling in. But I tell you, I've been going crazy here, trying to keep a lid on Mum and Dad. Anyone would think they didn't still have a son at home, the amount of time they spend worrying about how you're getting on, why you haven't called, et cetera.'

A cocky kind of pleasure crowed from her scalp to her toes. 'But have *they* called?'

'Yeah, though they said they didn't want to leave messages in case you thought your flatmates would decide you were having an eye kept on you.'

A small lurch of shame. Rose and Robinson so considerate, after she'd left in high and mighty, flighty dudgeon. She was so *readable*. 'So how are you all?'

'Uhhh . . .' She could immediately visualise him, turning his back on whichever parent must have just walked into the hallway, where he'd be rocking on the back of the wooden chair, or moving it around with one hand as if it were light as a paperback: an excess physicality that spilled over when he was uncomfortable. She caught the sound of a door closing, but caution still pressed at the edges of his voice.

'We're okay, mostly.'

'Mostly?'

'Uhhh . . . the usual. You know?'

She tried to feeler into the gaps between each phrase. 'So, is the problem . . . Mum?'

'A little.'

'Just a little? So is it mainly Dad?'

'A little, also. But different.'

'Really? Shit. What about you?'

'Uhhh . . . can I give you a call? Back? Sometime?'

She gripped the phone tightly, as if she were grabbing his elbow, trying to anchor him on the spot. 'What about you come over soon instead? Tomorrow?'

'Ummm . . . sure. What time?'

'Say, after my afternoon shift at the store? I don't have a restaurant stint tomorrow, I'm making sure I only do a couple of hours of work each day because ofmy arms. So you could stay for dinner.'

'Just a second.' There was the muffled sound of the receiver being masked, and voices strained through thick covering. It was odd to think that perhaps he still had to check with their parents. She felt a sense of distance stretching out as she waited, growing like the expanse of water between wharf and departing ferry. How would it be when they saw each other again? He came back on line. 'Yeah, that'd be great.'

The next day she was running late. She had to cover for someone else at the shop, and, by the time she was asked to do so, realised Jeff would already be on his way to visit. She tried to phone ahead to the flat to leave a message but nobody else was home. She was hot and flustered when she finally got back, clumping over the doorstep and into the lower foyer, carrying extra shopping in her satchel — feta, phyllo pastry, carrots, spinach, sunflower seeds — so that she could cook Jeff something more interesting than spaghetti and tomato sauce, one of the flat's staples. She called out up the stairwell, 'Anyone here?'

'Helloooo!' Jayshri's flushed, happy face appeared as she let her torso bow low over the upper balustrade. Her hennaed hair — usually worn scooped back in a simple plastic barrette — was loose and swinging.

'Hellooooo!' Jeff appeared next to her, leaning out over the stairwell too. 'Where've you been?'

Knees solid rock, she locked at the bottom of the stairs. The sight of them side by side did it. Radiant. Playful. The stony petrification crawled up from her knees and into her face, as if emotion were taking a concrete cast of her. The little muscles in her cheeks and lips there wouldn't even twitch. Ramming into her from the side, lunging out of her blind spot: *jealousy again*.

'Did you have to work late?' said Jeff. He started giving small hops, trying to lift his feet off the ground, balancing on his stomach on the upper landing balustrade. It was embarrassing. Juvenile. She wanted to warn him, somehow: tried to say, with a frown alone, *Cool it, Jeff! This is a* flat, *you know, not home . . .*

Jaysh gave a giggle, low in her stomach. Then she was up on the balustrade too, feet waving behind her. 'Do you remember the Bugaloos?' she said. Then they were both at it, craning their necks as if they were looking at the topography of a field, legs held out suspended behind them, singing, 'The Bugaloos, the Bugaloos, they're in the air and everywhere, flying high, flying low . . .'

The blood was draining into their faces but they still hung on, side by side. 'The Bugaloos, they were *great!*'

'Wasn't it kind of the same as Puff 'n' Stuff? Didn't they both have that witchy-wizardy character?'

Candy glared at them both. What were they *on* about? 'How long have you been here?' she said to Jeff, as if it were his mistake

243

that she'd only just arrived. He slid back off the banister. 'Bloody ages,' he said. 'I thought you said five-thirty, but I got here just before five because the bus was faster than I thought. Lucky Jaysh was here.'

So it was 'Jaysh' already, was it?

'She let me in, and we've just been hanging out.'

Obviously.

'Right. Are you home for dinner, Jayshri?' Said in a tone loaded with, it'll be bloody inconvenient if you are, because you're not usually, and I didn't cater for everyone.

'That'd be excellent, Candy, thanks.' Sweet as cinnamon, she hippity-hoppitied down the stairs. 'Can I help you carry something?'

'No, no, that's fine.' But Jayshri whisked the satchel off her shoulder and lugged it back on up the flight of stairs.

Perhaps the only thing that saved Candy from staying in a pissed-off funk with them both was that Jeff let Jaysh go on through into the kitchen alone, and scooped Candy up in a hug at the top of the stairs. 'My *sister*,' he said. And she felt an old warmth nudge its way back through the stone.

She reminded herself that this was supposed to have been what she wanted. For Jeff to see what her new surroundings were like, and for Jayshri in particular to meet Jeff — in the hope that there'd be a thaw. Right, she said to herself. So they like each other. So you've achieved what you wanted. Get used to it.

While Candy cooked, the other two sat at the chromium-legged, red formica-topped kitchen table — neither of them, she noticed, offering to help, though they both exclaimed over how good it all looked and smelled. She had to step on the toes of a sniffy response (*what about my cooking?*) when she saw that Jeff had brought over some rich-looking muffins, from a bakery called The Upper Crust (only half-jokingly named, it seemed: the counter staff there reminded Candy of jewellers' cabinets: square chested, they both incongruously wore black velvet and were draped and dripping in gold chains).

A little suspicious of Jayshri's new, honeyed mildness, a part of her wanted to push her from the room, speak to Jeff alone and get to the bottom of his cryptic answers on the phone the other day. It felt wrong only finding out news about him at the same time as Jayshri did. No, even *after* Jayshri had.

Jaysh delicately peeled back the crinkled paper cup that held her muffin, and with her long, thin fingers methodically extracted the white chocolate and the strawberry chunks, lining them up on her plate.

'So whereabouts are you looking for a flat?'

Jeff, looking for a flat?

He talked around a wolfman bite of food. 'Not sure yet. Somewhere central, I guess, to save on transport.'

'What are you doing at the end of summer?' asked Jaysh.

Candy tried to reassert her insider knowledge. 'He'll be going to university, won't you, Jeff? He's a bit of a boffin. The family brain.'

He bowed his head, chin resting on the back of his knuckles. 'I'm just not so sure any more. I figure maybe there are other ways of going about it.' His eyes caught the light from the large, rotten-silled kitchen window, which opened out onto a small lower-level porch roof where the flatmates sometimes sat to sun themselves, the heat beating up from the corrugated iron. His irises seemed like a green-gold foil, wrapping something hidden, which his level stare asked Candy to guess, to understand.

'Have you sorted out what you're doing yet, Candy? Polytech? Varsity?'

She leaned against the kitchen bench, studying him. 'Haven't really decided. I guess it'll be another year or so before I'm ready. I want to save as much as possible, first. But I'm thinking maybe journalism.'

Jeff's lower jaw opened on a small O of surprise. 'What about music?'

'But what if I really can't play again?'

'Aw, c'mon, Can-do. It's only been a couple of months!'

'Oh, well. I'm thinking maybe of going into music journalism.

Channelling what I know into something a bit more stable. Studying here, then taking off overseas, looking into the music press in the UK. Most of the stuff I read in local rags, it's just so crap. I swear, some of the reviewers in things like *Trash It* or *Rock Solid* seem like they don't even have fifth-form English. I'm sure I could do better than that.'

Jeff gnawed thoughtfully on the side of his index finger. 'Hmmm. Journalism.'

Candy turned away to rinse the spinach leaves. 'I'd like to see if I could get into a polytech diploma course, so I can start earning faster. But I don't know. Maybe I'd miss out by not going to varsity. Maybe I wouldn't even get into the diploma without a degree first. I haven't really looked into it properly.'

Jeff tilted his chair back on its legs, turning his gaze on Jaysh's profile and drinking her in. 'What about you? What are you going to do when you graduate?'

She shrugged, and slid the pieces of her demolished muffin around her plate. 'I'm thinking of carrying on to do a Masters or a PhD, if I can get a proposal accepted. After that — don't know. Probably end up doing what most of my friends have done — compromise all my principles and work for the government.'

Candy wiped her wet hands on the cloth she'd tucked into her waistband. 'Can't imagine you doing that.'

Jayshri leaned back in her chair also, so that she and Jeff again seemed to match. She began pulling her hair back into a self-holding knot. 'Yeah, well. Shit happens.'

Jeff glanced at her plate. 'Are you actually going to eat that muffin, or just disembowel it so you can read its entrails?'

Candy expected Jaysh to go cold, to shut down, but she rubbed her hands over her stomach. 'I've eaten *heaps* of it!'

'No, you haven't. You've systematically dissected it and rearranged it into pretty patterns. What's wrong with it?'

Jaysh gave a just-discernible pout. 'Nothing.' She eyed the muffin like a child forced to contemplate Brussels sprouts or broad beans. Then she snatched two hunks of strawberry and chocolate and crammed them into her mouth with an expression that made Candy think of someone bracing themselves for a band aid to be torn off skin.

'Mmm, millisshisss.'

Puzzlement crumpled Jeff's brow. He and Candy exchanged a look that reminded her of times when Rose or Robinson were trying to get them on side for some staff's-family-Christmas-party or mid-year potluck lunch, and she and Jeff would swap silent *whoopdy-poops, oh yeah rights*.

Jaysh began to jiggle nervously on the spot. ''Scuse me, I need to get a jersey.' She slipped out of the room.

Candy felt tension unknot all along her body. 'So, Jeff.' She sat down at the table with a pot of melted butter, a basting brush and the sheets of phyllo pastry, then began to coat each sheet with butter. 'It sounded like there was something up at home.'

He rested his chin on his arms, which were crossed on the table, so that he had the air of a dog resting his muzzle on his paws. 'Oh, well, nothing in particular, really. I guess it's just time for me to leave too . . .'

She listened to the silence that he let trail behind his words. 'But Mum's not bad again, is she?'

'Aw . . . well, not too bad.' He wasn't meeting her eyes.

'There *is* something going on, isn't there?'

'Well . . . no, it's not that she's ill again. It's just — you know what it's like. Actually she really misses you, but I'm not saying that so you'll feel guilty. I've just . . . realised I get really worried when I feel like I'm disappointing her. And Dad. Or could be a disappointment to them. I don't know.' His words sounded somehow narrowed, the frankness difficult for him. 'It's like, now that it's time to make some of my own choices, everything suddenly seems so loaded, you know?'

Candy waited.

'I don't know what I'm trying to say. It's just . . . I think I want my own time now, too. So I don't have to watch myself so closely. Do you get what I mean?'

She slowly striped the final pastry sheet with butter. 'Sort of.'

He sat up with an irritated shake. 'Ahh, I don't even know what I'm talking about myself. Maybe it's not even to *do* with them any more. I'm just . . . restless, I guess.' He gnawed at the cuticle on one of his thumbs.

Candy nodded. 'I know how that feels.'

He suddenly shot an arm out and grabbed her around the elbow. She thought he was going to say something like, *Hey, go easy on the butter!* But he grinned at her, his nose wrinkling up with boyish delight. 'It's just so good to see you again, Candy. It feels like it's been bloody years, not a month. And you want to know something? When you didn't call, I thought maybe you were angry at me. That I'd done something wrong.'

A blush flared into her cheeks. 'Angry?' she said, too brightly, immediately back to the long-ago habit of protecting him. 'Wrong? No! Of course not!'

'I really missed you too. It's not just Mum. This'll sound corny, you know. But I didn't expect your leaving to affect me so much. I mean, you were in the same city and everything, but it was chronic, man. Some nights before I went to sleep I used to convince myself I could hear your songs through the wall. I thought I could have practically learned them if I'd tried hard enough to catch all the words and write them down.'

He gave her arm a strong squeeze, and before she could say, *Jeffrey, that's bizarre, listen*, the sharp bleat of the wall phone in the kitchen broke them out of conversation.

It was Lewis. As always, she was caught off guard by the sound of his voice, which sent her body into a kind of freefall, the progress of some journey suddenly sped forward. Yet it was also a pleasurable consternation, a pain she almost pined for: *pine*, solitary tree on a hilltop, green cushion heart full of needling need . . .

'Lewis!' she said, voice a bird loop-de-looping from the pine and out through blue. He seemed to be used to it, though, as he didn't laugh, just asked was she busy, was she free tonight? And without thinking whether she and Jeff mightn't have finished talking, she said, 'Hey, why don't you come round for dinner? I'm cooking for my brother — you remember? You met him at the rock quest night. Some of my flatmates will probably be here too, so I'll be making heaps.' (Which she hadn't been, and it wasn't what she would have told Jayshri, but for Lewis she'd improvise.) 'Plenty. Loads 'n' loads.' *Oh, shut up, Candy, you'll put him off.* Her mind was already racing wildly ahead of her white lie to the sticky cupboards where the old lavender, seventies-floral print contact sheets were peeling up from the wood. Her thoughts shuffled through the supplies, throwing together a lentil goulash or a kidney bean chilli, something stolid and super spicy so nobody could eat too much of it anyway, perhaps confusing heat overdose for satiation . . .

'Sure,' said Lewis. 'Sounds good.'

Just like that: easy, chancy. She'd been imagining all kinds of elaborate ways to get everyone together: envisioning, say, a cocktail party with a 1920s theme, house lit with candles in jam jars starting at the front path and mounting the stairs, plinky piano music on the stereo to blend with the sound of glass with ice cubes, rattling strings of beads, bracelets and metal toe caps clopping over the floorboards. Introducing them all to one another — Jaysh, Lewis, Jeffrey — and feeling something ignite: conversation and connection moving through them all.

The image of a cocktail party had let her fantasise about poise too. She'd scintillate like a screen diva, all her lines witty, incisive. It would be like playing music, body following sound, sound following body, everything progressing to a conclusion with the smooth, satisfying turn of a new key in a polished lock. Nothing like tonight, then. Which was madcap frazzle, bump, clatter and sweat, scorched thumb, cut finger, *fuck! forgot about having chopped the chillies before I rubbed my bloody eyes!*, vision streaming, walk into the teatowel drawer left open at knee height, catch a tender part beside the kneecap on a sharp corner, hobble around cursing the fact there was no bench space, no time to waste, Jeff trying to help while chatting about some kind of disagreement with Mum and Dad about — what? — something to do with a guy he'd met at a bus stop who wore dresses to teachers' college. How their parents thought it meant the man was disturbed and shouldn't be training as a primary school teacher but Jeff said children are far more open-minded than that and — Christ, Jeff, watch out — his feet were at her ankles like mewling, winding cats — look out for these hot pans, would you? No chance to brush her hair, put on eyeliner, change clothes, light incense or candles before rapdiddy rap rap rap, there was a knock at the door.

The kitchen looked as if it had been ransacked by drunks. Candy glowed with sweat and her fringe clung damply to her forehead as Jaysh popped back in, sallow and shadowy in a thick cable-stitched green jersey, to check whether anyone else had heard the knock.

Jeff stood pressed against the fridge, eyes bulging at the way Candy stood paralysed in the centre of the kitchen, out of sheer mortification at the state everything was in. He hissed at her, 'Who *is* this guy? The Queen?'

Jayshri laughed. 'Royalty or raving? Let's hope not, for Candy's sake. That'd put an end to the romance.'

'*Romance*?' Jeff's eyebrows shot up and dropped with the sleazy exaggeration of a TV comedian lifting a French maid's skirt. Candy had to slap him.

'Stop it!'

He loved that.

'Stop what?'

'Being so childish.'

He puckered up. 'Diddums.'

They heard Jaysh opening the front door and a male voice saying, 'Gidday. Candy around?'

'Sure. Come on up.'

Candy ducked down to try to see her reflection in the side of the stainless steel electric kettle. 'How does my hair look?'

'With its "i"? Get it? The letter "i" and the eye your see with.' Jeff said.

She stoppered back a squeal of rage as Lewis appeared in the door dressed in motorcycle leathers and carrying two bright red helmets.

'Hi,' said Candy. 'Ummm.'

He nodded. 'Hi.'

'Wow. I guess . . . you've bought a bike!'

He grinned ruefully. 'I wish. Just looking after it for a friend who's gone overseas for six months.'

She nodded. The sight of him seemed to have caused some strange allergic reaction: now her voice box was paralysed. Why did liking someone so much do this? With Shane, the uncertainty about him had somehow made it easier — because there was less invested?

'I wondered if you'd like to take a spin, maybe after dinner,' Lewis said. The odd thing was, for a moment she genuinely couldn't tell who he was talking to. It was as if he were asking permission of the others — or was it that he was inviting everyone? His gaze drifted from Candy to rest on Jeff. There was a weird, wolverine, stiffening moment between them, their jaws set, their brows lowered, as if each were deliberately avoiding eye contact. Uh-oh. Then Lewis's expression grew a focused curiosity; someone searching for a memory of where they might have encountered this person before, perhaps. She darted forward a little, palms out like a boxing referee.

'You guys have met, remember? Like I said on the phone. At the rock quest night. Lewis, Jeff; Jeff, Lewis.'

Gradually Lewis's face cleared.

'Gidday,' the men said loudly to each other. They both shuffled and turned a bit on the spot, and now their postures seemed to be working at the same cause — pushing a boat out, getting a car started. A cryptic interchange, she thought: some recognition of each other's — place? It seemed there had been a shift from stand-off to acceptance, though they'd barely spoken. It was a relief. The evening could take care of itself.

At dinner, though, Candy couldn't eat much from nerves, and as she glanced at other people's plates, wondering if they'd notice that she couldn't seem to swallow her own cooking, she noticed, also, that Jaysh was toying with her food, eating the salad but leaving the sunflower seeds and boiled egg Candy had added, and pulling out the spinach from the spanikopita, eating that, but leaving the rest.

It helped to reinforce that Candy had cooked too much, in the end. Tracy and Nash were both out. When she said, doubtfully, 'I hope the food's all right,' Jayshri said, 'Oh, yeah, it's great. I've just had *sooooo* much fat today, you wouldn't believe.' And Candy was suddenly struck by the sight of her, wearing all green, green spinach perched on her fork: there was something vegetal and leaf like about her too. If you held her up to the light, perhaps it would shine through her, and you would see the veins running under her skin, carrying green blood like chlorophyll to all the secret chambers of her body. She was about to get started on, 'But someone as slight as you probably *needs* fat, Jaysh,' — the traditional feminine dance that would match the quicksteps Lewis and Jeff had performed earlier — but with a sudden giddiness she felt Lewis take hold of her wrist and tilt it to check the time on her watch.

'If we're going to take a ride on this bike tonight we should get going. I've got work early tomorrow. You want to come first, Candy?'

'Absolutely,' she said.

She kitted up in the thickest clothing she could find, including a leather jacket borrowed from Nash's room without asking. As she clung around Lewis's waist on the motorbike, Candy felt as if his body were a lens that focused heat through to her core, which, a flimsy scrap of rice paper, would start to smoulder any minute, giving away all her cool.

The ride was breathtaking, precarious, as he took corners with a low sideways sweep, the wind rushing past them. They biked to a scenic lookout point, from where they could see the city's lights come on as the sun plunged between the cold-looking green hills, a branding iron dunked in water. He told her that if she squinted until the lights blurred as they drove towards the cliff edge it would feel like flying. 'Hold on tightly,' he said. 'You might get spun out.' But she loved it. When they stopped on the cliff edge, she stayed clinging to him, marvelling at the outlook, as if a veil of the ordinary were removed from the city.

'Look at all that energy burning up out there,' said Lewis.

House lights, street lamps, neon signs, car headlights, sea

freighter signals out on the horizon, crane lights, lights on the city's tallest structures, TV transmitters, and all of it redoubled in the harbour.

'Sucking up the earth's resources,' said Candy.

'Exactly,' said Lewis. 'We're just as guilty, though, eh? Joyriding on a motorbike.'

'That's true,' said Candy. But the conversation only harmonised with the — dangerously luxurious — beauty out there. All those human-made lights glimmering, tonight, with potential and possibility: as if they signalled that humanity could also show the ingenuity to overcome its own mistakes. She had the sensation that she and Lewis were surfaces that could catch and reflect it back, the city's energy entering through the tiny keyholes of their pupils, where an inner circuitry could transform it to any good they chose. That was how Lewis had made her feel from the start: that wherever *here* was, on any scrubby hilltop creeping with gorse, lupin and foxgloves, littered with broken glass and marked with tyre burns, anything was possible, anything could happen, right here.

Lewis kicked down the bike stand, and slipped off the seat, wandering over to a park bench. She followed, hugging her arms to herself. They stood side by side, and there was the stirring of a tune she'd known once. She started to sing it.

> *. . . you showed me the city lights*
> *and it was like we were underground*
> *in a dark cave*
> *where fire flies danced*
> *and wrote our names*
> *and it was like we were flying*
> *high above the planet*
> *looking down on other suns . . .*

He turned to her. 'What's that?'

'A song I wrote once, when I was pretty young. About eleven, I guess.'

He turned to scan the harbour. 'Are you still writing songs?'

'Not really, no.'

'You should keep at it, you know. How many people have that kind of head start? Writing songs at eleven?'

'Oh, okay, actually, maybe I was twelve. Or thirteen.'

He shrugged, smiled. 'Still.'

A certain quality in the smile meant that she didn't take a deep breath. She didn't even swallow, cross her fingers, curl her toes. No preparation whatsoever. 'You know what, Lewis? You're . . . very special. Really. I mean it.'

Did she say it too fast? Too high? Too breathily? Too soon? Too non-sequitur? It was a pin to a balloon. His smile locked away. Shoes crunching on the gravel, he headed towards the bike again as he said over his shoulder, 'We should get back so that I can take the others out if they want.'

She felt a stunned disorientation. Subdued, she edged back onto the seat behind him, swallowing and swallowing: insecurity a bitter capsule on the back of her tongue as they cruised home.

Once she was there she lingered in the kitchen, tidying up slowly while Jayshri and Jeff both went off separately for a quick tour. 'Just round the block,' Lewis said. 'I've got to get back pretty soon.'

Yet when Jeffrey, who went last, came inside, unwrapping the scarf of hers he'd borrowed, he had the wild look of an animal just back from the chase, eyes still filled with the night outside, its vague merging shapes, sudden looming images, fleet reversals. Lewis slipped off to use the bathroom before he said goodbye.

As soon as he was out of earshot Candy said, 'What's up, Jeff?'

He blinked. 'Not much.'

Yet clearly something out there had worried him. It tilted in his thoughts, sunk lower for camouflage.

When Lewis reappeared he said to Jeff, 'Ready?'

'Yep.'

Candy was jarred by the sound of her own annoyance. 'For what?'

'Giving Jeff a lift home. It's sort of on the way.'

It wasn't. It wasn't at all.

Jaysh drifted into the hallway where they were all standing, coffee mug in her hands. 'Thanks for the ride,' she said. 'And hey, look. We still haven't had a proper flatmate warming for Candy, and we're thinking of having one in a couple of weeks.'

Oh, they were?

'You'll have to come.'

Jeffrey zipped his coat up to his neck. 'That'd be great.'

Lewis leaned over and gave Candy a quick hug, clamping her arms to her sides. 'Happy to warm this flatmate of yours any time.'

Bafflement roiled in Candy's head. For some reason she wanted to sob.

When the men had gone, Jaysh said to Candy, 'They seem like nice guys.'

And isn't that just the trouble? Candy wanted to say. Instead, she feinted. 'So when's this party?'

'I was thinking about Saturday week. There's a big meeting on that some out-of-towners will be coming to at the student union, and it'd be good to have something to do afterwards.'

'Will everyone else be free?'

'Ah well, who cares. We've postponed it long enough. Let's just say we're having it, and perhaps it will motivate them all to get organised and make it.' Jaysh brushed Candy's shoulder. 'G'night.'

Candy felt that her ability to read people had gone haywire: a needle on a metre, spinning loose on its axis, trying to gauge hot, cold, like, dislike, slow, fast, but touching on all and nothing at the same time.

ON THE SATURDAY of the party Candy was still walking around with a strange distended feeling: an aquarium whose glass was only just containing the weight and pressure of its contents. She came up the front path of the flat after an afternoon shift at the restaurant, trying to force her thoughts away from *Jayshri, Jeffrey, Lewis* — knowing they'd be taking up too much head space during the party anyway. Instead she tried to concentrate on clarifying her plans for applications for more study. Without having done so much as phone the local polytech to order a prospectus she was concocting her own ideal programme: a diploma in journalism with some sort of practical component in music — performance, composition, appreciation. Did it exist? Could she cobble it together somehow if she sweet-talked some admin staff and lecturers? Or would she have to do two separate qualifications and take that much longer, maybe even move towns? She wandered slowly up the stairs, satchel and work-weariness dragging at her step, and made her way heavily to the kitchen so that she could fix herself a strong coffee.

The sight of Jeff and Jayshri in the kitchen pulled her up short. She blinked. 'Hey, you two.'

Jaysh, rolling a cigarette with her natty little metal contraption, said languidly, 'Hey, you one.'

Jeff beamed at her. 'Been waiting for you to get home.'

Candy dropped her satchel and pulled up a chair. The others shuffled a pile of papers, glossy brochures and pamphlets on the kitchen table to clear some space for her. She wished Jaysh weren't there: her immediate urge was to bombard Jeff with questions about how the ride home with Lewis had gone the other night, why he'd offered the lift in the first place, what did Jeff think of him, what had they talked about (had Lewis mentioned her?) — but knew the onslaught of curiosity would sound anything but natural.

'You're here kind of early, aren't you?'

Jaysh finished preparing her smoke. 'Thought he could help us out with some of the preparations.'

She managed to stop herself from asking, *he* thought, or *you* thought? Knowing that it would sound possessive, inspector-like. 'Oh, great.'

'Hey, Candy?' Jeff reached over to touch her shoulder.

'Mmmm?'

'D'you mind if I doss down on your floor tonight? That way I won't have to worry about the trek home if I stay late. I've brought a sleeping bag and Jaysh has said I can borrow her camping bed roll.'

Candy had been battling with herself for at least a week, trying not to hope that Lewis might linger at the party, that they might work their way up to her room, alone . . . an image of him sprang up in her mind and barrelled away again with the mocking speed and clarity of the lucky pictures on a jackpot machine. Tartness sat in her mouth. 'Foregone conclusion, then.'

Jeff laughed. 'Yeah.'

She caught Jayshri's blunt scrutiny and tried to deflect it. 'Sure. You can stay. No problem.' She pointed at the table. 'What are you looking at there?' The leaflets appeared too slick for the productions of Jaysh's socialist crowd.

'Oh, just some ideas for courses and things.'

'Really? Weird. I was just thinking about that, on the way home.' She tilted the printed material to an angle where she could read the titles.

You've got to be fucking joking.

Diploma in Applied Arts: Journalism. Postgraduate Certificate in Practical Arts: Journalism. Department of Media Studies: Print and Radio Journalism. Career Guidance Services: So You Want a Career in Journalism?

She stared at Jeff. His irises, flat as nail-heads, pinned her down. Why couldn't she say it? *You can't do journalism. That's what I've chosen. Why are you even thinking about it? You're a sciences person. It's my idea.* Because it sounded petty, grasping, childish? Or because he really had got her tongue, taken her words, as if his body fitted around her, skull and bone?

Jayshri swung her legs away from the table. 'Can you help me set up those lights now, Jeff?'

'Sure.' Oblivious.

They sloped off to the lounge together. Through the old-fashioned serving hatch that connected the two rooms Candy could see them start to untangle large ropes of coloured lights. She could feel a vibration deep in her limbs, the way the structure of a building will thrub with the heavy bass in a piece of music. It was a kind of shaking. Dazed by it still — things took so long to sink in for her sometimes — she walked away. She sat on the edge of her bed, entranced by an almond-shaped knot in the floorboards. At the time she would have called it mild aftershock, perhaps — the response to assumptions being juddered off foundations that hadn't even set yet. Later, it would seem instead like the tremor of warning, the merest prelude.

She felt an urgent need to tell Lewis about Jeffrey and the brochures, even about Jeffrey and Jaysh, their sudden chumminess, and to recapitulate the conversation they'd never quite restarted after the Raggedies night: about how . . . robbed she'd felt by the sight of her brother in her place. Would Lewis understand? Would anyone understand how deep it ran, this love lined with jealousy lined with love, that made identity seem no more solid than a hand puppet, limp, hollow, so easily turned inside out?

The sight of the brochures, Jeff's casual camaraderie with her new flatmate: it all rushed her back in time to those overheard phrases, those little family mysteries that were usually kept hidden high in the locked-up cupboards of the adults' memories, but which she occasionally surprised them at, before they could box them back up. *Of course, before the twins came, Rose's moods were so much brighter . . . the difficulties should be more widely recognised . . . twice the work . . .*

She saw again, flashing in her mental vision, her mother entering a Barnados store, parking the double stroller under a gas heater. Her brown leather boots walking along a motorway. Her beige raincoat spotting with water drops.

The wind made branches scratch against the side of the house and Candy's attention slowly wheeled back to her attic room. Recently there had been much discussion at her two jobs among the older staff, about people they knew who had been made redundant in the New Economic Climate, in Restructuring Exercises, in the Slim-lining and Rationalising of Big Business. In her own coffee breaks she'd read newspaper interviews in the paper of middle-aged men who talked about loss of confidence, of meaning. There was even one who confessed he put his suit on every morning, packed his briefcase and ducked into the stream of rush-hour traffic at both ends of the working day because he didn't want the neighbours to know he'd lost his job. He sat, for eight hours, in his car down near the wharves, windows fitted with little detachable venetian blinds so no one could see in. He'd read, and sleep, and scan the job pages. But he couldn't find anything. The journalist called him an articulate man, described his close-cropped, grey-sprinkled hair, his slow demeanour. 'I'm truly redundant,' he said. 'There's an excess of me. A superfluity.'

Underneath that particular brand of distant sadness felt for strangers, and concern about how long her own job might last even though the lay-offs most often talked about weren't in the service industry, Candy had experienced the vicious pinch of recognition.

First there had been Jeff, and that was good, but whoops — here came another, just a girl version, most of her brother's carbon, copied. And though her folks had really made a pretty good go of it, had risen above Rose's early difficulties, still, twins weren't what they really wanted . . .

And now it was as if she and Jeff were caught in some odd revenge or payback cycle. Whatever Candy wanted, Jeff wanted too. And she knew — just knew — he'd nearly always do it better. True, he'd given up guitar, but look at his grades at school. Look at his scores in the twins research programme. Look at how The Raggedies had loved him. Look at how, when he filled in for her, the band had still done so well in the finals. Okay, the award was hardly for his playing, but the judges still listened, even though he'd only *mimed* his part. He could seduce anybody. Look at how the prickly Jayshri warmed to him, when Candy seemed to have committed some unspoken, cardinal flatmate social blue that meant they couldn't have a proper conversation any more. And now, supposedly, he was even going to pre-empt her plans for study.

She wanted something to hitch on to, something that would feed her with a sense of herself. The only situation at the moment that seemed to bring her close was when she was with Lewis. How even the fleeting sensation of his body pressed against hers, his hesitant kisses at her cheekbones, grounded her right in the present, drew a heavy, dark outline around her body that confirmed her to herself: I sit, I stand, I lean, I breathe, I feel, I am here. When they talked about the Big Things (oh, democracy, ecology, equality, nationality), the cells in her mind levered towards him, green stalks seeking light — eager to learn, to soak up knowledge like vitamins. And when he said, 'You should keep up your music,' there was a tingling around her hands and throat that brought to mind an image of a bird unfanning its wings to reveal vibrant down.

She'd browsed over some of Jaysh's and Tricia's dog-eared copies of *Broadsheet* and a copy of the Boston Women's Health Collective *Our Bodies Our Selves*, had read a section in one of Jaysh's anthropology textbooks on matriarchal societies, had attended a public lecture downtown given by the national director of women's refuge, visited the women's sections of second-hand bookshops, bought the pink stickers *Girls Can Do Anything*, wondered what Women's Studies at university would be like, hadn't read a fairytale in years, and here she was: enraptured. Wrapped in the glow of hope, which transformed everything she saw. Silly Cinders. Cotton-Candy, head filled with insubstantial spun sugar . . .

She heard Nash call her name up the small flight of stairs that led to her room.

'Candy? You up there? I'm heading out to get some beers and snacks for tonight. You wanna ride if you wanna buy anything?'

She gave her cheeks a couple of half slaps to wake herself out of maudlin mooning. 'Yup,' she called back, glad her voice didn't betray her. 'Coming right down.'

When she passed Jeff in the corridor — as he carried two cups of instant coffee into the living room — he looked surprised to see her putting on her jacket and slinging her satchel back over her shoulder.

'Hey, Candy. I wondered where you'd disappeared to. I was just going to come up and ask if you wanted a coffee.'

'No, thanks. I'm heading out for a bit. But you just go right ahead and help yourself, won't you?'

The edge in her voice made his expression falter somewhere between injury and embarrassment. 'Jayshri said I . . .'

'I'm sure Jayshri did.'

She turned on her heel and began to thump down the stairs. He followed her to the landing. 'Candy, what's up? Don't be like that.'

'Like what?'

'Annoyed or something.'

'Why not? Because you don't feel like duplicating it?'

Hurt clouded his face, so she had that sense of rushing into the past again: instantaneously back to all those occasions in his dim bedroom, where he'd hidden buried under the covers, hammered flat by a sadness she used to dread would spirit him off the way it had their mum.

She lingered on the stairs. 'Look, Jeff. I'm sorry. There's just . . . a lot for me to sort out in my head right now.' She didn't think she sounded in the least bit convincing but he looked relieved.

'Anything you want to talk about?'

Jayshri wandered out and leaned against the banister a little above where Jeff stood.

Candy sighed. 'Maybe. When we get a chance to be alone.'

Jaysh swung out of her slouch a little. 'Shall we go thirds on a cask of wine?'

Candy shook her head. 'Nope. I'm getting beer.'

'Halves?' said Jaysh to Jeff.

'Sure.'

'Grab one for us while you're out, will you, Candy?'

Candy held out her hand. 'Cash.'

Jayshri shrugged. 'Haven't got it right now.'

'Well, I can't cover it.'

Jaysh looked mildly surprised. 'Haven't you been paid this week?'

Candy had read that if you breathed through your nostrils when you were running, it minimised stitch. So she did it now, to filter out the hard knot of irritation that compacted right under her chest bones.

Jeffrey set the coffee cups down at his feet and dug around in his pockets. Then he passed Candy a couple of notes. She took them. 'You still getting an allowance?'

'Nuh-uh.' Examining one of her fingernails, Jaysh answered for him. 'He's just got himself a job, haven't you, Jeff?'

'Yeah. This is from my first pay. Got a job at a restaurant actually.' His eyes were fired with happiness and he was automatically nodding, apparently fully expecting Candy to proffer her impressed congratulations: *Oh, really, just like me!*

Should she laugh or groan?

Nash stomped into the corridor from outside the front of the flat. 'Hey, Floss-head, are we going or what? I've been in the bloody car for bloody yonky's years.'

'Sorry.' She gestured to the others. 'I'm waiting on their orders. Red? White?'

'Dry white,' from Jaysh, and, 'Whatever,' from Jeff, simultaneously.

So of course she deliberately came back with a sickly sweet red, Velluto Rosso, and said to Jeff, 'Here's your whatever,' avoiding Jaysh's eyes. 'I'll come back down to help with the food after I get changed.'

Upstairs, she tried to physically wrench herself out of the bitter mood by concentrating on what to wear. Her clothes had to be a web, body a scented stamen to draw the admiral butterfly . . . Heart on the sleeve indeed . . . *heart felt*, she thought in a flash of self-irony: how suitable a term. A heart made of dense, soft, woolly fabric: a big scarlet cut-out shape, a sponge to soak up any extra attention that Lewis might spill. But the flash of sour humour didn't really release her; it just made her feel all the more ridiculous — head over heels, how ungainly, as if she were permanently caught out halfway through a backwards somersault on the carpet.

Finally she chose some second-hand black satin pants that were woven with a raised pattern of Chinese dragons, and matched it with a peacock blue silk shirt, also second hand, which was trimmed with black piping and fitted with black acorn-shaped buttons. She found a little gold safety pin and worked a trick that her mother had shown her once, of hiding the pin under the shirt and pinning it to the middle of the bra so that you showed nothing but suggested much. Candy hardly ever wore any makeup apart from eyeliner, but had bought a liquid silver-green eye shadow that seemed to make her eyes shine like lamps, and a liquid gold lipstick called Hot Blonde. Pondering whether she looked like a completely overdone turkey, she was startled by a knock at the door. She'd been listening to a Tall Shrubs tape on her cassette deck, and had been so absorbed in trying to magic up any fairy godmother traits hidden in her own genes that she hadn't heard footsteps on the stairs.

'Come in?'

It was Jeff, laden down with his overnight gear. 'Hey, can I just leave my stuff in here now so it's out of the way for the party?'

'Oh, okay. Sure.'

'Is that what you're wearing?'

She looked down at herself. 'What's wrong with it?'

'Nothing! I just meant, you know, were you thinking of changing again, or was that it?'

She smoothed the fabric over her ribs. 'It's all I've really got.'

'Let's have a look.'

He went to her wardrobe and began shuffling through her hangers as self-assuredly as the proprietor of a clothing store. He pulled out a long-sleeved, seventies-style turtle neck, machine knitted in stretchy copper lurex, which Candy knew from experience would make her itch all over if she wore it directly against her skin.

'*Jeff*,' she said, hands in fists at her sides: miniature demolition balls she'd have liked to have swung at the thick-as-bricks of him.

'What?'

'Would you *ask* first? Just back off!'

'Jeez, excu-u-u-se me! What have you got hidden in there that you can't show your own brother? Chocolate-flavoured condoms?' He giggled and misaimed a few times as he tried to get the coat hanger back on the metal rail.

Realisation hit her. 'You're pissed already, aren't you?'

'Tipsy. Getting pissed, I hope.'

There was a deep dong-bong at the doorbell. Candy's nerve endings flared with the sound: she imagined them lit up like fibres of light. 'Shit. Someone's arrived already. I better get downstairs to help with the food.'

'Can I get into my things in here?' He gestured to the small backpack he'd brought up with his sleeping bag and the borrowed bed roll.

'Go ahead. Oh — and Jeff?' There was a worming of regret in her head even as she began to say it. 'Try not to make a fool of yourself tonight, will you? This party's actually quite important to me.'

He looked at her with sleepy eyes. 'Man, you sound like a jumped-up cow.'

She did. But he was acting like a selfish little prick. She felt years older than him as he fumbled to undo his backpack straps, laughing a broken tune to himself. And she dreaded him coming down and throwing himself around like a rottweiller that assumes it's cute as a shitsu, and having everyone turn to look at *her*, too, stares lining them up, side by side, seeing him in her, as if somehow one twin had an obligation to reflect the other.

Like the time when they were about eleven, and Jeff, who was on lunch duty, was caught stealing two of the potato top mince pies from the Styrofoam delivery carton from which he was supposed to dole out lunches, matching up kids' order tickets with the paper-wrapped packets inside. Some new entrants forgot where they were supposed to go to collect their orders, and instead of telling the headmaster — who was on playground duty that day — that there were two meals left over, Jeff hoed into both pies.

Each of the twins was banned from supervising the handing-out of lunch orders after that — even though Candy had performed the duty several times before Jeff's crime, and the little kids liked her, used to hang around, looking at her with their big eyes. And what's more, whenever there were other roles of responsibility the intermediate-age students were asked to volunteer for, the twins were always considered last.

Candy hadn't been mad at Jeff back then: not really. She'd been mad at Mr Yates, the headmaster. So furious that whenever she saw him she couldn't quite believe that he didn't melt into a puddle of water from the vehemence of it burning away at him from deep in every battery of her being. Now it was as if the old and the new fury had scrambled, heading straight for Jeff: a part of her own wiring crossed in on itself, threatening to fuse.

Down on the lower floors, a few small groups of people were milling around already: loosely connected to Jaysh, they were from a national tertiary students' association retreat that had finished early that day. The local politicos had bragged so much to the out-of-towners about what great parties Jayshri's flat threw that they'd all skipped the pub and come straight to the flat in case they missed out on any action. The out-of-towners were cheesed off, as Nash was having trouble with the stereo, all the main house lights were still on — no candles, no fairy lights, no atmosphere — and Jaysh's flatmates seemed to be the only people who weren't from their own sub-set.

'Where's the party?' asked one blond, ex-head-boy, ex-proxime-accessit-to-the-dux type, in blue and white striped business shirt and acid-wash blue jeans.

'Well, *you're* here, aren't you?' Candy answered, expecting him to be too obtuse to pick up the sarcasm. He blushed so much it threatened to stain his shirt pink, so she said, apologetically, 'Actually, it wasn't really due to start until around nine.' But for the rest of the night, whenever their orbits came remotely near, he looked at her like a panic-stricken possum: eyes wide, ears back, turning tail and scuttling back into a dark corner.

Candy managed to distract herself from wondering whether the party would be any good by concentrating on preparing cracker toppings and homemade dips, and chopping up crudités to arrange in a wagon-wheel pattern on a couple of dinner plates. One reason Jayshri's parties were famous among the student set was that food was usually on offer. There were always hollow-eyed, grey-skinned guests who just couldn't budget in more than baked beans, cheese and toast to their weekly expenses. Even carrot and celery sticks disappeared from Jayshri's dos, and the dip bowls usually looked as if they'd been licked clean.

The party seemed to follow the laws of the sauce bottle Candy fought with when she made a fast tomato-coating for a pizza base. Nothing, nothing, nothing, a few spurts arriving, and then — voosh — the building was swamped, overcrowded, the noise, temperature and clutter all up in a single rush. There was hardly room to move: people were still arriving and there was a guest-jam on the stairway, people crushed together still in their coats, looking up the stairwell expectantly, until the message was telegraphed down that there was no room anywhere else, either, so they may as well claim a place on the stairs. Couples hunkered down, awkwardly took off coats in confined spaces, cracked open beer cans they'd brought, or called up for a corkscrew to be passed out from the kitchen and down the chain. Some people spent the whole night trying to get from the ground floor to the turret room they'd all seen from the outside, but were wedged in so tightly next to strangers that they were forced to talk: which immediately made it seem like a 'really friendly party, eh?', as people kept saying, with enthusiastic nods.

It all seemed to be going well so, already a little squiffy, Candy couldn't work out why it felt as if something was missing. She found herself scanning the living room and corridor through the kitchen serving hatch and doorway, thinking, is it the beer? Maybe the beer's off or I chose the wrong brand. Maybe it's Nash's choice of music — I knew I should have hidden his Bucks Fizz album. Should we have done more decorations? Chosen a theme?

She tried to concentrate on what a woman pressed up near her was saying about a nightclub that had just opened. The Grimelight. 'Very *underground*. A mixture of Goth and fetish,' she was saying. 'People *really* get into the dressing up, it's fantastic.'

'Oh, right. Are you heading off there tonight?'

She was in pink and black striped knee-high socks, a black pleated mini-skirt and a hot pink lace-up corset, which showed she was probably wearing white foundation over most of her torso. Over her arms she wore pink fishnet tights turned into something of a cross between evening gloves and detachable sleeves, and her dyed black hair was in braids that looped up into an incredible shape like a hybrid of birdcage and wicker basket. Inside it she'd pinned a little fake bird with hot pink feathers, to match her outfit. She wore four distinct shades of pink eye shadow drawn in clear lines from eyebrow to eyelid, fake eyelashes, a hot pink diamante sticker on one cheek, baby pink lipstick outlined in black pencil, and her re-drawn eyebrows looked as complicated as Japanese calligraphy.

She laughed at Candy. 'No, no. When you go there, you have to make an effort.'

Part of Candy admired such self-elaboration, the ability to turn every public encounter into an act of performance art, being bold enough to put up with the sidelong glances and crude comments she could just catch from some of the straight-laced politicos who'd tagged on to Jaysh's friends. Or maybe it was an armour? So upfront and in-your-face that actually the only harassment you'd get were those cowardly whispers and guffaws: nothing more directly confrontational. Candy seemed to be the only person outside the — similarly dressed up — group who was willing to try to get past what one of the politicos mumbled was 'fucken freakin' war paint'.

Maybe it was the tension she could feel between the Goths and the politicos (whom the Goths called the 'quartics' — 'You've heard of squares, right? Well, those guys are more than squares. More than cubes. To the power of four, man. They're quartics.') that made things feel off-centre. Or had she actually had too much beer to drink — marinating her in melancholy? She caught sight of Jaysh and Jeff trying to push their way through the crush in the corridor. Jeff was wearing the coppery lurex top he'd pulled out of Candy's wardrobe, her Hot Blonde lipstick and, knotted into a makeshift cummerbund, a shimmering yellow scarf she didn't recognise. At the same time as she felt a click — memory and the present sliding together, right, clean and smooth as a film cartridge slotting into a camera — she felt herself wilt against the kitchen bench.

'That little shit,' she said.

'What?' the woman — who said her name was Salomé — peered out into the corridor.

'My brother. He's wearing my clothes and makeup.'

'Which one is he? Oh — obviously. Didn't need to ask really, did I?'

'The little *shit*.'

'Oh, well. It does suit him.'

Candy groaned, covered her face with a hand. 'I didn't need to hear that.'

'Hey, Candy?'

She surfaced, blinking, from where her hand had pressed a swirl of darks and lights, golds and blues, over her vision. Lewis. The party wheeled, revolved and steadied into position. Everything was going just fine! Her strange mood raced out like a tide. The night was a hit; what had she been so *worried* about?'

'Lewis!'

'You okay there? You looked like you were having a bit of a spin-out. Not back to your old boozing ways, are you?' He looked at Salomé. 'When I first met this little girl she was dancing on table-tops.'

Salomé — flatteringly — seemed impressed. 'Trippy!' So Candy held back protests about his exaggeration.

'Mmm. I had a whole routine.'

'You'll have to show us,' said Salomé.

'I would if there were room.'

The shape of the party dilated and swelled with a slow, viscous rhythm, so by sheer force of the crush, Lewis and Candy were kept talking together for at least an hour. And there were so few other people she knew there that once Salomé and her 'spooky crew' (another overheard wisecrack) had begun the slow ooze out of the kitchen, Candy was emboldened by the anonymity. Not caring who eavesdropped, and fighting off all the confusion she'd been feeling over things with him, she leaned against Lewis, upper arm to upper arm. She tried to find a way to work him on to a personal topic. 'Okay, so tell me, Lewis. Did you ever play truth or dare as a kid?'

He rolled the cool body of his beer bottle against one of his cheeks, pondering.

She envied that beer bottle . . . 'You haven't heard of it?'

'No, I definitely played it, but I was just thinking. When we played it as kids, dare was always the hardest option. Truth seemed easy.' He took a swig of beer. 'I was just wondering whether that'd be the case now. You know?'

Watching the curve of his mouth, the small, dark gap between his lips as they set a little apart, all she could think of were two equally nerve-wracking options to offer him. *Truth:* how do you really feel about me? *Dare:* stay the night, skin to skin.

She swallowed. 'I think it would depend. But don't you think it's pretty sad that truth could be harder?'

He shrugged. 'When you were a kid it was like, 'Dare you to go and ring old Mr One-armed-Retired-Policeman's doorbell and run away,' or 'Dare you to swim in the banned creek in winter'. But truth — we couldn't even come *up* with a truth question most of the time. 'Is it true your mother doesn't wear a bra?' That was the most challenging one I can remember, and the answer was no, she *does* wear a bra, anyway. I mean, what have kids got to hide? Half the time if they have got things their families want hidden, they don't even realise it themselves yet.'

Candy found herself twisting hard at a strand of hair, then feeling a surprisingly abrupt stress-niggle in her forearm — which she hadn't really experienced for a while. She'd been thinking about her mother, and the little girl from school who'd seen them at the hospital once. She put her hands in her pockets to stop her nervous twiddling. 'I think kids pick up more than that.'

Lewis took a white plastic cup from a stack lying on its side on the kitchen bench and poured her some of his beer. As he passed it to her he asked, 'So, your family had something to hide?'

She raised an eyebrow at him as she accepted the cup and drank. 'We're playing, are we?'

He took a deep breath through his nostrils, held it, and closed his eyes. Then he released the air in a great rush, batted his lashes at her. 'Okay. Okay, I think we are.' There was such a warmth in the way his grin collapsed the lines around his eyes — his expression said, ah, let's just scrap sadness altogether, crumple it up, start again — that she felt her own caginess unlock and breathe with a shake of stiffened limbs.

He gestured at her with his beer bottle. 'So, you first, as it was your suggestion. Your family had something to hide?'

'Ah.' She knew she gleamed at him again: no holding back. 'You haven't asked the real question.'

'Which is?'

'Truth — or dare.'

'Ha!' This time his gesture was so vigorous, that although the bottle was less than half full, beer fountained up in a foamy brown plume that slopped onto his wrist. 'There you go, you see? *Truth* is what you want to shy away from. It's too much. *You'd* rather have the dare.'

Laughter tingled in her feet and palms. 'I didn't say that! You just — have to play by the rules. So . . .'

'Right.' He dried off his wrist, crossed his arms, bottle held in the crook of one elbow. 'Truth. Or dare.'

She ran a thumb knuckle over her lips, wondering how the mere sight of someone could seem to press itself into the body like a letter-seal in warm wax: how just from looking at the angle of a jaw, a brow, pleasure could fill in between skin and bone like a drug, drowning all other memory.

'Chicken!' he said. 'I knew it. You're *chickening* on me!'

She narrowed her eyelids, tilted her chin and shot out her response, as if she were the one presenting him with the challenge. 'All right, then. Truth.'

He swallowed a fresh mouthful of beer. 'Okay. Is it *true* that your family had something to hide?'

The words struggled, large bees caught in the narrow neck of a foxglove. She cleared her throat. 'Well, other kids sometimes thought so, when they found out about us. But it wasn't really something to hide — I can see that now.'

His eyes took her in carefully. 'Is that all the truth I'm going to get?'

She shrugged a little. 'Okay. The full blow by blow? My mother used to get a kind of cyclical depression. I remember one kid at school asked me if my mum was mental. It seems laughable now, but at the time I was so upset, though tried to play it very cool. Jeff and I — we used to worry about Mum a lot, and probably didn't talk much about that to our parents. Because we thought it would upset her more.' There was a heaviness in her chest: a warning that she might have said too much. But to hold back — wouldn't that prove his point, about truth?

'I guess we sort of felt . . . responsible for it, a lot of the time.'

'Jeff did too?'

'What do you mean?'

Lewis's bottom lip gave its own small shrug. 'It's just interesting that you say "we". It sounds like you were quite . . . together as children.'

'On this, yes.'

In a break from the music coming from the living room, Candy heard a laugh that was unmistakably Jeff's. She ducked down to see if she could catch sight of him through the serving hatch, then wondered why she had: some concern, the old protective urge, had gripped her for a moment. She shook it off when she saw him cross-legged on the carpet, head bowed but grin still visible as he listened to what seemed to be a debate between Jaysh and one of her friends. When she recognised her shirt again, a wish not to be noticed by him chased away the sheltering instinct — in case, she realised guiltily, the conversation with Lewis looked more interesting, and Jeff tried to muscle in.

She bobbed up. 'Baby brother's okay,' she said, slightly sourly — though she meant half the sourness for herself.

Lewis raised an eyebrow at her. 'Baby? I thought Jeff said he was born first.'

Sarcasm made her lean on her words. 'He *told* you that? Oh, and he hardly ever tells *anyone* that.'

Lewis crossed his arms, face lively with fascination. 'I can't believe it's such a big deal for you guys. There was what — a whole seven minutes' difference?'

'Six.'

He laughed. 'Six. But you both act like it really means something.'

'I don't.'

'Well, why did you call him baby brother?'

'I just meant . . . sometimes I still feel like I ought to be looking out for him. You know. He hasn't left home yet, and —'

Lewis smiled. 'That's kind — but don't you think Jeff can look out for himself?'

His words made her reconsider the sight of Jeff, relaxed and laughing with Jayshri. He was making his own way, she understood in a flash; his happiness or unhappiness wasn't her responsibility. With two sharp prongs, the image of Lewis with Jeff as his pillion passenger on the motorbike pushed into Candy's heart. She tried to deflect it by getting Lewis off the subject.

'So, anyway, Lewis, back to the choice. What's your decision? Truth or dare?'

And regardless of the choice, what the hell would she ask him?

He looked at her knowingly, in a way that suddenly made her feel very exposed. 'Truth or dare. Hmmm. But what about a situation where you weren't sure what the truth was?'

Idly, Candy took a handful of Bombay mix from a snack bowl and savoured the crunchiness against her teeth. She wondered what he might be surmising about her intended questions. She almost hoped he had no idea, if he wasn't sure what the answer would be — but then, if he had no idea, did that mean she'd totally misconstrued all the signals? No, she can't have. Unless — maybe he'd been interested in more-than-friends once, but now that he'd done some . . . exploring, he'd decided it had all been a mistake.

She toyed with a beer cap on the bench. 'Well, maybe that would be a part of the truth. Maybe you'd have to say, "I'm not quite sure where the lines have to be drawn," or whatever.'

He gave her an appraising look that seemed to say she was either a striking — or a perplexing — curiosity. It unsettled her, yet made her want to try harder to rearrange herself, her words and the spaces between them, to find the pattern that would make his smile slide home like the solution to a brainteaser.

He placed his beer bottle very neatly inside a ring of condensation left on the bench. 'You're a pretty clever cookie, you know, Sweets.'

She laughed — high, tinkling, an unfamiliar sound of silver spoons and platters which she immediately wanted to deny: that's not me, that's not me at all! She'd meant it to be warm, lush and gravelly: *Sweets* somehow made her think of a blues singer, generous-bosomed, scarlet dress tight as a stocking, heavy black eyelashes, long and languid. Instead, she piped, 'Sweets?'

He gave her a crooked grin. 'Candy — Sweets. Nobody's ever called you that before?'

'No. But I like it.'

He was holding her gaze, wasn't he? He wasn't distracted by other activity in the kitchen, wasn't scouting around for other conversations. She pressed the side of her hip against his, experimentally, heart doing a steeple race.

'Okay, Lewis Tillerman. You're taking an extra long time to choose your options here. Are you trying to tell me that *you* might be chickening?'

Infinitesimally — yet also, to her hopes, by gargantuan proportions — she felt his hip draw away from hers. 'Are you threatening me, Candice Marshall? Are you *mocking* me?'

She raised both palms. 'I wouldn't dream of it. Not in a zillion.'

'Just as well. All right. Put it to me again. I need some extra time to think this through.'

The urge to touch him again reopened painfully in every single pore. She managed to constrain it, channelling it into one small, unsatisfactory teasing gesture: knocked him on the chest with the back of her hand, and clucked, *bawk, bawk bawk*. Then she tapped her forehead. 'I mean — excuse me. Truth. Or dare?'

The rim of his beer bottle resting up against his mouth pressed away the colour from his lips. His eyes — usually a light periwinkle blue — were choppy, sea-dark with whatever he was thinking. He lowered the beer bottle and said, 'Dare.'

She didn't blink. She let him think he'd got away without a ribbing. 'All right. I dare you to — ' she looked at the ceiling, pretending to contemplate possibilities. 'I dare you to *tell the truth about . . .*'

He roared, and heads turned. Candy laughed, and he waved them off. 'Sorry, folks, nothing serious.'

She touched his elbow. 'Sorry, Lewis. I do have a dare for you. A real dare.'

Arms behind him, he leaned against the kitchen bench again, staging a relaxed pose. 'Go on.'

She thought she might be sick. Her heart was no longer racing but sat in place, expanding slowly. The space her feet were taking up seemed to shrink to the thin cord of a highwire. She gripped to the edge of the bench hard, but forced herself to look right into the dark tunnels of his pupils.

'I dare you to — ' she took in a sharp breath. 'I dare you to — stay the night tonight.'

There was a silence. A small, puzzled smile curled at the edges of his mouth, giving him an almost hurt appearance. 'Candy.'

Through the serving hatch a hand gripped her forearm and she nearly leapt out of her shoes. Jeff's face poked through the frame, grinning. He tilted his head to the side so that he could get a better view of Lewis.

'Yeah, Lewis. Dare you to stay the night tonight. I'm bludging a bed here too — probably safer even than walking, after the amount I've had to drink, eh? And in that leather —' he tugged on the silver zip at the cuff of Lewis's biker jacket, which he still hadn't taken off, though Candy felt warm in her shirt sleeves — 'you wouldn't be safe, mate. Did you read in the paper about that guy who got knifed on Princes Street the other night? Just for his jacket. You should kip here, with us.'

The odd smile, which had seemed somehow to twist Lewis's eyes with pain, lifted from his face. 'You're a pair, you two, aren't you?'

Candy couldn't believe her heart hadn't exploded and sent her whizzing around the room like a deflated scrap of rubber. Jeff was impossible. Couldn't he read her face? All those myths about twin telepathy — if only they were true, he could see, in neon written on her brain, *Fuck off, Fuck off, Fuck OFF!* And what was she going to do about this rush of tears coming, which the men would think was so inexplicable?

Lewis was looking from brother to sister. 'All right,' he said, now with a couldn't-care-less shrug. 'You've convinced me. I'll stay. It means I can have a few more beers, after all.'

'Cool!' Jeff rested his chin on his elbows, looking up at Candy through his fringe like a cherub in a Renaissance painting.

With both hands in his jeans pockets, shifting his jacket aside a little, Lewis gave a small grimace. 'There is something I have to warn you about, though.'

Candy swallowed: her throat thoroughly bee-stung now, no sounds escaping past the swelling.

'And this means I'm taking two turns in a row, Candy.'

She shaped what she hoped was a questioning look.

Jeff angled a thin arm out through the serving hatch and checked a couple of empty cups and beer bottles on the bench, hunting for drink to pilfer. 'Two turns at what?'

'Truth or dare. So this is an unsolicited truth, okay? And it means you might change your mind about me staying the night.'

Jeff mimed a look of scandal. 'Don't tell me. Underneath that jacket and those jeans you've got wings and a tail.'

'Not quite that bad.' Lewis cleared his throat, fist up to his mouth. 'The thing is — ah, shit, this is really embarrassing.' He swept a palm over his face.

Jeff actually achieved a serious look for a moment, which seemed to let Lewis continue. 'Or, actually, maybe it's nothing. It's just . . . aaarrrgh.'

Candy gave him a quick consoling squeeze on the elbow, managing to say, thickly, 'You don't have to tell us if you don't want to.'

'Well, no, but I should, really, if I stay. It's just . . . there's this kind of issue with me. It's trivial really, but just in case . . . actually, I guess I was going to tell you about it once. You know I said there are some things about me that'd be pretty hard to live with?' He gave a short, dry laugh and Candy vaguely began to recall a session in his car . . .

He waved a dismissive hand. 'It's just that I tend to sleepwalk. That's all. It's a bit . . . unpredictable. Though it seems to be when

I'm more stressed than usual.' He gave them both a helpless look. 'So, if you notice it: Point (a) — '

'You're not responsible for your actions.' Jeff grinned.

'I guess you could say that. But, just try to talk me gently back to bed. And make sure I'm not . . . wandering out of the house, or doing anything . . . risky.' He judged their faces, then said hastily, 'But I'm sure it won't get that serious. It never has before, not really.'

Candy's mind had slowly been unpicking the muddle that Jeff had made, and she'd realised that, well, at least Lewis was actually going to be near her, in the same house overnight, even if it wasn't exclusively *with* her. And that had to be a positive step. Her throat unclouded. 'Not really? It sounds like there's a story there.'

'Well, there was, I guess, once. Yeah, once I was found — sort of — outside, without much on.'

'You're being a bit evasive.'

He slumped against the bench. 'Whoa. This is way too much truth for one night, Candy. You're sucking me dry!'

She shut up, and let the men start up some talk about motorbikes — with some fairly crude, fast-tongued jokes about men in leathers — that Candy let wash over her. She spent the rest of the party in a state of suspended animation, numb and drowsy with alcohol, only half listening to the conversations around her, just wanting things to wind up and for everyone to go home so that the crunch could come: the sorting out of sleeping arrangements. Would Lewis maybe *need* someone to watch over him?

As it happened, there wasn't any sorting to do. At four am, when the house had finally emptied, and she trailed through the corridors looking for Lewis and Jeff, from whom she'd somehow become separated as the crowd thinned out, she discovered Lewis was slumped, comatose, on a couch in the living room. She gazed at him for a moment, then knelt next to him. He was so close, so quiet. She whispered, 'Are you okay there?' Not even a flutter of consciousness. 'You know where my room is if you need me, don't you?' She waited for several more minutes, then had to slip away quietly to her bed.

Jeff was also already asleep, burrowed into his sleeping bag, which was heaped with a couple of spare blankets he'd taken from the end of Candy's bed. Beside him there was a saucer full of ash, paper rubbish and a joint that was still glowing. He can't have fallen asleep at all long ago then, but she was still furious as she took a quick draw on it, then stubbed it out. 'Dickhead,' she hissed at him. 'You want to set the whole place alight?'

She tumbled into bed and, although she was exhausted, found herself tossing and turning, lurching in and out of sleep: as aware of Lewis's presence in the house as if he'd been in the same room. She kept waking and listening for him: afraid he'd head away before she could get a chance to talk to him again, alone. When Jeff rustled in his sleeping bag she felt fury beat in her chest, cursing him for staying the night too, wishing it had been Lewis on her floor, the two of them talking until the sun came up — and wishing maybe for more, maybe for more. Once, when she woke fully after what must have been a fitful hour or so of sleep, she wondered if she could sneak out of bed, visit Lewis in the living room, tell him there how she felt, the bluntness of the words somehow cushioned by the darkness. She got as far as swinging her legs over the side of the bed, shivering in the cold, but Jeff stirred, and she shrank back under the covers.

She was awake again instantly when she heard the stairs crack and creak, the house sounding like a ship moving out from the doldrums into a fresh breeze. Her heart gave an axe-thud as she tried to work out whether the footsteps were those of a flatmate or an intruder, but then Lewis appeared, outlined in the doorway.

She sat up slightly, so that he'd know she was awake. But it was difficult to tell if he could see her, so she whispered, 'Hey, you.' He paused, and stood stock still, except for the rise and fall of his shoulders. Did she see Jeff move then? She could hear him and Lewis breathing, in a steady duet. And it was in listening to this, the rhythms like the small, foamy waves of the shallows dissolving on sand, that she realised Lewis was still asleep. His breaths were long, sighing. The question and response of the two men seemed so attuned, that she was unnerved. She instinctively drew the blankets up closer around her shoulders, then held motionless. The airy, hush-shush of their unconscious conversation continued, as she whispered, 'So, shit. What am I going to do now?'

Lewis had said to try to guide him gently back to bed, but could she cope with getting him down the stairs? And would he settle on a strange couch again anyway? She'd have to try. Maybe she could stay with him until daylight, to make sure he was all right. She started to ease herself out from under the covers, not wanting to make any sudden movements that could disconcert or startle him. As her feet touched the cold floor Lewis moved forward. He knelt by Jeff's sleeping bag. She froze.

In the moonlight and street light that filtered through her flimsy curtains she saw him reach out and touch Jeff's hair. Jeff definitely did stir this time. She was about to whisper his name in warning when he reached out in return, cupping Lewis's shoulder. The silhouettes of their heads were still for a moment, then exploring, tentative, before they became hungry, nudging, tasting. Then Lewis drew his face away. He curled up next to Jeff, who remained unmoving for a few beats. Eventually he cautiously shifted the blankets off his sleeping bag, and placed them over him. He let Lewis nuzzle up to him — and then, gradually, he, too, seemed to fall asleep.

A wild misery climbed through Candy. She tried to talk it down, saying, Lewis didn't know, not really, and now Jeff's just trying not to disconcert him, he's just glad Lewis is sleeping, what else could he have done? *But he didn't have to respond, did he? Though I'd have done the same* (*But it wouldn't have been the same!*) ... No, Lewis doesn't really know what he's doing he — he warned us, he's not responsible for his own actions ...

But there was the conviction, solid and strong, that those unconscious gestures told a deeper truth. That all of this was written on Lewis in an invisible ink that sleep and darkness brought out, his real desires legible now. Like the stars, moons, and comets people use to decorate ceilings: transfers almost concealed during daylight but which at night, when the lights are turned off, blaze with fluorescence.

Candy sat immobilised on the edge of the bed, cool air slipping under her thin nylon nightgown, raising gooseflesh on her arms. A series of moments rushed at her. All those hesitations, the constant awkwardness of their touching, that night in the car, *Sometimes I don't even know what . . . type I'm attracted to . . .* and his line during the party: 'What about a situation where you weren't sure what the truth was?' Offering Jeff a lift home, even Jeff's teasing theft of her shirt and lipstick — it all seemed so obvious now. She felt so stupid, so thick, so crudely deluded. How could she not have *seen*?

She stumbled up from her bed, dragging off the blankets and catching up her pillow. Shame, and a heart that felt as if a fracture were running across it, bent her in the middle. She bumbled her way over the sleeping bodies of the men, tripped and staggered down the stairs — not caring who she woke — and blindly found her way to the couch in the living room. She lay down inchingly, as if all her muscles were strained from over-exertion, and curled up, nursing a knot in her stomach that just wouldn't release.

CANDY WOKE AROUND midday the next day, head tight with hang-over, and her perspective still jangled by the strange dislocations of the night-time dumbshow in the turret room. She lay there, watching the colours cast on the living-room wall by a prism in the window, and tried to sift through the events she'd seen, and the weird versions of them she'd dreamed once she had plunged into an emotionally exhausted sleep. But she was here, on the couch, not in her room, so it must have happened . . .

How would they confront one another now? Would there be a chilly, detached lack of discussion? Might Lewis and Jeff have already left, sneaked out while the coast was clear? Would they even try to dismiss it all as off the wall drunkenness, nothing serious — or had it even been a set-up, right from their conversation about Lewis's sleepwalking? All those options made her angrier and angrier. A feeling of double betrayal geysered up, before she was fully conscious that she'd made the decision. She wrapped herself in a blanket, running a hand through her hair, and made her way to her room as quickly as the hang-over would allow.

She half expected the men not to be there, or for one of them to be in her bed, and for the denials to start. But they were still both on the floor, fully dressed and still asleep, though they'd rolled away from each other in the night.

At the sight of Lewis's sleeping face her anger receded, though she'd wanted to hold on to it, tight as a sword, as a shield. His face, his eyes, his lips. All she could do was stand there, bereft, unrequited: redundant again. A stupid, loud, ugly vowel escaped before she could clamp a hand over her mouth.

The noise woke Lewis, and the sound of him shifting on the floor, murmuring, 'God, man, what's the time?' helped to rouse Jeff also. Both of them raised their heads, swinging their gazes around the room, reminding Candy absurdly of beached sea elephants.

She shuffled over to her bed and dropped down on the mattress.

'Hey, Candy,' Jeff said, rubbing his eyes. 'Sleep any?'

Lewis rose to sit, head in his hands. 'God, man,' he said again. He tousled his hair and looked up. 'How did I get in here? I thought I went to sleep downstairs.'

Candy nodded, took a fragmented breath in, and said, 'Look, you guys.' She paused. 'Something happened last night that I think . . . I want you to talk about. To explain to me. I deserve . . . I just . . . want to know.'

Rubbing his eyes again, Jeff frowned, then his glance darted from Lewis to her before he busied himself with the zip on his sleeping bag.

Lewis appeared genuinely bamboozled. 'What's going on? What do you mean?'

She pushed out her hands, as if feeling for rain. 'Well, look where you were sleeping.'

He massaged his temples. 'Yeah, yeah, I know. Bizarre, eh? Did you hear me come in?'

Brother and sister both nodded.

'Hope I didn't do anything stupid.' He gave a half laugh.

Jeff continued to pick at his sleeping bag zip, face impassive, which made Candy bridle. 'Jeff, *you* weren't sleepwalking, right? So maybe you can tell me what's been going on here.'

He talked to his hands. 'Going on?'

'What happened here last night.'

He coloured.

Lewis's forehead creased into even deeper corrugations. 'I'm sorry, Candy. You'll have to backtrack.'

She waited for Jeff to say something, then closed her eyes before launching into it. 'You and Jeff were pretty . . . intimate last night.'

Silence floated down.

'And either way, intended or unintended, I need to understand.' She realised her hands were shaking so she sat on them. 'I think I deserve that. Not because ordinarily I think it's . . . wrong. But because —' she had to stop again. 'I mean —' She looked at Lewis. 'I thought that you and I . . . that it might be going somewhere.' She nodded to herself. 'I wanted it to go somewhere.' She pressed the backs of her knuckles against her face to try to cool it down.

There was another highly uncomfortable silence. It stretched on, and she began to feel like no words made sense any more, that her understanding of certain concepts was all skewed, that her attitudes to friendship and openness were alien, or antiquated, that these men — like her flatmates — knew some language she'd never been privy to. There was some gap in her education where everyone else had learned how to do this: how to cope with other people.

Lewis pushed the blankets off and came up into a crouch, hands on his knees. 'Look, I'm really sorry, Candy. Whatever happened — I don't really remember. Maybe I even . . . thought Jeff was you.' But his tone of voice was void: he seemed to be testing whether she would buy an idea he had no truck with himself.

'Yeah, right.'

He ran a hand through his hair so his fringe stood up like a shock of tussock. 'Okay, look.' Still squatting, he swung around on his heels towards Jeff. 'I need to talk to Candy alone. I agree it's only fair. Would you mind?'

As at a starter's gun, Jeff virtually leapt out of the sleeping bag. 'Yeah, sure. I'll wait downstairs. Maybe make us some coffee.'

Candy didn't want to acknowledge him but gave a minimal nod before he hived off.

Lewis stood up slowly. 'Can I sit next to you?'

She repeated the nod.

He came over beside her, and they both stared at their knees.

'I guess I've been . . . wondering for a while how to tell you about things, about how I am. Only . . . you, you seemed so sure. So convinced.' He brushed one of her knees swiftly — it might have been unintentional. 'And I guess that was . . . exciting. Flattering. I know that's unfair of me. I'd never met anyone else who was so sure, themselves, about me.' She felt the movement of the bedsprings as he shifted in place. 'I should have stopped it sooner, or explained so you'd know how . . . complicated it could be.'

She struggled for something to say. Empathy and despair twisted together, a thorny scrub: generous red flowers alternating with tough spikes. There was relief, too, that she hadn't been completely misreading everything — had instead been (although perhaps not deliberately) misled.

Nodding seemed to be all she could manage. Lewis cautiously held one of her hands and said, 'I'm sorry, Candy. I'm really fond of you, you must know that. I couldn't have . . . done what I did, all those times, and not been. That's the thing, you see. Sometimes you were what I wanted. But there's this other part of me, that will always need —' He tapped the hand that held hers on the air a few times, as if searching for how to say it. 'That needs men, needs both. That's just who I am. I'm not gay, I'm not straight. I'm both.'

He seemed to find her silence crushing, as he clenched her hand more tightly. 'I wish you'd believe me. This has all been pretty fucking hard for me too, you know. It's not fun finding out you can be a bastard.' He gave a small laugh.

Although the blade of selfishness in what he said caught her, she weakened, leaned her head against his shoulder, partly so he couldn't see the dampness on her face. 'You're not a bastard, Lewis. You're not.'

He leaned his head on hers and they sat there, perhaps the

closest to lovers they'd ever been. 'You're such a good, good kid, Sweets. I don't deserve a friend like you.'

She snuffled, cuffed tears off her face. 'Yes, you do.'

'Please don't cry. I'm not worth it.'

'You bloody are.'

He laughed, a little icy desperation threaded through it.

Candy tried to dry her face again and said, 'But I need to ask you something else. Why *Jeff*, for Christ's sake? That's the cruelty, Lewis. I mean, could it *be* any closer?'

Again his voice sounded hollowed out, insubstantial. 'Jesus, I don't know how to psychoanalyse what I do in my sleep, Candy. I don't know. Maybe some part of me thought it would be a safe way to experiment. Because Jeff is so like you, maybe I thought you'd forgive me the confusion and then . . . we could talk. Or maybe I thought Jeff could tell you. Take the pressure off me.'

Her stomach corkscrewed and she pulled away to give him a hard look. 'Sounds like you know exactly how to psychoanalyse what you do in your sleep.'

His knee jiggled nervously.

'It was pretty cruel,' she prompted again.

Sombre-faced, he gave a downwards tilt of his chin. It seemed that was all she'd get. And if she wasn't going to hear a full apology; there didn't seem to be anything else to say. They sat in a silence that was going nowhere, until Lewis finally stood up and walked away from the bed.

He hesitated at the door. 'I'll give you a call later in the week. We should go to a movie or something. There's that French film showing next Friday. We could go to that.' She nodded, and he stepped back towards her and gave her a long, warm kiss on the cheek, which left her feeling tossed and torn, a ripped sail, where he was both ocean and wind. She listened until she caught the sound of the front door slam, then forced herself to make her way downstairs, driven finally by the need for water and Panadol, coffee and fruit juice, or even fried food — anything that would stop the seasick, dehydrated feeling.

As she passed the living room she saw Jeff on a chair, face in his hands. Obviously feeling pretty much as she did. He raised his head when she got into the kitchen, and talked to her through the serving hatch.

'Hey, look, Candy. I'm really sorry.'

She concentrated on the water as it filled a plastic tumbler, trying to block off her sense of smell as the reek of old alcohol, cigarettes and the overflowing black rubbish sack in the kitchen nagged at her hang-over.

Jeff shifted over to the couch near the opening that joined the two rooms. 'It's no excuse, I know, but . . . I've just been really confused lately.'

'I've already heard the best lines today.'

The cold water spread through her throat, stomach, and started to dampen the throbbing in her temples.

'I guess I do owe you some kind of explanation. This whole thing is one of the reasons I wanted to get out of home. Space to think, sort out my own head, sort out these . . . feelings.'

She refilled her glass slowly, noticing the bluish, dark half moons under her brother's eyes. 'What's to sort out? If you're attracted to men, that's the way it is, Jeff. I don't think you owe me an explanation for that.' Then she gave herself credit for a steadier insight than she really deserved: truly, the real click, the final sinking in, had only come the night before. 'I've kind of wondered for a while, you know? I guess maybe Mum and Dad have too.'

'That's what I couldn't handle. It's like they wanted an answer, but I haven't been too sure I've wanted to ask the question yet. I just wanted to work it out for myself. At my own pace.'

Candy carried her glass through to the living room and stood opposite him. 'But your own pace still involved other people, didn't it?' She walked over to the window and glanced out. 'This is hard to say, but I do think . . . you've done a wrong thing.'

His face grew mottled, the patchwork colours of mingled hurt, anger, fear. 'But you just said, "that's the way it is".'

'It doesn't excuse you from what you've done to me.'

'To you?'

She looked at him with disbelief. 'Why *Lewis*? You must have guessed how I felt about him. I mean, why that way? If you'd even told me first, talked to me about it first —'

He broke in on her. 'But it was all so surreal. I mean, I was barely awake,' (*Liar*, she thought) 'And I was still pretty high, and soaked on drink, I guess. It was just . . . a thrill, smashed, crazy. But innocent, really, on the scale of things. It's not like we had sex, Candy.'

But that almost didn't seem to matter to her. It was sexual: a line was crossed, that meaning was there in their actions. It seemed just a matter of nuance, of emphasis. As if — full-blown wouldn't have been much more of a shock, somehow. What there had been was heads and bodies moving over each other, silhouetted in the dark: the overture to sex, the message given. She tried to arrange the words in her mind to make that clear to him, but, greenish-yellow, his face dipped then buried in his hands again, before he was up with a lurch and sprinting out of the room. Candy heard the toilet door slam and, through the thin walls, the desolate sound of guttural retching.

Her world seemed scoured, emptied, everything a little pointless. She told herself it was just the alcohol talking: that she shouldn't even think about grand abstracts like 'her world' until she'd had a drinkless day and a long sleep that night to clear her thoughts.

When Jeff surfaced from the bathroom she asked if he wanted to rest on the couch until he felt better. There was a kind of formal politeness between them: Jeff obviously jaded and drained, not really wanting any more interaction — with anyone — at all that day.

'No thanks,' he said. 'I'll catch a bus home and get to bed there.' The things they'd talked about sat between them, heavy, unwieldy. They both shied from them. He was gone without any more discussion, and Candy was highly relieved.

She spent a morose day of deliberately avoiding her flatmates, taking Panadol, drinking large beer handles of water, lying on her bed trying to read, and even trying to jot down phrases for a song, though she knew the night before was still too raw to make sense of, even at the remove of lyric or melody. In between efforts to distract herself she drifted off to sleep, waking now and then with a dry mouth and a persistent pinched sensation in her head.

The bouts of daytime sleep meant that in bed at first that night, after the grey, nothing, post-party day, Candy was restless. The wheels in her brain wouldn't stop turning out duplicate answers to duplicate questions: some anxious managerial voice at the stalk of her brain just wouldn't listen, kept barking out the questions again. Thinking over Lewis and Jeff, warm confused tears hurried their way up, out, away, as if she were transparent and smooth, and they found as little obstruction as stormwater racing over a large pane of glass. Maybe she'd been attracted to Lewis precisely because of the elusiveness, evasiveness, ambiguity? Qualities she'd sensed but not understood: the gentle boy who liked boys, but hadn't yet said. When she looked back over the last couple of months with Lewis, they reflected the life lived alongside a brother who had always alternately held her at arm's distance, but then needed her, right up close. Was a game of attract and repel all she'd ever know? The harder she ran to escape Jeff's image, the more clearly it came into view.

At last the crying rusted the ticking, irritating watch-jewels in her mind. Candy was still. The corrugated iron roof and wooden timbers of the house gave small pops and cracks as they too settled down for the night. Slipping into real sleep at last, she knew the whole structure was built of paper, and pebble-sized birds had flown in through the window, their wings strumming chords she wanted to write in the dew on the lawn outside . . .

How long — hours? — later she was woken by a ripe, distended moon splitting a grey skin of cloud, and a sweetish pressure in her bladder after a surprisingly good dream. She padded out to the bathroom, then felt too awake to head straight back to bed. She walked quietly to the kitchen, planning to pour herself a large glass of milk and take the mug back to her room, where she would read a bit, perhaps scribble in her notebook, trying to net the mist of the dream images that still lingered with her. In the dream, manuka petals had fallen into her hair, melted like snow, then walked down her shoulders: platinum butterflies that an amphibious man who'd surfaced from a pond was trying to collect from her skin, hands cupped at her. 'Quick, the hurricane lamps,' he kept saying. 'Hold very still: they think you are a *menorah*.' Menorah: she'd actually forgotten what the word meant. She'd need to look it up after she'd poured her glass of milk.

She reached the kitchen and turned on the light. Backlit, sprung, Jayshri was there, shivering. Cheeks and eyes swollen, her body showed through her thin mint and white striped cotton nightgown, like bones through the blue haze of an X-ray. There was dark icing around her mouth, her fists closed around something. Cake: the broken cake on the bench looked as if hands had plunged and torn into it. Next to it was an open jar of peanut butter, chewed bread crusts, the empty wrapper from a tube of crackers. Half a yoghurt-coated muesli bar sat there too, alongside an almost empty jar of olives.

'Jaysh?'

Jayshri stared blankly, her focus difficult to track — as if she stared inwards. A rivulet of alarm electrified Candy. Jesus Christ, was she sleepwalking too?

'Jaysh, can you hear me?'

She dropped the fistfuls of cake into the sink, spat out the food into a hand. She dumped the chewed sludge in the rubbish bin, then with one movement swept all the scraps on the kitchen bench along after it. She was still shivering, nose running, eye whites pinky, bruised.

Candy gestured at the kettle, voice low, still a little unsure whether Jayshri was awake. 'Do you . . . want a cup of tea? We could talk.'

Jayshri ran the back of a slim-knuckled hand across her nose, sniffed, took the great, shuddering inwards breath of a child who has been sobbing. Recognition made Candy's stomach flip-flop. 'Oh, Jaysh.'

Her flatmate's eyes sizzled. 'Just fuck off, Candy.'

Candy held back, but showed Jayshri her empty hands. 'I only want to help.'

'Just want to snoop and spy, more like. You're a nosy bitch, you know. You make me totally claustrophobic.'

They'd barely spoken for weeks, and hadn't seen each other for at least twenty-four hours: it was a bizarre accusation. But again the alarm Candy felt was strong, should have been as visible as the fine, hair-like stings that bristle over the surface of a small cactus.

Jayshri bolted from the kitchen, leaving the mess and debris around her as if it would just vanish on its own. Methodically, dumbly, Candy began to clean it up, helping Jaysh in her concealment without knowing why.

The next morning Candy slipped down to the kitchen and made herself tea and toast. She took it upstairs to her bedroom, still not feeling robust enough to deal with talking to Jaysh — or any of her flatmates — as if nothing had happened. There was a knock at her door soon afterwards, and when she saw that it was Jaysh, an irrational guilt bubbled up at the presence of her own breakfast: melted butter, marmite, full-cream milk in her tea.

Jaysh's face was hard, sculptured. There was no preamble at all. No apology. Just, 'I want you to leave. I want you out of the flat. And I don't want a scene about it.'

Anger ricocheted around Candy's body. 'Oh, for Christ's sake, Jayshri, *look*. I am so sick of this and the weird mood in this bloody place. All I was trying to do last night was help. That's hardly a flatmate crime, is it?'

'So we're both sick of it. It's not working out. It's obviously time for you to go.'

Though she was so small and slight, it was as if she were merely the visible section of the struts in a pier or breakwater, and there was great strength buried deep under the surface, making her indominatable, unbudgeable.

'You've stepped over a serious boundary,' said Jayshri. 'There has to be a line between sharing and privacy in a flat situation. And you just don't know where that line is. You're too naïve, Candy. I should have known it as soon as I saw you. I was shocked when I met Jeff. You and he aren't real twins, not in spirit. I actually think your family must be quite sick, Candy. I think you're like a sort of infection that's been screwing with my mind while you've been here.'

Her speech was green poison, pouring into Candy's ears, burning against her eardrums. It was all a ludicrous fiction, she knew that: she knew Jaysh was losing it, had some hot, swollen unhappiness locked away in her that was saying all of this, just to drive Candy away after the hyper-real encounter in the kitchen, the unanticipated self-exposure. But in the moment all Candy wanted was for the voice to shut up.

'All right,' she said. 'That's enough. I get the message. Have it your way.'

Jayshri actually seemed back-footed for a moment: floored by the fact that the result she'd wanted had come about so easily. After a stunned yet hard scrutiny of Candy, she quickly drew up the mask of composure again and gave a terse half pucker, half smile.

'Good.' She turned on her heel and clattered down the stairs.

Candy paced the room, then went to one of the windows and pressed her cheek against the glass, as if asking it to take her temperature and tell her what was wrong. The sensation against her skin helped to bring a sharp rage to the surface. People couldn't treat her this way. They just couldn't. All she'd done was . . . care about them. That was all. No pressure, no demands, barely any expectations. And they did — this. Well, stuff them. Stuff them all.

The tenancy agreement said she was supposed to give at least two weeks' notice before she left. But what did she really owe these people? Jaysh and the others would expect that time so they could set up flatmate interviews and cover their costs until they found someone else for the room. But up theirs. Up Jaysh. Pulse thudding, an insistent fist at a door: Candy felt a swoop of something like desire. It was the urge to run. The flight instinct in full throttle, still laced with savage anger. It was all she could do to weight herself on her bed, grasping a handful of the covers, and try to formulate a skeletal plan.

She'd move her things back to her parents'. Take a couple of weeks' leave from both of her jobs: who cared if she lost them? When she really thought about it properly, grotty jobs like hers were a dime a dozen and the staff turnover was pretty high, anyway. She just had a vision of herself driving somewhere — filling her head with shades of blue, green, yellow, brown, washing away the last few days and months: images of ferns, sand, totara, rata, farms, rivers, lakes, small towns, all working like a compress, muslin that soaked up the heat and ugliness of the events in this flat.

She rushed headlong into it, still the startled, disturbed bird, plunging into open air — just up and away, no thought for what other obstacles her poor, addled, thin-boned feather-head might hit.

She snatched up a jacket, her satchel, ran down the stairs and headed out to the corner shop. The bluff, 'Another lovely day in paradise!' store owner, whose moustache was the colour of wholemeal toast, seemed to pick up her mood. He spared her his usual cheerful small talk, whipping out a phone card and her change as soon as she made her request. He nodded at her with a crease of concern between his eyebrows — which surprised her with a pang for the dad she'd had when she was very little . . .

She swung away from the anchor of that memory, out the door and along the road to the privacy of a phone booth, where, within about twenty minutes, she had changed everything. Rebooked the one-man-and-his-van moving firm, and forewarned Rose that the family home was going to be used as a halfway house. She knew she had a cheek, giving such short notice, but Rose had been lark-like: blithe and sing-song. 'Of course! As long as you don't mind your gear being stored in the shed. And you know you can stay here for as long as it takes for you to find somewhere else.'

But Candy explained that she was sorted out for a while: was heading off on a holiday.

'Oh, really? I don't think we knew that you had something like this planned. Where are you going?'

'Not sure, really. Just a bit of a road trip. It's all a bit spontaneous.'

She could hear her mother reading the airiness, the dropped off-key stresses in her voice: cursed herself for not being better at deceit. Yet when Rose responded, Candy could hear how her mother, too, chose to be oblique, kindness coded into the hesitations and avoidances. Instead of saying, 'Are you sure this is all organised enough? Don't you think you should book ahead? Are you sure you should be travelling alone?' Rose asked, 'Do you need to borrow a car, or are you using coaches?'

'I'd sort of half thought of hiring a car . . .'

'But you can't afford that.'

'No, not really.'

'Look, how long will you be away for?'

'I don't know. Probably a couple of weeks.'

'You can borrow my car. We'll manage. I've often told your father that being a two-car couple feels like an excessive luxury anyway, now that you kids are independent. As long as you promise to return it with a full tank. And of course, no damage. Any damage, you pay. All right?'

Candy found herself nodding like a toddler who hasn't worked out that people can't see you on the phone.

'Candy?'

'Mum, that's great. It's just what I need. You're . . . I don't know. Restoring my faith in people.'

There was a careful, calculating pause from Rose. Then the rising intonation of worry. 'Candy? You are going to take it easy on this holiday, aren't you?'

'Of course, Mum. That's what holidays are for, isn't it?'

Rose made a distinctively maternal noise at the back of her throat: a murmur that was soothing, cooing but concerned — a sound that always made Candy want to reassure her in turn that she didn't need looking after, Rose mustn't worry, she mustn't take on board anything that could bind her into anything like that old state of grief.

'You're a star, Mum, you know that, don't you?'

'Well, then. You must be a starlet. When will you come to collect the car?'

The van was booked for the next morning. She'd complete her one-room move by noon, and head away then.

'But we'll be at work, Candy love. I won't get a chance to see you.'

'Maybe we could have a meal when I get back. And I could tell you all about my adventures.' She didn't want to talk much longer. She was struggling to keep her manufactured cheerfulness afloat: could feel it being sucked towards a vortex, like a flimsy piece of costume jewellery in a draining sink, dragged towards a plughole.

'That sounds good, Candy. Take photos, will you? You can borrow our camera too, if you like.'

Her mother's easy generosity was in such stark contrast to the world Candy had been absorbed by recently: it made her feel she'd been neglectful, an unnatural daughter. She vowed to spend more time with Rose — once she'd sorted herself out, worked out what she was going to do with her life.

With an unexpected sheen of perspiration gathering on her skin, Candy collected empty, collapsed cardboard boxes from the corner shop and quickened her step back to the flat. She managed to slip upstairs and carry out a hasty, makeshift packing job — treading from shelves to boxes in stockinged feet to keep down the noise — without any interruption from flatmates. But then, if Jayshri had the others on her side Candy was probably persona non grata and she'd have a clear space maintained around her from now on: like penicillin warding off bacteria in a petri dish, she thought darkly. Bugger them.

She knew that the others all had work the next morning and would be out of the house by eight or eight-thirty, so she'd booked the van-man for ten o'clock. She woke and lurked in her room, waiting to hear the front door slam and echo up the stairwell three times. She suddenly envisaged one of her flatmates coming down with flu, or deciding their employer was a fascist bully boy, resigning in protest, spending the day lying in, slothing around in dressing gown and socks, reading magazines at the kitchen table. . .

But slam. Slam . . . slam. Her body eased. She was safe, home free: free to ditch the so-called home.

At her parents' house, when she let herself in after she and the moving man had stacked up boxes in their shed, she found a note from Rose sitting under the camera and car keys. It wished her luck, and said Jeff wanted her to give him a call there at home before she left town. Candy was surprised at how pleased she was that he wanted to hear from her — imagined them talking properly, sober. She felt a smile involuntarily lifting at her mouth. 'He's found a flat,' Rose wrote, 'and mentioned something about wanting to swap some furniture with you: apparently you've taken a bedside table he claimed before you left.'

Her smile landed with a thud. Little jerk. She should have known. The only reason he'd like to hear from her was when he wanted something. She scribbled her mother a quick thank you, retrieved the keys and camera, and loaded her pack and satchel into the car. *Outta here.*

FOR THE LENGTH of her drive north Candy worked hard at visualising all her entanglements unravelling, streaming out invisibly behind the car like so much mental pollution. She told herself she'd stop when she felt completely freed, but found she'd travelled all the way to Picton still caught in the same cat's cradle of confusion — and not at all ready to head back home.

Six weeks later she was still moored at Davies' Dosser, a backpackers' lodge a few minutes' drive from Picton itself. Staying there seemed both rash and a fitting stopgap — though she knew her parents thought it was just plain odd. In a complicated arrangement that had somehow worked out, she'd organised for a friend of her new boss to drive the family car — and camera — back to Dunedin. (She gathered she was going to have do something fairly major to redeem herself in her parents' eyes after entrusting the car to a virtual stranger, even though it was returned unharmed. She figured she could at least start by sending Rose some local crafts, and courier her some fresh honeycomb. The last thing she wanted was anyone thinking she'd taken advantage of them, after all the heartache she'd worked up over other people's faithlessness.)

Happily, Candy would be able to pay for the little gifts for her parents from her wages at the backpackers'. She had arrived as a guest at the lodge but discovered they needed someone to work on reception. Her male predecessor had fallen for a German woman who was planning to cycle the length of the South Island; he'd bought a bike and Candy had last seen him pedalling furiously after her, as she shouted comparisons between the New Zealand bush and the Black Forest. Candy had asked for his job before the hostel owner had fully realised he had a staff vacancy: which made him think she was enormously pragmatic, a problem-solving whiz, so she landed the work straight away. She was hugely relieved: had told herself on the warm, sun-rinsed afternoon of her arrival that this particular bushscape, this particular sea air, could be exactly what she needed to scrub away the grime and rime that had built up over her messy, stressy heart.

Once in a routine at her new job she soon found that although she still felt the dull ache of betrayal, of disarray over what she'd left behind, other pleasures quietly began to seed themselves. She liked the sense of constant change in the hostel, yet the idea that she also had her own small continuity within it. She had an easy role: plenty of time to read at the check-in desk, and there was a stereo there too, with an eclectic treasure of an album collection she was free to use. She enjoyed the feeling that she was a kind of DJ, choosing the ambience of the arrivals and departures nook that also opened onto a lounge and small coffee bar that guests could use. She liked trying to guess which music would suit which combinations of travellers in the lounge, and also found herself studying the chord changes and melody lines with a renewed concentration: as if, in fact, all music sounded more clearly now, in this fresh setting — the new environment a kind of silence against which she could also listen more closely to recent events. She found she loved hearing the lodge guests' stories: where they came from, why they'd taken this break, what they planned to do after this. She told herself she was gathering moods and personalities for the songs she might write one day — if, if, if . . . yet also half knew that she listened in the hope that she'd hear a version of a life she might borrow: each account a potential answer to the constant strain of questions that sat balled up in a clot of tension at the base of her neck.

When she let her family know that she'd be staying on for a while, Rose's letter back to her sounded surprised (and deeply irritated about the car) but also, in the end, encouraging: saying if she stayed long enough, they'd try to make it up there for a vacation themselves. Jeff had written a couple of times too, but she hadn't sent off a reply yet. She was still too angry, too overturned and lost when she thought about him: still too prone to feeling as if the edges of herself were dissolving, her mind turning into gas, the molecules leaking out and merging with him, so that he talked with her voice, moved her limbs from within, pre-empted and stole her every decision.

Time ticked on. Although she'd expected not to start study this year, when February wore away and she knew polytechs and universities would be starting up their timetables, she felt more and more agitated about her lack of focus. Two more letters arrived from Jeff, one saying he'd decided to stay on in Dunedin and go to Otago, that he'd flagged the passing flirtation with journalism and was now really keen on a BSc, which actually increased her agitation. There were even a few phone messages from him, left when she was off duty. She did start to write a reply, but abandoned it when she found she was deliberately censoring out the details of her job, her transient friends — and even her visit to the doctor, which was hardly one of the things Jeff would want to emulate.

The visit to the doctor hadn't happened because of her hands — they were basically okay now, although during waking hours the guitar was still forced away from the forefront of her mind, a promise to herself she never quite fulfilled, despite her renewed appetite for music. No, the visit had happened because since moving this far up the island she thought she had been — hearing things.

She remembered exactly when it started. It was a day when the lodge was fairly empty, which was surprising, as they were in the middle of a relentless end-of-summer deluge of rain, and her boss, Mike, told her that often meant people delayed the start of their cycle tours or other excursions and holed up in the hostel, so that bar sales rocketed.

Sitting on her own at the check-in desk, leafing through a magazine, but with her mind racing over and over the questions of how long should she stay, why exactly had she stopped here, what should she be *doing* with her life? Candy caught the fragment of a tune, and felt the seep of a strangely plangent happiness. In her fingers, lips and toes there was a light buzzing, warm. It was like there was a memory hovering, of people and a place. People sitting cross-legged in a green clearing surrounded by ferns, native beech and fuchsia, leaves in pointillist green, yellow and red here and there on the grass. The people were talking, slow and easy from the sun and the large bottle of wine held in a wicker carafe propped on a plaid rug. There were men and women, all with long, fringeless hairstyles, one blonde woman with a beaded headband. But when had Candy ever seen such a thing? Was that what the lyrics were talking about? She held herself as still as possible, whole body craning with her ears as she tried to place the tune, and found herself guessing the chord changes in advance but still not being able to give the song a name or a context. What were those words just then?

She was lured out of her seat to tread the narrow, boxy corridors of both storeys of the old wooden lodge — pressing her ears up against doors and walls, heart thub-thub-thubbing in case she was caught, as she tried to isolate the source of the tune. In a hallway, by a large sash window, she finally twigged that it must be coming from outside — probably from an old hippy bus or some other vehicle big enough for a proper stereo, which could project through the rain. It must be parked right outside.

She loped down the stairs, flung open the front door and was confronted by an empty street, swept with an enormous silver threshing machine of rain that seemed to mow down all the light, and to have cleared away all signs of life. Candy was stumped. She checked the empty street again. The rain drummed steadily on the tin porch roof directly above her head. She listened — and then she realised. Water was being funnelled from faulty spouting on the main roof onto the porch-overhang at a steady, rhythmic rate, and the drumming had the metallic, chinking, ringing echo of a wind chime. There was no song at all. She stood there for several seconds, disbelieving, then shook herself, as if trying to clear her skin of the fine, cold dust of rain.

The minor incident left her unnerved. Her mind had elaborated on the fragment of sound to such a degree: had invented melodic shifts, begun to grope for memory, hope, even to shape hazy personalities . . . built an almost entirely illusory reality, a mirage made of noise. What was happening to her?

That experience, and then a recurrent phenomenon that happened when tilting on the verge of sleep, partially surfacing in the small hours, or even when making the steady ascent at morning, began to make her afraid. The word *insane* crackled and whispered at her, audibly as voices behind her back. Near sleep, she often heard a run of dense language, sometimes music, usually a jumbled rush, as if a tap had been turned on, phrases and melodies in fast-forward.

The yellow moon
gives off pieces of herself
I can hardly hear her

A dream of cattle
with sad horns like pelvic bones

His hands leave invisible ink
on her skin
he walks in
the heart's heat
makes his signature legible
in red
light rides the water
as his name rides her mind

Sometimes words that were almost a song came with a speed that startled, even frightened her — because they were unasked for, because they weren't worked at. She shied from them as from a dark bird swooping.

Fancy man with your clothes all over you
how dare they hide your bones
fancy man with your words all over me
well now can I ever go fancy free?
When you're not here
you're my sweet nothing
like the hole in the doughnut
my substantial something
your apologies for absences
your name on my tongue
as close as you get
like a bolt of bridal silk
at the scissors' first kiss
I'm ruined
I'm ruined
by the bite of you

It felt like clutter, an incoherent manifestation of anxiety, with another layer of anxiety beneath it which just wanted the voices and songs turned off and silenced. It began to plague her more and more. She tossed and turned, fought the garble and noise, ended up sleepless, grey, drained, her days foggy.

She finally cracked when one phrase started to recur, like some kind of message from her subconscious that she couldn't decode. *Turn able, turn tables, wooden leaves lift in welcome, sit with the coin's spin, the nickel music it plays him . . .*

She went to a doctor, and told a white lie at first: said she just wanted some new moles on her arms checked out in case they were a result of careless sunbathing. But she was so fidgety that the young GP said, 'And you're sure there's nothing else?'

So she told him, and admitted, 'I'm scared if it gets out of control . . . that I'll go crazy.' As she sat in the midst of blood pressure charts, posters of musculature and skeletons, pink and white plastic models of the human ear and the female reproductive system, Candy felt a lump of shame in her throat, like a confused teenager fearing the doctor will think she's dirty for having thrush, or a bladder infection. Shame, despite Rose and her history. Shame *because* of Rose and her history? She didn't tell the doctor about her mother. He was very young, she thought: a touch wide-eyed, and unbearably good-looking. The years of med school and late nights had cut two powerful lines of concentration between his eyebrows. She was glad she hadn't come for anything that needed a physical examination. She might shake. Yet she also felt fraudulent, for coming about phantoms, and her mind leapt forward to small-community encounters with him — in the grocery store, in a bookshop, walking through the main shoreline playground or at a local barbeque — where he'd recognise her and recall, oh, another clown from the psycho circus . . .

'How can I help?' His very clean hands with trim nails and square-edged fingers played with a drug company pen and memo pad.

'Well, I . . .' Candy focused on the desk blotter, which said *Locoid: To 'X' out Eczema*. She found herself automatically trying to rearrange letters in the drug into other words, an exercise she'd often used to calm herself down, or fill in time: to give the air — in public places such as street corners, buses, stations — of someone happy to stare into mid-air with a bland expression. Lid. Cod. Cool. Oil. Coil. Loco, Doc. *Oh Shit.*

'Ms Marshall?'

'I'm sorry. For some reason this is hard.'

The doctor turned and turned the pen in his hands, those furrows in his forehead darkening. She shocked herself with the image of her thumb running over them, feeling the quiet intelligence burn through to her knucklebone. She clenched down with her stomach muscles and just started to talk.

'I haven't been sleeping well for a while now, and I . . .' She knew her eyes were darting backwards and forwards, as if she weren't concentrating on the topic to hand, but her nervousness was spilling over all the carefully maintained edges now, her hands dancing as if to stop up the leaks, but there were too many, her body was a colander . . .

'Have you been worried about something in particular? Or been under a lot of pressure?'

She chewed her lip, knotted her fingers together to keep them still. 'I guess, well, worrying, maybe.'

She couldn't tell him everything, of course: that she'd left her home town to clear her head because she'd had a sorry love affair that wasn't, because her flatmate had turned against her, because her twin brother seemed to have become a natural cuckoo who had nestled into her life, and — and *Doc, I have no sense of direction*. It would all sound as if she should be cultivating her own natural yoghurt, getting her Tarot cards done, or reading the self-help encounter group notices at the health-food store, not sitting in a GP's chair. So she told him the pieces that sounded almost medical: that she'd had to give up music for a while because of a problem with pain in her hands, and now she thought she was having . . . auditory hallucinations. Yeah, hearing things.

She waited for him to laugh, or to say, 'I have genuinely ill people waiting out there for my attention. Do you think that just because this is a small surgery I have all the time in the world to listen to neurotics?' But he watched her quietly, then asked a few questions about whether she'd had any weight loss, what her eating habits were like, had she noticed anything like racing heart, diarrhoea? When she couldn't offer him any more symptoms, he thought for a while, looking at the carpet so intently that Candy sneaked a glance down near his feet, half wondering if there was a sheet of paper down there that described medical protocol for her kind of case. But he swivelled his chair back to his desk and rested his steepled hands against his mouth. Then he wrote out a script for a short course of sleeping tablets, telling her that her thoughts had probably just become overactive through lack of rest. A simple and common problem. But she should come back again if the cycle wasn't broken. And then he said, 'Now, I'm no artist, so you might laugh.' And he seemed genuinely timid about making the next suggestion; a fine wash of pink lifted over his face. Candy had to stop from gaping moronically.

His eyes brushed over hers briefly. 'Have you tried airing any of these words, or songs, or whatever they are that you've been hearing? You say you used to write music — maybe this is just a sign that it's time to get back into it again.' He cleared his throat self-consciously. 'I'm not making light of how worried you've been, but maybe it's as simple as that. Maybe they're ideas that just . . . want to get out.'

Candy wasn't quite sure why she couldn't write to Jeff about this. She decided maybe she just had to get more distance — from everything. But after the visit to the doctor and a few nights of undisturbed sleep Candy found herself no longer kept away from her acoustic guitar as if an invisible force-field separated them.

One night, after work, she removed the instrument slowly from its case, realising as she touched it that she'd half expected some kind of repulsion: a static electric shock, a bolt to drive her backwards. And she *was* back-footed, but it was by how strongly she was affected by the scent of the wood, the feeling of its cold, smooth skin, the fit of the strings under her no longer toughened fingertips. She tried a few Raggedies' numbers and had that old sensation: of a key fitting into its lock, a foot into a comfy shoe. Her ears wanted the music the way tastebuds crave cocoa, cream, salt, the fresh juice of an orange.

Though she was rusty, and had to watch how often she played, after that night she even began to carry the guitar down to reception from the staff bedroom quarters, so that it was on hand when she had completed all her paperwork and just had to babysit the phone and front door.

Loosened up by the practice itself, perhaps, and by the feeling of having some kind of renewed focus, one afternoon when she had been tinkering away at an old song at the reception desk, she fell into easy conversation with one of the B & B guests who had sauntered into the café-bar area looking for a cappuccino and a recent newspaper. The guest was English: a very brown-skinned, outdoorsy sort, wearing black Adidas trackpants with the stirrups not hooked under his bare heels, a Yosemite National Park T-shirt, and sunglasses pushed back into his dark curly hair in a way that somehow made him look rakish and arty — slightly feminine and unthreatening, Candy thought. She agreed to make him the coffee although it was past the end of her shift, and her boss was already heading down the stairs to replace her as she set the guitar aside and hopped off her stool.

'Make yourself a drink too,' Mike said to her as she led the guest into the serving area.

'Okay, thanks.' Mike gave her the smile that she half wished he wouldn't — it made her know it would be hard to tell him she was leaving if she ever made up her mind about what to *do* with her life.

'How long have you played guitar?' the guest — Richard — asked, as Candy made herself a flat white. They were soon joined by his French girlfriend, Séverine, who in sleeveless yellow cotton shirt and navy blue Brigitte Bardot pedal-pushers, was the same nut-brown colour as Richard. She managed to look as if she'd just stepped out of a photo shoot for a laundry detergent ad. Noticing Candy's glance at her clothes, perhaps, she immediately claimed she was wearing the only other set she'd brought on holiday apart from cycling gear.

Richard raised a finger. 'I was just asking — Candy, is it? — how long she'd been playing guitar for. She's pretty good.'

'Ah, it was you we could hear from the room?'

'Oh, you're on the ground floor? I'm sorry, I hope it wasn't too loud . . .'

'No, no, too loud, no! Actually we left the door . . . how do you say, popped?'

Richard gazed at her. 'Propped.'

'Propped open to hear better, more.'

'You could say popped open, couldn't you?' said Candy. 'You can ask someone to pop open the door . . .'

Richard made a face as if a sip of cappuccino had burnt his lip. 'Don't confuse things. It's complicated enough as it is.'

Séverine laughed. 'He likes it better when I get some words wrong. He likes still to feel he is helping me, he is my teacher.'

'Can you speak French?' Candy asked Richard.

Séverine rolled her eyes. 'He thinks so, yes? But I'd rather he did not. My friends think a man speaking with accents is sexy, but to me it sounds like . . . errr . . . a cat on his claws on the blackboard.'

Richard shook his head at his cappuccino. 'Defamation.' He hunched up a little as he drew his stool in closer to the bar. 'But we're sick of us. Sick of our own company on this trip, isn't it, Séverine?'

She flicked back her hair. 'Oh, so sick of it, yes. We are bored with ourselves. Fed full . . .'

'Fed up,' nodded Richard.

'Fed up of the sound of our own stories. And that is even when most of the day we are many *mètres* apart because Richard cycle so fast. So. You can tell us about your music?'

Candy began a standard reply — 'Oh, I've played guitar for a few years, I guess' — but found Richard and Séverine's insistent interest egged her on, and talking became like pulling on an apparently endless chain of magician's scarves. She told these strangers about her one-time aspirations, and even about her old tutor, Julian — which made her feel she'd swallowed two grey rocks: nostalgia and guilt, as she realised how she had stopped all contact with him so abruptly. She told them about The Raggedies, the injuries to her hands, even Jeff's joke stage appearance. And, in edited, listener's digest form, everything that followed: Jaysh, Lewis, her thoughts about journalism . . . with Jeff always winding through it all. The hand holding her coffee cup trembled a little, like a needle registering sound levels, her own body apparently thrown off balance by this rush into confessions with people she'd only just met. But Richard and Séverine nodded, eyebrows buckled in concentration.

This couple just a few years older than her seemed to know how to ask all the right questions, in all the right pauses. Still, Candy was flustered when she stopped: even found herself checking that the buttons at the front of her shirt weren't letting pink loops of skin show, the sense of self-exposure was so great.

Séverine made a tsking, clucking sound, and — in some kind of reward, or mark of acknowledgement of all Candy had poured out — Richard said, 'You need a beer.' He ordered a plastic jug of Lion Export and three glasses from the new barmaid who'd come on duty for the evening session.

Séverine took a delicate taste of the foamy head and said, frown lines puckering on her forehead still, 'You are very young.'

Candy felt irritation swarm her skin. She'd thought, from their faces, that they had understood. Thought they could see this wasn't about youth, naivety, inexperience, but about — what? Bloody life, with a capital bloody.

Séverine held up a hand that had a silver ring set with a green stone on its pinky, so Candy noticed how it brought out the green flecks in her hazel eyes. 'I don't mean that as it seems. What I mean is . . . you mustn't . . .' She glanced questioningly at Richard. 'Cut off yourself?'

He looked puzzled in response.

'You mustn't cut off yourself from chances. From what *you* really *want*.' She balled the ringed hand in a fist and pressed it hard into her chest to stress the words. 'And it sounding now to me —'

'Sounds,' corrected Richard, and she gave him a withering look, which said grammar was now trivial compared with the vehemence of her argument.

'It *sounds* now, to me, that you are the one who knows. You *know* that. You know that exactly. You know that you want.'

He couldn't help himself: Richard mouthed *what*, but only Candy noticed.

'It's him, Jeffrey, yes? Who does not know. He follows you, but he does not know. You see?'

Candy drew on her beer, wanting more of the sweet, heady,

floating feeling — the sensation of coming to understand something, of a landscape moving into sharper focus, a coastline seen from a low-flying plane when the sun begins to lift. Séverine's accented voice was a telescope lens, the filter of her unfamiliar vowels and pauses somehow starting to bring things closer: world rightly distorted.

Richard poured himself another glass of beer and said glumly, 'I'll tell you what. I could go a real Guinness.'

Candy smiled at him in sad, tipsy apology for the bar's stocks. Séverine gave him a small slap on the arm. 'The Englishman travels just so he can miss home, yes?'

'Guinness is Irish.'

Ignoring this, Séverine stared at him with an austere expression at her mouth. 'But I am right about this brother, you think?'

He opened his shoulders slightly, expanding into his subject. 'I suppose what I don't really understand, right, is how it would be so much of a problem even if your brother did, say, follow the same line as you.' He began to fold a soggy beer mat. 'I don't see how it makes what you do any the less . . . important, or any the less right for you. You can't help what you are; he can't help what he is.' Richard shrugged and looked at Séverine for approval. 'So, yeah. If that's what you are, you can't just pull the plug on it, or nail a board over it, or whatever. It's you.'

Séverine nodded. 'This brother you say isn't even *un vrai*, a true musician. So perhaps there is no real problem. Only a ghost problem, a phantom. And even if not, even if that is to say, some bizarre thing happen, and he decide one day to sing or something like . . .' Candy could feel Séverine's eyes travel over her face, back and forth — 'it is not a piece of pie to fight over. It is your lives you decide to lead. There is enough pie for both. I mean, you make your own pie. Inside.'

Richard began to laugh. 'The metaphor's a little gooey, Reenie.'

Séverine crumpled up a paper napkin and swept away a few drops of beer from the table, as if she'd like to swipe away their laughter. 'My words are maybe wrong. But the idea? Maybe no.'

Candy bought another jug of beer — at staff rates, which meant she handed over a ten dollar note to the barmaid, Kiri, who grinned and gave her two five dollar notes in return. 'Nice folk, those tourists?' Kiri asked.

'Yeah, better than average.' Candy tried to sound casual but felt her grin expand.

Head and limbs light with beer, Candy felt she could almost say she'd been to the French alps after a late night of gradually cajoling Richard and Séverine for some of their own stories. How they met at a ski chalet in Bourg St Maurice, where he cleaned the rooms for guests and staff and she acted as tour group hostess for the English-speaking clientele . . . Candy held images in her mind of snow like slices of wedding marzipan on dark wooden eaves. Houses in small hamlets where the modern descendants of peasant ancestors still kept the goats, sheep and cows inside in winter, the heat from their bodies rising through the floorboards, an extra insulation. Chubby brown muzzles of marmottes nosing out of burrows. People muffled up in padded layers of clothing, baguettes tucked under their arms like rolled-up newspapers as white speech balloons billowed in the cold.

Candy was almost glad of the hang-over the next day. The morning was dramatically sunny again — puddles and boggy mud steamed in the heat — and when she came downstairs to grab a strong coffee for a late breakfast she discovered that Richard and Séverine were doctoring their bicycle tyres outside, shifting baggage to and from panniers, stretching calf and thigh muscles, ready to get going towards the Nelson lakes. She was surprised at how disappointed she was to be saying goodbye after just one night, and when the dazed, alcohol-sour headache took over, she gave it a kind of resigned welcome. It was a distraction from an odd tearing feeling, the urge to fold caution into a light paper dart and blurt, 'But can't I come with you?'

The couple called out to her through the open ranchsliders that separated the café-bar area from the patio where they'd leaned their bikes. They exchanged addresses — their flat in London, Candy's family home — though she doubted either she or they would ever use them. It was a goodwill gesture, a goodbye that somehow postponed itself, and pretended this was other than a fleeting, almost anonymous encounter.

Although Richard was impatient to get going, Séverine seemed to feel the tinge of melancholy. 'We meet a good person and still must carry on away. So. You must come to London one day.' She gave Candy a kiss, from cheek to cheek, then called from her bicycle seat, as Richard slowly got momentum going ahead of her, 'Good luck for the music!'

CANDY WOULD THINK, later, that there were three things that turned her back home, and towards the beginnings of a decision. There was the almost-chance conversation with Richard and Séverine. There was the phone call from Jeff. And there was what happened as she passed through the children's playground on the main foreshore, on a deserted Sunday afternoon, after the crowd from the latest ferry sailing had dispersed. Maybe any one element alone would have been enough. But they all seemed to work together, a gathering wave, realisation breaking over her head with clean, drenching force.

Jeff's phone call came a couple of days after Richard and Séverine left, when Candy was picking away at a lyric she was trying to write about the mood their departure had left her in: the melody still blocked and clanged at some points, the words stubborn too. Although maybe that was because she was also trying to fit in some lines from an old, mildewed paperback copy of Shakespeare's *Comedy of Errors* that she had found in the hallway 'Travellers' Bookshelf': a collection to which trampers or cyclists donated books when they'd finished them and wanted to lighten their packs or panniers.

She'd finished struggling through the introduction, the notes, the play itself, a day or two before meeting Richard and Séverine. She'd persisted with it — despite wishing she had someone to ask about some obscure lines — because one early passage had given her the oddest sensation. As if hot feathers had run up her ribs, under her arms, and then immediately . . . dissolved. She'd written on a spare piece of manuscript paper: 'Act I, Scene ii, Antipholus of Syracuse. This man lost his twin as a boy, and has gone out to search for him'. Then, set out neatly:

He that commends me to my own content
Commends me to the thing I cannot get.
I to the world am like a drop of water
That in the ocean seeks another drop,
Who, falling there to find his fellow forth
(Unseen, inquisitive) confounds himself.

She'd thought, at first, that Antipholus talked about the opposite of what she'd done. But later she wondered: was it really? She'd thrown herself out into the ocean of the world to flee her brother: but was she any less confounded? A drop of water running away, but running into its likeness at every turn, not just the recent eerie fortune of chancing on the old play, but everywhere over the past few months: reflections of and on herself, reflections of and on her twin. Thoughts of Jeff, discussions about Jeff (and, unbeknownst to her then, what was to happen on the foreshore . . .)

So it was hardly a coincidence, really, that she was re-reading the lines to try to seal the metre in her head when Mike called out to her to say she had a call. An extension cord meant the phone just reached the double doors between bar and patio where she sat on the doorstep, legs in the sun, a seesaw of weird apprehension in her stomach.

'Hello?' As if she hadn't guessed who it was.

'Hey there, Candy girl.'

Her 'hi' came out flat and angry, though she'd intended it to be neutral.

Jeff was undeterred. 'So, what's up? It's been ages since you've been in touch.'

'Yeah, well. I've been busy.'

'Doing?'

'Working.'

'Beautiful area up there?'

'Pretty much.' She swallowed as he chattered on a bit. Then emptiness barrelled down the line — lengthened, thickened. 'Ummm — hey, Jeff? This is a toll call, right? So maybe I shouldn't take up too much of your time . . .'

'Hey, don't worry about it. I'm in this vacant office space, above my friend Tim's new flat. One of his flatmates found out there's a phone line working in here, even though nobody's moved a business in yet. So everyone's trying to get as many toll calls in as they can before Telecom or whoever's paying the bill finds out.'

'Dodgy.'

'Nah, cruisy. Especially for me, not even living here.'

'Hope the line's not tapped.'

'By who?'

'Look, Jeff?' She rubbed at her bare knee. 'Did you call for something? I mean, sorry, but this is really a work phone . . .' It was, but most business calls came through on two other lines: Mike had put the call through to this phone deliberately. He was now carrying a dishwasher rack of clean glasses to the area behind the bar; shook his head and mouthed, 'Go ahead!'

Candy smiled at him stiffly, glad Jeff couldn't see.

Now it was Jeff's turn to sound annoyed. 'You're my sister. That's enough reason to call, isn't it?' Candy was clipped back, his short tone reducing her stature, her boldness. 'Besides, we've got plenty to talk about. I found out last time I called when your days off were, so you've got time?' Telling her, really. Her spine folded; she leaned against the door-frame.

'Yeah, yeah. Okay. I didn't really mean . . . I just . . .'

He was impatient now: the pushy urgency in his voice made Candy wonder briefly if there were something serious about their parents he had to say. 'Don't worry. Forget it. Look, Candy? It hasn't been hard to guess you're still pissed off with me. And I understand, though, to tell the truth, so much has gone on down here since you left that the whole . . .' He stopped, as if he had to go backwards to get a run-up for what he had to say next. 'The whole Lewis thing seems a long time ago now.'

Right. Easy for him to say. The old desire she'd been consciously blocking out, damming back, roared in her heart again, defences whipped away like so much tissue paper artlessly used to seal over a broken skylight in a storm.

'God, there's so much to talk about.'

Candy had an image of him: propped up against a white wall, legs stretched out but jiggling on an oatmeal-coloured carpet, white phone in his lap, a bundle of tension in an otherwise bland, characterless office space.

'But look, first of all, about that night at your party. I did a lot of thinking about it afterwards. About how you said what I'd done was cruel, there was no excuse for it, why hadn't I talked to you about it first, instead of letting it just happen. I still feel really lousy about what went on. I guess I did know how you felt about him. It was selfish; I just got carried away by the looseness of getting out of home, all the debating in my head about Mum and Dad, where was I going, what was I doing with my life, blah blah — I know, pathetic excuse. But also' — deep breath — 'Can-do . . . I guess I just . . . wanted to sort of . . .' Again, the sense of run-up in his hesitation — 'belong where you were or something.'

He waited. But the wheels of her understanding ground on slowly. 'Belong?'

Another sudden picture flashed in her mind: of Jeff passing his hand over his face, like their father did when he was very tired and had to trawl down deep to find the energy to explain something. 'I've felt a lot of these things for such a long time. I guess I thought you might know.' A shade in that of *you, of all people*.

She watched a spider lumber over her toes, carrying a white egg sac on its back. Its slow, pregnant progress, lurching when it struck the strap of her sandals, somehow seemed to rhyme with the hitch and halt in the conversation. The beleaguered spider made her feel a stab of empathy for Jeff. Gently, she nudged the small creature off the difficult leather bridge. 'What things, Jeff?'

An airy whistle — like the sound of someone looking over the safety rails at a steep drop — came down the phone first. 'I guess, when I think really hard about it, I've been trying to show you — or let you know — for a while now.' He gently cleared the back of his throat. 'How I've felt about men, for a start.'

Although they'd already begun this conversation after the flat's party, memories only bubbled up afresh now, in a string. Jeff's serious face, from years ago, in a circle of pines. Jeff leaving a hockey field, a clear circle of space around him, subtly ignored by the other guys. Jeff and her guitar. Jeff nearly in tears the day she went to Shane. Shane's offended snarl as he said, 'Your brother's . . . soft.' Jeff on stage, Jeff in her coppery lurex.

'And over all that,' — the phone spat static, making Candy think of kindling taking fire, as if Jeff were using his words to set something off — 'I really for a long time felt so totally out on a limb.' He cleared his throat. 'I didn't know anyone else at school like me. I had an idea about some guys, from a distance, but the risk in actually asking them about it, at my school? You'd have to be some kind of suicidal masochist.' Boys hung from bus straps, boys carried like battering rams into the changing rooms, boys having their heads flushed in the public toilets . . . 'I used to feel so out of things. Except, maybe, around you.'

One of Candy's hands knitted the air, trying to net something.

'Yeah. I guess I knew where I was, around you.' He started to talk rapidly, as if to outrace his own embarrassment. 'I belonged, was part of something. Thought it was maybe even who I was.'

Candy felt responses rush in a clump to her throat. It was the shock of hearing him speak so frankly about all the years of silent thrust-off and tug-back between them. It was the shock of realising how much had been both concealed and revealed, all along. Hide-me Find-me, she thought to herself. The topsy-turvy doll. She spoke thickly. 'But you turn me away too. It's all mixed up. You turn me away, then no warning, you're right back on my heels.' She bent her head and saw how her legs threw a shadow on the patio. 'Like you're *stitched* to them.'

He went quiet. Candy watched a number of wasps dart around the lavender spikes of some bushy flowering plant opposite the patio, their fiery bodies spinning and looping Catherine wheels. She tired to bring back some lightness into the conversation, putting on a mock boy's voice. 'You remember. Even from way back. "I was born first. I'm the oldest."'

Funny how the quality of silence could alter. She could feel him thinking.

'That was years ago. When we were just little kids. But all that started to matter less than wanting to fit in. Since intermediate school, I've been shit scared about what I'd found out about myself. I kind of knew that if other kids saw how close you and I were they might start to guess, and, I don't know — get hostile, weird on me, scared or whatever.' A form of fatigue stretched his voice. 'And like I said, I just wanted to fit in. And you — you always seemed to know, for yourself.'

Candy gave an involuntary *huh*, which Jeff misinterpreted. 'You're sceptical?' Irritability leapt in him again. 'Look, none of this is exactly easy to put into words, Candy, I —'

'No, no. Not sceptical. It's just so . . . odd. What we can miss, or ignore. And how other people see us. You know?' she paused. 'Lewis said a similar thing to me, and some people I've just met also — about how I seemed to know what I wanted. And the whole time it's felt more like —' she searched the patio for clues, 'like I've been in a long game of Blind Man's Buff. Not knowing where or what I'm aiming at.'

He sounded closer now, as if he'd adjusted his sitting position. 'That's hard to . . . that surprises me.'

She thought over her whole time in the rented turret room. 'I mean, compared to someone like that girl in my flat, someone like Jaysh —'

'But you've heard about her?'

Candy blinked. 'No.'

'Oh, right. Well, that was another thing I was going to talk to you about. Apparently she had some kind of meltdown. I ran into Nash the other week at the university caf — he said she'd moved out, gone back to her parents, I think. Had been working way too hard on her PhD proposal. It was on — how'd he put it? — something to do with media representation of racist hate crime. She wanted to get into overseas universities and Nash said she'd just . . . cracked. Stopped eating, was exercising obsessively — she got pretty sick.'

Candy clutched and unclutched the handset. 'Really?' She recalled Jaysh's thin bones illuminated through her nightgown. Didn't know what else to say — could feel it all still gradually registering, like dry soil absorbing water.

'Yeah. It's a huge one, eh? Especially — I don't know — I had this really strong impression of her as sussed, totally sorted out, onto it, etcetera, etcetera — even though I guess I hardly knew her. It makes you think, like you say, about how we see each other.'

Candy shuddered, wished she'd brought out a long-sleeved jumper to the patio. Gradually their conversation began to wind down, as if they were long-distance runners finally feeling the kilometres drag at their muscles, though they talked briefly about how Jeff was finding university, and he even told her — coyly — that actually he was seeing someone — the 'friend', Tim — nearly ten years older than him. 'But hey, that does mean he's still in his twenties.' He still hadn't properly broached the subject with Rose and Robinson. He sounded edgy. 'I'll get there, when I'm confident about it. I just . . . need more time. Tim says it's a poor attitude, but I want something else to show them first.'

'Oh, God, Jeff. Can you hear my eyes rolling? Like what?'

'Like all 'As' this year, or something.' He started to laugh. 'Mum, Dad, I'm bent. But my grades are still straight!'

It had been good to hear him relax at the end of the call. Afterwards Candy could feel a slow, infinitesimally small shifting and turning within herself — but of what to what, she could still only partly sense. She thought about something else he'd said.

'About that whole Lewis thing? I guess . . . I didn't like the way you were pulling away from me, without talking about it. That probably sounds selfish again. But you've always been there, you know? Even as something to work against, or an arrow pointing in the direction you decide not to take. It was hard when you moved out; I didn't really understand it. And then I realised it was what I wanted too. So I guess you've been the right signpost a few times.'

So much to think about, to absorb properly, that she even declined an invitation from Mike and his wife to go to a party on a yacht owned by some American friends of theirs that night. Instead she went to her room and just — doodled. Lay on her bed and went over it all, with the deliberateness of someone who'd taken a fall testing all their bones, probing for tenderness, for bruises. What harm, what anger, was left?

She still couldn't really answer until the next day. That morning she woke from a horrible, wrenching dream. In it, Jeff had died, and before she could get home to see him she'd found herself in a sterile room, which had a shiny black coffin propped up as if standing against a wall. She kept telling a man who wore a corsage of live, interchanging bees and beetles pinned to his lapel that they had placed the wrong person in the coffin. 'It's me in there,' she explained rationally. 'I'm sorry, but you'll have to let me out.' Then her parents arrived and turned to her with bland faces. 'How kind of you to come. Are you one of Jeff's friends?'

'It's Candy,' she answered. 'Your daughter.'

They swapped a look. 'Who?'

And the funeral man leaned over. 'Little water drop, you've confounded yourself.' Then the man had Jayshri's face, smeared in cake and crumbs.

She woke feeling jangled: was grateful to realise she had another day off. She needed to get out, get down to the sea. Maybe it would wash her head clean of all its snarl and fray.

The morning looked as if it could grow a little overcast, grey clouds starting to rise — like the scum on a pot of lentils — from what had seemed a permanent blue the day before. She made sure she took a long-sleeved sweatshirt and a light windproof jacket in her straw shopping bag, along with her pens and stationery, a couple of pieces of fruit and some oat and raisin cookies, so she could spend a few hours trailing around and exploring.

After a long walk up into the hilly bush behind the port she sat down at the foreshore where she tried, for an hour, to rework the Shakespeare lyrics, which seemed to have turned ingrown, gnarled, as she stayed bound up in recollecting the phone call and the dream. Uncricking her neck and back, she looked up to realise that the area was deserted and a wind was picking up. She decided to use the women's toilets near the children's playground before she headed back to the lodge. She walked past the swings, see-saws, the paddling pool — with the statue of Donald Duck straddling the middle — and the large concrete whale that children could enter through the mouth — though it smelt badly of urine and beer and was in dire need of a clean-up and fresh layer of paint. Nobody was playing anywhere in the playground; just a few gulls that lifted, light as bubbles, as she walked by, echoing the bob of white skiffs anchored in the port. And that was when the third thing happened. Terrible, shocking, random. And yet . . . and yet. When she looked back over it, the message she accepted from it was far from random. Synchronicity? A twisted luck? As if even our lives will double, if we don't learn enough first time.

A strange thing was, when she first walked into the dank, eerie little stone toilet block, whose metal door was tapping slightly in the wind, there was no other sound. The light, channelled in by a row of small high windows, was dim and she had to take a few seconds for her eyes to adjust. She'd just ascertained that both narrow cubicles were empty, and there was nobody at the oval steel sink in the corner, when she heard the lonely, wan mewling. She thought, for a moment, that it came from the far corner — that a cat had wandered in and become trapped — then, as the cry repeated, realised it must have been the strange acoustics of the empty concrete cube. She turned around to acknowledge the woman who had walked in behind her with her tiny child. But there was nobody there. Was her mind distorting things again? The cry repeated from the far corner, opposite the main door. Piercing now, high-pitched. She shook her head, as if to clear her ears of water after a dunking. Then — of course — the sound must be coming from outside, through the narrow high windows, which were open just a slit — there was nothing at all in the corner except a tall, swing-top, plastic rubbish bin. The cry wrung at her nerves so desperately then, she felt screwed down to a tight thinness by the noise. Oh, my God. Oh, my *God*. She had a plunging sensation, as if the unsavoury little public toilet were airborne and had suddenly jerked to one side. In the bin. Over there. The cry.

Pulse hurtling, Candy went to the corner and gingerly swung open the lid of the rubbish bin. It looked as if a clean sack had been inserted recently — it was empty except for a number of dry paper towels that had been made into a kind of circular nest or padding at the bottom. And empty except for the cry; except for the one that was crying. It was dressed in warm enough clothes, though they seemed slightly too large for it. Red-faced, lick of dark hair, crying, crying.

Oh, my God. Oh, my God. Candy's knees and arms were shaking, and she fumbled her movements, forcing the lid off completely, with a clatter that probably startled the baby more. Clutching the baby tightly, she managed to tip over the rubbish bin one-handed, and crouched down to sift through the paper towels. There had to be a note, a bag of clothes, money, a baby bottle filled with milk. She knew there would be; she knew there would be some sign. She cleared the bin. Paper towels scuffed, fluttered, blotted up drips of tap water someone had shaken on the floor. There was nothing else. She pulled the black rubbish sack right out, then even began to turn over every paper towel, expecting something scrawled on one — a name, an age, a request: *Please take care of my baby because I cannot* — a message that helped to give another kind of start, another kind of foundation. Every paper towel was blank. Nothing. She crouched down again, saying *hussh, shh, hussh, sssh, sssh,* and looked under the slats of a small wooden waiting bench. Leaves, dust, a dead bee on its back, all legs curled up tightly to its chest. The fear from the dream the night before came up like backwash. And then Candy ran. Up the steps of the main entrance to the park, the stone archway built for World War One victims, under the sign that seemed so incongruous in this moment: *Peace Perfect Peace*. Straw bag over her shoulder, baby held to her chest, one hand to its head as a protective helmet, to keep it from falling missiles of worse misfortune, she ran.

Candy reached a public phone booth, and paused. Her thoughts still pelting on, she wasn't sure how long an ambulance would take to get here, where it might have to come from, nor even what the local police could do for the baby straight away. She checked her watch. Quarter to five. The doctor's surgery closed at 5.30, and it wasn't far. It was warm there, there was her doctor, a nurse and another older woman — the receptionist. They would know what to do. Candy carried on running, biting down sobs because there wasn't time for them: they took too much energy, she needed all her breath, the breath that burned in her chest like a fuel.

She crashed through the surgery door, startling an elderly man who sat in cap and tweed jacket in the waiting room, leafing through a magazine. She drew back the sliding glass panel that at chest height separated the receptionist's desk and office from the waiting area, though you were supposed to ring a bell and wait for someone to attend to you.

'Something terrible's happened,' Candy said to the alarmed-looking woman behind the desk. 'We need the doctor. I found this baby.' The images of how she had chanced upon the child were so appallingly clear, it took Candy a moment to realise that the woman wouldn't automatically know what had happened.

'It was in the women's public toilet down at the beach. No belongings, no name, no anything.' She looked down at the baby nursed in the crook of her arm. Candy stared at the woman, as if the true awfulness of the site where the foundling had been stowed away was just dawning on her.

'Good God.' The woman picked up a phone, turned her back on Candy, dialled an inside line, spoke for a few moments, then covered the mouthpiece. 'Dr Bryant will be straight with you, love.

We'll have to call the police. You'll be able to talk to them?' It was phrased as a question, but with her tightly permed glossy brown curls, her glasses on a silver chain, the receptionist exuded pragmatism and calm, not expecting any response other than a yes.

Candy nodded, and the receptionist stood up, clutching a handful of soft, apricot, perfumed tissues. She quickly, unfussily, wiped at Candy's sudden tears and runny nose, saying, 'You're a brave young woman,' the incongruity of which made Candy give a choked laugh.

'There, you see? That's the spirit,' the woman said. She leaned over the reception bench, touching the baby's cheek. 'Poor little thing.'

The young doctor who had seen Candy a few weeks before strode out at last, behind a stocky Maori man with a long, lush ponytail, who wore blue electrician's dungarees over a bare torso, a tiny cottonwool pad taped to the pit of his arm. Dr Bryant took the baby gently from Candy, fingertips already assessing it here and there as he led her in to the examining room.

She couldn't stand not being told what the doctor was checking for, and what conclusions he was arriving at. 'It's all right? It's not malnourished, is it?' Anxiety made her voice girlish, high-pitched.

Dr Bryant gently unsnapped the baby-grow jumpsuit and unfastened the cloth nappies, which were done up with little pins that had yellow plastic ducks' heads as decoration. Candy whistled under her breath at the detail: it seemed a sign of caring, of someone who had thought and prepared, choosing the playful, frivolous option before the practical and common-sense . . . She hoped the baby would be allowed to keep the pins, the only clue so far to the fragments of love and concern its life had begun with.

Dr Bryant checked the nappies, giving a grim murmur when he saw the way the umbilical cord had been cut; concern compacted by disbelief when he discovered that the nappies were dry. Over several tense minutes while he attended to the umbilical cord, he had the practice nurse prepare what might have been the baby's first feed. 'Dehydration,' Candy heard, through a buzzing headache that flared and stopped, flared and stopped. Encouraging the newborn to suck on his pinkie, Dr Bryant then slid in a small sterile syringe of formula beside his finger, and all three adults watched anxiously for the fluid level to drop. Once the baby started suckling, Dr Bryant managed a smile. 'Now at least we know he's a he,' he said. 'Little laddie, hey? Where's your momma gone?' He gently stroked the baby's head.

'He seems all right, considering — and as far as I can tell — but we'll need to get him to a hospital quickly, for a proper examination from a paediatrician. And get him looked after until something is sorted out.' The doctor hadn't taken his eyes off the baby the whole time he spoke. 'He's a very new little specimen. I'd be concerned about the mother right now.'

'The mother?'

'Well, she's obviously not in a good state if she's done this.' He frowned. 'But my guess is if she thinks she's going to get away with it, it's likely that nobody close to her even knew about the pregnancy. She's probably not had any medical care right throughout, let alone during the birth. She could be putting herself at physical risk right now, just by not telling anyone.'

Candy was startled by the salty, silvery taste of blood; she had bitten through a layer of skin on her bottom lip. Of course. So much she hadn't even thought about . . .

The baby gave a funny little peep, a kind of high sigh. Candy swallowed. 'How will they — I — who will take care of him if they can't find her?'

Dr Bryant buttoned up the baby's stretch-and-grow. 'In a situation like this the authorities will have to get involved. I guess if they can't find the parents there are probably dozens of couples out there already, on waiting lists, who'd want to adopt. But we'll see.'

Her heart felt like a giant earth ball, tossed from hand to hand, airborne for short moments and dropping instantaneously with sickening lurches in between. She couldn't say why, but whenever she looked at the tiny boy's creased face she found herself searching back into the phone call she'd had the day before, as if probing, still, to find out what residual dismay remained. Mentally, she kicked herself — what was she thinking? This event was of such a different magnitude of seriousness, of urgency. Yet when she reached out to touch the baby she startled herself by whispering, 'Are you all right, little Jeff?'

Puzzled, Dr Bryant looked over his shoulder as he retrieved a small, thick flannel sheet from a drawer below the examination bed. 'Named him already, have you?' Embarrassed, as if she'd talked in her sleep or spoken over some social taboo, she didn't answer. He folded the blanket into a shawl to swaddle around the baby.

There was a knock at the door and the receptionist's face appeared around the corner, as she checked whether it was all right for a local constable to come in and speak to Candy. 'No more appointments left today, Colin,' she said to the doctor, who nodded.

Then, in a hurried blur, Candy had been taken back to the public toilets to show the constable exactly where she'd found the baby. She'd answered all his questions, half noticing phrases like 'the mother's probably on the move', 'could have caught one of the inter-islander ferries, of course, perhaps both before and after the birth', and she'd also given him her contact details both at the lodge and at home.

When she was dropped back at the lodge, having been reassured the baby was on its way to a neo-natal unit in Blenheim, only an hour and a half had passed for the whole episode. Yet exhaustion hummed in her limbs. Dazed though she was, she already had a strong feeling that the hostel was the wrong place to be. By the time she was walking down the path to the front entrance, the impulse to run had resurfaced. But this time it was the boomerang drive: the homing instinct. And the form it took was unexpected — an overwhelming urge to see Rose. Just to hug her, first of all: but also, to tell her about what had just happened. The impulse was both simple and largely incoherent at first. The thought of her mother just sat there, like a separate emotion, at the forefront of her mind, the name of a destination. So it was hard to explain to Mike why she wanted to leave. She managed to mumble that she'd had an important phone call — err, from her family. That, and the shock of finding the little boy meant she just 'had to see people at home'.

Arms folded, Mike spoke to his feet. 'I'm not surprised you need a break. We're all stunned about that wee one,' he said. Candy imagined the township on their doorsteps, faces bowed as was

Mike's, words failing to ignite. He scuffed the toe of his shoe at a crack in the wooden floorboards. 'It's fine, Candy. We'll be moving into a quieter season soon, so won't be too rushed. So we'll see you — what, in about a week?' He nodded several times, trying to lead her to the answer he wanted. She didn't have the energy or the heart to tell him she just didn't know if she'd get back. Still, she said, 'That's really generous, Mike, thanks,' and he looked so uncomfortable that he verged on angry. 'No, no. No, no. Now, you go on and take a rest. Too much drama for one week, eh?'

The reasons she wanted to see Rose only gradually floated to the surface when the coach that Candy had caught on the long journey south rose to the top of the highway entering Dunedin. But when she saw the city's lights beading the dark hills that sat like lumbering shadow puppets against the purple sky, she knew she needed to have Rose retell the old stories, unpack the rumours caught around door-frames, under open windows, in the corridors, throughout all those years at home. The stories about how different Rose was before she'd had twins. How hard it was . . . Rose leaving both children (*Or was it just one?* Gram had said) parked in the stroller in the Barnados shop.

Here she was, having left home and even home towns, and yet needing to hear, as much as ever, that it had been a mistake, that Rose hadn't really wanted to walk away. Yet perhaps most of all, that she didn't regret that someone had found her, had brought her back to the twins.

Too late for public transport to be running regularly enough to her parents' house, Candy had to fork out for a taxi. The driver treated her guitar as if it were a cage with a small vulnerable animal in it. 'Will it be all right in the boot?' he asked, looking at it askance and concerned. 'Fine,' she said, grinning at him. When they pulled up in the driveway she was dumbfounded for a moment. The porch lights — and the two extra driveway lamps — were on, the house floodlit as if on display. Candy saw it as if she'd been away for years, and changes had been wrought that she hadn't been forewarned about.

The taxi driver gave an impressed whistle, and then laughed as he glanced at Candy. 'You all right? Sure this is the right address?'

'What? Oh yeah, yes, I'm sure. I'd just . . . forgotten some things.'

Poker flowers stalked up the driveway lamplight in a blaze of hot orange that she could imagine would warm your hands if you stood close and cupped them around the heads. The garden was scattered with bursts of colour that seemed to rush and flow like fountains. Candy didn't know the names of many of the plants, although she thought it seemed late in the season for so much to be in bloom. On the porch roof and the veranda railings here and there the light caught Rose's spiked and glinting collection of weather-vanes. Roosters and hens of all sizes and designs, made of wood, copper, steel, tin: painted or plain. And all the other variations — less like weathervanes than like wind-clocks and windmills — whirred and danced in the evening breeze, on the lawn and in the flower beds, trying to keep up with one another. Kermit the Frog pedalled on a bicycle, an anatomically absurd ladybird's wings spun, dozens of wooden sunflowers twirled their petals around their black hearts, a dalmatian's four paws wheeled ludicrously, a cartoonish kiwi ran on the spot, beak flapping a red plastic tongue, made of the same material as the strings of flags at Robinson's car sales yard. A penguin, a Bugs Bunny, a flamingo, a Wily Coyote, a Road Runner — dozens of critters whirled in place. Only the flock of iron and wooden butterflies — red, purple, yellow, green, blue — that trailed up the one wall near the downpipe of some spouting managed to keep still.

'Someone a bit of a collector, eh?' asked the taxi driver as Candy hunted for change.

'Sort of. My mother makes a lot of them. She loves bright and busy things.'

He laughed again. 'You don't say.'

She remembered, with an old sour lunge of dislike, Phil Redshaw, the boy who'd vandalised Rose's chicken-shaped letterbox, and Shane, the short-lived boyfriend who'd said 'It's beyond kitsch!' as if she'd find her own life small, funny and a little repellent too. Some urge to refute it started her talking now.

Reminiscent of the night-time conversation with Séverine and Richard there was a candid moment with the cab driver, which happened despite the fact that he was a total stranger — or perhaps exactly because the intimacy had no real ties, risks, potential costs. Candy sat back in her seat and gazed out at the scene again. 'You know, my mother told me once — it's so bizarre, but I've only just remembered this — that after she'd come through a long phase of unhappy times, she'd decided colour and motion were a way to celebrate the fact of every day we were alive.'

Gazing out into the darkness beyond the pools of light on the garden she felt back into the past. 'It seemed to me like — I don't know — like her eyes have always had a faster metabolism than most of us. Like they crave more vibrancy than the average person.'

She and the taxi driver both contemplated the garden. 'She needed visual intensity the way some people need extra calories, just to survive. I think she wanted to fill herself up to the brim. Like making up for lost time.' The taxi driver nodded slowly, and Candy felt the silence unroll like a soft black bolt of cloth. 'And it's totally weird. I'd completely forgotten it until now.'

The driver (Stan, his ID photo stuck to the sun visor said — Cab Number 56) counted out Candy's coins and filed them away in a small stacking abacus. 'Sounds like a wise woman, your mother. You're blessed there.'

The tone of mellow resignation told Candy that Stan was used to people half talking to themselves, with him there as a kind of faceless confessor, divided from his flock by the gear stick and the sickly scent of pine from the plastic deodoriser that sat on his dashboard — which perhaps acted as a deterrent for conversations like this that started to go on too long: Candy had begun to find it a bit oppressive. She opened the car door to show him she was letting him off the hook. 'Yeah, I am,' she said. 'You're right. Hey, I can get my luggage myself. Have a good night.'

'And yourself,' he said, flicking off the inside light and waiting for her to retrieve her belongings.

Candy walked up to the front door and rang the doorbell — an action that felt stiff and unnatural after all those years of just bursting in through the door, calling out hello and dumping her schoolbag on the floor, but that also seemed the least deference she could show after her parents' annoyance over how she'd returned their car and camera.

Rose answered. She was carrying a book, magazine, brightly painted watering can and even a half-finished square of cross-stitch which dangled needle and thread — as if she'd somehow been managing to do four things at once. She had the stopped, then slowly astonished, look of someone who'd just walked in on a surprise party.

'Hi, Mum,' Candy said, and the grin fitted like a comfortable coat she'd lost and rediscovered.

Rose tried to hug her but succeeded in pricking herself with the needle and slopping water from the can over Candy's foot. 'Oh, hell's bells, look at me, I'm all turned around! When did you get back? Why did you decide — are you all right? Oh, look, I should be asking you to sit down, not leaving you to stand there like you're some door-knocker from the God Squad. Come in, come in.'

They were both exclaiming and laughing at nothing, their noises like the pirrups and cries of small birds.

Rose ushered Candy into the kitchen, where she finally discarded her clutch of objects and automatically began to fossick in the fridge for cheese, tomato, lettuce and eggs, to make her a snack dinner.

'I'm all right, Mum. I grabbed a pie from a dairy before I jumped in the taxi.'

'That doesn't sound like enough.' She carried on, and seemed happier with her hands busy, so Candy kept quiet. A thick, warm contentment settled on her to see Rose so readily turned back to the small, ministering actions of habit. Yet it also made her hesitate a little over the questions that had driven her here like a tail wind at a yacht.

'Where's Dad?' she asked. The false nonchalance felt easily detectable. She had a suspicion Robinson might pack away the conversation she wanted to have, leave it on a high, inaccessible shelf — protecting Rose, as he had so often done when they were a young family.

'Robinson — oh, he's taken up bowls, would you believe? He's at a tournament committee meeting for the local club.'

'Bowls? I thought that was for retired people.'

'Well, he tells me there's a fifteen-year-old girl who's in the top three down there' — she moved her shoulder as if Candy would be able to tell the general location from the gesture — 'and Robinson figures if he's going to be any good when he does retire, he should start training now.'

'Amazing.' Candy blew on the hot, sweet cup of tea that Rose had set down in front of her without asking if she wanted one. And now, the satisfaction that had settled on her before began to make her feel a little drugged and sluggish, as if her autonomy were leaching away, somehow, helped oddly by the accompanying sensation of being left outside things, after hearing that her father had taken up a completely unexpected hobby. Without . . . well, not without asking, that would be ridiculous to expect. But without . . . Candy knowing. She shook herself a bit as her mind flicked back to the scene in the taxi — that sensation of only now really seeing her family home, only now hearing something that Rose had once said, as if a recording had been made all those years ago, which her memory saved to replay until she could take note of it properly. She watched Rose's profile, and the way her hands — which seemed more heavily knuckled with age than Candy remembered — worked at sponging down, then drying the bench. As she watched her movements, with a slow but honed ache, Candy wondered how clearly she'd ever known, or how deeply she'd ever tried to understand, the people she'd grown up with.

Rose handed her a plate of food and ushered her out to the dining-room table, where she drew up a chair as well and poured them each a glass of cheap cask wine. 'Château Cardboard doesn't taste like much,' she said, 'but it'll do the job of helping you to relax after that long drive.' She sampled some herself. 'So. You seem to have come back in a hurry — everything all right?'

Candy speared half a boiled egg. 'Yeah, pretty much all right.

No accidents or emergencies. For me at least.' A long pause grew between them, and tension spread on the air, silent static. Candy swallowed, then tried to confront what she wanted to say. 'But . . . something fairly heavy did happen, Mum, which I guess . . . I guess helped to motivate me to get here. I haven't promised Mike I'll go back, but he said the job will stay open for me.'

Rose smiled down at the tabletop, like someone bashful of her happiness. 'Of course he did. You'd have made a fine impression.' She shifted in her chair, and eventually led Candy back to the topic again. 'So, something motivated you to visit.'

Setting down her fork, Candy clutched both hands in her lap, leaning over her plate slightly. 'Something . . . awful. But lucky at the same time.' She found herself reliving the quick press of chill emptiness that had moved in over her at the Picton foreshore — and how now it seemed the papery drift of gulls, the hollow call of the wind, the grey sea that stirred as if the fists and feet of a distraught life were held under it, were all a forewarning, even a reaction to the dark little cube at the perimeter of it all: the furtive, rushed and desperate disposal that must have happened — minutes? An hour? — before Candy chanced upon it. She rubbed at her upper arms quickly, to chafe away the traces of retrospective fear, and told her mother about the little abandoned boy.

She discovered she couldn't say exactly where she'd found him — her mind winced from it as from a blade. Instead she said, 'He was so . . . tiny. And alone. You know? So totally alone.'

That was it. It was like looking at an illustration that gradually shape-shifted as her focus adjusted, so that she saw a second shape that shared exactly the same outline as the first, yet was also different. An owl hidden inside flowers. A young girl within the trunk of a tree. An urn, a clock, inside the opposing profiles of a man and a woman.

Alone. Whereas, for Candy, in a way, there had always been another. Right back, back deeper than memory: almost the very source of memory. Not just the envelope and nourishment of the mother's body, but a second, beside her. Mirror, partner or opponent; playmate, rival or time thief — at last she understood what she'd been testing herself for repeatedly over the last three days. After Jeff's phone call, the baby, even the night with Séverine and Richard, whether her brother was her opposite or her copy — or rather, she his — had begun to seem so much less urgent than it had.

She wondered again how many minutes or hours the newborn boy had existed in that state — total isolation. And again the thought instinctively retracted, as physically as the senses would turn away from a wound or an overpowering smell.

Candy saw such a simple fact: she had always had another presence beside her, a kind of thought companion — or even, as Jeff had implied in his phone call, a mind to measure herself against. And in the strange, torn light thrown by her discovery of the orphan boy, that (alongside the very fact of her family) seemed not like trouble and struggle, but like luck, beneficence. There'd been a protective membrane around her all her life. Thinner at some times than at others — but there.

Rose's fingertips had pressed briefly against her mouth, pushing a breath or a word back down, Candy thought. She looked at her own fingers, thinking of the small fists of the newborn and the shock of how cold they'd been.

'I took him to a doctor there, and he's being looked after. They drove him to Blenheim, and as far as I know, everything's up to the police and social services now. If they can't find his family, he'll be up for adoption, I guess. But I've asked them to record who found him, so if he ever wants to talk to me, or find me, he can. In case he wants to hear his story, you know?'

Like someone on the edge of swift water, trying to gauge the depths, Rose stared into her glass of wine. Then she lifted her head to meet Candy's gaze. 'You've really been through the wringer, love. But it sounds like you handled it well. You should be proud. And you're right, in a way it is lucky. That he met kindness on the way somewhere so — different.'

Candy barely acknowledged what she'd said, hurried on. 'The thing is, afterwards? All I really wanted to do was talk to you.'

Rose's face seemed pale, still — the expression of someone

sitting on a bus, stonily waiting for the journey to end. Candy felt a flutter of embarrassment contorting into anger. As if she'd burst in here, a clown covered in cherries and cream, hooters blaring, only to find herself not in a circus ring with the audience she'd expected, but somewhere more sombre: a waiting room, a court. But Rose's stillness began to register something, emotion pulling at the surface like a lake prickled with minute raindrops. She shifted forward, nodded. 'It brought up some memories.'

Candy nodded back.

Rose reached out and stroked Candy's hair, as if she were nine or ten again. 'It sounds like the mother must have been very distressed.' Her hand rested for a moment, her voice low but steady. 'There but for the grace of, eh?' And somehow that, with the look in Rose's eyes, became all the reassurance Candy needed.

In a series like a contact sheet of stills, again she saw the story she'd known of her mother. Water-blotted raincoat, double stroller, wheels sending a fringe of spray up from the pavement puddles, gas heater, metal fretwork glowing under the heat of flames, and then, anew, as if she'd been hunting through a drawer she thought she knew all the contents of — a moving image this time. Of two pairs of white, crocheted booties. They were threaded at the top with yellow satin ribbon, which helped to tie them closed. One pair of the woollen boots kicked and stretched next to the other, which then followed in a similar series of airborne steps. The four feet kicked and lifted: chattered and bantered in some sort of silent, humorous sign exchange. She homed in on the image, held on to it, tightly.

That night she stayed up for a while over brandy with her parents. She had been startled by Robinson's initial greeting of her. When he came home he gave her a hug that made it seem as if her bones were a walnut shell under a nut-cracker; there was some sweetness in her he wanted to get right down to. He'd said, 'Candy, my girl, you've been gone too long!' It made her wonder, again, how harsh her own judgement of her family had been, how well she'd really let herself know them. It was, perhaps, another realisation that helped to make her feel so drained. She was deeply drowsy by ten, so excused herself and went to sleep in the guest room — her own former bedroom.

Yet once her door was closed, the valve of sleep was shut off. She found she couldn't settle: it was as if the tiredness were brought on by being in other people's company, and having to rethink her position with them. She pressed a palm up against her old bedroom wall, remembering how she and Jeff used to scratch messages to each other through it, feeling, now, for any residual heat or movement the house's memory might store.

Right from the start they've been different. When did Candy begin to translate that into better and worse? Was it because different meant *not-me*, and automatically seemed to mean judgement? Or was it because, conversely, when people like her dad had insisted on their similarities, their very differences became a kind of failure? The funny thing was, now Candy remembered that when Rose had said, 'Right from the start — they've been different,' she and Jeffrey would meet each other's gaze and hold it steady. And an understanding gleamed there, between them, that said, *She can't know. She can't know how close.* Something they barely acknowledged at other times: something she'd ignored, and then fought against, maybe to her detriment.

A wired energy churned through her now, and she doubted she'd sleep unless she did something with it. Voices, words and images were tumbling in her head: Picton, the lodge, its travelling guests, Jeff's phone call — its apologies and news of Jayshri, then the baby boy. It all mixed and intermingled until her view of the world seemed awash in an entirely new colour. And that shade said that the mistake had been hers: to think there was a choice between sameness and difference, that a choice of two meant good or bad, Jeffrey or Candy, lesser or better.

The sudden rush of energy made her restless, made her want to walk and walk into the night, past the solemn blocks of shadowed houses, through the trees lining the suburb's gardens, out to a park, or way, way out, up one of the hills surrounding the city, so she could sit among the chilly, sharp blades of spear grass, under the cold white stone of the moon, feel herself peeled back to some nub of meaning, of clarity. But she couldn't leave the house — Robinson and Rose would hear and, if they checked on her, would worry themselves into compact knots of nerves.

She opened her window quietly and leaned out, trying to name some of the garden scents that came to her, pores sipping on a smaller draught of the coolness promised by the bulky outlines of the city's surrounding bush and peaks. It helped clear her head a little.

She'd call Jeff first thing tomorrow. Because — she could have said, if he asked — after all this, this long summer, she could begin to see, now, that one plus one meant both. Same but different: same and different. Like the very genetics she and Jeff shared: DNA, the double helix or spiral.

She reminded herself to tell him, somewhere in the long conversation she envisaged, about the abandoned child she'd found: how somehow it had made her think of him. (And how she would try to stay in touch: in years to come she could tell the little boy about Rose, and maybe he'd be able to rescue a starved kind of love from their own story.) Maybe she and Jeff would even talk again about Lewis, and about the way brother and sister saw each other: leading and following, copying and diverging, encroaching and freeing. She had confidence now that they'd start to sort it out together. Because sometimes, she'd say to him (the sop pop song not too far under her breath), it takes two.

Hearing echoes of that chewing-gum tune made her want something grittier, more deliberately dissonant. And then, at last, she recognised the sensation of tightly wound, frenetic energy that had come on since closing the bedroom door. It was a long time since it had charged her up exactly like this. She ferreted around in her bag, came up with notebook and pen, scrawled and scrawled (hands not even feeling it) until the words, notes, chords, all of them, had drunk her dry, left her and themselves sated. The fumes of sleep finally began to trail again into her head.

She'd have to chip away at the lines for weeks before they were ready, but it felt like a corner turned, back into a richer, denser, more complex space: a space she knew she finally, fully wanted to live inside in some form — be it through journalism, composition, or both . . .

She'd seen the man so physically: close as a face blurred by candlelight and reflected in the window the night sat just beyond. Shades of Jeff, shades of self? Maybe even the man the little foundling boy could become.

She unpacked her guitar for a few moments before sleep. Pool of happiness beginning to fill, she started to pick up and put down the muffled notes and chords.

Lucid Companion

Came to my table
frost brittle on his mouth and stubble
his eyes blue snow, his eyes grey horizon

sat down at my side, uninvited guest
carried roll-your-owns, hot black coffee in a chipped juice glass
wore a knitted cap, gold and silver on his fingers
leaned close at my table, tall and easy stranger,
offered food and comfort, offered ginger and wine.
So we talked a little while, until he said

'Have you heard of lucid dreams
when you dream what you dream
but know you're dreaming all the time?'

And the winter sun caught his rings,
sent a hoop of light to dance across the floor,
to run along the tablecloth, slide towards the door.

'That's Jack o' the Wall,' he said. 'Twin of Jack Frost,
Jack o' the Wall,' he said, and tipped his rings so the light fell on my
hand,

Jack o' the Wall danced on my knuckles, stepped on my palm.

My uninvited guest he said, 'Do you know what lucid dream means
when you dream what you dream
but know you're dreaming all the time?'

And he pulled out a pack of playing cards
to give his lonely hands quiet company
and his fingers cut and shuffled, they dealt out Solitaire
and Jack o' the Wall waltzed on my sleeve, Jack o' the Wall brushed
past my hair

and my uninvited stranger said, 'Can you feel what lucid dream
means
when you dream what you dream
but know you're dreaming all the time?

Your name, I didn't catch it,' he said.
'But you remind me of a friend of mine:
her eyes were brittle blue, her eyes were snow horizon.
Tall and easy, she chose my table; we talked a little while,
she tasted like honeyed ginger, she tasted like apple wine
when the winter sun caught her hair, when the winter sun caught
her hands.

No, I didn't hear your name', he said.
'But I'd say it will echo sadness
for you remind me of a friend of mine,
Jack Frost on her lips, but Jack o' the Wall behind her eyes.'